I0819208

Praise for

Home No Matter Where

"In *Home No Matter Where,* we travel to beautiful Whelk's Island, where a close-knit community puts us right at home. Along the way, we meet compelling characters caught in realistic storms and learn faith-filled lessons about weathering them. Naigle's tenderly told tale is sure to leave you satisfied and hopeful, and ready to book a trip to Whelk's Island!"

—Denise Hunter, bestselling author of *More Than Friends*

"In this third Shell Collector novel, Naigle beautifully explores, with honesty and insight, the depth of family bonds. Rich with forgiveness, love, and friendship, *Home No Matter Where* both charms and entertains while reminding us what matters most—one another. Well done!"

—Rachel Hauck, *New York Times* bestselling author

"Tender, uplifting, and beautifully real, *Home No Matter Where* captures the messiness of family and the miracle of second chances. Nancy Naigle's Whelk's Island is the kind of place—and story—you'll want to return to again and again."

—RaeAnne Thayne, *New York Times* bestselling author

Praise for

To Light the Way Forward

"Bringing to life characters you can't help but fall in love with, Nancy Naigle goes straight to the heart with this story of tragedy turned to triumph. A poignant reminder to never give up hope."

—SHEILA ROBERTS, author of *The Best Life Book Club*

"An emotional and uplifting story about surviving—no, make that thriving—after great loss, thanks to connection, friendship, and love (of all kinds!). Nancy Naigle truly understands the human heart and its incredible capacity for resilience. I came away wishing all the wonderful characters from Whelk's Island were my friends too!"

—MIRANDA LIASSON, Amazon bestselling author and author of *Sea Glass Summer*

"A beautiful, tender, uplifting novel about love, loss, and the courage to embrace new beginnings. Nancy Naigle crafts a story that will touch your heart and inspire your soul."

—RAEANNE THAYNE, *New York Times* bestselling author

"Naigle returns to Whelk's Island in this charming tale of loss, love, and taking chances. *To Light the Way Forward* shines hope on the strength of family and friendship—and the power of coming together. Well-paced with rich detail, this story will delight readers."

—RACHEL HAUCK, *New York Times* bestselling author of *The Wedding Dress*

"Nancy Naigle creates characters who are so multidimensional and real that it's like you are walking along the beach with them. It's a joy to go on their journey of miracles and weathering the storms of life.

To Light the Way Forward beautifully illuminates how resilient the human spirit is. Naigle splendidly captures the journey of love and loss through laughter, tears, and all the feelings. This book is an uplifting story of miracles and human connection. I want to live in the world of Whelk's Island!"

—Erin Cahill, actress, Hallmark

Praise for

The Shell Collector

"This is a beautiful story full of love, loss, and second chances. A collection of vivid characters, an inspiring setting, and heart-held hope for a better tomorrow."

—DEBBIE MACOMBER, #1 *New York Times* bestselling author

"As an avid shell seeker, I enjoyed this tale of surprises deposited among the tides, with its underlying message of finding just the shells we are meant to discover. A tender story of faith, love, and friendship that will warm the hearts of beachgoers and lovers of the sea."

—LISA WINGATE, #1 *New York Times* bestselling author of *Before We Were Yours* and *The Book of Lost Friends*

"A touching story of hope and renewal—proof that you can find more at the beach than shells."

—SHEILA ROBERTS, *USA Today* bestselling author

"An amazing emotional story of putting one foot in front of the other, of overcoming heartache, and of learning to live—and love—again. You'll cry—and smile—and you'll close the book with a very full heart."

—LORI FOSTER, *New York Times* bestselling author

"Nancy Naigle is at the top of her game with *The Shell Collector*. A compelling cast of characters—all acting in accord with their best lights—tackles the issues of loss and grief with wit and grace. 'The Wife' is my favorite new character. An uplifting, hopeful page-turner that shouldn't be missed!"

—BARBARA HINSKE, author of the Rosemont series and *Guiding Emily*

"A touching story about love, loss, and healing, *The Shell Collector* gives you all the feels. I enjoyed spending time at the beach collecting seashells—and pondering the encouraging messages inside them—right along with the characters. Don't miss this uplifting, faith-affirming read!"

—Brenda Novak, *New York Times* bestselling author

"*The Shell Collector* is a beautiful, emotional story about the glorious sunrise that can come after a dark night, about surviving loss and finding hope and joy again. Amanda, Maeve, and the entire cast will break your heart and then heal it all over again. I loved every word."

—RaeAnne Thayne, *New York Times* bestselling author

"In *The Shell Collector*, Naigle takes readers on a hopeful journey of healing after unimaginable loss. A tragic past, lovable characters, and a charming small-town setting align for a meaningful beach read. Don't miss this tender tale full of wisdom and insight!"

—Denise Hunter, bestselling author of *Bookshop by the Sea*

"*The Shell Collector* is utterly charming. Naigle's story of restoration, love, and hope is a perfect read any time of the year. The characters are fun if not a bit quirky, and the setting evokes so much peace. Well done. I loved it."

—Rachel Hauck, *New York Times* bestselling author

"*The Shell Collector* is an unforgettable story of love, hope, and healing. This inspiring novel has found a place in my heart."

—Jane Porter, *New York Times* bestselling author

"*The Shell Collector* gives voice to the profound truth of grieving and learning to come alive again. Nancy Naigle beautifully shows how love can come in so many different forms, as long as you're open to the unexpected miracles life has to offer. In her own words, 'Life is rarely predictable if we're doing it right.'"

—Erin Cahill, actress, Hallmark

Other Novels by Nancy Naigle

Adams Grove Novels

Sweet Tea and Secrets

Out of Focus

Wedding Cake and Big Mistakes

Pecan Pie and Deadly Lies

Mint Juleps and Justice

Barbecue and Bad News

Boot Creek Series

Life After Perfect

Every Yesterday

Until Tomorrow

Seasoned Southern Sleuths Mysteries

In for a Penny

Collard Greens and Catfishing

Deviled Eggs and Deception

Fried Pickles and a Funeral

Wedding Mints and Witnesses

Christmas Cookies and a Confession

Sweet Tea and Second Chances

The Shell Collector Novels

The Shell Collector

To Light the Way Forward

Stand-Alone Titles

inkBLOT

Sand Dollar Cove

Recipe for Romance

The Secret Ingredient

What Remains True

And Then There Was You

The Law of Attraction

Christmas Novels

Christmas Joy

Hope at Christmas

The Christmas Shop

Christmas Angels

A Heartfelt Christmas Promise

Mission: Merry Christmas

Christmas in Chestnut Ridge

A South Hill Christmas Keepsake

Home No Matter Where

Home No Matter Where

A Shell Collector Novel

NANCY NAIGLE

WATERBROOK

WaterBrook

An imprint of the Penguin Random House Christian Publishing Group, a division of Penguin Random House LLC
1745 Broadway, New York, NY 10019

waterbrookmultnomah.com
penguinrandomhouse.com

A WaterBrook Trade Paperback Original

Copyright © 2026 by Nancy Naigle

Penguin Random House values and supports copyright. Copyright fuels creativity, encourages diverse voices, promotes free speech, and creates a vibrant culture. Thank you for buying an authorized edition of this book and for complying with copyright laws by not reproducing, scanning, or distributing any part of it in any form without permission. You are supporting writers and allowing Penguin Random House to continue to publish books for every reader. Please note that no part of this book may be used or reproduced in any manner for the purpose of training artificial intelligence technologies or systems.

WATERBROOK and colophon are registered trademarks of Penguin Random House LLC.

Library of Congress Cataloging-in-Publication Data
Names: Naigle, Nancy author
Title: Home no matter where / Nancy Naigle.
Description: New York, NY: WaterBrook, 2026. |
Series: A shell collector novel
Identifiers: LCCN 2025047215 (print) | LCCN 2025047216 (ebook) |
ISBN 9780593601068 trade paperback acid-free paper |
ISBN 9780593601075 ebook
Subjects: LCGFT: Christian fiction | Fiction | Novels
Classification: LCC PS3614.A545 H66 2026 (print) |
LCC PS3614.A545 (ebook)
LC record available at https://lccn.loc.gov/2025047215
LC ebook record available at https://lccn.loc.gov/2025047216

Printed in the United States of America

1st Printing

Title page art from stock.adobe.com/Christian Hinkle

The authorized representative in the EU for product safety and compliance is Penguin Random House Ireland, Morrison Chambers, 32 Nassau Street, Dublin D02 YH68, Ireland.
https://eu-contact.penguin.ie

Bookmaking Team: Production editor: Helen Macdonald • Managing editor: Julia Wallace • Production manager: Richard Elman • Copy editor: Cara Iverson • Proofreaders: Jean Bloom, JoLeigh Buchanan, Aria Fischer

Home isn't always a place—it's the comfort of being known,
the courage to begin again, and the love that lights the way.
May you always know when you've found your home
and feel it in your heart forever.

Home No Matter Where

Chapter One

NINA HADN'T EVEN REACHED THE BRIDGE TO WHELK'S ISland and was already questioning everything. This trip to Mom's beach house wasn't a vacation; it felt like a surrender. A last-ditch effort to fix what she had no idea how to repair: her daughter Kendra, herself, and everything that had gone unspoken since the divorce. She prayed this time away was the right answer—that the ocean breeze would carry away their hurts and the waves would wash the slate clean. A break. A fresh start. If only finding home was as simple as leaving one behind.

The steady hum of the engine filled the silence between mother and daughter on their drive from Pennsylvania to North Carolina, broken only by the pounding bass thumping from Kendra's earbuds. Nina tightened her grip on the steering wheel, resisting the urge to tell her daughter to turn the music down.

Be patient. Nina rolled her shoulders to shake out the tension that had settled in hours ago. Her fingers ached, but she wasn't sure if it was from driving or the weight of everything she'd been carrying lately. The wall Kendra was building between them was becoming impossible to penetrate, and Nina felt like she would break if she had to face one more problem.

Calling Mom—Rosemary Palakiko—had been Nina's last

hope. She'd hated to do it. Admitting that she couldn't handle her own daughter revealed an even bigger failure than the divorce. Slipping grades, missed curfews, and a sassy attitude were becoming Kendra's norm. But if anyone could help, it was her mother. Wise, warm, and never afraid to say what needed saying, Rosemary had a way of bringing clarity to chaos, even from four hundred miles away.

Kendra slouched in the seat, arms folded, chin jutting out—her fourteen-year-old armor against the world and an attitude that took up all the space in the car.

Nina's beautiful girl made her heart ache with both pride and sorrow, caught somewhere between the little one who used to snuggle close, her I-love-yous floating like butterflies, and the stranger now riding shotgun. "You okay?" Nina asked, loud enough for Kendra to hear when her daughter caught her gaze.

Kendra's hazel eyes flickered in annoyance. They were impossible to read, shifting with the light: green when she was mischievous, gold when she was angry. Was it just the afternoon sun glinting off them right now, or had she mustered up more anger in the hours of silence on the drive?

Her daughter had barely said a word since they left. No complaints, no conversation, just silence except for the occasional exaggerated sigh that made Nina's skin prickle.

Nina drew in a long breath, counting to five, the kind of breath meant to steady oneself.

This trip needed to be a fresh start. Whelk's Island—Mom's house, the ocean breeze, sunshine, vitamin D, and space to heal. It had all sounded so perfect in her head. But now, with Kendra beside her practically radiating misery, she wondered if she was fooling herself.

Could any place really fix what felt so broken? They'd been through a lot this past year, and they needed to find some peace.

Her and David's divorce had taken way too long, and it was

already ugly before he'd met the new girlfriend and stopped spending time with Kendra. In an attempt to reduce the disappointments David could inflict on her daughter with the every-other-week handovers, or lack of them, she'd fought for and gotten full custody. David was a good man, but he was dropping the ball on being a part of his daughter's daily life, so having Kendra in one home seemed best for her emotional well-being. And, frankly, Nina's own.

The divorce was tough on Kendra, but the anxiety of being a teenager added to the situation. Without two parents to keep her constantly on track, she was losing interest in sports and was left grappling for outlets that weren't to Nina's liking: reckless friends and getting into trouble. Kendra didn't understand that Nina's fight for custody had been to protect her, not punish her, and that hurt had fueled her anger.

Nina and David had balanced all their responsibilities like champs. Despite being workaholics, they'd somehow always found a way to compromise and handle everything together, making it work. Until it didn't.

When David announced he was moving out, she was completely blindsided. That's when the conversations became less civil and his participation in their daughter's activities became a passing priority. Then Dad died and she and David agreed to hold off on the divorce for a while. That pause lasted longer than planned, and the dissolution was only finalized last year.

The ink on their papers had barely dried before David announced his engagement to a woman closer to Kendra's age than hers, all glossy hair and acrylic nails, who could make him her entire focus.

Nina took a deep breath to clear her mind of all that had gone wrong. *Please, God, let us find a new healthy and happy normal on Whelk's Island. Is this too much to hope for?*

At the very least, she'd be thankful for a good night's sleep, and she was sort of guaranteed that by staying at Mom's beach house. Nina needed a break from hearing her daughter sigh dramatically every five minutes. There were worse ways to spend the summer. She'd still have to work, but walking on the beach and watching the waves crash on the shore sure sounded good.

Kendra let out an exasperated grunt. "Mom, are we *ever* going to get there?"

Nina's jaw clenched. She recognized that tone in her daughter's voice. It said, *I don't really care. I'm just letting you know how much I hate this.*

"Think of it as a family vacation." Nina tried to keep her tone upbeat, though the strain in her voice felt like a frayed edge she could barely smooth.

"I'm already going on a vacation with Dad the second week of August." Kendra crossed her arms, her gaze locked on the road ahead as if willing it to speed up. "I'm counting down the days."

"This will be just as fun," Nina offered, knowing even as she said it that Kendra wouldn't believe her.

"As fun as an epic national park tour?" Kendra's snort added the extra twist. "Dad has it all planned out. Yellowstone, and we're renting this cool camper van, hiking waterfalls, and going to see real cave dwellings built into the side of a mountain. We'll probably see buffalo in the wild." Her voice softened as she drifted into this fantasy of her vacation, her fingers flicking across the screen of her phone. "Look, Mom. Hikes, a train ride, and even a dude-ranch cookout. Just me and Dad. It'll be the best time of my life."

Nina looked over, taking in the momentary delight that replaced the scowl on her daughter's face. *If only I believed that trip was going to be all about you.* But she forced a smile to mask her concern. "It does sound amazing. I'm glad you have something special to look forward to."

However, Nina knew her ex well enough to know it wasn't really "all about Kendra" as her daughter was imagining. But that was for her to find out. Maybe by some miracle, David would surprise her. She swallowed hard. "Maybe both trips will be wonderful. You're lucky to have two cool things on your summer calendar."

Kendra's voice turned sharp again. "This trip? This is just a free ride to see Grandma. It's not the same."

Nina drew in a slow breath, working to steady her words. "Kendra, it's not about how far you go or how much you spend that makes a trip worthwhile. You know that."

Kendra slumped against the door, staring out at the endless stretch of highway. "It's going to be boring," she muttered, but the fight had drained from her voice, leaving behind a trace of something Nina recognized all too well: disappointment, plain and raw.

"Your grandmother will spoil you. It'll be great." *And me? I'm going to try with all my heart to let her.*

"I don't want to be spoiled." Kendra turned further toward the window and retreated once again to silence.

Nina swallowed her frustration over the silent treatment, the heavy sighs, the eye rolls. But, she reminded herself, this trip wasn't just for Kendra. It was for *both* of them.

The hours stretched on, exhaustion settling in, when finally the road signs started looking familiar. Now all she wanted was to cross that bridge and breathe in the salt air, if her daughter would let her enjoy even that.

She stole another glance at Kendra, who was still staring out the window, now with her lip caught between her teeth, a sign she was trying not to cry. The tough shell cracked for just a breath, and Nina could almost see her little girl again—the one who used to reach for her hand on long drives. Nina's heart ached for her.

"Kendra," she said quietly, "I know you don't want to be here, but I'm asking you to give it a chance. Please."

Her daughter's shoulders stiffened. She opened her mouth like she was going to say something cutting, then seemed to think better of it.

Finally, Kendra let out a heavy sigh that almost shook the car. "I just don't get it. Do you think the beach is gonna suddenly make everything okay because you forced me to take a trip with you?"

Nina bristled, but she softened her voice. "Just *try* to enjoy this."

Kendra didn't answer.

The road stretched on. The waves would be waiting, and maybe, just maybe, they'd give both of them a little room to figure things out.

Finally, the highway signs listed Whelk's Island among the beach destinations. The road narrowed as they approached the three-mile Wright Memorial Bridge, the only road onto Whelk's Island from the north. The waters of the sound shifted between blue and gray, catching the sunlight in a dance of fleeting glimmers.

The salt air drifted in through her open window, mingling with the faint scent of coconut from the hand lotion Kendra had spilled in the console weeks ago.

Her daughter slouched, earbuds still in, eyes fixed on the endless scroll of her phone. Nina's heart ached, the weight of these past three years pressing hard against her chest. The drawn-out divorce and the loss of Nina's father had really taken a toll on both of them.

"You still okay over there?" Nina asked softly, hoping for something more than a shrug.

Kendra didn't look up. "Fine."

That word. It had become Kendra's shield. Nina reached over, squeezing her hand. "We're almost there, sweetheart."

Whelk's Island felt like a promise. In Nina's mind, this bridge was the path passing from one world into another, leaving the chaos behind.

She slowed the car as the road narrowed ahead. They passed a bait shop with a carved-wood pelican out front, an ice cream stand already gearing up for the summer rush, and expanses of scrubby dunes that felt more foreign than familiar. There was no nostalgia here—just a quiet hope that maybe this place, her mother's new home, could offer the fresh start they both so desperately needed.

"Look at that big old oak," Nina said, nodding toward a gnarled tree with branches stretched wide as if attempting to hold the world together. "Your grandma was telling me that it's one of the oldest trees on the island."

Kendra barely glanced at the tree. "Its branches are all twisted up funny, like a dancer's arms." She lifted her own arms, striking a wobbly ballerina pose, tongue stuck out like some kind of wild little creature.

But when she dropped her arms, her shoulders sagged, and she quickly turned back to the window, leaving Nina to wonder what Kendra's silliness was hiding.

Kendra spat her next words like an accusation. "Looks kinda creepy, if you ask me."

Nina bit back a sigh, searching past the attitude to find the sweet girl she knew was still in there somewhere. She gave her daughter an encouraging grin, holding tight to hope. "If you ask me, it looks like that tree's trying to give the whole road a big ole hug. And, you know, sometimes the things that look the most tangled up are the strongest of all. And sometimes we could all use a hug." She patted Kendra's leg.

Kendra didn't even bother to look her way. "If you say so," she mumbled, her voice as flat as a pancake.

But Nina wasn't ready to give up—not on the mood, not on this trip, not on her daughter. "Well, I do. And I'm hoping that's how we're gonna feel staying here this summer—like we're right where we are meant to be."

She took in a deep breath. The clean scent filled her lungs, and for the first time all day, she felt her chest loosen just a little.

Kendra tugged out one earbud. "Shouldn't we be there? Are we lost?" Her voice was as weary as Nina felt.

Nina said a silent prayer, asking that she and Kendra would meet halfway soon. She cleared her throat. "It smells like the ocean already, doesn't it?" She faced her daughter and lifted her brow in what she hoped would appear playful.

Kendra cocked her head, but as she turned, she pulled her other earbud out and muttered, "Because it *is* the ocean."

A small victory. Nina fought back a smile. "Look at the way the sun dances over the surface. It's so pretty."

Kendra huffed but didn't put the earbuds back in. Another victory.

Encouraged, Nina pressed on. "Your grandma's excited to see you. She's been baking all week."

Kendra shrugged. "Fine. How much farther?"

Not exactly a warm response, but it wasn't a fight either. Nina would take it.

Purposely adding enthusiasm to her voice, she said, "Not even thirty minutes to go. Just a couple little beach towns before we get to Whelk's Island. Remember when we came last year and you couldn't stop pointing out all the cool shops on the way? Ice cream, mini golf, the surf shops?"

Kendra's gaze traced the water stretching out on either side. Boats bobbed in the distance, their white hulls like tiny seashells scattered on blue-green glass. The marsh grass rippled at the edges of the water, and gulls wheeled overhead, their cries carried on the wind.

"Looks the same as it did last time we were here," Kendra grumbled, tucking her hair behind one ear.

"You loved it last time," Nina said, struggling to keep her voice even. "You didn't stop talking about the beach for a month."

Her daughter shrugged, shoulders sinking like they were too heavy to lift. "I don't know why you think coming here is supposed to fix everything."

"I love you, and I have to try *something*. I hate seeing you like this." Nina could argue. She could remind Kendra that it was about trying, about survival, but she was too tired for a fight. "I don't think the island's magic," she said quietly. "But I do think a fresh start can help. And your grandmother's waiting for us. That counts for something, doesn't it?"

Kendra didn't answer. She just turned back to the window.

They drove in silence, but finally the **WELCOME TO WHELK'S ISLAND** sign rose ahead like a promise, its hand-painted letters weathered but steady, just like Nina hoped *she* could be. She steered the car around the curve that hugged the coast and took the turn toward Mom's house. Two more turns and they'd be there. Her heart thudded as she eased off the main highway, the tires rumbling over the shell-speckled road, the ocean glinting between the dunes like it was waiting to greet them.

Then, just before they turned onto the beach road, Kendra straightened. "Wait, isn't that Hailey and Jesse's house?"

"Sure is," Nina said. "We're almost there."

Kendra dropped her earbuds into her backpack, rubbing her hands over her jeans like she was shaking off the last bit of her bad mood.

Nina stole a glance at her, her heart swelling with something she hadn't felt in a long time. *Hope.* It was just for a second, a flicker of light, but it was there.

And as they rounded the bend toward her mother's house, Nina whispered another silent prayer, this time asking that Whelk's Island would keep that light burning.

Chapter Two

NINA'S FINGERS TAPPED LIGHTLY ON THE STEERING WHEEL as she counted the houses, her heart lifting with every pastel porch. One, two, three more and they should be there. The sight of her mother's house brought a rush of relief and nerves all at once. The seafoam-green two-story beach house with crisp white trim proudly stood out from the others.

Kendra bolted upright in her seat, her eyes wide.

"There it is! Look, Mom! Grandma's house!"

Her voice rang with the kind of excitement Nina hadn't heard from her in ages, and it was sweeter than any ocean breeze.

Kendra straightened and pointed. "That's it. It's the flag we bought her!" The bright-pink hibiscus on the fabric fluttering in the breeze beneath the mailbox had been their housewarming gift to her.

"It sure is. I knew she'd love it when you picked it out."

Kendra practically bounced in her seat. "Look! Grandma also got a sign with the name of the beach house on it!"

Nina followed her daughter's gaze, her stomach tightening at the sight of the wooden sign arching above the mailbox: **PALAKIKO'S RETREAT.** Nina's maiden name, painted in soft beachy blue. Flower boxes spilled over with petunias and beach daisies, and the sweet sound of chimes played in the breeze.

Seeing her mom's place made the reality settle in. This wasn't just a vacation—this was an important step in positioning her daughter for success. She pulled into the driveway, the car's tires crunching against the oyster-shell sand. Mom must've been standing at the window, waiting, because she came breezing out the front door on the second story before Nina could even park.

Nina cut the engine, relieved that the long drive was over, and turned to Kendra, but she'd already jumped out of the car.

Mom was on the porch, hand braced on the rail, the late-afternoon breeze lifting the ends of her still-vibrant auburn hair. Dressed in a flowing turquoise tunic that shifted like water around her frame, she was the picture of effortless elegance as she came down the stairs.

If only I could feel half as relaxed as she looks.

Even from here, Mom's ocean-blue eyes sparkled with that mischievous twinkle Nina had known all her life, a look that said she was both wise enough to guide them and young enough at heart to stir up a little trouble if the moment called for it.

"There you are!" Her mother's face split into a grin. "I was starting to think you took a wrong turn and ended up in Florida."

"Me too. I thought we'd never get here." Nina opened the driver's door, stretching her stiff legs before standing. "Longest drive ever."

Rosemary walked over. "You two are on island time now, honey. The only thing in your way is a stop sign and maybe a sunbathing turtle."

She barely got the words out before Kendra tucked her phone in her back pocket and launched herself into her grandmother's arms.

"I love you!" Kendra's voice was muffled against her grandmother's shoulder.

Nina froze, stunned that Kendra could flip a switch so

quickly. Her daughter wasn't a hugger. At least, not lately. She tried to push down the little feeling of jealousy that Kendra could turn into that sweet angel Nina used to yearn to see at the end of a tough workday.

Rosemary's expression softened as she pressed a kiss to Kendra's temple. "My sweet, beautiful granddaughter. I've been missing you something fierce."

And to Nina's complete shock, Kendra didn't pull away.

It wasn't a bear hug, but it also wasn't the stiff, obligatory kind that teenagers did just to be polite. It was *real.*

Nina blinked, swallowing the lump in her throat.

Maybe this wasn't such a far-fetched plan after all. This was the only glimpse of hope she'd witnessed in her daughter in weeks.

Carrying her small backpack, Kendra raced past Nina and her grandmother, up the stairs, and into the house.

"You can never really predict a teenager. Thank you, Mom, for having us for this extended visit. I just didn't know how to reach her on my own anymore."

Rosemary shrugged off Kendra's behavior and pulled Nina into a warm hug, one that smelled of lavender and sunshine. "Lord, I've been worried sick."

"We made good time," Nina said, her voice catching with emotion she hadn't meant to let slip.

Rosemary leaned back to look at her, eyes full of knowing. "You're exhausted. I see it in your eyes, darlin'. That mossy green, dark like the marsh after rain . . . carryin' all that storm. But you're home now. We'll get you rested."

Nina's throat tightened. How did her mother always see through her so easily?

Kendra double-stepped back down the stairs and stopped right next to Rosemary. Nina appreciated the knowing look in her mother's eyes.

"I made up your rooms. Kendra, you're in the bedroom right across from me. We'll be like college roommates."

Kendra's eyes lit up. "Cool!" She hurried to the back seat to scoop up a small suitcase and duffel bag. "I'm ready."

"Great. Go put your bags in your room. I'm going to get your mom squared away down here in the studio apartment."

"Mom's not even going to be up there with us? Sweet!" Kendra smirked and took off for the stairs again.

"Did she just say 'sweet'? Glad she'll miss me," Nina said. "She knows I'm still technically in the house, right?"

"She's being a teenager. It's easier when you're not in it." Rosemary's smile shifted into a smirk. "You were a handful too. Trust me, I've been where you are."

"I don't think I was ever this bad. Dad would've set me straight if you didn't."

"Guess we'll soon find out." Her mom laughed and touched Nina's arm. "I know it wasn't easy for you to ask to come here, but I'm glad you did. You've been holding yourself together with glue and grit so long, Nina. It's time you let somebody help."

Nina felt tears begin to pool and blinked them away. "I didn't want to be a burden."

"Oh, honey." Rosemary's smile crinkled the corners of her eyes. "You could never be a burden. I'd have come and dragged you down here myself if I thought you'd let me."

"Ha, like I tried to drag you from Whelk's Island? That didn't work so well for me."

"That's different. I'm the mom." She gave Nina a wink. "Plus, this is an unexplainable place. You're going to experience it, and I'm so glad you will. I put you downstairs so you could get some peace. Go and get yourself settled in. I'll fix us a snack and meet you upstairs when you're ready. No hurry."

"Thank you, Mom." Nina grabbed her suitcase from the car.

"My pleasure. Oh, I made you a desk out of a folding table. I hope it'll work for you, but if it doesn't, Tug said he could put something together for us. He's super handy like that."

"That's so sweet of him. I'm sure it'll be fine. Thanks, Mom." Once again emotion caught in Nina's voice. Her mother was so thoughtful.

Rosemary turned and headed upstairs. "I'm going to check on Kendra."

Nina stood for a moment, watching her mother until she walked inside. Then she lifted the handle of her suitcase and rolled it toward the glossy-white ground-level cottage door, catty-corner from the one that hid the elevator to the second floor.

The moment she opened the door, a soft peace settled over her like a favorite quilt on a chilly night. The whole space felt kissed by the coast, from the creamy-white furniture to the walls in shades of sea-glass green, shell pink, and that pale green that reminded her of the ocean first thing in the morning.

The bedding was simple and inviting, layered in those same gentle hues as if the colors had been gathered right off the shore. Near the window sat the folding table Mom had mentioned, dressed up with a cheerful tablecloth in a print that hinted at sand dollars and driftwood, and a glass vase that held a single daisy.

Her mom had thought of everything, and it showed. In the simple comfort of the room. In the way it felt like home the minute she crossed the threshold. It wasn't fancy, but it was perfect.

She placed her suitcase on the end of the bed and quickly put her clothes into the dresser drawers. Even after years of corporate travel, she'd never been one to live out of a suitcase. She tucked the empty case into the closet, then walked over and opened the plantation shutters on the window behind the desk. All she could see were the dunes and sea oats, but that was enough.

With a grateful sigh and high hopes, she walked out and, just for fun, took the elevator to the main floor.

When the lift stopped, she opened the metal gate and stepped into the hallway. The scent of buttery biscuits and something sweet—maybe Mom's delicious pound cake—hit her with childhood memories of how that warm aroma used to fill the house.

She lingered in the hallway. Mom had negotiated keeping all the staged furnishings with the purchase of this house last year, and it had been stunning, but she could see her mom's personal touches were warming things up.

A collage of mismatched frames in various sizes filled one hallway wall. Some of the photos were old: beach days from Nina's childhood, the macadamia farm in Hawaii, her graduation picture, a cheering squad photo, Christmas mornings, Dad's old fishing boat. But there were new ones too: a picture of Mom with her fiancé, Tug, at a lighthouse; a selfie of Mom with Amanda's kids; a photo of a hefty black-and-white English bulldog kissing her mother. That photo of Amanda's pet made her laugh, because her mom had never been the kind to let a dog kiss her. But she was so close with Amanda and her family that the kids probably rubbed off on her a little. *Denali. That was the dog's name.*

As she got closer to the living space, she noticed more colorful pictures dotting the wall. In a photo of the northern lights dancing so vividly from Mom and Tug's first big adventure together, the way Tug looked at Mom showed there were true feelings at play. Nina's heart pinched as she stood there, feeling joy for the happiness her mom had stumbled upon.

"Something on your mind?"

Nina turned to find her mother watching her, a knowing

smile playing on her lips. "Sorry, I was just enjoying the pictures, both old and new." She hesitated, then shrugged. "Just . . . a lot to take in."

"It always is, honey." There was a tenderness in her mother's voice that Nina had craved for weeks. "But you don't have to have all the answers today. We will sort it out together."

Nina wasn't sure if her mom was talking about Kendra or the new pictures in the hallway.

A loud yelp erupted from the kitchen.

Nina's eyes widened. "What—what happened? Kendra! Are you okay?" From the sound of it, she couldn't tell if her daughter was laughing or crying.

"Calm down." Rosemary swatted the air as if shooing a fly. "You're wrapped as tight as a clam. Relax. It's fine. I bet Tug surprised her. He's fixing my dishwasher, and I forgot to warn her."

"Well?" Tug walked in from the kitchen, wiping his hands on a red shop rag and then tucking it casually into his back pocket. He gave Nina a nod. "I about scared your daughter to death, but then I told her she could have some of the cake. Your mom's cake can fix anyone."

Nina narrowed her eyes. Had Mom been confiding in Tug about Kendra?

Tug grinned, shooting Rosemary a playful glance. "It's the best pound cake, hands down."

"She makes *my* favorite cake for *you* too?" Nina teased, folding her arms. "You two must be *more* than serious."

Tug smirked. "I like to think so. The truth is, she trades cake for handyman work. I'm on to her scheme, you know."

Mom rolled her eyes, but the warmth in her expression didn't waver. "It's a fair deal."

"No complaints from me." Tug patted the doorframe. "Dishwasher's as good as new. Just needed a little TLC."

"Don't we all," Rosemary said.

"I do what I can," Tug said with a grin. He turned back to Nina. "It's good to see you."

"You too." And, strangely, she meant it. Gone were the bitter and admittedly childish feelings of jealousy. Or maybe all this with Kendra had left her with no more capacity for controversy.

"Let's get you something to eat," Mom said. "Then you can sit out on the deck with me. I'll pour us some tea. We can just breathe for a bit."

Nina followed Rosemary into the kitchen, where the windows framed the sea like a living painting, and for the first time in a long time, she felt as if maybe the storm was passing. But deep down, that little voice, the one that only a mother hears, warned her to stay ready.

Chapter Three

CHEERFUL CONVERSATION FLOWED LIKE LYRICS TO A MELody, the soft rush of waves filling The Tackle Box. Fisher turned down the music, preferring the sound of life being lived in his modest seaside bar. This place was one for gatherings—more than he could have dreamed of.

The air carried the scent of the Atlantic with a trace of the lemon oil he'd used on the bar top. He breathed it in, letting it settle him the way only the ocean ever could.

Nights like this suited him. Easy. Familiar.

He ran a rag along the teak bar, his palm trailing the smooth wood he'd reclaimed and sanded until it gleamed like sea glass beneath the soft light. Hurricane Edwina had tried to take this place from him last year—ripping off the roof and leaving nothing untouched in the flood. But he'd rebuilt it with the help of good folks in the tight community of Whelk's Island.

One of them was Paul Grant, Amanda's husband and the military veteran who'd opened Paws Town Square in their sleepy beach town. Paws wasn't just a place for people to kennel their animals while they vacationed on the North Carolina coast. Rather, Paul had a bigger true-value proposition: Bring home and reacclimate military working dogs. Fisher had no idea at the time that the then-stranger would end up being such a tremendous help in restoring The Tackle Box. This place was now stronger, Fisher was wiser, and the bar—like him—knew what it meant to weather a storm and come back standing. He wanted to make sure it stayed strong not only for himself but for the people he kept on as employees.

And since then, getting to know Paul and his selfless approach to helping others had made him wonder if his quiet existence that he'd worked so hard to create was really what was important in life.

There would be no answers tonight, though. Whatever came next, he'd pivot, and maybe that would lead him to what was gnawing at him for attention. *I'm ready to withstand the next storm. The rest will fall into place.*

Fisher wiped his hands on a clean towel and poured a soda, sliding it down the bar to Chase, who looked sunbaked and worn out in that satisfied kind of way that came from a full day working at Paws Town Square.

"Long day?" Fisher asked, picking up a lime and slicing it clean in one smooth motion.

Chase groaned, stretching his legs. "You have no idea. Between the tourists, their spoiled dogs, and one fella insisting on a gluten-free-dog-biscuit tasting. And not for his dog. For *himself*! Today was the kind of day I'd rather trade places with one of the boarders. Maybe a happy-go-lucky doodle of some sort. They always seem chill."

Fisher chuckled low. "Careful what you wish for. I hear tell Denali's got first dibs on the best spot in the shade and all the belly rubs he wants at Paws since Paul and Amanda got married."

Miss Myrtle let out a cackle from the end of the bar, where she sat like the queen of the castle, eyeing the crowd over her drink. "That's because Denali's got more sense than most folks."

Fisher winked at her as he shucked oysters with an easy

rhythm. "You'd know, Miss Myrtle. You've been keeping us all in line for years."

He worked the blade under another shell, tossing it open in one practiced flick, then stacked the last of the dozen on a round tin tray, crackers and hot sauce nestled in the center. He carried it over to a couple tucked in close, whispering as though they were the only two people left on earth.

"Here y'all go," Fisher said, setting the tray between them. He couldn't help but grin at the way they barely noticed him, lost in their own little world. "Crackers in the middle. Hot sauce, too, in case the conversation isn't spicy enough."

"Nice." The guy gave his girl a flirty wink. "Better get us another dozen."

Fisher watched them lean in even closer, sharing a laugh no one else could hear. He'd once thought peace was all a man needed, but maybe what he really craved was that kind of belonging. "You got 'em."

He returned to the bar just in time for Chase to gesture around the place, his soda in hand. "You know, I tell folks The Tackle Box is like a home away from home."

At that, a fella with city polish, still in his golf shirt, leaned on the bar with a smirk. "Feels like home, huh? Maybe if you grew up in a trailer park or spent summers at a campground."

Fisher tried not to take exception to the smug tourist. "Well now, I don't see anything wrong with that. The way I see it, The Tackle Box is like the best parts of a campsite: good company, simple pleasures, nothing fancy but plenty of heart."

Miss Myrtle raised her glass. "And no mosquitoes."

Fisher grinned as he began shucking another batch of oysters. "And if you stick around long enough, you'll find the drinks are cold, the breeze is free, and the stories are better than whatever's on your phone."

The visitor hesitated, observing the flirty couple, the cozy bar, and the soft sound of laughter mingling with the sea breeze. "Didn't mean any offense." His face reddened, but, surprisingly, he didn't bolt.

Fisher poured him his beer, sliding it over. "None taken. Stick around. The charm of this place washes over you, same as the waves."

He plated the oysters and carried them over to the couple who had finished off the first batch in short order.

"Incoming!" Fisher announced loudly, hoping to interrupt the romance of the couple's moment, but they didn't seem to even notice him. He placed the oysters between them. "Enjoy," he said, knowing that even if he'd placed sand pancakes in front of those two, it couldn't ruin what they had going on.

When he was behind the bar, the work came naturally. What he didn't expect tonight was the restless feeling that had crept in lately, and that couple so lost in each other had pushed it to the top again.

Is this all there is?

For years, he'd thought so. Simple life, steady life. A bar, a board, a roof over his head, and the sea at his feet. But lately, watching Tug soften under Rosemary's smile and seeing families on vacation and couples leaning in close over shared plates, he'd begun to wonder if maybe he'd been fooling himself. Maybe peace wasn't the same as being alone.

He leaned against the bar, listening to the easy rhythm of the night, and let his gaze drift to the porch, where the sky bled coral and gold into the sea. If there was one thing he could always be grateful for, it was nature. The sun still set and the waves still came regardless of what a man had done right or wrong that day—the ocean didn't hold grudges.

Fisher slid a cold one across the counter to one of his regulars without waiting for his order, nodding toward the pastel sunset. "That's the best show you'll see all week," he said to himself.

"And this is the best place to see it," the customer said as he lifted the beer in a salute in Fisher's direction. "Thanks, man. Been a long day."

"All summer long," Fisher said. "The hotter it gets, the longer the days. You just take a load off. Not a single expectation of you here."

This was his favorite part of the job. Not the income. Not even the business itself. Just giving someone the room to exhale and seeing the weight of the day slip from their shoulders as the ocean reminded them that nothing in life is permanent. Not stress, not heartache, not even bad weather.

The buzz of conversation faded to the background as his gaze wandered to the driftwood sign above the bar. The letters, painted in weathered navy blue, spelled out the reminder he'd carved into that sea-worn plank long before he ever opened The Tackle Box. The writing was so old and permanently waterlogged that it looked nearly black: **THE SEA GIVES, THE SEA TAKES, BUT IT ALWAYS LEAVES SOMETHING TO BE THANKFUL FOR.**

The wood's soft grain caught the last of the setting sun, and for a beat, Fisher let the words anchor him. Gratitude had seen him through storms worse than Edwina. Tonight, it kept his restlessness at bay, reminding him that whatever he was missing, the ocean would help him find it, one tide at a time.

His gaze flicked toward the entrance, a habit he picked up when he first opened The Tackle Box. He was determined not to let his little seaside oasis be one of those bawdy bars. He monitored who bellied up to his bar. And although there were no doors, he politely led the undesirables right out the nonexistent exit with a coupon to one of the rowdier spots in town. A better fit for everyone.

Truth be told, most of his customers were the locals, and that's how he liked it, because that was year-round. Occasionally, tourists would poke their heads in and then back out when they realized how small the place was. He could only guess it was the lack of anonymity in the tight space that sent them fleeing, but if he could work in a quick hello, most of the time they came in and then always returned.

Tug ambled in, a grin on his weathered face, his ball cap pushed back like always. "Hey, partner. The usual."

"Well, if it ain't the legend himself," Fisher teased, grabbing a clean glass and reaching for the cherry syrup. "Didn't expect to see you tonight. Isn't this your night for romancing Rosemary?"

Tug laughed, settling onto his favorite stool. "Normally, yeah. But we're shufflin' things around. Her daughter and granddaughter are staying for a while at her place. The kid is having a rough patch, so they're looking to hit pause on real life for a bit."

Fisher raised a brow, sliding the cherry limeade across to him. "Ah. So Rosemary's got her hands full. And here I thought you two had the island all to yourselves. Guess this'll cramp your style, huh?"

Tug chuckled. "Nah. Well, maybe a little. But I'm glad they're here. Hopefully, Whelk's Island'll work its magic on them."

"I don't know. You and Rosemary spend all your time together these days."

"Don't knock it till you try it." Tug's look was matter-of-fact.

"Are you sure you're not at risk of some kind of withdrawal?"

"She's worth it. And I'll be fine as long as you keep serving me these delicious cherry limeades."

"Cures everything, huh?"

Fisher watched Tug take that first sip of his drink like it was the best thing on earth. "Always does."

"Well, you let me know if there is anything I can do, Tug."

"I will." Tug clucked his tongue and winked, the universal sign for "Later," before starting to head out, but then he turned back and placed his hand on the bar. "I know you're just teasing about me and Rosemary spending so much time together, but I'll tell you, I have never been happier than when I'm with her."

"So, I'm the last confirmed bachelor of Whelk's Island over forty?"

"You might be the only confirmed bachelor, period. Get smart. Don't miss out for so long like I did."

And with that, he headed out, leaving Fisher to the quiet hum of his bar with the weight of words that felt less like friendly ribbing and more like a challenge. Maybe it was time he stopped telling himself he was content and started figuring out what was missing.

The evening rolled on easily. Locals trickled in, grumbling about tourist traffic and sharing updates about where the fish were biting. Fisher listened, poured drinks and served appetizers, and let the rhythm of the place settle over him.

He stepped outside for a breather as the night deepened, leaning against the weathered railing and watching the moon's reflection shimmer on the water. Tomorrow he had a surf lesson booked with a group of kids visiting from Raleigh. He loved thinking about how their faces always lit up when they caught that initial wave. Nothing like it. He still remembered the day he first rode a wave as clearly as if it had happened this morning.

A breeze washed over him. The sea was calm tonight, but he knew that calm never lasted. And sure as the tides, a storm would come knocking.

Chapter Four

NO SOONER HAD THAT GUT FEELING TOLD HIM A STORM was brewing than he turned to see a girl standing near the end of the bar, a look of hesitation on her face. Her eyes darted around as though she was unsure if she belonged there. She was much younger than the usual crowd, early teens at best. Her red hair was pulled into a messy ponytail, and a denim jacket swallowed her small frame. She was trying too hard to blend in with the grown-ups.

So, this is the storm tonight, huh?

When Fisher returned to the bar, the girl took a slow step forward, her sneakers squeaking against the floor like they didn't belong there either. She squared her shoulders, trying to sell the role she was playing. Her fingers curled around the strap of her oversized bag, as though she needed something to hold on to.

"I'll have a beer," she said.

Fisher gave her a careful once-over, not reaching for a glass. The words had come a shade too rehearsed, and her voice was just a little too bright and forced.

Before he even opened his mouth, she fidgeted.

He didn't so much as flinch. He just gave a slow, easy grin like he'd seen this play before. "Tell you what, kiddo. Why don't I save you the trouble of making up a birthday and doing math in public? I'm guessing you're here for the world-famous soda special tonight?"

He reached for a glass, already filling it with ice and something sweet and fizzy. "It's what all the cool kids order when they're trying to look grown." He slid it across the bar, the ice clinking softly. "No ID required, and you'll leave with your pride still intact."

She stared at him, caught off guard. Her shoulders sank just a little, her fight fading. "Whatever," she muttered, but she took the glass, her eyes locked on the beer bottles behind him.

Fisher kept his voice light but his gaze steady. "We've all had nights we thought we needed to prove something. This isn't gonna be one of yours."

He watched her become uncomfortable, his mind working behind his calm exterior. He could tell by the way she held herself that she was more interested in proving a point than in actually enjoying a drink. A rookie move.

"How old are you?" he asked finally, his voice casual but probing.

The girl hesitated for a second too long before speaking. When she finally did, she rushed her words: "Twenty-one, almost twenty-two. My birthday is August twenty-third. I just moved here."

Fisher raised an eyebrow again. "Uh-huh. And what's your name?"

"Kelly?" The way the name lifted at the end seemed more a question than a response. The story was written all over her face. She was looking for a way in, trying to break through whatever walls the town had built to keep out the inexperienced and naïve. And she wasn't quite ready to face the consequences.

He leaned back and took a slow look around the room. The

customers were all lost in their own conversations and the rhythm of the place. No one else had even noticed her walk in. But he wasn't about to let it slide.

"So, I guess I'll need to see your identification after all," Fisher said firmly.

She opened her mouth, but he raised a hand to stop her.

"Fine, my name isn't Kelly. Besides, I'm drinking soda."

"But that's not what you ordered. Are you here on vacation with your family?"

"No. I'm here with my mother, and we're staying at my grandmother's house. They'll vouch for me."

And with that, the pieces fell into place. Fisher had a good idea who this young lady was.

The girl lifted her chin. "Are you going to sell me a drink or not?"

Fisher kept his voice steady. "I'm not selling you a beer."

She pulled in a deep breath, mumbled something he couldn't make out, and stormed off.

"No, ma'am." He whisked around the counter so fast that she bumped right into him. "You're not leaving yet." He wasn't about to give her a moment of hope that he would let this go. About now, she should be sweating, and she had a look on her face like she might make a run for it.

She scowled but stayed put. "Change your mind?" Her voice carried a smug edge.

"Hardly." He pointed to a tall two-topper. "Take a seat."

She looked confused but hoisted herself onto the barstool.

Fisher tried to keep a close eye on her as he pulled out his phone and texted Tug. It was more than just the drinking; it was the defiance, the need to prove herself to some unseen force. He was determined to uncover the truth, and once he heard from Tug, he'd know for sure.

"What's going on here?" Fisher asked her.

"Nothing. I just wanted to buy a drink. Quit giving me grief. I'm thirsty. If you don't want me to be here, just sell me a bottle. I'll be on my way."

"It's a bar, not a liquor store. I don't sell bottles that leave this property. It's against the law."

She pulled out a twenty-dollar bill.

"I also don't serve anyone underage. Put that money back in your pocket." His phone buzzed with Tug's reply. "And by the way, you trying to buy beer is also breaking the law."

With his suspicions now confirmed by Tug, Fisher slid his phone into his back pocket and folded his arms across his chest with calm authority. "Come on, Kendra. Let's go."

Her eyes flew wide, the glass he'd given her pausing halfway to her lips. "How do you know my name?"

Fisher just gave a small, knowing smile, the kind that said he saw more than she wanted him to.

"Small island. Folks look out for each other."

He went outside, the heat of the summer air heavy on his skin, and Kendra followed. Then she cocked her hip and crossed her arms, tapping her foot in the sand.

"You're not fooling anyone," Fisher said, his voice still calm but with an edge of authority. "This little game you're playing can be dangerous."

She shot him a glare, the anger in her eyes simmering. "It's none of your business."

Fisher let the girl's anger wash over him. "It is more than a little bit my business. I'm responsible for what goes on in here." He paused. "And I am well versed in getting into trouble. Rethink this path now while you can. Believe me, it's not a fun hole to dig yourself out of."

"What are you gonna do? Call the cops?"

Kendra's scowl deepened, but Fisher caught movement in his periphery as Nina stepped into view behind her daughter. Her red hair caught the porch light, and her shoulders were drawn tight. Taller and more graceful than he remembered, she carried a beauty that could quiet a room. But tonight it was the fire in her green eyes that spoke loudest. He'd had only one interaction with the pretty redhead during her last short visit to town, but he could tell she was a force to be reckoned with. Someone ready to right wrongs.

Fisher turned just as Nina stepped closer, and for a beat, he took her in. She didn't look like a local. She was polished, tailored, controlled. Even in jeans with her crisp starched shirt tucked in beneath a belt with a golden buckle, she seemed dressed up.

Out of my league.

But Fisher could see the cracks. Like the way she brushed her hair back a fraction too fast, as though she were too tired to even care if it stayed put.

He felt bad he'd had to be the one to rat out her daughter. Doing the right thing didn't always make you feel like a hero.

Behind Kendra, Nina's voice cut through the humid night air: sharp, precise, but carrying the weight of exhaustion. "What are you doing here?"

Kendra spun around. Her defiance faltered for a second, but she recovered and doubled down. "I'm fine, Mom. What?" She let out a low aggravated grunt and turned back to Fisher. "Guess you ratted me out, huh?"

"She tried to order a beer," Fisher said gently to Nina, not wanting to pile on but not willing to sugarcoat it either.

Nina looked at Fisher as if ready to apologize.

He stopped her. "Happens more often than you'd think. Kids experimenting. Come on, I'm not the only one who did that at her age, am I?" Nina was out of place in this easy, sun-worn town, yet something about her made him curious to know more.

Nina blinked. "No, you're right. But it's different when it's your kid." She let out a breath. "I'm so sorry about this. We haven't even been here a whole day yet."

Fisher didn't want Kendra to think it wasn't a big deal, but he did want Nina to relax a little. "Look, kids test boundaries."

"I can hear you," Kendra said.

Nina's breath hitched, and Fisher wasn't sure what she was going to do or say. He tried to tame the moment that was building quickly. "Now that you know what's going on, it's less likely to happen again."

Her eyes softened, and for a brief second, Fisher could see the strain beneath her beauty. The quiet exhaustion of a mother struggling to hold it all together.

Nina leveled her gaze on her daughter. "Kendra, what were you thinking? Get in the car. Now."

Kendra gave her a sharp look, then got in, slamming the door hard enough to shake teeth.

"I don't know what's gotten into her." She glanced over at Kendra. "Thank you for contacting Tug."

"He mentioned earlier that y'all were coming to town to stay with your mom for a while. When I realized she might be your daughter, I texted Tug. I'm sorry we had to meet again under these circumstances, but I'm sure it'll shake out. Looks like you have your hands full tonight, though."

"You have no idea." She laughed. "Mom doesn't know what she's in for." She brushed a shaking hand through her hair, swallowing back her frustration.

"I can let the other bar owners know to be on the lookout."

"That would be great."

"Happy to do it." Fisher's eyes lingered on Nina. She was beautiful, sure, but it was a beauty tempered with something that went beyond her physical appearance. She possessed a quiet strength despite being on the verge of a breakdown.

Fisher's phone pinged. He glanced at the message and typed something back.

When he looked up, he noticed Nina's hands shaking. She was holding it together, but she shouldn't have to work so hard at it.

"Let me drive y'all home," he offered, but the words came out a little softer than he intended.

Nina glanced up, her green eyes sharp, assessing him. She hesitated, as if she wasn't sure she trusted him. Then she nodded. "Yeah. Yes. Thank you." A long sigh followed. She held out her shaking hands. "I'm probably better off not driving."

"Great. I'll drive you in your car. Tug can probably give me a ride back."

"Yeah," she said with a smirk. "You already texted him and asked, didn't you?"

He grinned. "What can I say? Whelk's Island operates on inside information. Let's get you two home."

He got behind the wheel. Nina got in, and he caught Kendra sulking in his rearview mirror, looking anywhere but toward them during the short drive. Fisher was glad Nina had accepted his help. Something in her sigh told him she'd been carrying too much for too long. But he wasn't sure she realized that.

She sat tense in the passenger seat, and he could feel the emotion swirling around the teenager in the back seat without even looking. As he turned onto Rosemary's street, his gut tightened at the strangest thought: *I've never been one to step into someone else's storm uninvited. But tonight? I'm already standing in the rain.*

Chapter Five

FISHER CRESTED THE DUNE JUST BEFORE SIX THAT MORNING, his board tucked under one arm, the familiar weight of it a comfort against his side. The breeze met him first, carrying the promise of another perfect morning. He paused at the top, his bare feet sinking into the soft sand, and took in the view below.

The first look at the ocean's morning mood never got old. The Atlantic sparkled beneath the rising sun, waves rolling in lazy sets but with just enough chop to make things interesting for the crew of kids he was teaching today.

Down on the stretch of beach where the tide had only recently retreated, the group of teens stood waiting, boards planted upright like fence posts across the damp sand. The wet ground glistened where the ocean had smoothed it, dark and packed firm. They'd chosen the right spot: high enough that the waves wouldn't sneak back up on them but close enough to feel their pull.

The kids' chatter floated up on the breeze, enthusiastic and peppered with the kind of good-natured banter that only young boys could pull off at this hour. They made dares, one-upped each other on who'd catch the biggest wave, and tossed around nicknames like they'd known one another forever.

Bright rash guards and board shorts made a patchwork of color against the pale backdrop of the morning sky: reds, blues, neon greens, and oranges that stood out as bold as a basket of beach balls. The boys shifted from foot to foot, itching to get started, the sand already darkened where their excitement left prints.

Some had slathered on sunscreen in streaks that caught the sun's early rays, while others fidgeted with their shiny new gear: leashes coiled just right and decals untouched by salt or sand. It brought a smile to Fisher's face. The boards were the kind that cost more than a few birthday wishes, and he'd bet good money most of the kids hadn't seen more water than a backyard pool, if even that.

What struck him most was that they were there. Early. Eager. Before their scheduled sunrise lesson—the best time to hit the beach, in his opinion. They stood on that cool, wet sand with their eyes wide open, ready to learn. Fisher's heart tugged, full of quiet pride. *This is gonna be a good group.*

He moved his board to under his other arm, his gaze sweeping the shore, and started down the dune, the soft crunch of his steps lost beneath the steady hush of the waves. As he walked, that old familiar ache settled low in his chest—the kind that always came when he saw kids like this, full of wonder, given a chance to fall in love with the ocean and the sport the way he had.

He thought about what it might've been like if, all those years ago, some patient soul had handed him a board and said, "Here, try this instead." Maybe he wouldn't have made half the mistakes he did. Maybe the weight he carried wouldn't feel so heavy on quiet mornings like this.

That's why he showed up. It's why he gave kids surfing lessons in exchange for help around The Tackle Box or odd jobs at his properties. Because he knew, deep down in his bones, how different things could've been. He'd do his part to make sure these kids had better.

Fisher drew in a long breath, letting the salt air fill him, settle him. The past was the past, but out here—on this beach, with these kids—he could shape something good. Maybe even something lasting.

This time it was one of those high-society types from Raleigh who'd contacted him about setting up the lessons, planning the half day for their teens as part of summer vacation. Word of mouth brought him more lessons than he could take on after all these years. The woman's motivation may have been less about the kids and more about buying the moms some uninterrupted time in the sun, but that didn't matter.

The parents clustered farther up the beach, perched beneath massive umbrellas, with fancy beach wagons and coolers lined up, like they were at a weeklong expedition rather than a morning lesson. Fisher grinned. He'd seen it before: city folks trying to master the art of beach life.

"Good morning, y'all." He waved as he approached.

The kids responded with a mix of "Hey!" and "Good morning!" as they straightened up.

Fisher set down his favorite board: a longboard with a hand-painted sea turtle on the nose, edges worn from years of rides. He tapped it affectionately. "This old girl's seen more sunrises than I can count. Ain't fancy, but she's true. And that's what counts out there."

The kids leaned in, listening. He could tell they were trying to soak it up, trying to figure out what made him seem so at ease with the world.

"All right, now. First things first," Fisher said with his hands on his hips. "Y'all are fortunate to be here this morning. These lessons? That gear you're holding? That's thanks to the folks sitting up the beach who will be sweating it out under those umbrellas while you try to catch your first wave. So, before we do a single pop-up drill, I want each of you to promise me you'll make a point today to thank your parents. Lotta kids don't get this kinda shot. Always show your appreciation for the opportunities you're given."

A few kids exchanged sheepish glances. Fisher hoped they'd take the lessons seriously. "It's easy to forget, I know. But gratitude's like wax on a board. It helps everything go smoother."

They laughed at that, and the mood lightened.

"Now, let's talk about what makes a surfer. Fancy boards and shiny stickers don't mean a thing if you don't respect this water, respect your body, and respect the people you're sharing the waves with." He scanned the group, seeing their excitement simmer down to focus.

"Sharing the waves?" one boy said, then snickered.

"Yes, sharing, and that's serious business, because you can get hurt out there if you're not paying attention. Staying healthy, staying strong–that's your foundation. Hydrate, eat right, and stretch. Before and after. The ocean's a mighty teacher, but she won't go easy on you just because you skipped your veggies."

The boys grinned, some nudging one another.

Fisher led them through a warm-up, the sun climbing higher as the air grew heavier. They did pop-up drills on the sand and learned paddle positioning and balance stances. He moved among them, adjusting a hand here, shifting a foot there.

"Feel your board. Know where your center is. Never fight the wave. It'll win every time. Work with it."

After a good half hour onshore, it was time.

"All right, let's hit the water," Fisher shouted. "Remember, look where you want to go, not at your feet. Also, remember to breathe."

They waded into the water, squealing as the cold hit their bodies.

"Let's do this," he encouraged them as they rehearsed what they'd been practicing on the sand, and now the boards were bobbing beside them. Fisher watched them try their first rides. Some wiped out spectacularly, boards flying, bodies splashing. But they came up laughing, salt stinging their eyes, hooked on the thrill.

A boy named Mason, maybe thirteen years old, caught a small swell and rode it all the way in, his arms flailing. The beach erupted in cheers.

Fisher paddled over. "That's what I'm talkin' about, Mason! You earned yourself a title today, my friend."

Mason's eyes went wide. "A title?"

Fisher grinned. "You bet. You're officially the 'Whelk's Island Wave Wrangler' for best effort of the day."

The other kids whooped and clapped, and Mason beamed like he'd just won a trophy.

As the lesson continued, Fisher kept pace with them, calling out encouragement and demonstrating on his sea-turtle board. His movements were fluid and easy, a man at home on the water. It would take years before they reached that level, and he hoped they would.

"Remember, y'all—respect the lineup. Wait your turn. Cheer each other on. That's how surf families are made. Out here, we're all on the same team."

And sure enough, when one boy finally got his pop-up right and rode his first clean wave, the whole group applauded as though they'd done it themselves.

Out of the corner of his eye, Fisher saw Rosemary, Amanda, Hailey, and Jesse making their way down the beach. Amanda carried a bag, Rosemary had a sun hat tilted just so, and the kids skipped along, collecting shells and treasures.

No Nina.

Fisher's heart sank, though he kept his focus on his students. He wondered if Amanda had seen her that morning and if Nina had found a little peace after last night's storm.

When the lesson wrapped up, the parents converged, full of praise.

"You're incredible with them," one mom gushed, pushing sunglasses up the bridge of her nose. "They had the best time!"

"Can we book you again before we leave?" another chimed in.

Fisher rested his hands on his board. "Glad they enjoyed it. My week is pretty booked up, but we can talk about that."

As they crowded around, snapping photos, Fisher's eyes drifted past them. And there she was.

Nina.

She was standing just beyond the group, her hands loose at her sides, hair tousled by the breeze, watching him. How long had she been there?

The way the sun lit her hair made his heart stumble. Their eyes met, and for a breath, the noise around him faded.

Chapter Six

LAST NIGHT STILL PRESSED IN ON NINA, THE WEIGHT OF IT mingling with concern, gratitude, and a whole lot of embarrassment. She stood there at the dune, barefoot in the warm sand, her skirt lapping at her calves in the light breeze, watching Fisher stride toward her from the water. With his board under one arm, he moved like a man who belonged to this place, as much a part of the ocean as the town itself.

Was it a mistake to have come here to see him? Anxiety rushed over her. Tug had said this was where she'd find him, and at the time it felt right. But now, with him closing the distance, she wondered why she hadn't just called. Or left well enough alone.

Then he smiled. An easy, genuine smile that somehow made her feel steadier and more nervous all at once.

His damp brown hair caught the morning light, his blue eyes crinkled at the corners, and his sun-warmed skin stretched across his broad shoulders. He looked so at ease out here, as though the sea itself had shaped him. She hadn't meant to notice how fit he was, but it was hard not to. He was so athletic, strong and steady. She blinked, pulling her thoughts back to why she'd come.

She tried to hide her anxiousness with a smile, hoping it came across as friendly rather than flustered. The truth was, she felt off-balance, like she'd stepped into one of those rip currents she'd been warned about. This wasn't the plan. She'd come only to say thank you, nothing more. But standing here now, watching Fisher with the sea at his back and that easy warmth in his eyes, she couldn't help but feel a gentle pull that was a little unsettling. Plus, she'd told herself, he was not her type at all.

"Good morning," Fisher said, stopping a few paces away.

"Hi." Her voice came out softer than she'd meant, so she cleared her throat. "I didn't mean to interrupt. I just . . . well, Tug said I'd find you out here this morning, and . . ." Her eyes dropped to his board, and a grin tugged at her lips. "Is that a sea turtle on your board?"

Fisher glanced down and gave the nose of his board an affectionate pat. "It is. Hand-painted years ago. She's been with me a very long time."

"She? The board or the turtle?"

He cocked his head. "Well, hadn't really thought about it that way before. I consider them one and the same."

"Does *she* have a name?"

His mouth pulled to the left in a grimace. "I don't really tell people her name."

Her brows raised and she stifled a laugh, but before she could say anything, he did.

"But it's a good question, and I don't think anyone has ever asked. Her name is Honu Honey."

"Honu? Honey?"

"*Honu* is Hawaiian for 'sea turtle,' and this sweet honey of a board is one I bought while surfing for a year in Hawaii, while I was finding myself."

She leaned closer and he twirled the board. "Wow! The view of the sea turtle on top and the belly on the bottom? That is really cool. Hawaii for a year, huh? Beats Europe, I'd think."

"Wouldn't know."

"Well, I grew up in Hawaii, and I've been to Europe. The islands win. So, it's . . . *she's* beautiful. I don't think I've ever seen a surfboard like that. The way it catches the light is mesmerizing."

"Well, then, you really should see the one I have with a pelican. That's my backup board. Not quite as lucky, but it's got character."

"Two boards?" She laughed, the tension easing between them. "Oh, I'm going to have to see that."

"I'll give you the tour sometime," he said, his smile widening. "And brace yourself. There are about a dozen of them. Not all with personality, as you so politely put it."

Oh no! Did I embarrass him? She shouldn't have made light of his surfboard. She knew better. After all, David couldn't golf without The Green Reaper, his lucky putter. *Men and their weird sports habits.*

"I didn't mean to offend you," she said.

"No offense taken. It is a little funnier now than it seemed when I thought of it. Being a sea turtle surfing the waves just seemed so epic, and it tied into my whole Hawaii experience."

"Epic." He's a real-deal surfer dude. "I, uh, came to say thank you. For last night. You didn't just stop Kendra from making a mistake. You helped me step in, helped me see it for what it was. And that kind of help—that's rare these days."

"You don't owe me anything. That's how we do things here. Folks look out for each other."

"I know, but still—I'd like to show my appreciation properly. Would you join us for dinner tonight? Nothing fancy. Just something simple. Mom and Tug will be there too. I'll handle the cooking, and Kendra can apologize."

For a second, he didn't answer. He just watched her as a light gust teased a strand of hair across her cheek. His eyes, kind and sure, held hers. "I'll be there. I'd like that," he said, and it sounded like he meant it.

She found herself glancing past him at the kids out in the surf, their laughter carrying on the breeze, boards bobbing in the gentle swell. "You're great with them," she said quietly.

"They're good kids. And the ocean—it brings out the best in folks."

"You make it look easy," she admitted, unable to keep her eyes from lingering a little longer on him, from his sun-kissed skin to those strong arms and the way he stood like he and the sea had some unspoken understanding. "And you look pretty good out there."

Fisher chuckled softly. "Thank you for that. Truth is, it's not just about surfing for me. It's the peace the water brings. The rhythm of the tide reminds me life's always in motion, always changing. When storms come, you learn to stand firm, like those sandbars out there. I find clarity here. Some people jog or go to the gym. I surf. This is where I feel most at home."

Nina's heart softened. She could see it now—the connection between him and the sea, the way it shaped him—and she realized she liked seeing him this way. She liked it a lot, because having grown up in Hawaii, she understood what he meant.

"Well," she said, tucking that loose strand of hair behind her ear, "I'm glad you're here."

His gaze lingered. "Me too. So, where and what time for dinner, and what can I bring?"

"How about Mom's house around six-thirty? We'll probably eat around seven, and you don't need to bring a thing."

"I'll be there."

They stood for an awkward moment, trying to end the conversation. "Yeah, so I'm going to go." She turned, closing her eyes and wishing she hadn't been such a dork just then.

"See you tonight," he called after her.

Chapter Seven

FISHER PULLED UP IN FRONT OF ROSEMARY'S HOUSE RIGHT at 6:25 P.M. *If you're not early, you're not on time.*

He killed the engine, took a breath, and glanced at the covered dish riding shotgun. Showing up empty-handed just wasn't an option, and besides, Rosemary and Tug had become accustomed to him bringing his specialty whenever they invited him to dinner. It was cheap and easy to make, but that old cast-iron skillet made it look important. He'd perfected the recipe over the years. His secret ingredients, honey and mayo, didn't sound all that appealing, which was enough reason not to share the recipe.

He carried the heavy skillet up the stairs, balancing it in one hand, and rapped on the frame. Before he could second-guess his timing, the door creaked open and Kendra stood there, wide-eyed.

For a beat, she just stared at him, like she wasn't sure he was real. Then, to his surprise, her gaze softened, and she wrapped her arms across her chest. "Um . . . hi, Fisher. I—I'm sorry about . . . you know . . . last night. About everything."

Fisher smiled, easy and genuine. He didn't know if Nina had encouraged the apology or if Kendra had come to it on her own. Either way, he appreciated it. "Thank you, Kendra. That means a lot. And for what it's worth, I think you've got a good head on your shoulders. We all make mistakes. It's what we do next that counts."

"Yes, sir."

He stood there for a moment, then realized she must not have known why he was there. "Um, your mom invited me over to dinner."

"Oh!" She twisted to shout, but Nina was already walking through the dining area toward the front door with a stack of napkins in her hand. Kendra turned and walked away without another word.

"Hey, Fisher. Come on in."

He walked inside, the familiar scent of something slow-cooked and Southern filling the air.

"Right on time." Nina's words came across as sweet but slightly nervous.

Funny, because he felt the same way, and there was no reason for all that. It wasn't a date. Just a dinner with people who knew him well. He lifted the cast-iron skillet. "Brought my famous skillet cornbread. Figured it'd go with whatever's cooking."

"I'd say that would go with pretty much everything. Thanks," Nina replied, her eyes brightening.

Fisher followed a rhythm of playful laughter to the kitchen, where Tug and Rosemary worked side by side, surrounded by the aroma of roasted chicken. "That smells so good."

"Fisher! We're so glad you're joining us," Rosemary said.

Tug came over and clapped him on the shoulder. "How're you doing?"

"Good. Can't complain. What's on the menu?"

Rosemary piped in. "My slow-roasted chicken, greens with a hint of vinegar, fresh tomatoes from the farmers market this morning sprinkled with salt and pepper, a big bowl of buttered corn on the cob, and peach cobbler for dessert."

"Fresh peaches too?"

"You betcha." Tug grinned. "It was a harvest day, and no tractor required."

"Perfect timing, Fisher. Dinner's ready." Rosemary looked toward Nina. "Are we ready?"

"I was just putting the silverware in place when Fisher knocked," Nina said over her shoulder as she hurried back to the dining room, napkins fluttering like white flags.

Rosemary carried the platter with the chicken on it into the dining room. "Kendra, tomorrow it's your turn to set the table." Everyone carried something over, and then the chairs scraped against the wood plank floors as everyone sat down.

Rosemary reached for Tug's hand to her left and Nina's to the right. "Let me bless this food real quick."

Heads bowed as she offered the blessing.

"Lord, we thank You for this good meal, for the hands that prepared it, and for the gift of friends who are family in every way that matters. We're especially grateful tonight for timely help, for kind hearts, and for reminders that we are never alone. Help us walk with grace, speak with kindness, and fly straight when the world tempts us otherwise. Amen."

Fisher caught the gentle weight of those words and the way Kendra's gaze lowered a little, thoughtful. The clanging of serving spoons and soft chatter filled the room as plates were passed, butter melted on warm cornbread, and ice clinked in glasses.

Conversation flowed and laughter spilled over like the sweet tea from Tug's glass when Kendra made a surprising funny remark that cracked them all up. For the first time in a long while, Fisher felt that quiet peace that came with belonging.

They steered clear of the events of the previous night.

"I'm calling it quits," Fisher said, placing his napkin on the table. "Ladies—and Tug, of course—that was a wonderful meal."

"Well, a man can't live on skillet cornbread alone," Rosemary teased.

"It's pretty much the only thing I ever bring when I come over. I'm sure they're sick of it." Fisher leaned back and offered Nina a grin.

"We are not. We love it and we love you," Rosemary said. She then stood. "Kendra, you can help me clear the table."

Kendra's mouth dropped open, but she got up and started carrying plates gingerly from the dining room to the kitchen sink.

Rosemary picked up the serving platter. "Y'all go on out and enjoy the deck to continue the conversation. Kendra will do the dishes, and Tug and I will get dessert ready."

"Ouch. No hurry on the dessert, Mom. I think we can take a minute before that."

"Truly," Fisher agreed.

"Come on," Nina said, her eyes twinkling. "Let's not argue with her. I learned that a long, long time ago."

"Don't have to tell me twice." Fisher got up and they walked out to the deck, leaving Kendra, Tug, and Rosemary in the kitchen.

The ocean stretched before them, dark and endless, the waves rolling in like pounding thunder.

"That sound, and the coolness of the breeze off the water, can ease the tension out of anything," Fisher said.

"Thank goodness, because I'm wound up tight!" She walked over to the railing, looking out over the water. "I know this is just a beach. Just a house. But something about being here under Mom's roof, near the ocean, is making me feel like maybe we will come through this stuff with Kendra okay."

"You will. And Whelk's Island is special. It holds that old-fashioned moral compass. Remember how they used to say it takes a village to raise a kid? Probably more true now than ever, only there's no village most places. You've got one here."

"Yeah. This place has many special qualities," she said.

"That's true." Fisher's lips pressed into a thin line. "After my dad passed, I didn't think I'd ever find peace again. Couldn't stand to be still—couldn't sleep, couldn't think straight. I had an aunt with ties to Whelk's Island. She'd always been so encouraging, so I came here. Only it wasn't just her that was grounding. It's this place. The ocean was the only thing that could drown out everything else."

"Yeah, that's how it feels."

"It's like the tide knows just how much to take to leave us with what we need to start over." Fisher stepped next to her, leaning his forearms on the railing to get to her level. "Tug said you might need a friend right now. He told me about your divorce."

"Not a pretty story." Nina turned, then glanced at him, smiling. "Is Tug always this protective of newcomers?"

"Not sure," Fisher said with a shrug. "I think mostly for daughters and granddaughters of the woman he is madly in love with."

She laughed. "Fair enough."

"He's been sort of a father to all of us at some point. Join the club. It's a good one to be a part of."

"You don't think he's going to set a curfew for me while I'm here, do you? They aren't even married yet."

Fisher smirked. "He knows his boundaries. He's a solid guy, you know."

"I do. I can see it in my mom's smile." She looked like she was relaxing a little, finally. "It's so beautiful here. Like a dream. Do you ever get tired of this?"

"The ocean?"

"The view. It's breathtaking, and still different every day. Or is that just because I'm a newbie to the beach?"

"No, its appearance changes every day. Depending on the mood of the ocean, it can go from green to blue to black, and even the temperature makes things look different. Sometimes a storm's so far away we can't even see it, but it still shakes things up here on the coast."

"It's been a long time since I lived in Hawaii, and honestly, I was so young that I took it for granted," Nina admitted.

She leaned forward, gazing out over the water. "Yeah, I remember shelling as a little girl, and surfing, of course. I was actually pretty good."

"You?"

"Hey, don't look so surprised."

"Well, you just—"

"Just what?"

"I had you pegged as more of a beach-chair-with-a-book kind of gal than a barefoot board-under-your-arm thrill-seeking type."

She looked taken aback at first, and then she started laughing. "Yeah, well, I am that now. But there was a time."

"It's like riding a bike. If you want to get back out there while you're in town, I love having company."

"Oh, after this many years, I might be about as good as those boys you were teaching this morning. And I hate to say it, but only maybe two of them are even remotely the kind to keep it up."

"That's true, but if I can unleash even one new surfer a season, it's a good thing. It really changed my life."

"Nature can do that, can't it?" She took in a deep breath. "I've been locked up in an office for so long that I almost forgot what this felt like."

"Then enjoy it."

"I come bearing gifts," Tug said as he pushed through the deck doors. "Forgive the intrusion."

Nina took one of the plates and handed the other to Fisher. "I'll share."

"Thanks." Fisher took a bite. "I'm too full for this, but how can I resist?"

"Yeah. Rosemary can really bake—and cook," Tug said. "I feel like a rookie next to her."

"But you owned a diner for how many years?" Nina asked.

"More than seems possible." He nudged Fisher. "She's trying to make me feel old."

"No! I just meant you have to be an amazing cook too." Nina blushed and looked grateful for the distraction when Kendra walked out carrying her plate of dessert with Mom on her heels. "Hey, you two. Welcome to the beach party."

Kendra sat at the end of a chaise longue. "This is my second piece of cobbler. Grandma said she's going to teach me how to make it."

"Learn from the best," Nina said. "I'm sure you'll stir up some trouble in the kitchen together."

"If we do it right," Rosemary teased.

"Mom, can I have the keys to the car so I can get all my beach stuff out?" Kendra asked.

"Honey, we'll do it later. It's underneath all my boxes from the office. Remind me, and we'll do it when it cools down tonight."

Fisher set his empty plate aside. "I'll go get it." He motioned to Nina for the keys.

"No, Fisher, thank you. I loaded all of it into the trunk. I'm capable of unloading it too."

Is this what people mean about redheads being stubborn? He didn't mind it, really, but his old-fashioned manners wouldn't let it be. Plus, he kind of liked her spirit.

"I know you're capable," he said, trying not to sound condescending. "But I'm here and want to lend a hand. I like to lighten the load by helping my neighbors. Ask your mom. I carry stuff up for her all the time."

"Y'all know there's an elevator, right?" Kendra said.

"See, so it's not even that hard to do," Fisher said. "Just let me feel like I'm doing a good deed so I can check it off my list for the day."

Nina hesitated. "I loaded it. I can unload it."

Fisher met her gaze, steady as the tide. "I know you can. But I want to help."

Reluctantly, she grabbed her keys from the counter and tossed them, Fisher catching them midair.

"Thanks. That would be great. If you could get the boxes from my trunk and put them in the downstairs apartment, that would be a huge help. Sorry, Kendra's beach stuff is all the way at the bottom underneath them all."

He turned to leave, and Nina jumped to her feet. "Stop," she said. "You know what? Some of those boxes are pretty heavy. Maybe I should help."

"Nope. I'm *capable.*" He lifted his chin and stepped around her. "Hang out and have fun."

"Okay," she said, but the word strung out as if she doubted it. "Just set them inside my door."

"On it." He gave her a quick nod, feeling pleased he'd been able to penetrate her armadillo armor. "Come on, Kendra. You can sort out the stuff you want." Kendra followed him out the front door to take the stairs down to the driveway.

"I usually take the elevator," she said.

"Yeah, well, your body will appreciate the extra steps over summer vacation since there's no PE while school's out."

She shrugged but stood there ready to help.

He unlocked the car, the keys warm in his hand, hoping one day she'd see what he already knew: Some loads are meant to be shared.

Chapter Eight

THE NEXT MORNING, NINA WOKE FEELING MORE PREPARED to face the day than she had over the past few months. She'd left her window open to fall asleep to the sound of the ocean. After a productive day at work, she made her way to the kitchen upstairs and took a seat at the table. Across from her, Rosemary sat, as steady and unshaken as ever, hands wrapped around a mug of tea and a peaceful look of serenity softening the lines etching her face.

Nina ached to feel like that.

The light spilled through the window, casting a glow on Rosemary's fiery hair and cheerful coral wrap, seemingly brightening the whole kitchen. The gentle steam from her mug carried the soothing scent of chamomile. There was also something yummy cooking in a crockpot.

Even in her seventies, her mom radiated a youthful spirit. The way she moved, the way she dressed, the way she embraced each day made it easy for Nina to forget her age. It was like she'd uncovered the secret to staying young at heart.

As a kid, Nina had watched her mom dance barefoot in the sand more times than she could count, swaying to island melodies under the stars and never losing the rhythm. Mom had always known how to embrace joy.

Nina envied that calm, that ability to let go. She needed to borrow about half a cup of it right now because her entire life felt like a cracked foundation and she could barely hold up the walls any longer.

Thankfully, Kendra had gone with Tug to help at Paws Town Square, which would at least buy Nina a little more time before she had to deal with her and Kendra's issues. Nina made some tea, then sat at the kitchen table, stirring her tea absentmindedly as she watched the late-afternoon breeze play with the curtains. She needed a dose of her mom's steady spirit, especially as she wanted to talk to her about something that was still bothering her a bit.

"I'm not sure about all this, Mom," Nina said, finally breaking the silence. She couldn't keep it in anymore. The question had been eating at her ever since they arrived on the island. Rosemary's whirlwind romance with Tug seemed to be moving at breakneck speed. "Things are moving fast with you and Tug. I mean, are you sure you're ready for this?"

"Of course I'm ready. Why wouldn't I be? He's a good man, and we love each other." Her mother didn't look fazed by the question. She just took a sip of her tea. "You don't need to worry about me."

Nina wanted to believe her. But she also knew that love had a way of looking easy in the beginning. Hadn't she once believed her own marriage was built to last? She glanced at the engagement ring on her mother's finger. Tug had surprised her with it while the two of them were checking off the northern lights on their bucket list. Rosemary held her tea with the steadiness Nina had lost somewhere between divorce papers, her dad's death, and the recent late-night worries over Kendra.

How did Mom do it? How did she move forward so easily, while Nina still felt stuck in the wreckage of what should have been? And how did she know that Tug wasn't attracted to not only her beauty and fun-loving attitude but also the money that selling the macadamia farm had put in her pocket?

"Are you sure it's love?" Nina asked. The words slipped out before she could stop them, and immediately she regretted them. It wasn't her place to question her mother's happiness, especially when Nina knew deep in her heart that Mom and Tug did really love each other.

Rosemary's eyes softened, and her lips turned up in the slightest smile. "Yes, Nina. This is love. True love. It's different from what I had with your father, but it's just as strong."

Nina swallowed, feeling the weight of her mother's words. She knew her mom had loved Nina's father. She'd loved him deeply, but maybe their passion had faded over the years. That happened in long marriages.

"I just want to make sure you're happy," Nina muttered, the words heavy with all the uncertainty swirling inside her.

"I couldn't be happier with Tug," Rosemary said. "You've got enough on your plate with Kendra. Don't project your concerns onto me, please."

The mention of Kendra's name sent a fresh wave of exhaustion through Nina.

"Mom, you're right. That comment about Tug was misplaced. I'm sorry. I don't know what to do about Kendra, and I suppose I'm just looking for something I can fix."

Rosemary's brow furrowed, but her voice remained even. "It's not the end of the world, Nina. Kids make mistakes. She may have done it before, but you were given the chance to intercept her. Thank goodness Fisher put two and two together."

"It's just so embarrassing. And risky. What if she'd fallen prey to someone looking to take advantage of her in that bar?"

"She didn't, and it's not that kind of place. It's where neighbors go to catch up. The Tackle Box is like the town's unofficial living room. People gather to share stories, joke about tourists, and comfort each other. And Fisher is a good guy, which is why he noticed Kendra as soon as she popped in. Don't worry about things that didn't happen. Today is enough for us to carry."

"I'm so thankful Fisher was the one she approached."

"I like him. There's more to that quiet man than I've seen so far."

"Well, I guess that's something to be thankful for," Nina said, dropping her head into her hands.

"Let's count our blessings."

Nina rubbed her temples. "The whole town knows what happened by now. They'll all be judging me. I'm so sorry. They probably think I'm a horrible mother."

"Nina, you're doing your best." Rosemary's voice was soft and steady. "And you're there for Kendra. We know that, and that's really all that matters. Kendra will come around. Whelk's Island has a way of helping people work things out."

Nina's thoughts drifted for a moment. The idea of this small town doing something she hadn't been able to accomplish seemed like a lofty hope. She wasn't sure she was ready to embrace Whelk's Island and its easy, neighborly ways as a solution so quickly. And trusting it meant loosening her grip on that fear of failure—something she still hadn't mastered.

Nina said, "She's not exactly making it easy."

"I know." Rosemary's voice wrapped around the words like a hug. "Give yourself some grace. You both need a minute to let things simmer. Let the ocean air work its wonders on you. Be thankful and believe it can correct the course of things."

Kendra wasn't listening to even her grandma, although somehow Mom had snagged her to wash dishes last night. That was a start. Maybe Whelk's Island's slow pace would work in Nina's favor and Kendra would give up on fighting everything she tried to offer to help her.

A car door slammed outside.

"Tug and Kendra are back," Rosemary said, standing to peer out the front window.

Nina braced herself. Whatever mood Kendra was in would dictate the next few hours.

Tug's voice rumbled from the porch, his usual easy cadence filling the air. "You're just as stubborn as that pet fish of yours, kid."

Kendra stepped into view, shaking her head. "James isn't *my* pet fish. I just help feed him. He's Grandma's."

"Figures. She has a stubborn streak a mile wide too."

Kendra's laugh carried through the screen door. A heart laugh, not the sarcastic-edged one Nina had become used to. It was small, fleeting, but it sent a rush of relief through her.

"I haven't heard that joy in a while," Nina admitted, tears threatening to spill over her lashes, as she stood up from the table.

"Honey, don't take it personally. She's a typical teenager." She turned and patted Nina's hand sweetly. "Of course, I always took it very personally when your moods went wild. I know exactly what you're going through. You'll survive this. I promise."

"You wished this on me, didn't you?" But Nina was kidding, and Rosemary laughed. Yet it was true that as a teenager, Nina had heard this from her mom more times than she cared to remember: *"Wait until you have a daughter just like you."* "Was I *this* bad?"

Rosemary shrugged. "You were a handful. And you hadn't gone through all the family drama she's been through." She took Nina's hand. "Honey, it's life, and life is messy, but thank you from the very heart of me for turning to me for help." Her eyes became glossy. "You have no idea how much that means to me."

"You've always been there for me, Mom."

"I know we don't always see eye to eye, but I love you, and I'm proud of the woman you've become. You are so much stronger than I ever was."

"I don't know about that, but thank you for saying it."

The groan of the elevator behind them caused them both to turn just as the door opened.

"You knew she wasn't going to take the stairs," Nina said.

"Oh yeah. It's one of the best parts of this house. I'm still using the stairs for the exercise, but someday I'm going to be really grateful for that thing."

"If she doesn't wear it out while we're here." They shared the laugh. Nina understood everything that drew her mother to Whelk's Island. "The view, the weather, and the neighbors are all pretty spectacular too."

"They are." Rosemary tucked a wisp of red hair behind her ear, then gave Nina an encouraging look. "It feels even more like home with you here. I'm worried. You look so tired, dear."

"I am," Nina admitted.

Kendra strolled right between them. "How's James?"

"Land sakes!" Rosemary's hand fluttered to her chest as she turned. "He's on the coffee table. He's been blowing bubbles all morning. I told him you'd be back soon."

Rosemary and Nina followed Kendra as she raced to the table and dropped to her knees. The red betta fish, James, swam lazily in his bowl, pausing as he recognized her. She smirked, raising an eyebrow. "Yeah, I see you, James. I missed you too." She brushed her fingers against the glass. "Things are still the same with me," she muttered. "You get it, don't you?"

The fish, with his fin held high in what could be described only as a dignified nod, gave a flounce of his tail like he was acknowledging the unspoken struggle.

Kendra's lips twitched, and for a moment there, it looked like she might smile, but just as quickly, she shut it down and rose to her feet. "Is there anything to eat? I'm starving."

Rosemary shared a glance with Nina. "Dinner will be ready shortly."

"I brought some snacks. I put them in the pantry," Nina said defensively.

"Healthy snacks? They suck."

"Please don't use that word," Nina said. "You know it grates on me."

Kendra leaned down in front of the fishbowl. "Don't say 'suck.' It sucks to say 'suck.' "

"Hilarious."

"Go get a little snack, and you two be nice," Rosemary said, coming to the rescue. "This is Switzerland."

"Great, so basically I'm the only one who doesn't get an opinion." Kendra stomped off to the kitchen.

Nina raised her hand in mock surrender. "I'm sorry, Mom. I warned you. I don't know what I'm going to do about this."

"We'll take it step by step. One day at a time." The words snapped Nina's attention back to the moment. "I'll make her help me finish our dinner and calm her down."

Nina watched her mother's movements, fluid and graceful. There was something about the way Rosemary moved that made Nina feel like everything in her own life was out of sync. She couldn't help but feel a little envious of how grounded her mother was, how steady.

Dinner was a quiet affair. Kendra sat at the table with her arms crossed, her eyes darting everywhere except where they should have been: on the people who cared about her. Somehow Rosemary didn't let Kendra get away with the defiance. She gave her a pointed look and told her exactly what she expected.

"You will eat this meal with us." Mom's words were firm and final. "I'll hear no more complaints."

It was a command, not a suggestion, and Kendra reluctantly

picked up her fork. Nina was glad her mom wasn't letting Kendra get away with anything for once.

After dinner, just as Nina was cleaning up, there was a knock at the door. "Who could that be at this time of night?"

Rosemary laughed. "Only one way to find out."

"Since when did you become a smarty-pants?" Nina teased. She walked over and opened the door.

Fisher stood there, smiling. "Good evening. Mind if I drop in for just a few? I promise I won't be long."

"Sure. Yeah, come on in." She stepped to the side, and he strode into the room.

"I wanted to check in on you—and Kendra, of course."

"Business as usual." Nina didn't know what else to say. She hadn't expected him to come by again.

He looked as if he was expecting her to say more.

"She's in her room. Did you want to talk to her?" Nina couldn't decide if she was grateful for him or if she found his presence unsettling.

"No. I'm here to see you." Fisher's gaze drifted around the room, pausing on a stack of pamphlets on the coffee table. "You might have already found some local summer activities for Kendra. Some are really good, and they're specific to only teens on Whelk's Island. The surf shop has a program where the kids work in exchange for store bucks—earn a little money, gain some experience, stay out of trouble. I've seen it change some attitudes firsthand." He shrugged and handed the manila envelope he was carrying to Nina, his eyes warm with encouragement. "I don't mean to overstep. I just thought it might be good for her. For you both, really. I'm sure you could use some time not worrying about her. This might help do the trick."

"That was really thoughtful." Nina's heart caught somewhere between gratitude and hesitation. She hadn't expected this kind of help. And yet here it was, coming from Fisher, steady and kind, always one step ahead.

"Thank you," she whispered, wondering why it felt so awkward to accept help from him.

Rosemary walked back into the living room. "I thought I heard your voice." She hugged him. "What brings you around tonight?"

"Brought some stuff for Nina and Kendra. I was going to bring it tomorrow when we walk, but figured under the circumstances, Nina might get better rest knowing there are some good options."

Rosemary pressed a hand to Fisher's chest. "Is this guy the real deal or what?"

"Your mom is easy to impress," he teased. "We're still walking tomorrow morning, right?"

"Absolutely," Rosemary said.

When Fisher's eyes shifted to Nina, his smile widened. "You're welcome to join us. Once a week, we take a morning walk along the beach, searching for shells. It's a great way to start the day."

"Doubt it. I have to work, but we'll see," Nina said, beginning to thumb through the papers from the envelope.

She sensed his gaze linger a little longer than necessary, so she kept her head down and tried to pretend she hadn't noticed. After a few seconds, he said his goodbyes and left.

Nina let out a slow breath. "I've got bigger things to worry about than walking the beach with the local bar owner."

"Nina! That was judgy."

"I didn't mean it like that! I just don't have time to go for a leisurely walk. I've got a job and a daughter who is out of control."

"And a mother who thinks you need to lighten up a little

before you make yourself sick over this." Rosemary tilted her head. "Why don't you ask for just a few days off? Give yourself some time to unwind and find a routine."

"I'll think about it," Nina said, and she did, sort of, but her mind kept circling back to one thing. Not to the pamphlets, not even to Kendra, but rather to the way Fisher had shown up without her even asking.

Chapter Nine

MORNING SETTLED OVER WHELK'S ISLAND LIKE A THICK blanket against Fisher's skin, the salt-heavy air clinging the way certain memories refused to let go. The soft crunch of the crusted-over sand created a steady rhythm as he walked. He silently counted his steps, an absent-minded habit he'd never quite broken. It was quiet, just the way he liked it. Still, as he neared Rosemary's house, he couldn't help but wonder if Nina might join them on their walk this morning.

He climbed the steps and knocked on the door.

Kendra opened the door, shrinking back when she recognized him.

"I come in peace," he said.

She looked him right in the eye. "I'm sorry . . . still."

"Well, that's an excellent first step in the right direction. Apology accepted. Again."

Her lips lifted in a half smile. "Are you here to see Grandma?"

"I am. We have our weekly beachcombing date."

Kendra's eyes widened. "You do? She's kind of old for you, and you know she's engaged to Tug, right?"

"Yes." He couldn't hold back the laugh. "I'm well aware of that. It's not that kind of date. We're good friends. It's Tug's morning out for breakfast with the old men."

"Checkers and rocking chairs?" She laughed.

"Not quite, but almost. They tell stories about the good old days." He leaned in and whispered, "I've heard them all about a hundred times."

"Old people repeat themselves a lot." She paused, then added, "No offense."

"What?" Fisher smirked. "I didn't take any until you added the last part."

Kendra shrugged. "If the flip-flop fits . . ."

But this time, there was a teasing glint in her eyes, like she wasn't as irritated by his presence as she wanted to be.

She turned, calling into the house, "Grandma! You have company."

Rosemary called from her room, "Fisher! Come on in. I'm almost ready."

He peered into the kitchen. Nina sat at the table, drinking coffee and looking at her laptop.

She turned, pulling off her glasses. For a split second, he thought she might say she was coming. Then she said, "Enjoy your walk. I think I'm going to get these emails cleared out of my inbox."

The faint clink of her spoon against the coffee mug led to her fingers quickly dancing over the computer keyboard. Fisher took a chance. "It can't wait for just thirty minutes?"

"No." She looked up. "But thank you for the invitation." She turned back to her computer, leaving him standing there awkwardly dismissed.

"If you change your mind, I'll show you the hidden spots to find the best shells."

"Okay." She didn't even lift her eyes from her computer.

He realized he'd been looking forward to her joining them. He liked her energy, her presence, her quiet strength, but now, with the morning breeze and the expanse of the beach just ahead without her there, he felt the familiar sting of rejection.

Still, it wasn't the end of the world. He had Rosemary with him, and she was a steady presence in his life. They'd walked this beach together every week since he helped get her settled in the beach house. He'd even hung the Palakiko's Retreat sign for her. Fisher enjoyed the solitude of his mornings, but this time with Rosemary each week was something he looked forward to now.

He stepped outside to wait for her.

A couple of minutes later, she came down the stairs, smiling as she adjusted her windbreaker. "You want to ask Nina one more time?" Rosemary had a way of seeing through people, especially Fisher. He could never hide much from her.

He grinned. "Not this time. If she's not feeling it, I'll give her some space."

Nina was guarded, but not in the way people typically act when concealing something. She held herself like someone trying to keep everything from spilling over. Like she thought that if she let go for even a second, she wasn't sure she could put herself back together again.

He'd known that feeling before, and he wasn't sure what to do with the fact that he recognized it in her. He could tell there was more beneath the surface.

He turned his attention back to Rosemary. "Shall we get this walk going?"

She chuckled softly. "I imagine we will."

They started their walk along the shore, the morning sun spilling over them in golden swaths. Fisher's bare feet sank lightly into the wet sand as he walked beside Rosemary, the cold ocean water reaching his ankles with each slow step, and the gulls calling out in the distance. He had always felt a deep connection to this beach. It was one of the things that had kept him rooted to Whelk's Island. Here, it felt as though life could unfold at its own pace.

As they walked, Rosemary bent to pick up yet another shell, adding it to Fisher's pocket, which was her usual habit. Over the past few months, she'd come to rely on him for this, and he didn't mind at all. He was the one with pockets big enough to hold the beautiful little treasures she found scattered across the beach.

"You're a lucky man, Fisher." Her tone was light, teasing, but there was something beneath it. A question, maybe. "Tug said people are talking about our weekly walks," she continued, her voice drifting.

A smirk tugged at Fisher's lips. "When are you two going to set an official date and save my reputation?" A low, easy laugh slipped free.

Her laughter floated on the breeze. "Tug's a good man, and I love him." She pocketed another shell. "But, no, we haven't set a date. It's my fault, but he's not rushing me. Right now I've got Kendra and Nina to focus on."

"Ah, I see." Fisher stepped around a patch of seaweed tangled and forgotten by the tide. Something about it made his chest tighten. Probably that it was a reminder that people let things drift too far before thinking to hold on to them. "I guess love finds its way when it's ready, huh?"

Rosemary didn't seem to mind the deeper conversation. If anything, it only made her smile more, like she was letting him in on something. Maybe she was right. Did love always find its path when it was least expected?

They walked in silence for a while, letting the weight of their words hang between them.

Finally, Fisher said, "Kendra's a good kid." He knew how much Rosemary cared about her granddaughter, and he didn't want her to think he was ignoring the issue.

"She is," she agreed, her voice softening. "But a lot is going on in her mind. I don't know the whole story, but I know my daughter's perfectionism often makes it hard for her to see anything but the things she wants to fix."

Fisher's brow furrowed as he thought about Nina. From the moment he'd met her, there was an intensity in her that had caught his attention in ways he hadn't expected.

"She seems like a caring mother, though," Fisher said after a moment, glancing over at Rosemary.

"She is. But there's also been a lot of drama with her ex. I think anything that disrupts her carefully planned life right now is just one more thing she doesn't know how to handle." Her words had a quiet knowing that had Fisher turning his head toward her. "I'm glad she has work to focus on at least. Otherwise, she might just break under the pressure."

"Sounds like she's trying to keep it all together," Fisher said.

"Yes." Rosemary brushed her fingers through the top of her auburn hair. "But I don't think she's ready to let go yet. Not of the control. I don't know what her plan is, but I imagine that's why she's here this summer."

Fisher slowed his pace slightly as he absorbed the weight of her words. "She's trying to figure out more than just Kendra?" he asked, the question lingering in his chest, suddenly tangled with feelings he wasn't ready to look at too closely.

"Maybe," Rosemary said with a knowing smile. "Her divorce went on far too long, and it's been hard on them all. I think being in a new place might put some distance between her and those old wounds. The distance they need in order to heal."

They made their way toward the pier where Tug's Diner used to stand. The place Fisher had stumbled into all those years ago, starving and tired after a long drive, the town still a mystery to him. He remembered how Tug had made him a cheeseburger that night when the place was supposed to be closing. He'd seen Fisher's need for food and took the time to make it. That was Tug: always looking out for people.

"No matter how many times we walk this stretch of beach, I still expect to see Tug's Diner," Fisher said, his voice thoughtful about the destruction the hurricane had done. "I can't get used to it being gone."

"It's got to be strange for the locals," Rosemary agreed. "I miss it, and I only stepped foot in the place once, before the storm. It was the day I arrived. But Whelk's Island will never change, even if the businesses and landscape do. It can't change the people who make up this town."

"That's true," Fisher said, his gaze drifting out toward the empty spot where the diner once stood. "If I can be half the man Tug is, I'll be proud of how I've spent my life."

Rosemary turned to look at him, her smile warm. "Fisher, I think you're already doing that."

His chest swelled from her approval. "Thank you, ma'am," he said, trying to keep it light. "But I'm sure you're just being kind."

Rosemary chuckled, the sound musical and rich in the salt-kissed morning air. "You're so Southern, Fisher. I love that about you."

He laughed along with her, feeling the ease between them, the familiar comfort of the friendship they'd built. They turned at the pier and started walking back.

Then, ahead, a woman approached. He caught a glimmer of red in her hair. His pulse quickened. For a moment, he thought it was Nina. But it was probably just another islander out for a morning stroll.

"Well, I think I'll head back to the house," Rosemary said, breaking him out of his thoughts. "It looks like Nina is taking you up on your offer after all."

It is her. Fisher turned his attention to the woman ahead of him, a smile tugging at his lips. "I'll show her the best shell-collecting spots," he said, feeling a spark flicker inside him.

There was something about Nina Langley that had Fisher's curiosity piqued. Maybe it was the way she walked, like she had everything figured out, always keeping it together, even when it seemed like the world was falling apart around her. Or maybe it was something he hadn't quite put his finger on.

The slow pull of the water tugged at his ankles. Fisher was starting to realize this walk wasn't just about collecting shells—it was about seeing what the tide carried in when you stopped fighting it.

Chapter Ten

THE FOLLOWING MORNING, A SOFT BREEZE CARRIED THE scent of fresh-cut grass from the common green, where the townsfolk had gathered. Today wasn't just another sleepy coastal morning. There was a hum of purpose in the air. A beach cleanup and festival prep had folks bustling about, and Fisher couldn't help but smile as he shouldered a bundle of driftwood collected from the tide line.

He'd always loved mornings like this. No rush, no suits or city traffic—just good people working side by side to care for the place they called home. Fisher moved through the crowd with an easy rhythm, his bare feet sinking into the warm sand, his sleeves rolled up and hat tipped low to shade his eyes. His hands, rough from years of working with wood and water, made quick work of loading debris onto a waiting flatbed.

"Hey there, Fisher." Tug crossed the lot toward him with a grin stretched beneath his sun-creased eyes. "You keep this up and we might just make you honorary mayor of cleanup day."

Fisher brushed the sand from his palms. "Long as it doesn't come with a necktie, I'm in."

He turned back toward the tables and tents that needed setting up, his gaze snagging on a familiar figure in the distance. Nina, her hair tucked beneath a Phillies ball cap, was unrolling a banner with a determined set to her shoulders. Even from here, he could see the way she kept glancing up and down, as if making sure every edge lined up perfectly. That fierce attention to detail suited her, but it also tugged at something inside him. She was trying so hard to hold everything together. He knew that look because he'd worn it himself once.

Before he could think better of it, Fisher strode across the sand toward her. The chatter of volunteers and the clang of folding chairs being set up for them all faded into the background.

"Morning," he said, his voice smooth as the tide.

Nina looked up, surprised, her cheeks flushed from the sun. "Oh, hey, Fisher. I didn't see you there."

"Need a hand?"

She hesitated, then stepped back with a nod, tucking a stray wisp of hair behind her ear. "Sure. This banner's got a mind of its own."

Together, they smoothed out the long length of fabric, Fisher holding one end steady while Nina secured the ties. Their hands brushed once, and though neither spoke of it, the moment lingered between them, warm and quietly charged.

"You've got a knack for this," she said.

Fisher grinned. "For banners?"

"For making it look easy."

"Don't tell anyone," he warned, a glint of humor in his eyes. "I've got a reputation to protect."

They worked in companionable silence, the kind that felt natural, not strained. When the banner finally hung straight, Nina stepped back to admire it, shading her eyes from the rising sun.

"Looks good," she said.

"Not bad for a couple of amateurs," Fisher teased.

A laugh escaped her then, quick and genuine, and it surprised them both.

Just then, Kendra appeared, carrying a crate of bottled water. She stopped short when she saw them together, but Fisher greeted her with an easy smile.

"Hey, Kendra. Need help with that?"

She hesitated, then shrugged. "Sure. It's heavy."

Fisher took the crate as if it weighed nothing and set it down near the supply table. Kendra offered a quiet thanks before busying herself with stacking paper cups. For a moment, the three of them stood in an unexpected little circle of peace, the tension between Kendra and Fisher eased by the simple shared purpose of the morning.

When Kendra wandered off to join a group of teens sorting recycling bags, Nina exhaled, making Fisher realize she'd been holding her breath.

"She's warming up to you," she said, almost to herself.

"Or maybe I'm just good at lifting heavy things," Fisher replied, his grin easy, his heart lighter than it had been all morning.

The hours slipped by on waves of small talk, shared work, and the comfortable rhythm of community. When the last bag of trash was loaded onto the truck and the tents stood ready for the festival, folks started to drift away, calling out their goodbyes and promises to see one another at the evening's festivities.

Fisher found himself walking beside Nina as they carried the last of the folding chairs from the beach cleanup stations back to storage. The breeze lifted the edge of her cap, and for a moment, she pushed it down with a quick, almost shy motion.

"Thanks for today," she said quietly. "I didn't realize how much I needed this."

"We all need room to breathe now and then," Fisher said, his voice low, meant only for her. "Even you, city girl."

When they reached her car, she turned to him, brushing sand from her jeans. "You're always helping. You don't have to, you know."

"I know," Fisher said, leaning a shoulder against the doorframe. "But I want to."

She opened her mouth as if to reply, then thought better of it. Instead, she nodded, her gaze drifting to where the sun was on its way to the horizon.

"See you tonight at the festival?" she asked.

"I wouldn't miss it."

They went their separate ways, but after their short beach stroll yesterday and working together today, the air between them was charged with something unspoken.

Fisher walked back down to The Tackle Box, deep in thought. As he passed the dunes where the sea oats waved in the wind, the driftwood scattered along the tide line seemed to call to him. He veered off the path, pocketing a small, smooth piece, his fingers tracing its weathered grain as he walked.

By the time he reached his shed, an idea had already taken root. He fetched his sketch pad from behind the bar at The Tackle Box and settled into a lounge chair on the sandy side of the building. His pencil moved almost of its own accord. The outline of a piece took shape: a curve like the banner they'd hung together, a swirl like the sea, a quiet nod to the day. To her.

He set the pad aside and pulled a few pieces of driftwood from the crate near his workbench, turning them in his hands, already seeing how they might fit the sketch. It wasn't much yet, just the start of something he hoped would make her smile.

Fisher wasn't sure when he'd give it to her. Maybe not for a while. Maybe when the time was right. For now, it was enough to know it was there, waiting, same as he was.

And somewhere, deep down, Nina's walls had cracked just a little. He felt it. Did she? Would she allow it to continue?

Chapter Eleven

Nina held the shell and examined it again, a sweet memory from the walk she and Fisher had a couple of days ago. He'd pointed it out to her first. "This one's got a story," he'd said, brushing sand from its ridges before handing it to her.

She had nodded, pretending not to care. But she'd held on to it.

Now, sitting at her desk with her laptop open, she shook the memory away, forcing her attention back to the glowing screen in front of her.

Work. She had to focus on work.

Balancing an important conference call with her need to keep an eye on Kendra was already too much to handle. She couldn't add a single thing to her load. With Kendra home for the summer and their sabbatical to Whelk's Island in full swing, there was no escaping the fact that multitasking was going to be status quo for a while. No room for the likes of Fisher or seashells.

"Okay, everyone, let's focus on the backlog," Nina said, shifting in her seat and forcing her tone into something crisp and professional. "I need updates, especially on the new app features we discussed last week."

Her team started listing off progress reports. Exhaling slowly, her fingers tightened around her coffee mug. *I don't have time for journeys. I barely have time to breathe.*

She adjusted her headset, then tapped the table as her team members chimed in with their updates. But then she heard it. A sound that, at this point, could break her concentration faster than anything else.

Thud, thud, thud.

Kendra's footsteps. Marching into the room like she owned it.

Nina tightened her grip on the edge of her laptop. She had to focus. Not on Kendra's interruption or the tension that was still simmering between them. Not on her daughter's constant huffing or the mocking little noises she would make when she was irritated. Just . . . focus.

She shot a glance over her shoulder at Kendra, who stood in the doorway with her arms crossed. Her expression was one of pure exasperation, as if to communicate that it was Nina who had ruined her life by making her leave everything behind for this boring town.

Nina swallowed her frustration, forcing a professional smile as one of her developers spoke about timelines. Kendra was now mimicking her every word, exaggerating her lips as she made faces. Nina could feel the familiar burn of irritation creeping up her neck.

"Mom . . ." Kendra said dramatically, flicking a strand of her hair over her shoulder.

Nina muted her line. "I'm on a call," she said through clenched teeth. "Just give me a few more minutes."

Kendra flopped onto the couch, crossing her arms so tightly that it was a wonder she could still breathe. "You're always on a call."

Nina pressed her lips together. "Not now, Kendra."

Her daughter let out a long, exaggerated sigh before mumbling, "This place is lame. There's nothing to do."

But something in her voice didn't quite match the sharpness

of her words. Boredom, sure. Frustration, absolutely. But there was something else in there too.

Loneliness.

Nina bit her tongue, determined to press through the meeting. Her finger hovered over the laptop trackpad as she pulled her attention back to the screen.

"Now, as for the design updates . . ." She kept her voice steady, though Kendra's presence felt like a weight bearing down on her.

Kendra, clearly not interested in the conversation, stood and started pacing, her hands flailing dramatically. Nina forced herself to stay calm. She couldn't afford to snap. Not now. Not in front of her team.

Finally, the call wrapped up. Nina closed her laptop with a soft click, pressing her palms into her eyes.

"Great. I'm glad we got that sorted out," she muttered to no one in particular.

She turned to Kendra, who was now glaring at her from the couch, a frown deepening the lines on her face.

"You can't be serious," Kendra said, her voice thick with frustration. "You don't get it. I hate it here. You *ruined* my life by dragging me here."

Nina's stomach twisted, the words stabbing deep into her chest. Her daughter's anger was like a tidal wave that she couldn't outrun. She had hoped a summer on Whelk's Island would offer some peace for Kendra, but instead it felt like they were both stuck in the same relentless pattern of misunderstandings.

"I didn't want to uproot you, Kendra," Nina replied, her voice low and steady, though the weight of her guilt was beginning to seep in. "I thought it would be good for us both. A break from everything. Time to figure things out."

Kendra threw her hands up in that dramatic way that always

set Nina's nerves on edge. "I didn't need a break, Mom. I needed to be with my friends, not stuck here, where nobody even knows me."

Nina closed her eyes, drawing in a slow, measured breath. *Why does it have to be like this?* She second-guessed herself, wondering if coming to Whelk's Island had been the right choice after all. She'd hoped being here would help ease the unspoken tension that seemed to grow between them no matter what she tried.

As her thoughts churned, a tight knot of worry settled in her chest. What else could she do? Then, like a glimmer of light through the storm, Fisher's suggestion surfaced: the surf shop's summer program.

Maybe that *was* the answer. It would be a way for Kendra to fill the empty hours and find a little piece of herself again. Maybe a new surf hoodie or sneakers would help her feel like she belonged, even just a little.

It was an idea. She wasn't sure it was a good one, but did that even matter if it gave Kendra something to look forward to?

"Fisher mentioned a program down at the surf shop. You can work there and earn some store bucks. You know, get some cool gear," she said cautiously, hoping Kendra might latch on to the idea. Maybe something small could shift the mood.

Kendra scoffed immediately. "What would I want at a surf shop? That's lame. The gear they have is only cool to the boarders, and they aren't even cool. Which, you know, I'm *neither.*"

Nina's heart sank. "Oh, Kendra, I'm reaching for anything that might help you get back to yourself." Her voice shook with the vulnerability she was rarely willing to show her daughter. "I'm trying to help you figure out what to do this summer."

"Making me a weirdo won't help. I don't need your help! I just need to be me. Quit trying to turn me into you," Kendra yelled, standing and storming out. The door slammed behind her with a finality that left Nina feeling defeated, as if her attempts to bridge the gap between them had been in vain and now left a canyon even Evel Knievel couldn't cross.

What's so bad about being like me? Nina sat for a long time after that, the weight of the conversation hanging in the air like a thick fog. She wasn't sure what to do anymore. She'd tried, really tried, to make this work, but Kendra didn't want any part of it.

When emotions clouded everything, the best way to move forward was to lay out a plan and stick to it. If there was one thing she could trust, it was her problem-resolution skills. She just needed to remove her emotions from this situation. Nina turned back to her laptop, opened a new document, and began typing a list of things she could do to get Kendra back on track and help them both regain some sense of control.

1. Talk to Kendra more. Less surface, more heart.
2. Make time for fun things that Kendra likes.
3. Re-spin that summer program. Don't focus on the shopping.
4. Keep listening and stay present.

She stared at the list, but it felt flimsy. Nothing could fix the broken parts of their relationship, at least not easily. Kendra was hurting, and Nina didn't know how to heal that pain. She didn't have all the answers. But she had to keep trying.

Later that evening, Nina stepped onto the balcony, and the waves crashed loudly below, like the thoughts tumbling in her head. She drew in a deep breath, holding it until her lungs ached, then blew it out, hoping the tension in her chest would go with it.

If only life came with instructions. Not just vague advice or feel-good quotes but an actual process like the laminated emergency plans posted on airplanes. Clear steps. A glowing exit sign. A guarantee that following the arrows would lead to safety.

Her gaze drifted down to the beach. She spotted Kendra there, standing by the water, picking something up from the sand. Nina's heart squeezed. She watched her daughter hold the shell up to her face, studying it as if it held all the answers.

Kendra made her way back to the house. Nina opened the front door to greet her.

Kendra entered quietly, holding the precious find out toward her. "Look what I found, Mom. There's a message in it."

Nina took it and turned it over in her hand. It was delicate, worn by the waves, but still intact. The message inside was simple:

Embrace the journey.

"Do you think Grandma left it for me to find?"

"I'm not sure. Doesn't really sound like something she'd do, but you never know. You could ask her." Nina couldn't explain it, but something made her pause. The message was a subtle reminder that maybe they were both in the middle of their journeys and it wasn't always clear where they would end up.

Kendra crossed her arms, glaring at her mother. "I know you've been talking to Grandma about me. Stop acting like I don't know."

"Then you know we both care." Nina stared at the shell, the message echoing in her thoughts.

Running her thumb over the shell, she traced the letters of each word, then enjoyed the softened edges worn by years of tumbling in the tide. The message had found Kendra, but as Nina stood there, the weight of it settled somewhere deep in her chest. Maybe this wasn't just for her daughter. Maybe it was for *her* too.

Those words from the ocean, even as vague as they were, gave her a little hope. Maybe this wasn't the end of the road for them. Maybe it was a new beginning.

She looked up at Kendra. "We'll get through this. Together," she whispered, hoping that somehow they both could. "Deal?" She held out her pinky.

Kendra hesitated, then hooked her finger around Nina's, her expression softening.

Nina didn't even try to hide the joy flowing through her at that moment. *I'll take it. One step at a time.*

Chapter Twelve

THE AFTERNOON SUN STREAMED THROUGH THE OPEN sides of The Tackle Box, a weathered rectangle of a building—part beach shack, part community porch. Locals lingered at bistro tables on the beach side, sipping sweet tea and talking shop. The whole place looked like it might fold up and drift out to sea on the next strong tide, but it had heart—and a view no money could buy.

Overhead, fans worked overtime, swirling the thick, salt-heavy air that crept in from the ocean like a slow-moving fog. It didn't offer much relief, but it was something.

Fisher wiped down the counter, enjoying the quiet lull before the evening rush. Old beach music played from the speakers behind him. He glanced toward the far end of the bar, where Kendra stood, arms crossed, shifting awkwardly on her feet.

She had been working there for almost an hour now, cleaning tables, straightening chairs, and restocking the cups and coasters. She wasn't exactly enthusiastic about it, but she was trying.

It had been Rosemary's idea for Kendra to work for Fisher a couple of days as a way to make amends for the whole underage-drinking stunt. Not just to him but to the town. He hadn't expected her to show up, yet here she was.

"You don't have to stand there looking miserable." Fisher stacked clean glasses on the shelf behind the bar.

Kendra let out a dramatic sigh, dropping the rag she'd been twisting in her hands.

"I'm not miserable," she muttered. Then, after a pause, "I didn't think you'd let me help here. I figured you may secretly still be mad."

Fisher leaned against the counter, folding his arms. "I was never mad."

She raised an eyebrow, clearly skeptical.

"Okay," he admitted. "You frustrated me. I hate seeing people get in their own way. Especially young people who could have a bright future ahead of them."

Kendra didn't answer right away, but something in her expression changed. "I'm not sure I understand." She frowned. "What does that even mean, 'getting in my own way'? That sounds anatomically impossible."

"Big words." Fisher straightened. "Let me make it simple for you. It means making life harder for yourself than it has to be."

She huffed. "Yeah, well, life's already hard."

"It is. But sometimes people make it harder without realizing it." Fisher paused. "Like when you walked into my bar the other night. Drinking isn't a healthy habit for anyone, but it is a terrible idea for a young mind. That's why there's a law against it. Who were you trying to prove something to? Me? The town? Yourself?"

Kendra didn't answer, but she didn't look away either.

He let the silence sit for a second before continuing. "Look, I've been there. Thinking I had to act a certain way to fit in or feel like I had control. But you wanna know the truth?"

She shrugged. "Sure."

"The only thing I ever proved was how much trouble I could get myself into. And trust me, that gets old fast."

Kendra looked down at her hands, tracing one finger over a knot in the wooden bar. "So, what? I just . . . stop?"

He shook his head. "No, it's about not fighting at every turn. You don't need to complicate matters because you don't like the way they are. You make a plan and shift your focus to achieve the results that will make you happy."

She sat with that for a second, chewing her lip.

"That's . . . kinda deep."

Fisher chuckled. "Yeah, well, don't expect me to start handing out motivational speeches. But since you asked, I want you to know you have choices. You always do. Don't let your own choices make life harder than it already is."

Kendra looked at him. Really looked at him as if she were replaying what he'd said in her mind. "Well, I *am* sorry," she said quietly. "Not for getting caught, but because I wasn't nice, and you seem to care." She turned, avoiding eye contact, and mumbled, "It's been a while since it seemed like anyone does."

"*I'm* sorry too. I'm sure a lot of people care about you." Fisher let the words settle. "You're lonely, aren't you?"

Kendra hesitated, then gave a tiny, reluctant nod. "Yeah," she admitted. "Kinda sucks."

He smiled a little at that. "Yeah. It does."

She studied him some more. "Have you ever gone through that?"

Fisher tossed a towel over his shoulder and leaned forward on his elbows. "All the time when I was your age."

Kendra scoffed. "Really? You have, like, a whole town full of people who know you."

Fisher let out a quiet laugh. "That came later." He tilted his head, considering. "Back then? I kept busy. Surfed. Rode my bike. Read whatever I could get my hands on. I didn't have any real friends."

At the mention of bikes, he caught the brief flicker of recognition in her eyes. "What?"

She shifted. "Nothing."

He raised an eyebrow. "I saw your eyes perk up. What did I say? It wasn't nothing. I'm not buying that."

She let out a breath. "Okay, fine. I saw this old bike out by the storage shed. Rusty thing with a flat tire. Looked kinda cool, though. Retro or something. At least it would be something to do."

He grinned, wiping his hands on his towel. "Yeah, I noticed you checking it out the other day."

Kendra looked genuinely surprised. "You did?"

"Sure. You kept circling it like a shark. Thanks for not stealing it," Fisher teased. "You wanna fix it up?"

Kendra hesitated, then shrugged. "I mean . . . if it's not a total piece of junk."

Fisher smirked. "Only one way to find out. Let's go take a closer look." He put his towel on the counter and gave a quick whistle to the summer help. "You've got the bar. If anyone needs me, just shout out. I'm going to be by the storage unit." He walked out without waiting for an answer. "Come on."

Kendra broke into a jog to keep up with him.

A minute later, they were next to the dusty old bike propped up on its kickstand.

Kendra stared down at it, her arms crossed, eyes skeptical. "This thing's ancient."

Fisher crouched beside it, inspecting the flat tire. "*Ancient* is another word for 'well loved.' And for what it's worth, they made bicycles way better back then."

Kendra rolled her eyes. "Is that supposed to be inspiring?"

He grinned. "Did it work?"

She groaned but didn't argue. Instead, she crouched next to him, watching as he tested the inner tube.

"So," Kendra said, clearing her throat, "what's the first step?"

Fisher glanced over, surprised at the shift in her tone. It wasn't full of sarcasm or resistance anymore. It sounded like sincere curiosity.

"Well, first things first," he said, handing her a wrench he'd retrieved from the shed. "We gotta get this tire off."

"You expect me to know how to do that?"

"I'll help. Go on. Anyone who can use the word *anatomically* in a sentence correctly should be able to turn a couple of nuts and remove a bicycle tire."

She took the challenge. For the next half hour, they worked together, Fisher guiding her through each step. Rather than hover, he coached her on how to solve the problem.

Kendra was quick to pick up on things, though she pretended not to care.

He grabbed a patch kit and repaired the tube. The simplicity of the task reminded him of his younger years. "When I was your age, I enjoyed the challenge of fixing things. This is pretty simple. Watch, and then you can probably do it yourself if it happens again."

"Really?" Kendra leaned in. "You really think I could?"

She still wore that hard teenage mask, but she seemed hungry for information.

Fisher glanced up at her while still working on the tire. "Definitely. I learned the hard way. I made a lot of mistakes as a kid. I didn't have a plan. I thought I could wing it. But some things don't work that way. You have to appreciate what you've got and take care of it. And sometimes that takes longer than it would've taken if you'd just taken care of it in the first place."

"Things? Or people?"

"Both."

Kendra frowned but seemed to consider his words. "Sounds complicated."

"It can be." Fisher shrugged. "But sometimes that's where the real lessons are. They're in the messes we make, not in the pretty parts." He handed her the inflated tire, now properly patched. "All set. Should hold up for a while."

She glanced up at him, brows raised. "That wasn't so hard."

"Most things aren't if you believe it can be done and you give it half a chance. You just gotta be willing to try."

She looked down at the patched tire, pressing her fingers along the rubber to test the strength. Almost inaudibly, she expressed her gratitude with a thank-you.

"You're welcome." Fisher handed her the air pump. "All right, kid. That tire's gonna need some air. Let's get this thing road-ready."

As they finished up, the sound of tires approaching caught Fisher's attention. He looked up to see Tug stepping out of his truck, hat tipped back, a grin on his face.

"What's this?" Tug asked, watching Kendra give the bike a test pedal.

"A little project." Fisher stood and dusted off his hands.

Tug gave Kendra an approving nod. "Nice job, kid."

"He's a good teacher." Kendra just shrugged, but there was a glimmer of pride in her eyes. "I want to test out this bike. Is that okay?"

"See if one of those old bike helmets in the shed will fit, and stick to the sand road in case anything breaks for now, okay?"

"Sure thing." She raced toward the shed and walked out with a huge smile, wearing a bike helmet covered in surf shop stickers.

Fisher watched her push off and ride away. He turned his attention back to Tug. "She really is a good kid."

Tug lowered his voice, although Kendra was too far away already to hear him. "I saw Nina earlier."

Fisher raised an eyebrow. "Okay? And?"

"Let's just say I wouldn't be surprised if you saw her again soon." Tug smirked. "You're welcome."

"Hey, I didn't ask for help. Have you been matchmaking, old man?" Fisher had to admit he didn't mind having Tug as a wingman in this case.

"Son, some things don't need matchmaking. They need direction and patience," Tug said with a nod toward Kendra, who was pedaling like the wind toward them.

"This bike is the best. Thank you so much." She skidded to a stop in front of them. "Whoa! I need to get used to these brakes."

"Good stuff." Tug patted Fisher on the shoulder, then turned his attention to Kendra. "Come on, kid. Time to head home."

Kendra hesitated for a split second, then glanced back at Fisher. "Can I leave now? Did I finish everything you needed me to do?"

"Are you coming back tomorrow?"

"Yes, sir." Kendra stood a little straighter. "Might even ride the bike here if Mom will let me."

"Sounds like a plan to me, and it'll get Tug off the hook for picking you up, if your mom says yes. And if she doesn't—"

"I know. I have some trust to earn." She and Tug shared a look.

The old man gave Kendra a nod. "You want me to follow you home in case you break down?"

"I trust Fisher's fixes." She turned to Fisher. "Guess I'll see you around?" The comment was shallow, in the way teenagers talked when they didn't want to admit they enjoyed themselves. "Thanks for letting me use the bike."

At that moment, Nina drove up and stopped. The look on her face was one of concern.

"Hey, we've been working on the old bike abandoned behind The Tackle Box," Fisher said. "Kendra's a great helper. You've got a good kid there, Nina."

Kendra beamed.

"Yay, awesome. I was on my way home and thought you might want a ride. Should I put the bike in the trunk and drive you?" Nina offered.

"Nope. I'm going to ride it the whole way."

"Deal. I'll meet you at home. It's a hot ride. We can celebrate with one of those chocolate fudge pops I saw in the freezer."

"'Kay. See you there." Kendra took a wobbly first pedal but steadied herself quickly.

Fisher hollered, "Take good care of it. See you tomorrow." He watched Kendra take off pedaling down the street, then looked at Nina, who was smiling. "Isn't this great?"

"The best. See y'all later. Hope Mom didn't eat all the fudge pops I just promised." She eased down the street.

Tug waved, and then when Nina was out of sight, he turned to Fisher for a fist bump.

Warmth filled Fisher's heart, and Tug's words lingered. *"Some things don't need matchmaking. Just . . . patience."*

Fisher pushed his hands into his pockets. *Patience, huh?* Maybe that's what this was about all along.

Chapter Thirteen

NINA REMEMBERED HOW SURPRISINGLY NICE IT HAD BEEN giving in to Fisher's offer to join the shell-collecting walk, so there was no telling how much good a simple dinner at Tug's might do for her and Kendra. Family, friends, and The Wife—that sharp-tongued African Grey he doted on as if she paid half the mortgage. The bird never missed a chance to toss out a sassy remark the second you least expected it.

Nina had every intention of saying no to the offer. But maybe that was part of her problem lately: saying no too often. So this time, she'd said yes.

I could get used to the pace of beach life.

She owed Mom. Nina had made such a lousy first impression when her mother first came to Whelk's Island. Every time she thought about how she'd acted, it made her cringe. Joining them for dinner showed her support for their relationship, but more important, it was a good way to get Kendra out of the house with people in a normal setting.

The invitation from Tug was just in time, too, because she desperately needed a break from the constant drama with her daughter. She felt a deep sense of gratitude for her mother and Tug's support in Kendra finding her joy again.

She herded Kendra to the car, not wanting to be late. Nina couldn't believe she wasn't pitching a fit. A day with no drama was almost too much to hope for, but she parked her doubts and said a little thank-you to Jesus for the reprieve.

Tug had written directions for her and included a hand-drawn map. She glanced at it and headed north up the beach road.

"He drew you a map?" Kendra snorted. "Has he never heard of GPS?"

"I think it's sweet of him to take care of us like this." She knew her GPS probably could have taken her there in a snap, but she appreciated the effort Tug had put into the old-fashioned routine of helping her not get lost.

"If you say so." Kendra let out an exaggerated sigh, slumping in her seat. "Mom, do I really have to go? I'm not even hungry."

Nina glanced at her, arching a brow. *Well, I almost got her there without a fight.* "You're already in the car, Kendra. That ship has sailed. Just relax. I bet you'll be hungry when you see what they've fixed. It's going to be your kind of food."

Kendra huffed dramatically and crossed her arms. "This whole town is obsessed with eating. It's weird."

Nina bit back a laugh. "It's not about eating. It's about being with friends and family. Something we should be thankful for. Something we can both work on a little."

Her daughter rolled her eyes so hard that Nina half expected them to stay that way.

"Yeah, well, it's intense."

Still, despite the attitude, Nina saw it. A slight shift, but it was there. Kendra was showing less of her usual defensiveness, and that was something.

"I think we're almost there." Nina reflected on how Mom and Tug had a certain rhythm to their pace and how nice it was that they were including her and Kendra in it. It felt right in a way Nina hadn't quite grasped until now. Kendra needed to see a relationship that worked, a partnership that felt easy. Tug and

Mom had a relationship that seemed effortless. She'd never seen two people so happy together. They were a real-life example of how those romance novels weren't completely far-fetched, even if Nina hadn't experienced that kind of happiness herself.

Tug's house was massive but welcoming. It looked sturdy, a good thing since hurricanes felt like an annual occurrence on Whelk's Island. The faint scent of thyme and grilled pork emanated from the large wraparound deck.

"This place is huge. Is Tug rich?" Kendra looked to Nina for an answer.

"I have no idea, honey." A note on the front-step railing instructed them to go through the back entrance. "He treats your grandmother like a queen, and that's what's important."

They followed the path to the back of the house. The deck wrapped around the entire thing. *Maybe he* is *rich. And here I'd been worried he was after Mom for her money.*

The aromas of home cooking got stronger as they climbed the stairs to the landing.

A sudden burst of chatter interrupted the quiet. "Hello, sweet cheeks!"

Kendra froze and then whipped her head around.

From the large cage on the deck, a sleek African gray parrot blinked at them, its feathers ruffling.

Nina smirked. "So, we finally meet. You, I assume, are The Wife."

"I'm The Wife!" The bird's sharp eyes locked on Tug, who was stepping onto the deck. "You're late, honey," The Wife squawked, flapping her wings dramatically. "Dinner's cold. Do it again."

Tug sighed as he turned to Kendra. "You'd think I was actually married to her with the way she nags. You don't think your grandma is ever going to do that to me, do you?"

"No. Definitely not." Kendra stared, wide-eyed. "The Wife talks like that all the time?"

"Oh, she doesn't just talk." Fisher's voice carried from behind them as he stepped onto the deck, his hands in his pockets. "She gets downright judgy."

"That is too funny." Kendra gave the bird a thumbs-up.

"There's my sweet granddaughter." Rosemary practically skipped out to greet them, grabbing Kendra in a bear hug.

"Hi, Mom," Nina said. "Everything smells so good."

"Hey, Kendra, would you set the table for us in the dining area? I have everything right there on the sideboard. You just need to arrange it all."

"Sure, Grandma."

The Wife tilted her head and narrowed her eyes at Fisher. "Yo, Fisher, catch anything today?"

Kendra burst out laughing as she set the table.

Nina was relaxing and enjoying the casual banter with the guys when a loud crash came from inside. "Kendra!" She leaped to her feet.

"Clean up on aisle three," The Wife squawked, followed by a sharp whistle.

Nina ran into the house and found Mom soothing Kendra.

"I'm sorry," Kendra said. She was standing as still as a statue with broken glass around her flip-flops. "I didn't mean to."

"It's fine, honey. It happens," Mom said.

"It's just a glass, but don't move. You don't want to cut your foot." Nina started picking up the large pieces and carefully helping her daughter lift one foot out of her sandal for Nina to brush away any glass fragments.

"See," Rosemary said. "Good as new."

"Someone else needs to finish," said Kendra. "I'll just mess it up."

"Honey, you're fine. You can pick up right where you left off," Nina said.

"Sure can. I'll get another glass." Rosemary disappeared into the kitchen.

Nina pitched in, helping Kendra finish the task. By the time Rosemary brought in another glass, everything else was in place. Rosemary paused to take it all in, a smile blooming on her face. "This table looks beautiful. Thank you, Kendra."

"Mom helped."

"We're all just one great team!"

"Need anything else, Mom?" Nina asked.

"No, y'all go relax."

Nina was glad to see that even if it had been only a tiny little accident, they'd been able to quickly recoup and move on. That was more than she could have hoped for a couple of weeks ago.

Nina and Kendra walked back out to the deck where Tug, Fisher, and The Wife still were.

Fisher held out an apple slice, and The Wife snatched it with a speed that made him jump, tilting her head as if daring him to try to take it back. With a dramatic crunch, the bird chomped down, spraying juice as if it had won a prize. Then she leaned in toward Fisher, stretched her wings, and said, "Take a shower."

"Are you talking to *me*?" Fisher pressed a hand to his chest in mock offense. "Unbelievable."

Tug patted Fisher on the shoulder. "She's got no filter. You know that. We're just sitting here waiting for Amanda, Paul, and the kids. They should be here any minute." His eyes lit up as he cast his gaze toward Nina. "You know, I guess you being here makes your mom not the latest newcomer around here."

"What?" Kendra asked, looking confused.

"Well, newcomers happen onto our little island all the time. Some people die or move away, and others float into the day-to-day. This town has its own tide."

"I get it," Kendra said. "Since we're the most recent people to live here, we're the newcomers, but all the people who were new right before us, like Amanda and her family, are becoming part of the regular people."

"Sort of like that. Yeah!" Tug rubbed a hand across his stubbly beard. "You're a smart thinker, Kendra. Put that to good use."

"I didn't know Amanda and Paul were coming." Kendra looked pleased. "I hope Hailey and Jesse are with them."

Even though Hailey and Jesse were much younger than Kendra, she'd taken on a big-sister role the first time they met last year, when Nina had insisted that her mother come back home. *I was so wrong about that.* Nina would be forever thankful for Mom's hardheaded ways that brought Whelk's Island joy into all their lives.

Before Tug could respond to Kendra, Amanda's car pulled into the driveway, and the rest of them went inside.

Fisher leaned against the kitchen doorframe, watching the scene unfold with a simple confidence that made Nina's stomach flip. Tug pulled a tray of buttery biscuits from the oven while Rosemary chopped fresh herbs, humming softly.

"We're almost ready," Tug said. "If you want to grab seats at the table, we'll get this party started as soon as the rest get inside."

Nina sat down, her eyes drifting from her mother's gentle smile to Tug, who was now filling everyone's glasses with iced tea. There was a quiet intimacy in the way they interacted that tugged at Nina's heart. The familiarity was something she realized had been missing from her own life for a long time.

Fisher took the seat next to her. She admired his easygoing

nature, his craftsmanship, and his love for the ocean, yet they were from two different worlds. But tonight? She saw him in a different light.

Right now, he didn't look like a surfer. Instead, he looked like a handsome, capable man who rebuilt his bar after a hurricane and could calm a rebellious teenager, fix a bicycle, and still show up to dinner with a relaxed smile like it was no big deal.

And it shouldn't have been a big deal. But somehow it was to Nina. Could something with Fisher actually work for them both? The thought was swirling through her mind, like a roulette ball looking for the slot where it would land, when a yell from the front door snapped her out of those thoughts.

"Hey, everyone!" Amanda entered the room, carrying a covered dish.

Rosemary popped her head out from the kitchen. "Hey, darlin'. Wait, I told you not to make anything."

"It's just mac and cheese for the kids. Anything to keep them quiet." Amanda swept a dramatic hand across her brow. "Am I right?" she said to Nina.

"So right."

"I like mac and cheese," Kendra said.

"You're welcome to it. Everyone is," Amanda said.

Paul took the seat on the other side of Fisher. Kendra invited Hailey to sit next to her.

"Come on, everyone! Get it while it's hot!" Tug called, setting the food out on the long dinner table.

The meal was rich with laughter, conversation flowing between bites.

Halfway through dinner, Hailey leaned over to Kendra, her eyes sparkling. "Did you hear about the time Rosemary taught us all the hukilau dance down there below the deck?"

Kendra's brows pulled together. "You mean, like, the hula?" She looked at her grandmother with doubt.

"It's true," Rosemary confirmed.

Tug shook his head, a sweet smile on his face as he laughed at the memory. "That might be the night I realized I was falling in love with your grandma," he said to Kendra. "Her eyes twinkled like stars when she did that dance." His cheeks flushed.

"The hukilau? Like, seriously?" Kendra rolled her eyes. "Sorry I missed that." But she was being facetious.

Hailey wasn't at the age of sarcasm yet. "You've never done the hukilau?"

"Uh, not since I was a little girl."

Hailey sat up straighter, already grinning. "It's fun. We're totally doing it again. Come on, y'all!"

Paul groaned. "No, we are not. Let's finish dinner. Tug and Rosemary worked hard on this."

Amanda elbowed him. "Oh, stop that. It was fun, you party pooper!"

Paul shook his head. "If you recall, I only watched that night."

Tug sighed dramatically, then stood from his chair. "Fine. I watched long enough that I think I can make a go of it." He gave Paul a look as if daring him to sit it out. "I might as well show you how it's done."

Tug went into the area between the dining room and kitchen and rolled up his sleeves.

"Picture this," Hailey said, turning to Kendra. "Rosemary decides she's going to teach us this traditional Hawaiian dance, right? And we all go downstairs and—"

"Rock it," Jesse interjected, striking a ridiculous pose. "Sing it, Hailey! I know you remember it."

Kendra actually laughed.

Jesse next jumped into a warrior-like stance. "Let's do it!"

"Lead the way, Jesse!" Tug started following his exaggerated sways and hand motions.

Hailey jumped up next, tugging Kendra's arm. "Come on!"

"I heard that," The Wife said from the deck.

Kendra laughed at the bird's timing, and to Nina's absolute shock, Kendra went with Hailey.

They moved through the dance, Rosemary leading like she was meant for the stage, Jesse getting way too into it, and Kendra actually smiling.

The whole thing was ridiculous. Hilarious. And exactly what Nina needed to see. A tear slipped down her cheek. Somewhere underneath it all, her daughter was in there. Nina would find a way to get her back.

She glanced at Amanda, who was dancing with a soft smile. Nina remembered doing the dance in the elementary school cafeteria in front of all the parents.

"The island you grew up on is now alive and well here," Amanda said. "Watch out, Nina. This island will grow on *you* too. You can't tell me you don't know this dance."

Fisher leaned toward her. "I think you should show Amanda how it's done."

She placed her napkin on the table and stepped between Kendra and her mom, picking it up like she was back in elementary school in a grass skirt with strings of flowers around her ankles.

They danced and laughed, and then everyone crashed back into their chairs, winded from the impromptu dancing.

The laughter lingered like a melody in Nina's ears. This was what she wanted for Kendra. Maybe even for herself. A place that felt like belonging.

Chapter Fourteen

"I THINK WE ALL HAVE ROOM FOR SECONDS NOW," TUG said, his voice as warm as the tea in their glasses.

The second half of dinner was calmer. As they ate, Nina noticed how naturally the conversation flowed. Tug teased Rosemary about her habit of forgetting where she put things, and Rosemary shot back with a playful eye roll. There were shared jokes, memories, and laughter that filled the air without any pretense. It was clear that this wasn't just companionship between them. It was something deeper. A bond forged over time, with respect and care.

It was beautiful, and Nina couldn't help but feel a pang in her chest, a longing for that kind of connection. She hadn't realized how much she missed feeling seen, understood, until she saw it so clearly between Tug and her mother.

Later, when the stars had started to peek through the sky, Nina stepped onto the deck for some air.

Fisher followed her outside. "You looked worried."

Nina smirked. "That obvious?"

He shrugged. "I've got good instincts."

She exhaled, watching the moonlight dance over the waves.

"Relax." He spread his arms wide. "You're at the beach where everything is calmer."

"I used to know how to do this," she said, motioning toward the waves. "But somewhere between leaving Hawaii to go to college, divorce papers, and PTA meetings, I forgot how to just . . . be."

He cocked his head, giving her a playful grin. "No one forgets how to relax. Here, follow my lead. First, look at the stars." He paused. "Good. Now close your eyes and let the sound of the ocean nudge all the worries aside."

She did as he said, and it was actually sort of working. Her shoulders relaxed a bit.

Fisher placed his hand on her shoulder and gave it a soft squeeze. "That's better. See. Nothing to it."

She opened her eyes. "I wouldn't say 'nothing.'" She motioned all around her. "I wish I could live like you all do here, ready to embrace whatever comes your way. My brain is still firing off random ideas and to-dos."

"Hmm. Thinking still, huh?" He eyed her cautiously. "Walk with me?"

She hesitated but then placed her hand in his. "Okay."

He squeezed her hand gently as they took the back stairs to the beach.

Fisher walked alongside her, barefoot in the sand, the ocean breeze tugging at the edges of his loose button-down. He moved like the water itself: fluid, unhurried, as if he never fought against the current but always knew how to ride it. It was easy to picture him on a surfboard, cutting through waves with the same quiet confidence he carried now. There was something grounding about him, like a man who had already been through his fair share of storms and had no interest in creating new ones. That was a settling thought.

He looked at her then, that same steady gaze, the one that

made her feel like she wasn't as invisible as she thought she was.

"You don't have to have all the answers, Nina." His voice was a low rumble over the sound of the waves. "Just roll like the tide."

She swallowed. How long had she been waiting for someone to say that? Her thoughts wandered to her relationship with her ex-husband. They had loved each other in their own way, but they were so fifty-fifty on everything that there had been unspoken resentments, too many times when Nina carried the weight of everything on her shoulders when really she wanted him to take care of her, just a little.

One glance in Fisher's direction unveiled something she hadn't even known she'd yearned for. *I can't start something with someone here. I'll be gone before it gets anywhere, and I've got too much on my plate.*

Fisher lifted his arm and draped it around her shoulder. "Bring it in here, gal." He never broke stride, as if the move was as natural as breathing. The warmth of his side brushed against hers, steady and unhurried, reiterating, *You don't have to have it all figured out right this minute.* For a beat, she tensed, but then she allowed herself to lean into him. It felt nice to be the one taken care of even for a matter of seconds. Finally, she eased back, matching his pace, pretending her pulse hadn't just noticed him.

"Are you always designer T-shirt and fancy jeans?" He lifted his chin, eyeing her with a crooked smile. "You know, around here nobody's keeping score on style. You really can relax."

That made her laugh. "Relaxing isn't really something I'm good at."

"I'm happy to help you anytime," he offered. "I can even give you a shirt from The Tackle Box to get you started on the chill-axing vibes people pay to experience around here."

Nina opened her mouth to brush him off, but the words didn't come. The truth was, she was tired—tired of always keeping it together, of pretending she had it all figured out, when half the time she felt like she was barely holding on. The admission lodged in her throat, unspoken but heavy.

She offered Fisher a thoughtful smile. "I'll think about that."

"Hey, I'm not one to brag, but rumor is that my bar is considered the living room of this town. A place where laughter and tall tales flow as easily as the beer and my famous cherry limeades. The tall-tales part comes pretty naturally. I'm the son of a fisherman."

"Really?"

"Yep. Hard, honest work."

"My daddy was a macadamia farmer," Nina said. "He was the most hardworking man I've ever known. Hands as rough as the bark on those trees but a heart as gentle as a spring breeze. Losing him a few years ago was so hard. You mentioned your dad died too?"

"Yeah, he's been gone a long time. But I rarely talk about that stuff. Any of it."

The night air embraced them, sea spray heavy in the air, and something unspoken hovered between them.

Nina shifted, stealing a glance at him before looking to the darkened shoreline beyond Tug's backyard.

"I should probably get back inside," she murmured when they reached the deck, more to herself than to him.

Fisher hesitated, then tilted his head toward her. "You in a rush?"

Nina let out a breath, one that seemed to carry something deeper. "No, not really."

He paused, his gaze steady on hers.

Nina realized she'd drawn her shoulders tight without meaning to.

"You okay?" he asked.

She nodded too quickly. "I'm not even sure I know who I am at this point."

Fisher's fingers twitched against the railing, and for a second she thought he might reach out and place his hand on hers.

She held her breath, and when he didn't make the move, she was relieved.

He curled his fingers into a loose fist instead. "Yeah," he said, his voice softer now. "I get that."

A gust of wind swept in from the water, catching a loose tendril of her hair and sending it across her cheek. Before she could lift her hand, he reached over and tucked the strand behind her ear.

It caught her off guard. It was a gentle movement, and her skin prickled in response. She swallowed back the nervous feeling. *I can't make any more mistakes in my life right now.*

She took a step back. "Fisher?"

He dropped his hand, stuffing it into his pocket. "Yeah?"

Her lips parted to say something, but then she just shook her head, exhaling a quiet, almost frustrated laugh. "Never mind."

He stood there quiet for a long moment, and Nina knew he was wondering what she'd been about to say, but she couldn't put the thought together.

Finally, he spoke. "All right," he said, keeping his voice easy. "But for what it's worth, I'm glad you're here."

Nina's eyes lifted to his, something unreadable flickering there. "Me too."

The promise hung there, soft as the breeze, waiting. But tonight it was enough just to feel seen.

Chapter Fifteen

THE MORNING HAD BEEN BRIGHT AND CLEAR—THE KIND of day that almost convinced Fisher everything was as it should be. But he knew better. Storms always had a way of sneaking up on you.

As he walked down the main beach road with Nina and Kendra, the low hum of the ocean lapping at the shore in the distance played background to their footsteps. They were all in good spirits. It was supposed to be an impromptu hike with him sharing a brief history of the town. The world seemed manageable for Kendra today, but the air shifted as they rounded the corner. A cool, damp breeze signaled a change.

"Can you feel that?" He stopped, taking it in.

Nina frowned. "Feel what?"

"A storm brewing." He gestured toward clouds moving across the sky. "The shift in the air. Feel how heavy the air just got?"

"Not really."

He tilted his chin up and inhaled. "Smell the sharp scent? Rain's coming. We'd better get a move on."

"You're crazy! It's a beautiful day." Nina dragged her feet intentionally and then inhaled deeply. "Smells like salt and fish."

Fisher chuckled, shaking his head. "Nah, past that. It's in the wind, the way it picks up but isn't consistent. And see how the waves are flattening out?"

"You're just trying to freak us out," Kendra said.

"No. I'm serious. Come on!" He grabbed Nina's hand and they took off jogging.

"It's not going to storm. The sun is shining!" Kendra paused. "Hey, wait for me!" she hollered, running to keep up.

"Listen to your elders. We know stuff!" Fisher yelled to Kendra. Then he winked at Nina. After the bar incident and learning more about the drama between her and her daughter, this seemed like a good chance to share some wisdom to prove to the kid that elders knew best.

A moment later, before Kendra caught up, the breeze cooled and dark clouds rolled in, blocking the sun.

"You're right!" Kendra's expression immediately shifted to one of mild panic. "A random storm? It's not even supposed to rain today! How did you know?" Kendra squealed as the first heavy drops splattered down.

"Some things you learn from experience," he said.

Fat, cold raindrops pelted them, causing Nina to let out a yowl too. A gust of wind tore through, sending a cool rush over Fisher's skin as thunder rumbled across the horizon. He grabbed Kendra's hand and Nina's, pulling them both toward an old market stand building just ahead. "Looks like we'll have to run for cover now."

The rain picked up, and soon enough, the downpour was torrential. Rain swirled in sheets over them as they ran.

"You have got to be kidding me," Nina said.

Kendra covered her face with her hands, trying to shield it from the rain.

Nina let go of Fisher's hand.

Fisher turned, rain dripping from his hair. "What?"

She grinned up at him, breathless. "If I'm going to get soaked, why not enjoy it?"

Then she tilted her head back, her arms spread wide, letting the rain pour over her.

Fisher watched her, something deep and unshakable settling in his chest. In that moment, even with the storm raging around them, Nina looked free. And suddenly, he realized he wanted to be whatever she needed to feel that way.

He let her enjoy herself for a minute, but as another crash of thunder sounded, he caught her hand. "Come on, Good-Time Girl. Thunder and lightning are no joke."

The three of them reached the rickety shack of a building just as the storm hit full force. Fisher yanked open the door with one hand, pulling them inside. They all laughed as the wind howled and the pounding rain beat down on the metal roof. The warm, musty air of the building had filled his lungs as they'd stumbled inside. They were dripping wet and laughing like kids who had just narrowly avoided trouble.

"Well, that was something," Nina said, breathless but smiling. She ran her fingers through her hair, trying to fuss it back into place.

He hadn't meant to stare, but he did. Even with her hair plastered to her cheeks and her makeup gone, she was flat-out lovely to him.

Kendra, still panting, glanced around, her expression a mix of concern and disbelief. "That was crazy!"

Fisher shrugged, shaking the water out of his hair like a big dog. "Summer storms happen all the time. Especially when the humidity is so high. It'll pass as fast as it showed up."

"I hope so." Kendra still looked alarmed, her arms crossed defensively. "I don't like this. What if it gets worse? What if there's a hurricane or something?"

"No warning for these pop-up storms, but there's always plenty of warning for hurricanes. You don't need to worry about that." Fisher chuckled as he wiped his hands on his shirt. "Although we did get that real big one last year. One of the worst in a long time."

Kendra looked at Nina, then back at Fisher. "Like, how much warning? You mean, we could have one tomorrow?"

"No, hurricanes don't work that way. They build slowly. I promise, this is just a thunderstorm."

"Well, it seems like a hurricane to me. I heard about how that sand covered Tug's truck. That seems pretty intense."

"Yes, that was scary when Grandma came down," Nina said. "I'm sure glad you knew about this building, Fisher."

Fisher settled against a shelf in the corner. "The farmers market uses this building on weekends. I hunkered down at home during the hurricane last year, but I wasn't prepared to have a tree fall on my house and trap me inside. If it hadn't been for Paul and Tug, I'm not sure how long it would've been until someone found me."

"So, wait, there wasn't any warning?" Kendra asked.

"There was plenty of warning. I just didn't heed the evacuation. It was my poor judgment that got me into trouble."

Nina seemed to be trying to wrap her mind around the severity of it all. "That sounds terrifying. You were trapped?"

"When the tree crashed through the roof, an entertainment center fell and pinned me. It was like this impossible game of mousetrap, and I was the mouse," Fisher said, his smile fading a bit as he recalled the memories.

"I still can't believe Mom showed up in this town during an evacuation."

"A lot of people got hit worse than me. My insurance covered the roof, and once the flooding subsided, I got the place dried out and things weren't so bad."

"I was so mad when I showed up in town that I'm sure I

didn't notice most of it." Nina sucked in a breath. "I was laser-focused on getting Mom out of Whelk's Island and back home, where she'd be safe."

"She's always laser-focused on everyone but her," Kendra mumbled.

Fisher and Nina's eyes caught, but he had a feeling that not giving Kendra the satisfaction of any type of reaction was probably the best, so he continued with his story. "So much sand came ashore that it buried Tug's Jeep in his driveway. A total loss. I'm not talking about a little dusting of sand either. It was like a dune had swallowed it up. He and Rosemary had to climb up and over the Jeep to even get into the house. You couldn't see that there was a vehicle there. It was covered."

"I would have been worried to death if I'd known all that."

"You were pretty worried," Kendra said.

"That's true," Nina admitted.

"Tug has all the insurance pictures," Fisher said. "Get him to show you. Now that everything is okay, it's sort of funny. Wasn't at the time, though."

Kendra's eyes widened in disbelief. "Are you serious? I thought you were exaggerating about the Jeep being buried in the sand."

Fisher laughed, shaking his head. "Nah. We were all just kind of in shock at first. But what got me was the wind. The house I was in was just a little bungalow, and when the storm hit, the whole place was shaking. I could feel the wind lifting the roof. It was so loud. But I wouldn't say I ever felt scared."

Nina straightened. "You weren't scared?"

"Not really," Fisher said. "The sound of nature can be scary, no question about it. The way the wind screams through the trees. The way the waves crash. It can sound like the world is coming apart. It's powerful, sure, but there's also a strange comfort in knowing that nature's doing its thing. I wasn't afraid of the storm itself, but more of the things that break loose because of it, like that tree that fell."

Kendra's expression shifted to one of genuine concern.

"And let me tell you, treading water while stuck under a piece of furniture isn't as glamorous as it sounds."

Nina blinked in surprise. "Wait, *water*?" she asked, leaning in a little closer. "You had to tread water?"

Fisher grinned, his voice taking on a playful tone as he did a silly little dance. "Can you picture it?" He mimicked the motion of treading water, his feet shuffling dramatically as if he were swimming in place.

Kendra cracked a smile.

"Okay, okay, the water wasn't that deep," Fisher said with a chuckle. "It was just a few inches, but it feels like you're up to your neck when you're stuck in it. I just wanted to see if you were paying attention."

Kendra's laugh bubbled up, shaking her nerves loose. For the first time since the storm started, she seemed to relax a little, letting herself enjoy the absurdity of the moment.

Fisher shared, "The whole town pulled together after that storm. Pastor Qualls even led a prayer walk down Main to the pier. Gave people hope."

Fisher watched them both—mother and daughter—caught between struggle and grace. He didn't know what came next, but he knew one thing for certain: He wanted to be here for it. Storms, sunshine, whatever the day brought. Just here, with them.

Chapter Sixteen

AS THEY WAITED OUT THE STORM, FISHER WATCHED NINA with quiet amusement, feeling the room lighten along with Kendra's mood. Outside, the rain still came down hard, but inside, the storm had already started to pass.

"But seriously, it was a mess." Fisher remembered wondering how long it would be before someone discovered him. He had been hungry, waterlogged, and without many options. "Tug and Paul came by with the sheriff's truck to check on me."

Kendra was quiet for a moment, clearly taken in by the story. "Even without the treading-water part, it sounds insane."

"Mom didn't relay those details," Nina said.

Fisher grimaced. "Oh, she probably didn't want to worry you."

"Yeah, because I told her it wasn't safe to drive down here when they were talking about the potential of that storm coming up the coast."

"It's just another part of living here. You get storms, you get surges, and you get the occasional tree in your living room. But you know what? The community always comes together."

Nina nodded, her shoulders seeming to loosen as she began to see the town through Fisher's eyes. A place that wasn't perfect but was rich in its own kind of raw beauty. "I think I understand," she said quietly. "Living here is different from what I'm used to, but maybe that's not such a bad thing."

His smile softened as he gave her a thoughtful look. "Sometimes the best things come from the unexpected, Nina. You just have to give it the time to settle in."

Inside the little farmers market building, it felt like they were all anchored in a moment of calm. Fisher watched Nina with quiet interest as Kendra's voice broke through the storm again.

"So, you really think pirates used to hide treasure around here?"

His lips quirked into a smile, the playful edge to Kendra's voice tugging at something inside him. He couldn't remember the last time he'd been able to talk so carefree. "Oh, absolutely," he said, his eyes glinting as he let the story roll off his tongue. "The Outer Banks has a history of pirates. Blackbeard used to roam these waters. You've heard about Blackbeard, haven't you?"

"Yeah, the pirate."

"Yep. Some people think there might be treasure buried on this island. It could be right under our feet."

Kendra's face lit up as she took a dramatic step toward the door, her eyes scanning the ground like she was on the hunt for some long-lost bounty. "I'm gonna find it! I'm gonna find the treasure!" she declared, her voice filled with mock determination as she stepped out into the rain, looking back over her shoulder to see if anyone was watching.

"Is it safe for her to be out there?" Nina asked Fisher.

"Unless we hear any more thunder, she's just going to get wet." Fisher chuckled softly, but his gaze didn't leave Nina. She was watching Kendra, her lips lifting in the smallest of smiles. The tension that had been so palpable between her and Kendra earlier, between her and herself, seemed to slip away in the space of that simple playful exchange.

Nina's eyes softened as she watched her daughter disappear into the rain-soaked world outside, her figure already lost in the sheets of water coming down like a curtain. Fisher shifted his weight, drawing closer, his instinct to make her feel heard, to make her feel safe, always there, even when he wasn't fully aware of it. The way she let herself relax when she thought no one was watching struck him.

Nina slowly turned to face him, her shoulders still wet, her hair clinging to her face, her smile gentle but distant. The sound of the rain pounding against the roof filled the space between them, but it was their unspoken connection that filled the room.

"You know," she said, her voice quieter now, as if she was testing the waters of this new bond, "Kendra's been . . . well, a handful. I can't seem to get through to her. She's so angry, so closed off, and nothing I try seems to reach her. You dropped some subtle hints. Thank you for that. The 'Listen to your elders' and 'Knowledge comes with experience.' That was on purpose, wasn't it?"

"I may have been trying to help. Did I cross a line?" Fisher studied her, seeing the concern in her eyes, the deep worry she wore like a second skin.

"No, not in a bad way." Their gazes connected. "Thank you."

"She's a teenager." His voice carried the understanding he'd built up over years of watching families navigate struggles. "She's trying to figure herself out. It's difficult for all of them, especially when there's a lot of change. The good news is, you're still here. You're present. You're a wonderful mother, and she might not show it, but she notices."

Nina looked down, her fingers twisting the hem of her shirt, a nervous gesture that betrayed how much stress she was carrying. "I thought coming here would help. I thought getting away from the chaos of the city and some questionable new friends she'd started hanging out with might give us a chance to reset."

Fisher could feel the weight of her words settle in the air, and he could sense the cracks beginning to show beneath her tough exterior. For a moment, he said nothing but just let the silence stretch between them. He wasn't sure what else to say, but the pull to comfort her was strong.

The soft glow of the overhead lighting illuminated her face, and Fisher couldn't help but notice how the shadows seemed to make her look more fragile in that moment. She was so much stronger than she gave herself credit for. Maybe it was because of everything she'd been through, everything she was still trying to work through.

"You're not alone in this, Nina," he said. "You've got a lot on your plate, and it won't be easy. Give it time."

Nina blinked, as if what he said hadn't quite landed at first. Then she looked up at him, her eyes searching his face, seeming to look for any sign of insincerity. Then he saw a flicker of something in her—hope, maybe, or relief.

"Thank you," she said softly. "I'm trying. I really am."

"You're doing more than you think," he said, his tone quiet and earnest. "You're here, you're trying, and that counts for more than you realize. Kendra's got a lot going on in her world, and so do you. But you're in this together. You'll figure it out."

"You've been a tremendous help already." Nina exhaled slowly, her shoulders relaxing just a fraction as the words sank in. Fisher wasn't pretending to have all the answers. He was simply showing up in a way that let Nina know she didn't have to face her burdens all alone.

She wiped a hand over her face, the rainwater mingling with the tears she hadn't let fall. "I didn't know it would be this hard," she admitted, her voice breaking slightly. "I thought if I just kept going, just kept pushing forward, everything would work out. But I think I've been pushing her away. I didn't mean to. It's just . . . it's easier to hide behind work than deal with how broken I've felt since my divorce."

He gave her a gentle smile. "I think sometimes we think if we just keep pushing, things will get better. But that's not how it works."

He studied her, the storm's rhythm filling the silence between them. This was the moment to let her see him—not just the easygoing bar owner, not just the surfer, but the man who understood what it meant to lose your footing and try to find your way back.

"I get it," he said, his voice steady and thoughtful. "When I was eighteen, I thought I could outrun that feeling. I enlisted. Figured if I had structure, discipline, I could fix myself, figure out who I was supposed to be."

Nina blinked, seeming surprised. He realized she hadn't expected him to share something so personal, but she didn't interrupt.

"It worked for a while," Fisher went on, his gaze on the rain blanketing the window. "I saw the world. Learned to listen, to follow, to lead. But then my dad got sick—cancer—and suddenly none of it mattered. I left the military to come home, take care of him." He paused, choosing his words. "He wasn't an easy man, even after he recovered. Mean, most days. But living through that taught me what I didn't want to become. It was the hardest thing I've ever done, and it changed the way I pick my battles."

"I had no idea," she said quietly. "I'm sorry."

He shook his head gently. "Don't be. It shaped me. Made me see what kind of life I wanted—simple, close to the water, close to the people who matter. Doesn't mean I always get it right, but I try."

"Thank you for telling me that," she said, her voice barely above a whisper. "It . . . helps."

"We all experience storms, Nina. Sometimes the best thing we can do is stop trying to outrun them and just let them pass."

"I'm afraid I'm going to keep making things worse."

"You've got to take the time to let it breathe, to let it be messy and give yourself some grace along the way."

Nina met his gaze, her eyes softer than they'd been since he'd met her. "I don't know what I'm doing half the time," she confessed.

Fisher gave her a gentle smile. "None of us do. But we get through it. Together."

"It's been a long time since I've felt hopeful, but I believe things will be okay once we get through this storm. Not the rainstorm. The family one."

"I knew what you meant." He watched her, almost afraid to say anything that might spoil this sweet moment. "You know what I love best about storms?"

"What?"

"The quiet after. It's so extreme. Everything is in chaos, and then the stillest, most peaceful moments follow. Sometimes storms make way for better things."

As he spoke those last words, the rain stopped. Nina's expression made them both laugh.

Kendra raced back inside. "I didn't find Blackbeard's treasure, but I found a quarter!" She twisted the shiny coin in the air. The look on her face was pure satisfaction.

Fisher slapped her hand in a high five. "May the treasure hunt begin."

One glance at Nina told him she was relieved and happy to see her daughter having fun. She leaned back to look longingly into his eyes. That moment held for barely a second but amounted to so much more. Fisher felt the quiet wish rise inside him: more moments like this, where laughter came easily and hearts felt light.

He gave Nina a reassuring nod. "There's this quote I like. 'Not all storms come to disrupt your life. Some come to clear your path.' It's from Paulo Coelho. Am I wrong, or does it feel like that may be the case today?"

Kendra paused, a questioning look on her face, followed by a slow, broad smile. "Yeah. Maybe."

Nina blinked back tears, but her smile reassured him they were joyful ones. "You are absolutely right."

Chapter Seventeen

THE NEXT MORNING, THE MEMORY OF THE STORM STILL clung to Nina as she walked the shoreline, the cool water washing over her ankles, drawing her toward whatever treasures the sea had left behind. Maybe even Blackbeard's treasure. She giggled, remembering Fisher telling Kendra about that history. A beautiful shell would be the perfect gift this morning.

Yesterday's storm had washed up an abundance of shells. One caught her eye. The spiral-shaped whelk wasn't identical to the Pacific whelks she'd found as a child growing up, but the shapes were similar enough that she could identify it.

Its pattern, deep and intricate, was almost hypnotic, and the inside was the softest pink hue. She turned it over in her palm, tracing the delicate curves of the spiral, spotting a message. She couldn't help but wonder if it was a sign.

Her thoughts drifted back to the shell Kendra had found with the message tucked inside. So perfectly timed. So eerily fitting for everything they were going through. It seemed like a divine nudge, something more than just a random coincidence.

And now this shell. She swallowed, tightening her grip around it.

"Mom," Nina called as she walked inside.

Her mother sat in the recliner with a knitting project draped across her lap. She glanced up with a knowing smile. "Another shell, huh?"

Nina stepped closer. "This one is a smallish whelk. It has something written really tiny along the edge." She held it out, her voice soft but urgent. "Look. It says, '*Strength grows in life's toughest storms.*'" She stared at the shell, hoping it might whisper its secrets to her. "It feels too perfect to be random. The message in Kendra's shell was aligned with everything she's going through right now. And this one . . ." She looked at her mother, her brow furrowing.

Rosemary leaned back and gave a soft laugh, the kind that held no malice or frustration, just an appreciation for the tangible facts Nina relied on. "I didn't write that message—or Kendra's. I don't know where those shells come from, but I promise you, I don't have anything to do with them.

"I know it sounds impossible, Nina," she continued. "When I first heard about these shells, I thought it was just a town legend. A feel-good hoax, maybe. But they've been showing up for years."

Nina frowned, rubbing the shell between her thumb and forefinger. "But why? Who's behind them?"

Her mother just chuckled, shaking her head. "That's part of the mystery."

"What are the chances that two related people visiting from Pennsylvania would find shells with messages in such a short time?"

"No idea. All I know is that those shells bring people what they need. There's something about them. You've heard the stories, haven't you?"

Nina tilted her head, unsure. "Just that they exist."

Rosemary scooched closer. "There used to be an entire display of them in Tug's Diner. Letters from people from all different places and walks of life. There have been articles in the newspaper about them before. I found a shell myself back when I was in town the first time. Right after the hurricane."

"You didn't tell me about that."

"Like you said, they seem almost too coincidental. Too personal." Rosemary shrugged. "You wouldn't have believed it was random if I'd told you."

Nina snickered. "You're probably right about that."

"But experiencing it gives you a different perspective. Mine had a message inside that spoke to me. I questioned it at first, but I couldn't dismiss it, and I eventually talked to Amanda about it. For what it's worth, I do believe those special shells fall into the right hands at the right time." She glanced away, as if remembering the moment clearly. "You should really talk to Amanda if you're unsure."

Nina raised her eyebrows, intrigued. "And this whole shell thing has been happening for years?"

"Yes. They've been part of this town's charm for as long as folks can remember," Rosemary said. "People pass through, but those shells somehow find their way to someone who needs them."

Nina wasn't entirely sure what to make of it all, but the idea of these shells, and the suggestion that they could hold messages meant specifically for certain people, seemed too magical. "I don't believe in magic," she said absently as she rubbed the shell between her thumb and forefinger again. Strangely, the spiral pattern calmed her.

"Seriously, Nina, talk to Amanda about it," Rosemary suggested, her tone thoughtful. "She might tell you more. That woman has been through some huge struggles. The shell she found changed everything for her on her path to find peace in the middle of it."

"I'll think about mentioning it to her." Nina doubted she

would, though. “Thanks for sharing your thoughts with me, Mom.” She glanced at the shell again.

Rosemary held a knowing look in her eyes. “I’m meeting Amanda at the church this afternoon. We’re putting together toiletry bags for the homeless shelter. We can always use another hand. Come with me. It’ll be fun.”

Nina looked out at the beach, her mind swirling. Being part of something bigger than herself seemed like exactly what she needed. “Kendra is volunteering at the library, so I don’t have anything else pressing. I’d love to help out.”

Later that afternoon, Nina stood next to Rosemary and Amanda in the church’s small volunteer center, putting together toiletry bags. The church smelled of old wood and candle wax—a peaceful, comforting scent that seemed to wrap around Nina like a warm embrace. The room was quiet except for the rustle of plastic bags and the soft murmurs of the volunteers, working quickly and efficiently.

Amanda, who had been sorting items on a nearby table, paused when she noticed Nina. “Hi! Good! You’re here,” she said with a bright smile, stepping over to her. “Nina, I’m so glad you came. Extra hands make this task such a breeze. We’re putting together forty bags today. We’ll finish in no time.”

Nina was comforted by Amanda’s easygoing demeanor. Nina felt like less of an outsider here in the church and more like someone who belonged. “I’m glad I could be here,” she replied. Doing something helpful was satisfying, and it was very nice that it didn’t require a spreadsheet or have a looming deadline. She sat down at a table and opened a box of shampoo bottles, then started adding them to bags, the simplicity of the task strangely soothing.

Amanda took the seat next to Nina. "How are things going?"

"Good. Better." Now that Amanda was sitting right next to her, that shell was the first thing on her mind. "I was going to ask you something."

"Sure. Anything."

"I found a shell with a message in it. Kendra and I have both found one, at different times. Mom says it's a real thing. Do you think so? I mean, it all seems a little out there."

"I know how you feel. When the kids and I found that first shell, I thought there was no way it meant anything."

"Right?"

"But . . . it did," she said, her voice lighter now. "It had a message inside. It said, '*Interrupt worry with gratitude.*'"

"That's good advice."

"It was. I was so overwhelmed after losing Jack, and the kids were little, and I was drowning in my grief. That message was like a lifeline. A reminder that even in the darkest times, there's always something to be grateful for. That simple little phrase became my mantra, and I leaned into it."

Nina looked up from the bag she was packing, surprised by the intensity of Amanda's words. She saw the depth of emotion in the woman's eyes and how the moment transported her back. "That sounds powerful."

"It was," Amanda replied, nodding. "I wasn't sure how to move forward. But that shell gave me the push I needed. I stop and look for the good, even in my hardest days. And you know what? I always find it." She paused, her expression softening. "I haven't shared this with many people before, but after finding that shell, a new chapter began for me. That little message—and meeting Maeve—set me on a new course."

She smiled at the memory. "Maeve was a gentle soul, full of quiet wisdom. She passed away just before your mom came to

Whelk's Island, but she had a way of seeing people, really seeing them. She and Tug were close. Losing her hit him hard."

Amanda's voice dropped to something tender and certain. "Those two things—the shell and Maeve—saved me. Whelk's Island has that kind of magic. It draws in the right people at just the right time. This is the kind of place where you can begin again."

"We sure could use a restart." A lump formed in Nina's throat. She understood the weight of grief more than she'd ever let on. Still mourning the ending of her marriage, she desperately longed for a new beginning for her and Kendra. She hoped to reconcile the divorce with a fresh life pattern and find some healthier choices when dealing with difficult situations. Her daughter was maturing. It was time to treat her like the young lady she was becoming and trust that all she'd put into raising her right could hold strong in the real world.

Amanda squeezed Nina's hand gently. "It's difficult, and I'm sure it doesn't all make sense right now, but sometimes the pieces fall into place when you least expect it."

Nina swallowed hard, the words hitting her in ways she hadn't prepared for. She could hear the truth in Amanda's voice, could feel the depth of the journey she'd been through. Kendra's actions consumed her every thought, leaving no room for anything else. Not even hope.

Amanda encouraged her. "You got nothing to lose by trusting it, you know? The process, the timing, whatever you want to call it."

"Right." Nina squeezed Amanda's hand back. "I've been so focused on what's fallen apart that I forget to appreciate what's still whole."

Amanda offered a gentle, knowing smile. "Exactly. Whelk's Island, this community, Rosemary, my family, Tug, and Fisher, too—we're all here for you. And we'll help you find your way back to what you need."

A warmth spread through Nina's chest. A sense of belonging that had been missing for so long. She looked up at her mom, who had been watching the exchange from across the room, her eyes filled with a quiet pride. Being pulled into something so unexpected felt strange, but in a good way, because it was hopeful. "I think I'm starting to believe that," Nina murmured.

Amanda gave Nina's hand one last squeeze before letting go of it and stepping back. "You should. Whelk's Island can renew your faith in yourself. You just have to be open and let it happen."

Nina took a deep breath, looking around the room at the people who had unknowingly become her support system, her new foundation. And then her gaze landed on tall, handsome Fisher, smiling easily in conversation with the others.

She wished she had the courage to ask Amanda about Fisher, but even the thought of letting another man get close felt like stepping into the surf: beautiful but full of unknowns.

Chapter Eighteen

FISHER STOOD SHOULDER TO SHOULDER WITH TUG, CASTing his line beyond the break, hoping today the ocean might offer more than just fish. The weather was perfect, the gentle waves lapping against the shore soothing to his soul.

Beside him, Tug stood with his line already in the water, his shoulders relaxed and his ball cap pulled low on his forehead, shading his eyes. For a while, they just stood in calm silence, the rhythmic click of their reels the only sound other than nature.

Then Fisher shot a side glance at Tug's slack line.

"You ever gonna get serious about this?" Fisher teased. "Or just keep letting the fish steal your bait?"

Tug snorted. "Boy, I was catching fish before you were born."

"Yeah?" Fisher smirked. "Seems like you've been missing 'em all morning."

Tug shot him a look, but he didn't argue. They fell again into that comfortable rhythm, casting, reeling, watching the waves.

Tug adjusted his stance, shifting his weight as the water swirled around his ankles.

"You gave me a hard time about Rosemary for a while there," he mused. "How I took my sweet time makin' a move. I guess I should thank you for your encouragement. She's special."

Fisher chuckled, reeling his line in. "Well, I was afraid you were going to let her slip right through your fingers."

Tug exhaled, shaking his head. "I thought when Maeve died, I'd missed my chance at this kind of love."

His voice held a depth Fisher didn't hear often.

Tug cast his line out again, watching it disappear beneath the waves. "Spent my whole life loving Maeve. The problem was, I never had her heart."

Fisher let that settle between them. Tug wasn't one to speak about regrets too often, but there was something in his tone, an old ache buried deep.

"Surfers," Fisher said after a beat, his eyes still on the horizon. "We'll wait our whole lives for that one sweet ride. One that might never come. I guess surfers are the same way about women, huh?"

Tug let out a snort followed by a laugh. "That, my friend, is a fact." He tugged on his cap, lifting his chin to level a stare. "You seem to be waiting on your perfect wave too. Don't wait too long. You'll get to be my age and still be looking for your person. Believe me, if I had any idea how wonderful my life would be because of Rosemary, I'd have looked for it sooner."

Silence settled again. Not heavy, just with the weight of truths neither had spoken aloud before.

"But loving Rosemary?" Tug said after a long pause, his voice quieter. "Easiest decision I ever made."

Fisher agreed. "She's good for you."

"She is. We've been engaged for a while now. I'd meant to surprise her with a summer wedding, but the timing seems wrong with everything going on." He shrugged. "Maybe I was just feeling inspired by Amanda and Paul's sweet backyard wedding last year."

"That was seriously the best wedding I've ever been to," Fisher said. "Great food and so much fun." He glanced over, watching Tug's expression shift.

"I don't want to push her," Tug said. "She's got a lot on her right now with Kendra and Nina in the house. We love each other, no question about that. I just want to give her some space to get the kids on steady ground. We're all family, wedding bells or not. I love those girls. All three of them."

Fisher exhaled slowly. "Life's messy. Who said that?"

"Who hasn't said it?" Tug said with a laugh. "It's true, and I understand now is not the time to focus on the wedding of a couple of senior citizens, but I would be devastated if something were to happen and I hadn't been able to make her my wife, share my name and my home with her." He let out a humorless chuckle. "I have a history of falling for women who never get past their past, ya know. What if all this family drama makes her have second thoughts? What if there's no room for me in the picture?"

"That's not gonna happen. I'd bet my epic turtle longboard on it." Fisher knew Tug was thinking of Maeve. "You do know, Tug, that Rosemary is completely different from Maeve. I can't speak to Maeve, but I spend enough time with Rosemary to know she adores you. You both light up like Fourth of July fireworks when you're together."

Fisher understood that kind of longing. "It's like waiting all day for the fish to bite, and just when you're ready to pack it in, there's a tug on the line. Your heart skips a beat. The feeling is a mix of excitement and relief, and as you reel in the line, it's not about the catch at all. It's about the process or the journey, the patience, and the memories you're building with friends who understand that sometimes it's the waiting that makes the experience so much sweeter."

"When you put it like that, fishing *is* like falling in love." Tug laughed.

"Tug, I know Rosemary is in love with you. It's plain as the smile on your face."

"I believe that when we're alone. I guess I'm just afraid. Why would a beautiful woman like her want to spend the rest of her life with an old man like me?" Tug shifted his weight, giving Fisher a sidelong glance.

"You're only as old as you feel, and I saw you hula the other night. You don't have one foot in the grave, so stop talking like you do."

Tug shrugged. "Fisher, I've known you for years," he said. "How come you never come to me with your relationship woes? Or anything else, for that matter?"

Fisher kept his eyes on the horizon. He had a knack for blending into the background, keeping things cheerful and relaxed. It had once been a way to survive. But some things . . . some things a man couldn't keep buried forever.

"She's out of my league. What could I give her that she doesn't already have?"

Tug whipped his head around. "Are you kidding? Fisher, that's ridiculous. You are a good man. A giving man."

"Even when I had assets, it was hard to shake that old feeling that I'm not good enough, ya know?" He turned and looked down at the beach. "This town was my escape. And for a lot of those years, I was here for the wrong reasons. Running from bad things at home."

Tug stayed quiet, letting him speak.

"And then I had no choice but to be at home to hold it together, but I couldn't. When I came back for good, I was in a different place. But my past? That's not something I'm proud of. Shame, I guess. And fear. Fear that if I spoke it out loud, everything I'd built would fall away. That maybe none of it was real."

"Our past makes us who we are today," Tug said. "Do you think I made no mistakes? We've all made mistakes, Fisher."

"I had some deep-seated struggles, Tug. I didn't trust anyone." Fisher recast his line into the surf. "Some demons I had to fight off. There was a time when I didn't know where my next meal was coming from or where I'd sleep."

Tug didn't flinch, didn't seem to judge. "The school of hard knocks comes with one powerful diploma."

"That, it does." It was why he kept his success to himself, not even mentioning what he'd built since then or bragging about the properties he owned, the businesses he'd built quietly in the background. He was humbly grateful for the resources he'd been given and for his aunt's belief in him. Because he knew what it was like to have nothing. And for a long time, he lived with the constant fear that if his father found out he'd dug himself out of the hole he'd been left in, he'd show up to steal it from him. And he never wanted to be in that position again.

"I came here to Whelk's Island for sanctuary," Fisher explained. "As a kid, I didn't have much. I helped Mom clean the rental houses to pay the bills. Sometimes we lived in them secretly, only to have to move at a moment's notice because we weren't supposed to be there. Sometimes we even slept in the car. Tug, it was hard."

"Fisher, why have you kept this to yourself all this time? You never have to be ashamed of things that are out of your control. You have to know that. We do the best we can with what we have and know at the time. It's all we can do."

"Way easier to believe that now. Back then, I was afraid. I've never been able to shake that fear of my dad showing up and ruining everything I finally built for myself. It was like digging out of quicksand. I learned how to fix things by reading books and trying until I made progress. It's how I've flipped every one of my beach houses pretty much on my own, with the help of some kids who need work."

Tug lifted his chin. "All those rentals you clean—you own them, don't you?"

"I do."

Tug simply threw out his line again. The rhythmic sound of waves rolling against the shore filled the quiet between them as they stood side by side, their fishing rods balanced against the wind. The morning was clear, the kind of peaceful breezy day that made Whelk's Island feel timeless.

Tug cast his line out again, the reel humming, his movements slow and practiced. "You're usually so quiet," he finally said, his voice easy, "but I'm glad you opened up to me a little today." The observation wasn't lost on Fisher.

Fisher reeled his line back in. He considered brushing off the comment, giving a half-hearted response, but he knew Tug too well. The old man had a way of seeing through excuses. Maybe that was why the surfers, the wayward kids, and even stubborn old-timers always seemed to gravitate toward him. Tug didn't judge, but he sure knew how to get someone to talk when they needed to. Even when they didn't want to.

"I've been thinking," Fisher said, casting his line back into the surf. "About how I got here. Why I stayed."

Tug let out a chuckle. "That's dangerous territory, son. Could lead to self-discovery."

Fisher smirked, shaking his head. "Yeah, well, maybe it's time."

Tug tugged on the bill of his cap. "Yeah, we all need to do a little of that thoughtful introspection now and again."

The water shimmered under the morning light, and for a long moment, Fisher just watched it, remembering a younger version of himself, the one who had first come to Whelk's Island with nothing but a duffel bag and more anger than a teenager should carry around.

"My Aunt Claire lived here," Fisher said. "She was my dad's older sister, but they weren't anything alike. She owned the bungalow where I used to live with her. Nothing fancy, you know?"

"Yeah, sure."

"I don't have to live there now. I do because it keeps me grounded. Aunt Claire was the only person who ever believed in me. She saw me for more than my mistakes. Most of my family just saw me as in the way."

Tug reeled his line in slowly. "I remember her. Good woman. She took you in? I never realized you lived there before she died."

Fisher nodded. "I was fifteen when she convinced my mom to send me here. Dad was abusive and Mom was hardly home, probably because when she was, it was loud and dangerous at our house. She was tired and afraid that I was gonna end up just like him. I'd started hanging out with some kids who stirred up a lot of trouble. And when you've got nothing to lose, it makes doing stupid things real easy."

Tug cast him a sideways glance, but Fisher saw no judgment there.

"Aunt Claire was different," Fisher continued. "She didn't push. Didn't lecture. Just handed me a surfboard and told me if I wanted to be angry, I should take it out on the waves." He let out a soft laugh. "I thought she was crazy, but with nowhere else to go, I took that old board and paddled out and fought that ocean all day long. I'll be darned if that woman wasn't right."

"It's got a way of humbling a man," Tug said.

"She died when I was twenty," Fisher said. "Left me the house. Her family wasn't too happy about it. They figured I'd sell it, take the money, and disappear. Actually, I think they hoped I would. And I almost did to avoid the conflict, which I'd become pretty good at, but something made me stay and try to make her proud." He glanced out at the horizon.

Tug reeled his line in, the *click-click-click* of the reel filling the silence. "And you didn't leave."

"No," Fisher said, shaking his head. "For once, I didn't run. I stood there, staring at that sagging porch and those weather-beaten walls, and saw more than just a house. I saw myself—beat-up, a little forgotten, but still standing. Figured fixing it was my shot at putting myself back together too."

"So, you fixed it up."

Fisher shrugged. "Didn't have the money for contractors, so I learned. Read books, asked questions, and bartered work when I needed help. Meanwhile, I was learning skills. I volunteered on some mission builds for the church and learned from people who knew what they were doing. Picked up occasional temporary jobs on some of the big houses they were building around here. And something about being with the people from church felt like nothing I'd ever experienced before. I suddenly felt confident that I could do something."

Tug let out a low whistle. "And you did."

Fisher gave a modest shrug. "One at a time. Saved every cent. Lived cheap. Bought places no one wanted and made them something worth having."

"Such a shame," Tug muttered.

Fisher arched a brow. "What is?"

"That I never knew," Tug said, turning to him now. "That you were out here doing all that work, building something out of nothing, and I never got to celebrate any of those wins with you."

Fisher stilled, the words hitting somewhere deep, somewhere he hadn't expected. He'd never had anyone say something like that to him before. Never had someone acknowledge what it might've felt like to do it all alone.

"I've always liked you, Fisher. You were one of the first people to show up to help me when we had to board up for the storms. But I had no idea." Tug gave him an affirming nod. "I'm very proud of you, son."

Fisher swallowed hard. "Thanks," he said, his voice rougher

than he liked. "I guess I never thought much about that. Having someone to celebrate with."

Tug sighed, shaking his head. "You and me both. If you've never really had it, you have no idea what you're missing out on. You don't know what you don't know."

They stood in silence for a long moment, just the waves and the wind between them.

"What about Maeve?" Fisher asked quietly.

Tug exhaled a long breath. "She never saw me the way I saw her. I loved her. Well, I always thought I did, but it's different from what I feel with Rosemary. Woo-boy, I never imagined love so big! Maeve and I never had that."

"Maybe you never let her."

Tug let out a soft chuckle. "You've been taking notes on my mistakes, huh?"

Fisher grinned. "No. It seemed like y'all were family, but I never saw you two as romantic."

"Yeah, we weren't." Tug eyed him, then leaned forward, lowering his voice. "Let me give you some advice. Don't live your life being safe. You think you're protecting yourself, but really you're just keeping yourself from ever having something worth holding on to."

Fisher let the words sink in, rolling them over like the tide smoothing out the jagged edges of broken seashells.

"I'll tell you something else," Tug continued. "That redhead who's got you looking at the world a little differently? That's something to pay attention to."

Fisher stiffened but said nothing, especially because the comment echoed one he had made to Tug about Rosemary right after the hurricane.

"Those words fell close to home, didn't they?"

"You mean like the advice I gave you once upon a time at The Tackle Box?"

He nodded.

"Apparently, it was pretty good advice, because it looks like it's working out pretty nicely for you."

"Yep. And I see you stumbling around, almost dipping your toe into the opportunity," Tug said. "Don't be a fool like me and need advice from someone else to help you see what's right there in front of you." He paused. "You know I'm talking about Nina, right?"

"Yeah, I'm listening."

"You've built a good life for yourself, but don't miss out on letting yourself share it with someone. If you want a real legacy? Let yourself have more than just peace. Share it and build a family around it and fill it with love."

Fisher didn't respond right away. He just watched the waves, feeling something shift inside him. He'd never let himself think about it before. Never let himself want it. Images of family had been dark and hurtful in his life.

But now? Now he saw how different it was for others. He wanted more than just peace. Maybe for the first time, he wanted a family. And that terrified him more than anything ever had before.

"I hear what you're saying, Tug. Sometimes being alone isn't the brave thing to do. Sharing our life is, and with the right person, it's . . . well, it's right. It's more than I could ever be or feel on my own."

"Amen." Tug stretched and looked over at Fisher. "Guess it's not our day," he said with a half-hearted chuckle.

"Fishing is never over until the lines come in." Fisher's gaze drifted toward the distant horizon, his mind already able to taste how good a fresh-catch dinner would be later, with maybe a cold beer and certainly a story to tell. Just as he reached for his gear to pull up the line and call it quits, something jerked his rod. "Hang on. Did you see that?"

It was subtle at first, a quick twitch, a small resistance, but then it pulled again, this time stronger and more deliberate. His rod arched and his pulse quickened.

"It ain't over, old man," Fisher muttered, planting his feet in the sand, his fingers gripping the rod as excitement surged through his veins.

Tug looked surprised. Maybe he thought Fisher was joking, but Tug knew you couldn't fake the bend in a rod like that. He raced to Fisher's side.

"This day just got a lot more interesting," Tug said. "You've got something." He clapped Fisher on the back, cheering him to pull it in.

It felt like it took forever to bring the fish in, but every second only held more promise of what was coming.

Tug was steadily talking, offering tips and encouragement, his voice low but confident. "Keep it steady. Don't yank. Patience, now."

The fish fought, thrashing under the water, trying to break free. And then, with one last pull, it surfaced. The large silvery form broke through the water with a splash.

Fisher let out a short laugh of relief mixed with disbelief. "It's a keeper." Not just any fish, but one big enough to feed them and those women they were just talking about. A reward for their patience, for their perseverance.

And as Fisher stood there, feeling the weight of the fish on the line, he realized it wasn't just about the catch or the story they'd tell. It was about knowing he didn't have to face these moments alone anymore. Not if he chose differently.

"All right! Now, that's dinner!" Tug exclaimed.

There was a sense of shared triumph in the moment as both of them stared at the fish wriggling on the line, the promise of a hearty meal and a story for later hanging between them like an unspoken bond.

With a practiced hand, Tug helped Fisher pull the fish onto the sand, the two of them laughing now.

"Guess it was our day after all," Fisher said with a grin, his eyes glinting in the late-morning light.

"Yeah, maybe we'll both get the girls," Tug said.

"I said nothing about getting Nina."

"You didn't have to. It's all over your face with that goofy, swooning, doe-eyed look you have when she's around."

Fisher gulped. "I'm that obvious, huh?"

Tug sighed, shaking his head.

Maybe it was time to stop waiting for the next wave and trust the one already beneath his feet.

Chapter Nineteen

WHILE TUG HANDLED THEIR CATCH, THE WEIGHT OF THE old man's words sat on Fisher's shoulders as he watched the surf roll in. He'd spent so many years thinking he was just a guy on his own, building something for himself, making sure he owed no one a thing. But maybe that was just another kind of cage.

As Fisher stood at the edge of the water, each wave tugged at the sand beneath him, trying to carry away all the heaviness he'd been holding for too long. Maybe he should bid all that good riddance, anyway. The horizon stretched wide and endless, a quiet reminder that there was more out there if only he'd let himself look beyond the safety of what he'd always known.

He breathed in a little deeper, wondering what it would be like to admit he wanted a little more. More of Nina in his life. Her image was so clear: the way she tossed her head when she really laughed, and the way her nose crinkled just slightly when she worried. He hoped he wouldn't see the latter very often. Brewing inside him was an instinctive desire to be there for her. Then he exhaled, knowing he didn't just *want* her—he *needed* her.

And then he saw her. Nina. Standing by the dunes, her arms wrapped around herself as the breeze played with loose strands of her hair. She looked lost in thought, her gaze soft and distant as she stared out over the water. When she spotted him, she lifted a hand in a small wave, and something in Fisher's chest eased, as if he'd been holding his breath without realizing it.

Fisher didn't hesitate. He walked over, nodding toward the horizon. "This is one of my favorite parts of the beach. Did you come out here to unwind?"

"Something like that. Just taking a short break, but I have to get back to work soon," she said, her smile tentative. "Actually, I came looking for you. Mom said you were out here fishing with Tug. This isn't one of those no-girls-allowed guy things, is it?"

"Hardly!" He chuckled. "You have really good timing. I'm glad you're here. You're just in time to hear about my great victory."

Her brows lifted, curiosity softening her worry. "Oh? Victory?"

"I caught a fish big enough for dinner. Tug's already planning the menu."

As if summoned, Tug appeared, hauling his heavy wagon toward the beach. His face lit up as soon as he spotted them. "Well, well. Look who's here. I was ready to call it a day after feeding the fish my bait all morning, but your buddy here reeled in a whopper."

"That's wonderful," Nina said. "Sounds like a good morning."

"The best kind," Tug agreed. "Dinner's at my place tonight. Catch of the day à la Fisher, prepared by yours truly. I already texted your mom. She and Kendra are handling side dishes."

"Perfect," Nina said. "What about me?"

"You get to keep me out of the way," Fisher said.

"How did I get stuck with the hardest job?" she teased.

Fisher felt the warmth of it: the easy rhythm, the sense of

belonging he hadn't let himself want before. He turned to Tug. "You sure you don't want me to help clean the fish?"

Tug shook his head. "Nah. I've been cleaning fish longer than you've been alive. That's the deal: You caught it; I'll prep it. But I'm sending you two off to go have some fun and work up an appetite. Go on."

Fisher hesitated only a second before turning to Nina. "Do you have time for a quick ride? I want to show you something."

He reached for her hand.

After the briefest pause, she placed hers in his, and said, "Yes, I have a little bit of time."

He felt the promise of what could be in that simple touch. He opened the truck door for her, steadying her as she climbed in, and for the first time in years, he wasn't thinking about the things that had gone wrong. He was thinking about what could go right.

They drove with the windows down, the breeze carrying the scent of the ocean. Nina laughed as Fisher deflected her playful attempts to get him to reveal their destination.

"Come on," she said, grinning. "You can't give me even a hint?"

"Nope." Fisher tapped the steering wheel, his eyes twinkling. "Trust me, you'll like it."

Finally, he pulled up behind a weathered beach house, where a small shed sat tucked in the shade of an old oak. A hand-painted sign hung crookedly: FRESH CHURNED ICE CREAM—UNTIL IT'S GONE.

Nina blinked, surprised. "This is your big surprise?"

Fisher hopped out, his grin wide and boyish. "Not just any ice cream. Best you'll ever taste. And we're grown-ups. We can have ice cream for lunch, can't we?"

"I guess we could."

"You'll love it. It's hand-cranked right here every summer,

and it's only open from June until Labor Day. They open at ten and close as soon as whatever they made that day is gone, and then they're done for the day. Sometimes they are sold out before noon."

"What are we waiting for, then?" Nina rushed ahead of him, forcing him to turn it into a race.

The air near the little stand smelled of sweet cream and vanilla. Fisher grabbed his favorite pint without hesitation. Nina studied the options, then mentioned she was going to choose the flavor Kendra loved best, even though it wasn't her own favorite.

The small act made Fisher's heart tug. "You always think of her first, don't you?"

Nina shrugged, a little shy. "That's what moms do."

They drove back toward Rosemary's, the ice cream pints tucked between them, cool against their arms. As they pulled up, they spotted Rosemary and Kendra hanging a basket of bright blooms outside the apartment door. The flowers spilled over the edge, catching the sun.

The sight warmed Fisher clear through. "She looks happy out there. She's settling in."

Nina followed his gaze. "She is," she said quietly. "And I think . . . maybe I am too."

The four of them sat on the porch to eat the ice cream, spoons clinking and laughter spilling over like sunshine. The worries that usually hung between Nina and Fisher felt lighter, carried off on the breeze. No expectations. No pressure. Just the sweetness of a day well spent.

Fisher gave Nina a playful grin. *Sometimes the simplest moments are the ones that change everything.*

Chapter Twenty

A SMILE TUGGED AT THE CORNERS OF NINA'S LIPS AS SHE sat savoring the sounds of the beach that night. The early dinner at Tug's had been not only delicious but promising. The hope of better things ahead lightened the burden on her heart. Fisher had shared his story and then taken her to see a couple of the properties he owned on their way to Tug's. They'd even walked through a vacant one, and it was gorgeous. The details showed he had an artistic eye in both the craftsmanship and the way he'd decorated it in a minimalist way.

Fisher was not only handy but also humble. He was definitely not your average Surfing Sam. She'd gotten him all wrong.

But after their fun time together, reality crashed back down on her as soon as she stepped inside her mom's house. Kendra was grumpy, slamming kitchen cabinets, her frustration filling the space between them.

"What is going on, Kendra?"

"You know. You always know," she said, glaring at her.

Then Nina's phone rang. "Know what?" She glanced at the caller ID. Her ex-husband. All the air deflated from her chest. Answering David's call was about to no doubt extinguish the warmth her conversation with Fisher had given her.

She left Kendra in her dark mood and scurried out to the deck to take the call. David got right to the point after she answered, telling Nina he'd just informed Kendra that he would not be picking her up later this summer to take her to Yellowstone.

Nina couldn't believe it. She listened as David rambled on about how he and his *new* wife were going to Europe instead of him taking Kendra out West, and the kicker was that the plan change was because they were expecting.

"We're going to have a baby, so it's sort of now or never," he said. "I didn't tell Kendra that part. Thought you could help me out with that one."

She blinked, letting his words sink in. *Help you? We never took vacations when we were married, pregnant or not. Why are you getting a big do-over, and here I am being responsible for cleaning up the problems in your wake while you go globe-trotting?*

But none of that passed through her lips. She stood there shaking her head. "I'm not sure what to say."

"Well, your daughter has quite an attitude. She mouthed off to me when I told her I needed to reschedule. Who's the parent here?"

"Of course she mouthed off to you, David. You're letting her down again! You always do this!" She paced the deck, gripping the phone until her knuckles ached. "You make grandiose promises, then abandon them when something shiny grabs your attention. You give no thought at all to what effect it has on our daughter. What is wrong with you?"

"I—"

"No. I don't even want to hear it. If you called me because you think, for one happy second, that I'm smoothing this over for you, you've got another thing coming." Nina closed her eyes, unable to even process what he'd said. "Not this time, David. I've rearranged my whole life to bring her here and not interrupt your time with her to try to make things better for her. She is struggling. You don't even deserve her love."

Kendra walked out at the worst possible moment. Her face

twisted in frustration. "Why do you always have to be so mean to Daddy?"

Nina turned, startled. "Kendra, I–"

"He's trying. You just want him to fail so you can be the good guy!"

"What?" Nina sucked in a breath, reeling. "That's not fair." She realized that she was probably just an easier target for Kendra since her dad wasn't in front of her, but it still hurt.

"You hope I'll hate him!" Kendra accused, her voice shaking. Then, with a sneer, she added, "Just like you want me to like your new surfer boyfriend."

Nina stiffened. "What did you just say?"

Kendra crossed her arms, eyeing her mom. "I see the way he looks at you."

Heat rushed to Nina's face, not just in anger but in something else, something unnerving. Because there was a truth buried in Kendra's words. Fisher had been looking at her differently. And it was nice. She hadn't felt desirable in a very long time. But this wasn't the moment to unpack that.

"I don't know what's gotten into you, but you do not talk to me that way," Nina said, her voice low and controlled. "Your father is the one who let you down, so don't take it out on me. Go to your room. Now."

"It was fine when you were married. You loved him then, and everything was perfect." Kendra glared, then stomped back inside. Nina heard her bedroom door slam shut.

Oh, their marriage had been far from perfect, and she and David had been too busy to realize it until it was too late. Nina let out a long breath, pressing her fingers to her temple. She then lifted the phone to her ear. David was screaming what-to-dos, but she didn't care. *I can't believe I didn't hang up before all that.* She ended the call without another word and sank onto the couch inside, her heart pounding.

Later that night, the house was quiet. Too quiet. Uneasiness ran up Nina's spine. She went to Kendra's bedroom door, turned the knob, and peeked in. The room was empty.

Her stomach dropped. She raced from room to room, but there was no sign of Kendra. The back door was unlocked, but she wasn't on the deck either. Panic surged through Nina. *No, no, no!*

As she grabbed her keys, her first thought was to text Fisher for help, but that wasn't right. This wasn't his mess to handle, and she hated to ruin Mom's time with Tug if it wasn't an emergency. *Or is it?* Nina ran outside, calling Kendra's name. The salty wind whipped around her like a heavy coat, and the darkness pressed in close.

What are you thinking, Kendra?

As Nina raced for her car, she noticed the bicycle still leaning against the carport wall.

Please be nearby.

When she looked over to the beach, she saw Kendra standing knee-deep in the surf, her arms wrapped around herself, gazing out at the waves.

Relief battled anger inside Nina. She leaned over to catch her breath and regain her composure. Once her heart slowed down, she walked over to her daughter. "What are you doing?" Her voice came out sharp with fear. "Do you have any idea how dangerous this is?"

"Who cares?" Kendra turned to Nina, her face set in a defiant glare.

"I do." She held Kendra's hollow gaze. "Your grandmother does."

"I needed air."

"That's not how this works," Nina shot back. "You don't just sneak out after dark." She fought back tears, afraid to let Kendra see her weaken. "What is going on in that head of yours?"

Kendra's lip trembled, but she lifted her chin. "If you keep being mean to Dad, he'll never come back for us."

It was like a dagger to her heart to be reminded that her divorce was the tipping point of her daughter's distress. Nina stepped closer, placing a calming hand on Kendra's arm. "He's remarried, Kendra. Your dad has moved on. We have to as well."

"You're so busy making eyes at Fisher that you don't even notice me."

Nina's breath caught. "That is not true. You are always first in my heart. He's a friend of our family. I thought you liked him."

Kendra's eyes flashed. "It's me or him, Mom. Pick."

The ultimatum landed like a punch to the gut. Nina staggered back a step. "Kendra . . ."

Kendra shook her head and turned away, walking back toward the house and leaving Nina standing there, alone, under the vast, empty sky.

How could she possibly tell Kendra about her dad and Charlotte having a baby when she felt Nina was picking someone else too?

From the beach, Nina saw a light turn on at the house. Kendra had made it back safely.

Nina sank onto the sand, dropping her face into her hands. Tears burned hot against her palms until they finally gave way to a hollow ache. When she stood, heaviness hung in her chest, that gnawing guilt whispering all the ways she might've done better. She had to figure out how to reach Kendra before the space between them grew into something she couldn't bridge.

Praying it wasn't too late already, Nina walked back up to the house. Just as she stepped off the sandy pathway when she got closer, she heard the door of a vehicle shut. When she looked over, Mom and Tug were walking up the stairs.

Nina stepped back into the darkness at the corner of the house, knowing her mother would be able to tell she'd been crying. The irony struck her. When the going got tough, Mom was always there to help, but Nina rarely gave her the opportunity to, and here she was again, trying to hide that she needed support. Wasn't that exactly what Kendra was doing to Nina now?

This is an unexpected dose of my own medicine. Soldier on.

After Tug drove off a few minutes later, Nina took the stairs to the house at a slow pace, thinking twice that she should walk back down to the beach until the lights went out and sneak in unnoticed, but that wouldn't solve the problems she was facing now. She needed Mom's advice.

She punched in the code on the front door and walked inside. Mom poked her head in from the kitchen.

"Nina?" She looked sheepish. "Hey, sorry for locking you out. I assumed you were in bed. Sorry."

"I remembered the code." It was easy enough. Mom's birthday. She tried to lift the tone of her voice. "No worries."

"Honey, are you okay?" Mom's smile drooped, her brows pulling together. "Have you been crying?" She raced to her side.

"Yes. I keep letting Kendra down, and I want to fix this. I just don't know how. There's not a problem I can't resolve at work, but at home I'm a train wreck."

"You are not. Nina, don't beat yourself up. If you only knew how often I felt exactly like you're feeling right now. You can't spreadsheet your way through raising a teenager."

"If only. I'm great at getting projects from red status to green. Teenagers? Another thing entirely. I wish it were as easy as business."

"You're a great mother, Nina."

She shook her head. "I don't feel like a good mom. Kendra is so mad at me. And she's still dreaming about me and David getting back together."

Rosemary looked horror-struck. "Oh, heavens, no. I wouldn't wish that on anyone."

"She has no idea how bad it was. We did a great job hiding our troubles, but I think all we did was make it harder for her to realize that ending our marriage was necessary."

"Teenagers can't understand mature problems like divorce. And they shouldn't have to. You did the right thing by trying to protect her."

"There's more." Nina sucked in a breath. "She thinks Fisher is keeping me from getting back with David."

"That's ridiculous. David is with what's-her-name."

"Charlotte. I know. No matter what, I'll never get back together with David. And Kendra said I have to pick between her and Fisher. It's all so ridiculous."

"Well, Fisher has nothing to do with your marriage. He's a good guy, and he came through for you. Don't let your daughter wield that kind of power over you. It's manipulative. And what you do or don't do with Fisher is your decision."

Nina lifted her chin a fraction. Maybe she'd needed to hear those words more than she realized.

"I think Fisher's been good for this family," Rosemary added. "We need someone strong who can understand Kendra's crazy brain right now."

"Yeah, he's been a godsend. I really misjudged him in the beginning. He's nothing like who I had him pigeonholed for when I met him last year."

Rosemary tsk-tsked. "Well, if you recall, your first visit to Whelk's Island didn't exactly cast *you* in a favorable light either."

"That's true." Nina regretted how she'd rolled into town

with her attitude on her shoulder, giving Mom the what for like she was a runaway teenager.

What goes around comes around.

❁

The next day, Nina stayed in her room, working straight through, but her focus was shot. Her stomach ached from carrying the weight of the news that David had let Kendra down again. Things between mother and daughter were already fragile, and now this? The fact that he wasn't just canceling the trip but was also replacing Kendra with his new wife was more than disappointing—it was devastating.

Nina knew her daughter deserved the whole truth, but she couldn't bring herself to tell her about the baby—not yet. Maybe if they could just find their footing again and ease out of this storm they'd been stuck in, Kendra might be able to handle it better. Right now, it would be like piling heartbreak on top of heartbreak.

After closing her laptop, she went upstairs to check on Kendra. She'd tried to earlier, but Tug and Fisher caught her by surprise by showing up. A little irritated at first, she shook it off, considering it a little God wink to buy her time from having that difficult conversation with Kendra. *Maybe I should plan a nice vacation for just the two of us, to sort of soften the blow.*

For dinner that night, they ate grilled hot dogs and hamburgers and Mom's broccoli salad. It was quick and easy.

"I'll clean up," Nina said as everyone finished.

"I'm going back to my room, Mom," Kendra said.

"Okay, sweetheart."

Nina carried a platter to the kitchen, put it in the sink, and gave it a quick scrub. Through the open window, she could hear

Tug and Fisher on the porch, their voices low and steady as they talked about something that made Tug chuckle. The simple rhythm of it settled over her like a warm tide.

She glanced at her mother, whose gaze was distant.

"Mom?" Nina dried her hands on a dish towel and crossed the room to where her mother sat at the table. "You okay?"

Rosemary blinked, then offered a small smile. "Hmm? Oh yes. Just thinking."

Nina pulled out the chair across from her and sat down. "Everything all right?"

Her mother exhaled and set her cup down. "Of course. I was just thinking about Tug and I being engaged." She wiggled her ring finger, looking at it like it was a magic eight ball.

Nina tilted her head. "That's not the look of someone who's supposed to be setting a wedding date."

Rosemary gave a soft chuckle but didn't argue. She tapped her fingers against the table, a habit Nina recognized from her childhood. Mom would fidget when she wasn't saying what was on her mind.

"I'm happy to help with the wedding plans," Nina offered. "Or is it Tug?"

"No." Rosemary's smile turned wistful. "Tug is wonderful. Everything I never knew I needed."

Nina studied her, sensing her hesitation. "But?"

Rosemary rubbed her temple. "But I spent a lifetime being someone's wife. Being part of a 'we.' And when your father passed, I thought that part of my life was over."

"But you accepted his ring. That must have changed."

"It did. I didn't expect someone to come along. I was building something for myself here. I can't say I even knew what it was, except that it felt right. But now there's so much going on with you and Kendra, and I just don't know if it's a good time."

"You're sharing your life with someone again. That's precious, Mom. I love that for you. Don't worry about me or Kendra. We love Tug, and we love how happy you are together."

Rosemary traced her fingers over the ring. "It's not that I don't love Tug. I do. With everything in me."

"It shows." Nina sat back, letting the words settle. She understood her mom's fear more than she wanted to admit. Loving someone again after loss, whether death or divorce, wasn't easy. It meant stepping into the unknown and risking stability for the chance at something greater.

"You know," Nina said after a moment, "I think I understand what you're feeling. I've been telling myself if I let Fisher in, I might lose myself. But watching you and Tug makes me feel less afraid. I don't know. I've thought a lot about this, so hear me out. Do you think love might make us more ourselves than being alone does? Is that crazy?"

"Like God planned?" Rosemary's lips curved slightly, her gaze softening. "He created us, intending us to be coupled. Stronger when we are as one. But I don't want to add any complexities to your life."

Nina shrugged. "I'd hate for you to miss out on something beautiful because you were afraid of changing. Or, worse, putting us ahead of your joy. You've earned this beautiful time in your life, and we're happy for you. It's the one good thing working in the family right now."

Her mother let out a quiet laugh. "When did you get so wise?"

"Somewhere between burning grilled cheese sandwiches and navigating teenage meltdowns. Oh, and I had a smart mom who raised me to believe in hope and joy."

Rosemary chuckled, reaching across the table to squeeze Nina's hand. "I suppose we should set a wedding date, then."

Nina said, "I think Tug would like that."

Her mother sighed, but this time, it was lighter. "Yes. I think he would."

"And I would love nothing more than to help make that happen. Be brave, Mom," Nina said, her voice soft but sure. "This is the only good stuff I have going on in my life. Don't mess it up for me," she teased.

As the night breeze lifted the curtain at the window, she let herself believe—just for a moment—that maybe *she* could be brave too.

Chapter Twenty-One

A PELICAN GLIDED LOW OVER THE WATER, THEN DOVE IN one clean motion, disrupting the calm with ripples. It pulled up in a spray of silver droplets, off on its merry way, just as Nina stepped outside.

And yet even the disturbance of the bird crashing through the surface didn't offer a hiccup to the timing of the waves rolling in. Watching the effortless motion, she wondered if she'd ever learn to trust life's timing the way the ocean seemed to. *The tides come at specific times, to the point that a person can count on them. It's really amazing that so many miracles seem to fit into the ebb and flow of nature. So, why is it that we're always trying to control something that was never meant to be tamed?*

The rhythm of summer was taking shape on Whelk's Island. It was busier and the heat wave changed things too. Nina clung to the routine as though it were a lifeline, keeping herself busy between work, Rosemary's projects, volunteering, and helping Kendra settle into something resembling normalcy.

And to everyone's surprise, Kendra was trying. It didn't keep Nina from checking on her daughter in the middle of the night, but she was beginning to rest easier with the hopes that blue skies were in their future.

Kendra was still volunteering at the library a few mornings a week, and after a little nudging from Amanda, Paul had offered her a part-time job walking dogs at Paws. At first, Nina hadn't been sure Kendra was going to accept the offer, but she was relieved when she did.

Fisher had played his part, too, being the one to stress to Kendra how important working with military dogs was. He explained how they trained for service and how they were truly soldiers themselves. Some came home from missions with emotional scars due to losing their soldier or enduring their own combat wounds. Others retired because of the emotional impact that war can take on a soldier, both the two-legged and four-legged kind. He'd said to Kendra, "These dogs need extra care before placement. Someone with a big heart and understanding like you."

Nina still remembered the glint in her daughter's eyes when Fisher's words landed on her. It looked like pride, maybe confidence, had sparked inside her.

Kendra agreed to give it a trial week, and Fisher offered to drive her to and from work the first day. He ended up taking her the first two days, and, truth be told, Nina had felt a little left out. On day three, Kendra asked her mom if she could bike to Paws, but Nina offered her a ride, and she seemed happy with that option.

When Nina picked her up that night, Kendra explained she'd been assigned one particular dog to care for. She said it was like having her own and that he was so smart and she was learning German because that's the only language this dog spoke. *"I might take German in school next year,"* she'd announced. It was the first positive thing she'd said in a while. It blew Nina's mind that suddenly Kendra was not only thinking about a healthy change but also looking to the future.

Now it was already time to pick her up again. Nina adjusted the strap of her bag as she stepped into the huge Paws Town Square building. The place had become a sanctuary for Kendra, though her daughter would never admit it. Amanda had told Nina that Kendra was fitting in and how impressed Paul had been with her care and intuition in handling the animals. After all Nina had been through with Kendra, Nina needed to see Kendra there for herself, so she went early to catch a glimpse.

She walked inside and headed back to the work area. She spotted Kendra almost immediately, sitting on the floor in one of the larger kennels, her legs tucked up as she stroked the ears of a golden retriever. The dog nestled against her like he knew what she needed.

Across the way, Amanda waved.

Nina pressed her finger to her lips and then waved.

Amanda pointed to the door leading back out.

They met in the hallway. "Sorry. I should've asked for permission, but I just wanted to see for myself how Kendra is doing."

"She's good with all the dogs, but she has her favorite too," Amanda said. "I think that old retriever is good for her. They understand each other. Come here. We can watch through this window." She led the way down another hallway. "This is where the team leads can monitor things without disturbing anyone."

Nina's breath hitched at the sight. "This place is amazing. Did Paul design all this himself?"

"He did. He has such a powerful sense of purpose. I really admire him for that. He designed Paws Town Square to fill a need. As a marine, he worked with military dogs and understands them. He saw the problems that arose when the dogs were separated from their handlers and the challenges in getting the dogs the help they needed when they came back. I never realized they are just like the men. They are soldiers. Brave hearts too. He planned this whole business around his dedication to that arm of the military. The rest of the business—the kennels, walking trails, and retail—all self-funds the true purpose. I couldn't be more proud of Paul."

"That is so beautiful. Kendra is spending a lot of time here. I hope Paul is okay with it."

"He's happy to have the help. She even told him he didn't have to pay her, but, of course, Paul will not let that happen." A small smile played on Amanda's lips. "Kids like to pretend they don't need structure, but deep down they crave it. Trust me, Paul is a marine to the core. This place is a well-oiled machine with many rules. She's in a good place to get structure here. Everyone respects Paul and his rules."

Nina watched as Kendra leaned down and whispered something to the dog. He lifted his head and licked her chin, and for a split second, her daughter's face softened in a way Nina hadn't seen in months.

"I'm so afraid I'm losing our connection. She's always so angry with me," Nina admitted, the words barely above a whisper.

Amanda turned to her then, her eyes filled with something steady and knowing. "You're not losing her. She's just trying to figure things out."

Nina ran a hand through her hair. "She barely talks to me anymore. It's like she's shutting me out."

"I'm sure she's just scared. She's worried about where she fits in your life now that everything is changing."

Nina frowned. "She's my daughter. Nothing can change that."

"*We* know that. But kids? They don't have the maturity to see it. My kids didn't feel connected to our family after Jack died. It broke what was normal for them. Even when things aren't good, children like consistency, and even when it's consistently bad, it can feel normal. Kendra might feel like she's lost her role in the family with the divorce. Any break in the family unit—

divorce, death, whatever—can make kids feel all kinds of crazy things. Sometimes they try to shift into caretaker mode."

"Amanda, your family has had a huge positive impact on Mom and now on us. I couldn't be more grateful for your friendship."

"I feel the same. You watch. Kendra will see you adjusting, settling into life here, maybe even opening up to Fisher. Don't think I haven't noticed something there. But now she has her work here. It should leave her feeling fulfilled. She's likely struggling to find her place, a common experience for kids from divorced homes."

Nina's eyes returned to Kendra. It was so comforting to see her smile as she stroked the golden retriever's belly. The dog's feathery tail swished against the floor.

"Kendra demanded that I pick between her and Fisher," Nina admitted. "Fisher and I aren't even a real thing yet. I mean, aside from the fact he's sort of been like a superhero, showing up and rescuing us every day."

Amanda shifted her weight. "You know, that could be an actual fear for her, Nina. That she might lose you. Especially with David not putting her first. She may be acting out because she needs that place in your life, and bad behavior gets attention."

Heavy and undeniable, the words lodged themselves deep within Nina's chest. Had she been so focused on trying to fix their broken life that she'd missed Kendra's perspective entirely?

Nina exhaled, the weight in her chest easing just enough for a little hope to slip in. "So, what do I do?"

"First of all, don't worry. You're doing better than you think. Second, every day remind her she's irreplaceable."

As Kendra laughed, crouching to let the dog nuzzle her cheek, Nina felt the promise of something steadier. Maybe

Fisher had seen it all along: that love wasn't in grand gestures; it was in small, quiet acts that build the strongest bonds.

Nina let the moment settle in her heart. From now on, no matter what storms came, Kendra would never have to doubt how deeply she was loved.

Chapter Twenty-Two

THURSDAY NIGHT BROUGHT A RARE HUSH TO THE HOUSE, with Kendra tucked away in her room watching her favorite wildlife show. It left Nina alone with her thoughts and the weight of what she hadn't yet said.

The soft sounds of the TV drifted down the hall, blending with the rhythmic hush of the ocean beyond the windows. Nina leaned against the kitchen sink, staring out at the dark, endless stretch of water, wishing it could wash away the hard things she couldn't outrun.

She'd been putting off telling Kendra the full story behind David canceling their vacation together. Every time she pictured her daughter's face—Daddy's little girl—her heart clenched. Things had been better lately. Kendra was laughing more, connecting. She hated to think about how knowing about David and Charlotte's expanding family would feel to her. Would it shatter all the progress they'd made this far? How could she protect Kendra now?

And, worse, it could be bad for her personally. If it upset Kendra, she surely would lash out at Nina first. She knew she should be able to take it, but, honestly, she felt as fragile as Kendra lately.

The sharp sound of a car door interrupted her thoughts.

Anxiety washed over her. Mom was over at Tug's, and it was too early for them to be back. Who could it be?

She walked over to the window and peered outside. Below, on the driveway, a familiar figure stepped out of a sleek black SUV, and her heart sank.

David.

Before Nina could get to the door to intercept him, Kendra's bedroom door flew wide open.

"Dad's here!" Her face lit up with so much love and hope that it made Nina's chest ache. A foreboding feeling hung in the air.

David knocked, and Nina opened the door.

"Nina." He stepped inside without waiting for an invitation. His presence filled the room like a storm cloud.

Kendra launched herself into his arms, almost taking him off-balance as she rattled off details about dolphins, bike rides, and how she'd been working on her tan and learning some German.

A desperate fog settled over him, his eyes pleading to Nina for help.

Not this time, David. She stepped back, forcing him to wallow in the mess he'd made. And here she was in a front-row seat to see how he'd handle it without her help for a change.

David brushed his hands across his shirt, trying to get himself pulled back together. "Tanning?" he responded to Kendra. "Is that so?"

"It's okay, Dad. I always wear sunscreen." Kendra grinned, oblivious to David's reaction. "I knew you'd change your mind about our vacation. Thank you. This is perfect, because now I'll be tan for it."

Nina understood why Kendra would wish for that scenario, but she knew it was unlikely. She said a quiet prayer that David might surprise her. *Please say you're taking her on vacation. Please, David, for once do the right thing.*

He stepped away from Kendra, closer to Nina, dropping his voice to a low hiss. "Why does she think we can still go?"

Nina's pulse spiked. *Why must I constantly justify your damaging actions?* The words were on the tip of her tongue, but she decided to be the bigger person. "Is that not why you're here?"

"What?" Kendra's brows furrowed. "We really aren't going?"

David let out a heavy sigh.

"Kendra, sweetheart," he started, his voice softening. "No, we still aren't going on vacation in August, but you will be spending a week with me sometime this summer."

"But I wanted to go on that trip. You said . . ." Kendra's eyes teared up. "Did Mom say something to make you mad?" Kendra spun toward her. "Mom, you always ruin everything."

"No. This is not my doing." Nina leveled an icy stare at her ex, keeping her voice and tone steady. "I'm not taking this one for you, David. *You* tell her why." She stood her ground, trying her best to look calm and confident, but her heart was pounding so hard that it was hard to take in the conversation.

He stood there, his jaw pulsing.

Nina was determined to outwait him, but it was heartbreaking to see Kendra crumble under his bad decisions . . . again.

This wasn't new. David was a superstar at standing quiet until it was unbearable, and Nina stepped in to smooth things over and patch the hole he created.

I can wait longer than you this time, David. I've got nothing to lose.

Nina saw her daughter's face fall, her eyes glistening as reality settled in. Kendra turned to her dad, waiting for an explanation.

David cleared his throat, clearly uncomfortable to have to tell her. "Charlotte and I are going to Europe, so I still can't take you on the trip we'd planned. Maybe we'll do a trip like that at Christmas break." He cocked his head toward Nina.

"You mean *y'all* are going to Europe, and I might, maybe, get to do something with you at the end of the year." Her voice was sharp and unforgiving. "You and her. I'm not part of your 'we' anymore, am I? You haven't even known her that long. Why are you picking her?"

"She's my wife, Kendra." David dared to look pained. "It's complicated, sweetheart."

"No," Kendra snapped. "It's not that hard to figure out. You promised me, then broke your promise. I'm your daughter, but you're choosing to dump me."

"Kendra, that's not fair," David argued, stepping toward her. "Charlotte and I need time together before the baby comes."

"What?" Kendra's shriek ended in a bitter laugh. "A baby?"

Reacting on impulse, Nina reached out, but Kendra pulled back from them both.

"You knew, didn't you?" she hissed to Nina. "Why didn't you tell me?"

Nina sucked in a breath. Nothing she could say would soothe Kendra at this moment.

"He doesn't want me anymore, and you're fine with it, aren't you? I hate this place. I hate you both." She turned and ran past David down the front stairs.

"Kendra! That's not true. I don't want to see you hurt!" Nina called after her, but her daughter was already out of sight.

"Well, this has been a real slice of heaven, David. Why did you show up uninvited? Why did you come here, anyway?" She nearly choked on the irony. "For one happy minute, I actually thought you were here to tell me you were still taking her on that amazing trip. I'm as gullible as she is."

"I have to get going," he said. "I've got a meeting in Charleston, then I'm straight off to a flight out of Atlanta to the West Coast, and I wanted to drop off Kendra's birthday present in person, since I just finished up a meeting close by."

"You know her birthday isn't until August. You could've just mailed it."

"I was passing right through and . . ." He patted his pockets, then pulled out a slim box. "I hope she likes it."

David had a history of buying his way out of problems with jewelry for Nina too. She'd gotten way too much diamond and tanzanite jewelry from him. Necklaces, earrings, rings, bracelets, even a key chain. And who in their right mind uses a key chain with precious gemstones in it?

Nina stared at him, fury simmering beneath her measured tone. "All she wants is your time. Just a little confirmation that you love her." She shook the box at him. "Get a clue."

He sighed and edged closer to the door. "Nina, I'm tired and I have a big day tomorrow, and I have to go. I messed up. I get it."

"Yes. You really did." They stood there staring at each other for a long moment.

He cleared his throat, shifting his weight toward the steps. "Call and let me know when you find her."

"You're really leaving? Your daughter just ran from this house in tears, because of you, and you're not even going to stay to help me find her and settle her down? What is wrong with you?"

David shifted, clearly uncomfortable. "I . . . I really can't miss this flight. It's important."

"More important than your daughter?" Nina's voice trembled, but not from weakness. No, it came from the sheer force it took to choke back everything she wanted to scream. Her chest burned and her fingers curled into fists at her sides, nails digging into her palms. Her heart thundered with the weight of all the letdowns, all the times she'd had to patch up the pieces for Kendra. "Fine. You know what? You should go. Why man up now, when we really need you? Just go." The words fell hard, like stones, but her gaze stayed locked, daring him to say something–*anything*–that might make it right.

He opened his mouth, but no words came. He turned and slipped out the door, the soft thud of it closing behind him the only answer Nina received.

She leaned against the door, drawing in a shaky breath, her heart breaking not just for Kendra but also for the man David had turned out to be. Her hands shook as she watched him pull out of the driveway.

I'm so sorry he's hurt you again, Kendra. I wish I could protect you from every hard moment.

After stepping outside to see if she could spot Kendra anywhere nearby, Nina texted her mother, and Mom and Tug arrived at the house in record time.

"Have you heard from her?" Mom asked.

"Not a word. She doesn't have her phone with her. When she saw that her dad was here, she came running out of her room. She didn't have anything. Not a jacket, or even shoes."

"She's going to be okay, Nina. You have to believe that." Tug leaned in and gave Rosemary a kiss on the temple and then, for the first time, pulled Nina into a hug. "We're here for you."

Nina broke into gulping sobs in his embrace.

Rosemary inserted herself into the mix. Then Tug stepped back. "I know this town better than anyone. I'm gonna go look for her."

"Thanks, Tug." Rosemary stroked Nina's shaking shoulders. "We're going to catch a breath, and then we'll look right here around the house and concentrate on this block. Sometimes kids don't go too far from home. They just need an escape."

"How do you know that?" Nina asked, thinking maybe her

mother had been doing research on the topic, but Mom's response was unexpected.

"I heard it on a show. There was this episode called 'When teens think running away means freedom—but don't get much farther than the mailbox.' It was really quite informative. And comforting, right?"

Nina blinked back the tears and began to laugh. "Yes, Mom, in some weird way, that is comforting. I hope it's true."

They searched until after one in the morning. They were all exhausted, and finally Rosemary put the question on the table. "Is it time we call the police to help us?"

Nina shrugged. "I don't know what to do."

Rosemary got up and crossed the room. "I'm just going to check her room one more time." It wasn't but a moment before she walked back in and gave Nina a thumbs-up. "She must have snuck back in when we were out looking for her. She's fast asleep."

"She's safe." Nina let out a long breath. "Thank goodness."

The next morning, Nina sat at the kitchen table, her untouched coffee growing cold. The sky stretched out in brilliant colors as the sun began to lift above the horizon. But the beautiful sunrise did little to soothe the knot in her stomach.

She hadn't slept. Not really. Kendra's words kept replaying in her mind.

A shuffle of footsteps from the hall caught her attention.

Rosemary appeared in the doorway, her expression gentle. "You look like you've been up all night."

"Because I have." Nina rubbed her temples, then lifted her coffee to her lips. "I've been rehearsing speeches in my head all night long and still don't know what to say to Kendra."

As she crossed the kitchen, Rosemary pressed a gentle hand to Nina's shoulder. "She's hurting, sweetheart." Pain etched her face. "And when people hurt, they lash out at the ones they trust most."

Nina swallowed. "What if she stops trusting me altogether?"

A quiet strength settled into Rosemary's expression. "Then you keep showing up anyway."

A soft knock came at the front door.

"That better not be David again." Nina jumped from the chair, her hands in fists and her footsteps heavy. She flung open the door, coming to an abrupt stop when she was face-to-face with Fisher.

"Am I interrupting?" he asked.

"No. Of course you're not." She stepped aside to let him in. "How do you always know when I need you?"

"I didn't, but you can call me anytime you do. I'd be right here for you."

"Well, you're here now."

He stepped inside and she closed the door behind them.

"You look like you've been up all night. Is this about Kendra? Because that's why I'm here."

"Yes. What?" Her eyes darted between him and her mom.

"Calm down. It's fine. I was over at Paws, helping Paul with a new display for Amanda's shop, when I saw Kendra talking to Chase. I was surprised, because it was barely dawn."

"She's there?" Nina held her hand over her heart, trying to catch her breath. "Now?"

Rosemary took Nina's hand and squeezed.

"She didn't see me," Fisher said, "but when Chase told me she showed up asking if she could work a double shift today, I wondered if something was up."

Nina blinked, trying to process it all.

"She's okay, honey. That's all that matters." Rosemary moved her hand to Nina's shoulder. "Breathe." She turned to Fisher to explain. "Her ex-husband showed up last night and stirred the pot. It wasn't pretty. I'll make you some coffee," she said.

Fisher pulled out a chair at the kitchen table, lowering himself and speaking in a calm, low tone. "She was working with one of the dogs. She seemed quiet, but I figured maybe it was because it was so early. Teenagers and mornings rarely mix well."

"That's true. She's not usually a morning person," Rosemary said. "None of us got much sleep last night."

"I almost called to check on you before I went to bed last night. I felt like something was off." Fisher leaned in, studying her. "I'm so sorry I didn't." He placed his hand on top of hers. "What can I do?"

"You're already doing it." Nina exhaled. "David was here to give Kendra her birthday present since he'll be out of the country when the day rolls around. Only I hadn't told her all the details about that, and it all sort of came rolling out."

"Oh yeah, he was supposed to take her on that trip."

"She'd been looking forward to it all year, and of course when he showed up unannounced, she leaped to the conclusion he was coming to surprise her with birthday-trip plans after all. Honestly, I had the same thought."

"Not the case?"

"Hardly. I was so mad when he told me he canceled Yellowstone because he and his new wife needed time together before their baby arrives." She swallowed back the bitterness in her throat. "I'd been waiting for the right time to tell her, but he didn't know that she didn't know the whole story yet. It was a mess."

"Is there ever a right time for that?"

"Probably not. It all came out in the worst possible way. Kendra is so upset."

"Why didn't he man up and tell her the bad news himself?"

Fisher lashed out, then sat back with a controlled sigh. "Sorry. It just makes me mad that he put that on you. It's not helpful for me to bash him, though, and it doesn't matter."

"Yeah. She'd been so looking forward to that trip. The funny thing is, she was madder that I knew and hadn't told her. I was going to tell her. It was just hard to when she was already feeling so dejected." Nina shook her head. "Me knowing was just salt in the wound at that point."

Rosemary walked over and set a cup of coffee in front of Fisher. "You two worry. I'm going to step outside and try not to."

"Thank you, Rosemary." Fisher took a sip, then rubbed his chin, thinking. "For what it's worth, she's pouring her heart into those dogs. Seems like a good place for her to be right now."

Nina swallowed hard. "You think she's trying to work through it?"

"I do." Fisher's voice was steady. "And I think she's got a soft spot for that golden retriever who lost his handler."

"That's so sad." Nina's chest tightened. "I saw her with him yesterday."

"Paul couldn't say enough about her instincts with them," Fisher added. "Most of the dogs on that side of the facility have sad stories. Not so different from people. We all need some unconditional love in our lives."

Nina looked at him. "I feel like I'm starring in a sad story."

"Don't we all?" Fisher's lips tugged into a small smile. "She's in good company. We won't let her feel alone. Think maybe it would help if I took some breakfast over to her? Sort of a neutral ear?"

"I think that would be amazing." The coil of tension in her shoulders unwound just a little. "Even if she doesn't like it, I appreciate you so much for even thinking of it."

"Well, we'll make sure she knows that she has love here, over and over until she believes it."

"And if she doesn't want to hear it?"

Fisher chuckled. "Doesn't matter. We just keep driving it home." He gave her hand a gentle squeeze. "And you know what? Why don't we plan something more? A beach day. Just the three of us. No pressure, no big expectations—just sand, sun, and a reminder that joy is still right here, waiting."

Nina nodded, her smile soft. "I think that sounds nice. It'd be great to give her something good to hold on to, but let's be careful not to make any promises we can't deliver." Emotion tightened in her throat, then loosened as she breathed past it. "Thank you for stopping by. I can't tell you how much it means for you to be with me through all this. I'm so grateful."

Fisher finished his coffee and stood, giving her shoulder a reassuring touch. "I'll swing by and grab breakfast sandwiches, then take them over to Paws and just be available. We'll figure this out."

He stepped out into the soft morning light, and as he made his way down the path, hope settled on her heart.

Somehow, when life went haywire, Whelk's Island had a way of propping you back up by surrounding you with people who cared.

Chapter Twenty-Three

THE DINING ROOM BRIMMED WITH MORE THAN JUST ICED-tea glasses and Tug's famous peanut butter cookies crowding the table. It brimmed with hope. Hope that gathering these friends, who felt more like family now, might help break the spiral Nina and Kendra were caught in.

Nina's nerves hummed beneath it all, but she held tight to the belief that if there were a way through this heartache, she'd find it. And she wasn't about to stop trying until she did. A candle burned by the windowsill, emotions in the room swirling like the smoke from the flame. She'd bought the candle at a cute little boutique the other day when she and Kendra had been together, and they'd both laughed at the thought of carrying a candle that touted the scent as "more relaxing than a day at the beach," when they were there for real already.

But desperate times call for desperate measures, and she'd fallen right for the marketing ploy and bought it on the spot. And honestly, she didn't really know what a bergamot was, but it smelled nice, and she could use a little uplifting ambiance tonight.

Nina looked around the room at these people. She was so thankful for them. They'd all so graciously agreed to be part of this family meeting, even though they weren't family at all, and it was Amanda who'd suggested including Hailey and Jesse.

Kendra sat between Rosemary and Amanda with her head down and her fingers tracing shapes on the wood. Fisher leaned back in his chair, his arms folded loosely, offering steady calm without saying much. Tug drummed his fingers lightly on the tabletop, as if he wanted to fix everything but didn't know how.

Nina drew in a deep breath, determined to set the tone without it feeling like they were all piling on Kendra. "Sweetheart, I want you to look around this table. Everyone here loves you. And every single one of us is here to help you through this."

Kendra's eyes flew wide when she realized this wasn't just an evening with friends. She tensed up like a cat about to be tossed in the bath.

"Love you, Kendra," Jesse said from across the table.

That sweet boy had no idea how his kind little interjections could brighten so many without even trying, but it eased the moment, and for that, Nina was thankful.

Despite the difficulty, Nina covered all the details concerning David and the recent problems with the vacation. Somehow it all fell into something kind, honest, unrehearsed, and—by the grace of God—healing.

"Kendra, we can't help each other if we don't know what's going on. Let's all, everyone here, make a conscious effort to keep the lines of communication open. I'm not saying it's always easy to say what's not going well, but with the people we love, it should be."

Kendra's lips pulled into a thin line, but she finally nodded.

"We can't have any more running off," Nina said.

Kendra snapped her attention from the table to Nina.

"That's not how we do things—not in this family, not anymore. Do you understand me?"

Kendra peeked up through her lashes. "I wasn't gonna—"

Nina held up a hand gently. "I get it. Believe me. There've been times I've wanted to grab my keys and just drive until the road ran out. But you can't run from problems, or sadness, or anything. It all just follows you anyway, and that doesn't solve anything, does it?"

Barely a shake of Kendra's head was agreement enough.

"Right," Nina said. "So from now on, no disappearing. We'll face things together. And if you don't feel like you can talk to me about it, you've got all these people here in this room to choose from."

Gentle smiles and quiet murmurs of agreement rippled like a wave of support.

Amanda spoke up. "Anytime at all, day or not, Kendra. I'm always here for you. We all are."

Kendra sniffled, wiping her cheeks with the back of her hand.

Nina's eyes stung, her voice thick and cracking with emotion. "It's okay, sweetheart. We'll get through this. Together."

Even Amanda blinked away tears, squeezing Kendra's hand. "You're stronger than you know, Kendra. We all see it."

There was a long, quiet beat before Tug cleared his throat. "Well, sweet Kendra, you've been dealt a crummy situation," he said, a twinkle cutting through the mist in his eyes. "But if anybody's got a time machine, I'd be willing to trade one of my boats for it. We could go back and do it all better the first time. Anyone in?"

Kendra let out a watery laugh, a small smile breaking through the tears. "Thanks, Tug."

"Some bad stuff happened," Fisher said. "No one is exempt from having bad things happen to them. Or making bad decisions, for that matter."

"I've made my share of bad decisions." Tug's voice was steady but quiet, each word carrying weight. Then he turned to Rosemary, eyes softening as his tone shifted. "You're not one of them. You're my best decision."

She wrinkled her nose and smiled his way. "Who hasn't made

a bad decision in their life or made the mistake of trying to hide the pain, thinking it won't burden anyone else that way? We don't always think straight in the middle of a crisis."

"That's for sure," Paul said. "It's why planning for those times while we are not in the middle of them will prepare us to take more levelheaded actions when we're put in that situation. It's just like at Paws, Kendra. We've talked about the what-could-go-wrongs, right? So we'll handle them calmly if they do."

Kendra's face lit up with understanding. "Yes. Okay, that makes sense."

"No matter how bad you think it is, lean on us and we'll help you pivot and come up with a plan," Rosemary said. "Trust me, you'll get used to switching gears after you have to do it enough times." She paused, then added, "I finally know that lesson."

"Hope it doesn't take me till I'm like eighty to get good at it," Kendra said. The remark was innocent, but it caused a roll of laughter from everyone at the table, and that's exactly what they all needed at the moment.

She straightened, scanned the room, and then pressed her lips together before finally saying, "I'm really lucky to have all of you in my life, and I'm really sorry I've been so hard to get along with." Then she turned to her mother, and the tears spilled. "I love you, Mom. I'm so sorry."

"Nope. No more apologies," Nina said through sniffles.

Jesse ran over to Kendra, and she stood briefly and gave him a big hug.

"Don't be sad," Jesse said in a trembling voice.

"I'm good, Jesse. Better than I've been in a while. Thank you."

Fisher leaned forward. "I think we can all agree we are in a good headspace right now."

A few heads dipped in agreement.

"How about we change the channel, so to speak," Fisher suggested. “This has been a lot, so maybe what we all need is a break. A fresh view.”

“What do you mean?” Amanda asked.

“Maybe a trip or something. Like, all of us. We pack up and get away for a little while. Nothing but fun. No decisions. No drama. No strict itineraries.”

Rosemary clapped her hands together. “A getaway? Oh, I like that idea.”

In an instant, the spark caught. They talked about possibilities, everyone tossing ideas in like pennies in a fountain. Myrtle Beach? Too soon after the storm. Charleston? Not as kid-friendly, so maybe another time.

It was Kendra who said it first. “What about the mountains?”

Nina’s heart lifted at the hope in her daughter’s voice.

“Now, that’s an idea.” Tug grinned. “Cool air, trout streams, no cell service.”

Amanda laughed. “You’d love that last part too much.”

“Not long ago, I saw this ad about a glamping resort with tree houses and cool geo-dome cabins with almost a full wall that’s clear so you can see the stars,” Fisher said. “They were up in the Asheville or Blue Ridge area. I don’t know if they’d have enough cabins to accommodate all of us, but I could look into it.”

“Asheville is on my bucket list.” Rosemary bumped her shoulder against Tug’s in a little “hint-hint” gesture.

“So cool!” Kendra bounced higher in her seat. “Like real tree houses?”

“Right up there in the sky, looking out over the mountains.” Fisher sounded like the voice-over for a commercial about vacationing in North Carolina, and Nina could almost feel the cooler air and see the smoky blue haze over the mountains.

They settled on going to Asheville. They decided to visit Biltmore for some historical flavor on this grand adventure. Paul mentioned some hiking trails he'd like to explore. Amanda insisted they all go to Biscuit Head for homemade cathead biscuits as big as a cat's head and trout fishing that, according to Tug, would make a believer out of anyone.

"Waders for everyone," Nina teased. "Not exactly the boots I had in mind, but who's to say they won't be a fashion statement?"

The next week passed in a happy blur of planning. Nina caught herself humming while she packed, feeling lighter than she had in months. Fisher helped haul luggage, Tug mapped out the route like he was captaining a ship, and Rosemary made lists of everything to bring, from snacks to sun hats.

The morning of the trip, when they were all putting the last things into the cars, Nina pulled Kendra aside. "Before we go, I want to clear up one last thing."

Kendra's brows pulled together.

"Your dad left this with me to give you on your birthday, since he wouldn't be with you. I know it's still weeks away, but I want to say now that although he does some questionable things, he is a good man."

"Okay."

"He loves you, but he shows it in his own way. He's clueless that what is important to you is quality time together. I didn't open this, but I'm willing to bet it's jewelry. That's his love language, and I believe he assumes it's ours too. This is how he tries to show you matter to him. So, I don't want this to put a damper on things, but I think you're strong enough and mature enough to understand it."

Nina handed Kendra the box. It was neatly wrapped, probably by an employee at the jewelry store, not David.

Kendra eyed it like it might bite.

Nina stepped back to give Kendra breathing room. "I promised I'd be honest with you, and you know everything I know, and that will be the way we go forward. I've had this since he showed up unannounced that night. I was holding out until your birthday like he'd asked, but then I realized this is not about him. This is about you. Open it now or leave it for later."

With a sigh as heavy as the humid air outside, Kendra opened the box. A delicate diamond heart on a thin gold chain sparkled up at her.

She stared at it, her jaw tight. "It's pretty," she said, more a question than a reaction.

Nina reached out, resting her hand over Kendra's. "Honey, no necklace in the world fixes what you're feeling, but I hope understanding your dad will help, and it will look beautiful on you."

Kendra snapped the box closed, pushing it aside. "I know." She drew in a shaky breath. "I'm fine. I'm going to leave this here, but I'll send a thank-you note when we get back, or maybe after my birthday. Can we go on our trip now?"

Nina smiled, tears pricking her eyes. "You bet we can."

The caravan to Asheville was half the fun. Three cars, music playing, the road winding up into the hills. Kendra kept snapping pictures on her phone, sending them to Amanda's kids in the car ahead and laughing at their goofy selfies in return.

They'd booked a set of cabins just outside town, tucked among tall pines with a mountain view that took your breath away. They weren't fancy, but they had just enough tree-house magic with stone fireplaces, wraparound porches strung with fairy lights, and the kind of crisp pine air that made Nina feel lighter the moment she breathed it in.

Fisher had snagged the biggest of the bunch. A jumbo multi-level tree-house suite perched high in the trees and big enough for everyone to gather. It even had a big hot tub and a telescope pointed at the stars. It quickly became the hub for morning coffee, late night laughs, and everything in between.

Every day brought something new. They hiked Craggy Gardens, the path lined with rhododendrons in bloom, and collected flowers and leaves for a craft project with Rosemary later. Kendra and the younger kids scrambled ahead, calling out when they found interesting rocks or funny-shaped sticks. The senior pair, Rosemary and Tug, took it slowly, but their smiles said it all.

On one bright afternoon, they toured the Biltmore estate, taking a horse-drawn-carriage ride behind the steady power of two Belgian draft horses. Ben and Mike, to be exact. Ben weighed about as much as a VW Bug, but his eyes showed so much kindness. Mike carried himself more like a Smart car but had the strength of something far greater. The kids giggled at the clip-clop of the horses' hooves in the bouncy wagon, and Amanda snapped a ton of pictures when they got out to pet the gentle giants.

Another day, Fisher and Tug took the kids trout fishing at a cool, clear stream where Kendra caught the first fish, and Tug declared her the family champion, even though he said the real fishing took place in the early morning hours and demanded a second chance to steal the title.

Meanwhile, the women escaped to the Omni Grove Park Inn & Spa for spa treatments and a tea where they learned about the amazing gingerbread house competition that happened there each year.

Mornings started slowly with biscuits and gravy at the little general store café, and evenings ended late around the campfire where Tug's stories spun long past bedtime.

Nina hadn't seen Kendra so at ease in ages. And the truth was, she hadn't felt so at ease herself. Interestingly, somehow over the past few weeks living on Whelk's Island, her unsettled teenager seemed to have become a levelheaded and motivated young lady.

One night, as Nina and Fisher sat on the deck of the treehouse suite, he handed her a mug of tea. "You're doing a good job, you know."

She glanced at him, surprised. "Doesn't always feel like it."

"But look at her. She's smiling again. That's no small thing."

"She is. That makes my heart so happy." Nina let the quiet settle between them, the sound of crickets and the soft creak of the deck's swing filling the space. She was so grateful for him—for this.

Later that night, around the fire pit while they were making s'mores, Tug and Rosemary showed up, each balancing a cardboard box.

"Before y'all go turnin' in," Tug said, his eyes twinkling, "we've got a little surprise to properly gear up for tomorrow's trout-fishing adventure."

"We thought everyone needed a fishing hat." Rosemary grinned and started passing them out. "Or at least something to give those trout a good laugh."

Inside the boxes were plain canvas bucket hats—some hilariously large and some comically small—alongside markers, patches, bits of ribbon, stick-on googly eyes, and a rainbow of colorful fishing flies and lures.

"Serious anglers only, folks," Fisher teased as he grabbed a hat, looped a strip of red bandanna through its brim, and then showed everyone how to decorate a hat with the feathery, colorful fishing flies. "Be careful to only poke those flies through around these areas so you don't end up pricking yourself."

The kids dove in, giggling as they decorated their creations. Jesse stuck a foam fish on the front of his hat, while Kendra drew a cartoon trout with crossed eyes and added the words BITE HERE in blocky letters. Even Nina found herself creating a beautiful string of those flies around hers like a feathery hat band, grinning as she worked.

At the end of the night, they posed for pictures under the fairy lights, a wild assortment of headwear crowning their happy, tired faces.

"Okay, one more thing. No, two more things." Rosemary smiled at Tug. "First, I know Tug and I said we were only staying these first couple of days, but we are having so much fun that we checked and were able to extend our stay until the end of the week."

Everyone cheered.

"And, second, Tug, tell them what time we have to be down at the parking lot for the junket."

"Four forty-five," Tug said.

Kendra seemed to almost choke on a marshmallow. "In the morning?"

"Early bird gets the worm. Or fly-fishing lure, in this case," Tug replied.

"Can't we just catch the lazy trout that sleep in?" she asked, earning a round of laughter from the group.

The days slipped by faster than the group wanted. On their last morning, they packed up the cars, reluctant but refreshed.

Fisher helped Nina secure the last bag, and Kendra bounded up with a grin. "Best trip ever."

"Worth the planning headache?" Nina asked.

"Oh yeah," Kendra said. "Can we come back next year?"

"Maybe so." Nina glanced at Fisher, whose answering smile warmed her.

"Everyone being here made it twice as good," Kendra said.

"I've never done a big trip with other people like this. I liked it too." Nina pulled Kendra in for a side hug. "We're good, right?"

"Better than ever and we will be forever," Kendra said.

"Did you mean to make that rhyme?" Nina asked.

"She's a poet and didn't know it," Fisher teased.

Mother and daughter both rolled their eyes and laughed as they got into the car.

The convoy headed home, still three cars strong: Fisher, Nina, and Kendra in one; Tug and Rosemary in the second; and Amanda, Paul, and the kids bringing up the rear. They took the long way, windows down, letting the mountain breeze carry them forward for as long as the cool mountain air would allow.

Nina finally felt like she and Kendra were on the right road again.

Chapter Twenty-Four

Two weeks had passed since David had rocked the boat and sent Kendra reeling. But she was in a better headspace now, her mood lighter and her laughter more frequent. The change was noticeable, and Fisher felt grateful to witness it. Continued time spent with Nina had brought a new sense of peace for him, and there was something reassuring about how each day felt more comfortable.

He stood on Tug's deck, his hands resting on the railing as he looked out over the backyard, where Paul and Amanda were playing volleyball against Kendra, Hailey, and Jesse. Fragrant smoke billowed from the barbecue grill, and music played from Rosemary's phone.

The Wife, perched nearby, seemed to sense the playful mood of the day, her feathers rustling as she turned toward the speakers when the Miranda Lambert song "Bluebird" played. As soon as the chorus started, The Wife loudly sang along in a Southern twang, "Keep a bluebird in my heart!" in surprisingly good rhythm and cadence.

Fisher blinked in disbelief, then grinned. "Did she just . . ."

Tug stepped up beside him with a chuckle. "Rosemary's been teaching The Wife songs, especially some of her favorites by Neil Diamond. But The Wife doesn't quite have the whole pitch down yet. She'll get better. I'm surprised Rosemary could teach her anything this quickly, but she's got the magic touch."

Fisher smirked. "Remind me not to bet against Rosemary."

His gaze drifted back down to the volleyball game, but it wasn't the match that held his attention. It was Kendra. She had stepped away from the group, her fingers tapping on her phone. The tension in her posture and the way she kept glancing toward the dunes made it seem like she was considering making a run for it. That sent a flicker of unease through Fisher.

A subtle tremor in her hand looked as if her phone was a jolt of electricity, causing her shoulders to tense and then relax into a state of quiet resignation. *Is she texting with her dad?* Fisher's internal alarm rang out like a church bell on Sunday morning, warning him that something was about to go awry. Unable to ignore the signs any longer, he made his way over to Rosemary, who was watching Kendra with a steady, knowing look.

"You noticed, too, didn't you?" he murmured, his voice laced with concern. Nina was inside the house on a conference call for work.

"Kendra? Yes." Rosemary's eyes were as deep as the ocean on a stormy night. "Sometimes a girl's got to let herself wander a spell, even if it means teetering on the edge. But I'd sure hate to see her fall off that ledge."

Fisher frowned, the lines on his weathered face deepening. "I've been there, Rosemary. I don't want her to get so lost that she can't find her way back. She's got a family that loves her, and her job is going so well. It surprised me to see her like that."

Rosemary's response was gentle yet firm. "You can't prevent every misstep. We are all meant to learn our own lessons. We can't do it for her. All we can do is lay the foundation—which Nina has done—offer a hand when they stumble and be there to pick up the pieces." She paused, letting the words sink in.

"I'd like to be the guardrail when the road gets too slippery," he said. He sighed, his mind swirling with memories of his own past missteps. Watching Kendra, who was as unpredictable as a summer storm, he felt a tug on his heartstrings. "You're a good woman, Rosemary. I wish I could do more without overstepping."

As if on cue, a sudden vibration from Kendra's phone rippled through the air, drawing Fisher's attention back to her. Her expression shifted. As she looked at her phone, her lips pressed into a thin line. For a split second, something akin to alarm replaced the usual spark of mischief in her eyes.

It was that tiny, barely perceptible change in her demeanor that made his blood run cold. In that silent exchange between screen and soul, he saw a hint of trouble. "I swear I wish phones had an age restriction like driving a car."

"You sound like an old man now." Rosemary's laugh was light. "Welcome to the new age of technology."

"I do, don't I? When did *that* happen?"

Rosemary laughed. "I believe right about the time you realized you enjoyed spending time with my daughter."

"I'm not going to deny that. And I wasn't looking."

"That's when you find it. I'm thrilled you're interested in Nina. I like you being around. You're good for my girls."

"I haven't always been a guy worth rooting for. I was sort of reckless after my dad passed away. I'm not sure I'm really the kind of guy to be with someone like Nina. I've made a lot of mistakes."

Rosemary shifted, really looking into his eyes. "Fisher, the man you are today is all that matters."

He met her gaze, startled by the calm certainty in her tone.

"You can't undo the past," she said gently, "but you can decide who you want to be now, and what I see is someone who's already made that choice."

"I would never let them down," Fisher said. "I can promise you that."

"I know." Rosemary spoke with confidence. "I trust you."

She gave him that "run-along now" look. "Thank you, Rosemary. I'm gonna go check on Kendra and make sure she's okay."

"I think that's a great idea."

He walked down from the deck and strode over to her, his steps measured yet filled with a quiet urgency. "Hey, Kendra, I noticed you ditched the volleyball game," he said, his Southern drawl gentle yet earnest. "Everything all right?"

Kendra jerked her gaze up, startled. "What? Yeah, I'm fine," she said, though the tremor in her voice betrayed her calm facade. Her eyes darted back to her phone, seeking refuge in its cold, flickering light.

Fisher remained unconvinced. He noticed the way her fingers, which moments before had been tapping out an erratic rhythm, now clutched the phone as if it were a lifeline.

"You sure about that, kiddo?" he pressed, glancing toward her phone to give her a subtle hint he'd noticed that too. "Sometimes when we're pretending to be all right, our bodies shout out the truth."

Kendra's eyes narrowed, and for a moment, a spark of defiance danced in her eyes. "Do you always think you know best?" she snapped.

"Are we talking about now, or when you came into my bar?" He tried to keep the exchange light. But behind her defiance, Fisher saw a trace of worry. Or was it a silent plea for someone to understand?

Before she could reply, the volleyball came soaring over to where they were standing.

Paul yelled, "Little help?" as Hailey and Amanda bent over laughing. Jesse raced over to retrieve the ball.

Fisher took a step forward and booted the ball toward Jesse, buying a little more time for Kendra.

"Hey." His voice held a hint of humor. "I'm not trying to be 'Friend of the Year' here, but I couldn't help but notice that your body language wasn't so good when I was singing up there on the deck. I'm here to tell you it was The Wife who was off-key." He played it off with a laugh. "You believe me, right?"

She cracked a smile. "No. I didn't even hear you."

"Seriously, though, if something's bugging you, I'm here. You can always talk to me. No judgment."

"No ratting me out?"

"Deal."

There was a pause, longer than it needed to be. Kendra's gaze dropped to her phone, and for a heartbeat, silence reigned. Then, in a surprising burst of vulnerability, she let out a half laugh, a sound that mingled defiance with the slightest trace of relief. "Fine. Maybe I'm not as okay as I said."

Nina called down to them. "Hey! I'm done." She started moving toward them. As she got closer, her eyes shifted from her daughter to him, a look of concern shadowing the smile.

"I was just checking on Kendra," he explained.

Kendra stepped into her mother's arms.

Nina's eyes softened, but the tension was still there. She mouthed a worried, *Is she okay?*

He gave her a reassuring look.

"Can I get a soda, Mom?"

"Sure."

Kendra went inside to get a soda from Tug's refrigerator.

Confused, Nina turned to Fisher. "Okay, I'm glad to get hugs, but that was kind of weird. What did I interrupt?"

"She was playing volleyball, and then I noticed she bailed and was on her phone. She looked upset. Your mom noticed it too. I just felt like I needed to check on her. I hope I haven't overstepped."

"No. I appreciate it, Fisher. I do. But we need to be careful, especially with all this stuff going on with David. I wouldn't want her to feel that you're trying to act like you're her father."

"Oh yeah, I would never do that. I was just trying to help."

"No, it's fine. Things are messy right now. It's just tricky. You didn't do anything a friend wouldn't do. Don't worry about it. I'm sure it's all fine."

Fisher's heart sank a little. He knew she was right. This was a delicate dance, and he was still learning the steps. And he was an outsider. "I just worry about her. I've seen young souls get swept away by situations they weren't ready to face. I don't want that to happen to her."

A hesitant smile broke through Nina's concern, the surrounding commotion seeming to offer a moment of levity.

Amanda's dog, Denali, ambled over and tripped on Fisher's outstretched foot. The mishap sent Fisher into an unexpected tangle, a clumsy dance of arms and legs, and as he stumbled, a burst of laughter erupted from those nearby.

Even Kendra couldn't help but let out a genuine, if reluctant, chuckle. "Work on those dancing skills, Fisher," she teased, shaking her head as he regained his balance and grinned sheepishly.

The laughter, light and infectious, eased the tension for a moment. In that shared chuckle, he remembered that a good laugh was often the best medicine.

He recalled Rosemary's comment before, which hadn't hit home until this moment. *"The man you are today is all that matters."* That thought, like a warm ember on a cool night, reassured him. He was here now, doing what he felt was right. And while the delicate lines of friendship could sometimes blur, Fisher believed in the power of genuine care.

Later that night, since Rosemary wanted to stay and help Tug clean up after the busy day of entertaining, Fisher drove Nina and Kendra back to Rosemary's house. It had been a day filled with fresh air, and they were quiet on the ride back. He pulled into the driveway and put his truck in Park. "All set. It was a fun day."

"It was. Thanks for the ride. Good night." Kendra got out and ran over to press the code on the elevator instead of taking the steps.

Nina saw her and shook her head. "That girl is going to wear Mom's elevator out. I'm not sure she's taken the stairs twice since we've been here."

"It is pretty cool. A lot of these multi-level homes have them nowadays."

"Good thing. That's too many steps to haul groceries or luggage."

"Unless you have a strong, capable man like me around."

She gave him a haughty look. "Are you getting ready to flex to impress me?"

"Not anymore." He liked the banter with her, and the laughs came easily.

"Want to come in?" Nina asked.

"I'm sure you're tired."

"I could use some time to wind down first. Come on up. We can watch for falling stars."

They got out of the truck, went up the stairs, and entered the house. Kendra must've gone straight to her room.

"Want anything to drink?"

"No. I'm good. I'm so full I couldn't even swallow a sip of water."

"I know what you mean. Mom and Tug throw one heck of a

party." She led the way to the deck and stepped outside. Fisher followed her, closing the door behind them.

The sky displayed stars strewn like diamonds, and the cooler air carried a sense of both promise and uncertainty.

Nina cleared her throat before speaking, her voice soft and hesitant. "Fisher, I hope you don't misinterpret this, as I appreciate your company. I'm happy we met. However, I want you to understand that I am still sorting out some big life things. I don't know where any of this is going to take us." She regarded him for a long moment, the moonlight softening the edges of her worry. "I could use a friend like you who isn't afraid to wade into the deep end when it matters."

A gentle smile tugged at Fisher's lips. "Consider me your lifeguard, Nina."

Even as they shared this quiet moment of understanding, he knew that challenges lay ahead. Kendra's behavior was only one ripple in a much larger, unpredictable tide. In the days to come, there might be more moments when her body language spoke of inner turmoil she wasn't ready to voice. With each step Fisher took, he had to balance between being a supportive friend and an intrusive outsider, all the while measuring his feelings for her.

At that moment, Fisher experienced a sudden breath of hope. He could become part of something bigger than himself: a life connected with this family, filled with love and fresh starts. Being there for these women in both their challenges and moments of joy showed him he was fulfilling his purpose.

Fisher made an unspoken vow to trust his instincts. He'd monitor Kendra's behavior and look for the little signs that signaled trouble, and any humor he could muster trying to guide her away from the wrong turns he'd once taken himself would bring relief to Nina too.

"I don't know where all this is leading either," he stated,

breaking the silence, "but I've never felt as connected to a family as I do to this one. I know it might get messy, but I don't mind navigating the choppy waters. I mean, I'm a surfer." He struck a mock pose, his arms out like he was catching a wave.

She raised an eyebrow, the corner of her mouth twitching. "I see."

"Looks better when I'm on top of the board."

She laughed.

"Hey, have you thought any more about going surfing with me? You'd probably like it. It's a little different from in Hawaii, you know. These smaller swells are tricky, but they're fun once you get the hang of it."

She grinned. "It's been a long time, but it would be fun to take Kendra out with us sometime."

"We'll make it happen." Fisher couldn't hide the spark of excitement in his voice. "I've got a few boards at my place. Just pick the day, and we'll hit the water."

Rosemary's words echoed in his mind again: *"The man you are today is all that matters."*

That truth, like a steady tide, reassured him.

Like he'd admitted to Nina, Fisher wasn't sure where all this would lead, but he knew he was exactly where he was meant to be, offering care, laughter, and a lifeline when it mattered most.

Chapter Twenty-Five

NINA WALKED INTO THE KITCHEN, SHAKING OFF THE COBwebs from a hard night's sleep. She popped a pod into the coffee maker and pressed the button to let it work its magic.

She had a nagging feeling about how Fisher had described Kendra's look yesterday, holding her phone like a shield. He hadn't said she looked angry—just upset. But then Kendra had hugged her and went on her way.

But now the house felt too still, as if she should brace for bad news. She stretched and yawned, then spun around when something caught her eye on the kitchen island.

She reached for it. It wasn't a bill or one of the many postcards Rosemary received from far-off relatives. It was just a single stark-white note card with no envelope, the paper crisp.

Probably a note from Mom. She and Tug were probably cuddled up in a booth over coffee and omelets. The thought made Nina smile. The two of them were so cute together, each energizing the other like a personal solar pack.

The coffee maker gurgled as she picked up the card and read the note. The air around her suddenly felt too thick. There were only a few words. Scribbled in jagged, angry force, it read,

You ruined everything, Mom.
Your mistakes are destroying my life.

Nina's heart pounded so hard that she thought she might choke. Each word stung like a cut. She clutched the note in her shaking fingers, praying, *Lord, please keep her safe.*

Nina read the note again, then ran through the house, yelling for her mother.

What have I done now?

She raced down the hall to see if her mother was actually home, in her room, then checked the deck. Maybe she was walking the beach, but as Nina leaned out over the railing, she didn't see any sign of Mom or Kendra.

She rested against the doorframe, her thoughts swirling. Just yesterday, Nina believed they were strengthening their foundation. Fisher was right. Something was going on with Kendra, and Nina hadn't even seen it. How did it all collapse overnight?

For a long moment, Nina stood there holding the note, an accusation too heavy to bear. Her breath hitched and her vision blurred with unshed tears. In that fragile instant, she felt the familiar weight of failure settling in. Failure as a mother trying to build a new beginning for her daughter.

Her fiery Kendra had always been the unpredictable storm in her life, but this felt like something catastrophic on the horizon.

This better be a joke.

She went back inside and dropped the note on the counter. Her heart slammed against her ribs as she bolted for the hallway, praying for the booming bass to come from the other side of Kendra's bedroom door. Looking behind her, she double-checked the living room. Kendra wasn't perched on the corner of the couch, scrolling through her phone.

Nina knocked as she entered her daughter's room. "Kendra?"

The bed was untouched, and drawers were half open, as if she'd grabbed a few things in a hurry. The room smelled faintly of sunscreen and the sweet strawberry shampoo Kendra favored.

Her gaze swept the space—hoping, praying—when she noticed the spiral-bound notebook lying open on the nightstand. She stepped closer, sank onto the mattress, and started reading. The pages were filled with Kendra's tidy handwriting, with stars and hearts doodled in the margins.

Yellowstone geysers.

Wild horses.

Old West dinner cookout with real cowboys on a ranch.

Etchings in the cliffside dwelling—Dad says they're thousands of years old.

Roadside-diner milkshakes (where Dad's dad took him at my age).

Page after page, Kendra's dream trip was mapped out, right down to a sketch of a horse she'd clearly worked hard on, its mane flowing as though the animal were caught mid-gallop.

Nina's throat burned. All that hope. All that belief that David would come through.

She closed the journal gently, tucking away a piece of her daughter's heart. Then she stood, scanning the room again, willing herself to think, to *move*. Wherever Kendra had gone, she needed to bring her home, before . . . She wouldn't even go there.

"My sweet child, I'm so sorry," she whispered. "Where could you be?"

Nina grabbed her keys and ran outside to her car. She revved the engine and peeled out of the driveway, scanning the street for Kendra. One quick zip through town didn't take long, and she realized she didn't really know where to look. She raced back to the house.

Once back inside, she hurried to the kitchen and grabbed her phone. It felt slippery in her grasp. She dialed Kendra's number, but the call went straight to voicemail. She looked at her daughter's social media accounts. No new posts.

Whelk's Island was supposed to be their sanctuary. A place filled with gentle tides and the easy hum of everyday life. It had been a rocky start, but now the whole idea was slipping away like water through her fingers.

Nina sank onto the cool tiled floor. Raw tears rolled down her cheeks, and the taste of salt mingled with the bitterness of regret. How could she have failed?

Summoning a strength she barely recognized as her own, she again reached for her phone. Her fingers were slick with tears as she scrolled through her contacts to Fisher's name. Even as the overwhelming sense of failure threatened to pull her under, she clung to the hope that his calm presence might be the lifeline she so desperately needed right now.

The phone rang, each tone echoing in the hollow silence of the empty house. When his familiar, gentle voice answered, it was with a welcoming hello. "Nina. Good morning."

Nina's voice came out halting and raw. "Fisher . . . I . . . I need your help. Kendra's gone. I found a note."

Fisher's tone shifted to one of tender concern, warm and reassuring, as if wrapping her in a comforting embrace. "Nina, take a breath for me. I'm right here with you. Tell me what happened."

Between quivering breaths, Nina recounted the events. Her words wavered, and she could almost feel the weight of each syllable like a stone in her chest. "I don't know where she could be, Fisher. I don't even know when she left. And I'm so scared. I thought we had turned a corner. I really did." Her voice broke as she whispered the admission, raw and painful.

"I'm on my way," Fisher assured her. "You're not alone in this, Nina."

His words steadied her for a moment, even as the storm raged inside her, threatening to drown her in her own tears. Nina closed her eyes tightly. "Fisher. Please help me." She let go of a shaky breath.

"I'm on my way," Fisher repeated. "We'll find her."

She ended the call, her mind whirling. She then dialed her mother's phone, but no answer. Her fingers moved almost on instinct to call Amanda.

Her friend's voice was as warm as the morning sun when she answered. "Hey there, Nina. You okay?"

Nina pressed a hand to her forehead. "No, I'm not okay. Kendra left a note. Ran away. She's out there somewhere, angry and lost."

"Oh no. Okay, we'll start looking for her."

"Amanda." Nina's voice cracked. "I don't even know where to begin."

Amanda's voice held no hesitation. "You don't have to, sweetheart. We're all here for you. Let me call Paul and check if she's at work today. He can pull some of his local employees off to help us look. Maybe she said something to one of them."

"I hope so," Nina said, pressing her fingers against the counter to steady herself as Amanda spoke with a gentle yet firm voice.

"You're a good momma, Nina. Trust your maternal instincts."

Nina shook her head, her vision blurring. "I feel like I've failed. She left a note, and she's blaming me for something. I don't even know what exactly."

"That's because every good mother does things kids don't like. We can't take it personally. You're okay. I promise we're here for you and we'll find her." Amanda's voice wasn't just kind—it was knowing. "And when you love someone as much as we love our kids, it's impossible not to feel like you should've done more. But it's not always in our hands."

Nina swallowed. "Amanda," she whispered, her voice raw but resolute, "thank you for getting the wheels turning. I think Mom's over at Tug's. Could you let them know what's going on? Fisher's coming to help me search. I have my phone with me. I tried to get in touch with Mom, but she didn't answer."

"I'll get in touch with her. No need to stress. Tug knows this island better than anyone else. We'll coordinate the search."

"Pray for her, and for my strength. I need your wisdom. Fisher just drove up."

Then, soft as ever, Amanda said, "I get it. You call me if you need me. I'm so glad Fisher is there for you. Take a breath. Know that we're praying for you."

"Thank you."

"Let us know if you find her or hear anything."

Nina nodded, her grip on the phone steady now. "I will. I gotta run."

She whispered a silent prayer as she raced to the front door, and she wanted to believe everything was going to be okay, but her thoughts turned darkly introspective. She replayed the sharp sting of Kendra's words. The betrayal her daughter felt wasn't just a moment of anger. It was a culmination of years of trying to mend what had been torn apart. And now, with her missing, Nina felt the full, crushing weight of her perceived failures.

She thought about Kendra's laughter on summer afternoons, the sparkle in her eyes, the soft murmur of shared secrets. "I've ruined everything," she whispered to herself. Perhaps she had lost her way as a mother. The very foundation of her identity, someone who always strived to nurture and protect, was shattered.

She got to the door just as Fisher was about to knock. "Thank you for coming. I'm so sorry. I just didn't—"

"No apologies. I'm glad you called me. I want to be here for you. For Kendra too." His eyes scanned her face like he was trying to read all the words she wasn't saying.

"Nina." Fisher's voice felt like an anchor.

She didn't realize she was crying again until he reached out, his thumb brushing a tear from her cheek.

"I'm here," he said.

She gulped a breath. "Thank you."

Fisher pulled a folded map of Whelk's Island from his back pocket. "Let's make a plan." He unfolded the map as Nina cleared a place on the table for him to lay it out. Creased and worn from years of use, it had fishing spots and notes inked in different places.

Nina quickly told him everything. Every fight, every shattered piece of the past that had led them here. The fear. The guilt. The helplessness. Anything and everything that might give clues to bringing Kendra back.

Fisher never interrupted, never looked away. And when she was finished, he didn't tell her she'd done everything wrong. He just reached across the table, his fingers closing around hers.

He jotted quick notes in the margins, marking spots they should check first: the pier, the dunes, the path behind the old church.

"We're gonna bring her home, Nina," he answered, his voice strong and capable. "She's out there, and she's hurting. But she's not lost forever. She knows there is love in this house for her. Once she sees past whatever is driving her, she will see that."

Nina wanted to believe that.

Chapter Twenty-Six

HAD KENDRA BEEN OUT ALL NIGHT? FISHER WISHED HE'D asked her more detailed questions about what she had been up to on her phone yesterday, but it wouldn't do any good to talk about should-haves now.

"Come on. We're going to check the perimeter. She may have just nestled down nearby."

He took the lead, looking in the carport and shed. Then he and Nina went out to the beach, searching the dunes and behind the tall sea oats along the way. They were perfect places to hide.

The rhythmic crashing of the waves felt too slow, too steady, a stark contrast to the anxious energy thrumming through Fisher's veins. He was used to reading the ocean, to trusting its shifts and patterns, but today the water felt unreadable, like it was hiding something just beneath its surface.

Nina's breathing was quick beside him, uneven, as she tried to keep up with his long stride. He slowed, noticing the sharp focus in her eyes that didn't quite mask the panic.

"She's got to be out there somewhere," she said. "Please let us find her."

A siren sliced through the humid air, making Fisher's gut twist with a fear he didn't want to name. But by the time they reached where they thought the noise was coming from, there were no flashing lights, no signs of emergency responders, only Paul and Amanda, scanning the shoreline. The couple said that Rosemary and Tug had taken the back roads to check the streets leading out of town, but no one had seen Kendra yet.

Fisher's heart pounded, but his voice stayed steady. "Okay, Paul, can you take Amanda and check the south trail by the inlet? She might've headed that way if she wanted to stay hidden."

Paul directed everyone. "We'll fan out, stay within sight lines. I'll text if we see anything."

Amanda touched Nina's arm briefly. "We'll find her. Don't let your mind run ahead of you, okay?"

Nina gave a quick, jerky nod, though Fisher could see the fear still storming behind her eyes.

He crouched, pulling the map from his back pocket. "Nina, look—here's where the dunes flatten out, and here's the stretch that's sheltered from the wind. If she wanted to hide, she might head there. There's an old lifeguard stand just north of that. We'll check it, and I'll bet she knows it's a spot no one uses much anymore."

Her breathing hitched as she focused on the map. "Okay, let's do it."

They moved quickly, their feet sinking into the soft sand. The rising sun threw long shadows over the beach, and Fisher felt sweat beads at the back of his neck and sand sticking to his arms. The air smelled of salt and seaweed, and the tide pulled away slowly like it carried the weight of their worry.

"Look!" Nina pointed at something half buried near a clump of beach grass.

Fisher jogged ahead, his heart lurching. He knelt, brushing away sand, but it was only an old sun-bleached flip-flop, cracked and long abandoned. "False alarm." He stood and laid a hand on her shoulder. "Let's keep going."

They pushed on, the beach stretching out ahead of them. Fisher scanned for footprints, for any sign. The tide had erased most of the morning's marks, leaving the sand deceptively smooth. Finally, at the base of the old lifeguard stand, he called a halt. He motioned for Nina to sit.

She sank to the bottom step, heaving with exhaustion and dread.

"We'll get a better vantage point here," he said, climbing up a few steps and shading his eyes against the brightening sky. From the height, he could see Paul and Amanda, small figures at the edge of the inlet, their paths crisscrossing. Further down, Tug's truck bumped along a back road, kicking up dust.

Fisher pulled out his phone, checking tide charts and timing the next surge. He mapped where the waterline would've been at dawn, trying to read the shore like he would read a wave.

"Nina," he said, his voice low but sure, "we're narrowing it down. We're gonna find her."

She looked up at him, her expression weary. "I don't know what I'd do without you right now."

He didn't answer but just offered a small nod, already scanning the horizon again.

"She used to do this when she was little," she murmured, almost to herself. "Run off when she was upset. But she'd always come back in about an hour. And the last time we had to look for her, she snuck back to her room and went to sleep. But this time . . ."

Fisher glanced at her. "She'll come back again, Nina."

She swallowed, blinking against the wind that sent sand pelting them. "Will she?"

He didn't answer. Instead, he focused on the subtle shifts in the sand, looking for any sign of movement.

Then, he saw a shape. Something small and hunched near the edge of the dune.

Nina's fingers gripped his arm. "Look! Fisher!"

"I see it." He raised his hand to her arm, trying to keep her calm.

They ran down the steps and onto the beach, the crunch of their footsteps deafening against the stillness of the morning as they made their way toward the object. The shape remained unmoving, curled into itself like a forgotten bundle of clothing abandoned by the tide.

Fisher's stomach clenched as he moved ahead, and he motioned for Nina to wait. Then, just as he got close enough to see, the shape moved.

Nina gasped and her hands flew to her mouth, but then she realized it wasn't Kendra. "Is that a goat?"

A scrappy brown dog, thin and matted from the damp sand, lifted its head, blinking up at them with sleepy, confused eyes. It let out a small yawn, then gave a whole-body shake, ears flapping like it was flicking off the last remnants of sleep. With a huff, it trotted off, tail swishing as if annoyed they'd interrupted its nap.

"No. Just a dog." Fisher rubbed his hand over Nina's shoulder, trying to calm her.

He exhaled, forcing his heart rate to slow.

Nina let out a shuddering laugh of half relief, half frustration. "You have got to be kidding me."

Fisher ran a hand over his face, glancing at her. "False alarm, again."

She huffed out a breath. "I don't know whether to be relieved or throw something."

He gave her a sideways glance. "I'd prefer you didn't throw something. I'm a little too close to dodge right now."

She chuckled and shook her head, but her expression sobered just as quickly. "We have to keep looking."

They moved farther down the beach, past a patch of scattered footprints leading toward the water. At first, Fisher thought they were remnants of someone's morning walk, but something about them felt fresh. The tide hadn't smoothed the edges of the prints yet. His gut twisted. "Nina," he said, letting her name settle low.

She turned to him, and as soon as she saw where he was looking, her breath hitched. "Footprints. Small feet. It has to be her!" She sprinted toward the water's edge. "Oh no. Do you think she—" She froze, scanning the waves, her breath coming fast. "She's a strong swimmer, but I don't see her."

The tide surged forward, washing over Nina's ankles and throwing her off-balance.

Fisher caught her arm. "Stop." His grip was firm. "Look at the footprints."

Her chest heaved.

"They turn back," he said, softer now. "She didn't go in," he said, willing her to believe it.

Maybe a yard beyond the tide line, the footprints turned away from the water, back toward the jagged rocks. Nina and Fisher followed them to where the water lifted, spraying into the sky as the tide rushed against the rocky man-made ledge meant to protect that part of the coastline.

Fisher scanned the area. Then he saw it. A small hunched figure perched on the rocks at the far end. "There." He pointed.

Nina rushed to him, trying to see what he was pointing out, and then she didn't hesitate. She took off, running toward her daughter, her voice raw and desperate. "Kendra!"

Kendra flinched but didn't turn around.

Nina reached her first, her hands shaking as she grabbed her daughter's arms, pulling her closer. "Baby, you scared me. I'm so sorry for whatever I did. I love you. You have to know that."

Fisher stayed back, giving them space.

Kendra's eyes had dark circles under them and were red from

crying. She held her body tense, looking lost and confused. "Why are you here?"

Nina's voice was thick. "You left me a note."

Kendra winced, her gaze flickering toward the sand. "I know what I said."

Nina couldn't understand. "Then why? You can always come to me."

Kendra's jaw clenched. "Because everything feels impossible."

Fisher inventoried the emotions he saw. Rebellion. Pain. Fear. Grief. He stepped slowly forward. "We've been looking everywhere for you, kiddo."

Kendra's lips pressed into a thin line. "I didn't ask you to."

"You don't have to," he said. "People who care show up."

Something in her eyes flickered, and she stood and took a step farther.

"No! Kendra, don't go. Please don't." Nina knelt on the rocks, barely able to hold herself. "I don't even know what I did, but I will make it right, no matter what it takes." She held her arms out.

Kendra stood there shivering for a long time. "You don't get it. Nobody does."

"Please let me help," Nina said as she extended her hand as far as she could.

Finally, Kendra stepped toward them and then fell on the rocks next to her mother, both of them in tears.

Nina brushed the damp hair from her daughter's forehead. "You can run," she whispered, her voice breaking, "but I'm always going to find you, because I love you. Please never scare me like that again."

Kendra trembled as she clung to her mom.

Relief washed over him, but he was worried the walk might be too much for Nina and Kendra. "I'm going to text Tug to bring his car up to the road for you. Let's get you both off the beach." He texted Tug and then walked ahead to give them a little space.

"Kendra, let's go home." Nina wrapped her arm around Kendra's waist as they walked up the beach together.

Their steps were slow on the hike back, the weight of the morning clinging to them like mist. Kendra wriggled free to put a single stride between herself and Nina.

Sensing they'd stopped, Fisher turned back to see Nina watching as Kendra knelt near a washed-up pile of seaweed and driftwood. The girl stood, brushing the sand from something in her hand.

Concerned, he jogged back over.

Nina hesitated as Kendra dropped a shell into her hand. A small pale-lavender whelk. Nina ran her thumb along its ridges.

"It caught my eye as we were walking," Kendra said. "It's so pretty. I thought maybe you should have it."

Nina's throat tightened. "You don't have—"

"It's not an apology, Mom," Kendra cut in, glancing up at her, her eyes wary, defensive. "I'm still mad."

Nina closed her fingers around the shell. "Sure. You have every right to be mad. I should've told you about the baby as soon as your dad told me. I wasn't trying to hurt you. I wanted to protect you."

Kendra kicked at the sand. "I always thought Dad loved me more than you did."

"Your father loves you, Kendra. We both do." Nina tucked a strand of damp hair behind Kendra's ear. "Always."

"I can't believe he keeps hurting me. Why didn't you tell me?"

A tear slid down Nina's cheek. "I knew it was going to hurt you, and I hated to be the one to tell you."

"He always makes you tell me the bad news, doesn't he?"

Fisher spotted Tug pull up at the street and gave Nina a quick hand motion to head to the car. He walked alongside without a word.

"I didn't think if I left that . . ." Kendra looked back at the waves.

Nina's heart squeezed. "That what?"

Kendra hesitated, twisting her fingers together. "That anyone cared enough to come looking for me."

"But we did, and I always will." Nina pulled her into her arms. "I love you more than I could ever put into words."

Kendra didn't pull away, but she didn't lean in either. She just stood there, her expression caught somewhere between anger and something softer and fragile. "I don't know how to do this, Mom."

"I don't either," Nina said, still gripping the shell. "But we'll find our way, the two of us."

Fisher jogged ahead to open the car door. Nina helped Kendra get in, and Fisher closed the door.

"You okay?" he asked Nina as they walked around to the other side.

"Yes. Thank you for being here. I couldn't have done this without you."

He put a hand on her waist and helped her in. "You could have, but you never need to. Let me get y'all home."

They weren't where they needed to be, but Kendra was safe, and that was a start.

Chapter Twenty-Seven

BACK AT THE HOUSE, WITH KENDRA CURLED UP ASLEEP ON the couch upstairs, Nina did what she'd been dreading: She called David.

He answered on the second ring. "Nina?"

"She ran away," Nina said, her voice raw but low, trying not to wake her daughter. "Because of you. Because of all this."

David's voice faltered. "Nina, I . . . I didn't mean for . . ." He exhaled sharply. "Is she okay?"

"She's safe."

He paused, then said flatly, "I take it you know by now why she was mad?"

Nina frowned. "Besides not telling her about the baby . . . again? I'm not sure. She's all over the place and so upset. I can't imagine what I did this time. I'd never—"

"You didn't, Nina." David sighed. "She got into a text volley with Charlotte yesterday afternoon."

Nina's stomach dropped. *With his new wife?* "She what?"

David controlled his words, but frustration laced them. "Kendra reached out. Told Charlotte she was angry about the vacation and had a few other choice words. And Charlotte . . ."

His hesitation made Nina's hands clench.

"What did she say, David?"

He let out a slow breath. "She told Kendra it shouldn't have been a surprise that the marriage broke up. That you'd always put work before family. That maybe if you'd wanted more kids, Kendra wouldn't have been so lonely and had to fight for your attention."

Nina's vision blurred with rage. "She said that?"

"It gets worse. Charlotte said that now that I was so happy with her and that we are having a baby, Kendra would always have a little sister or brother and never be lonely again."

Nina's grip on the phone tightened, her heart pounding. "Tell me she didn't."

He sighed. "I don't know what Charlotte was thinking."

"David. I can't believe this."

"It's not great timing. I get it, but we're newlyweds, and Charlotte wants children. It's a happy time for her. But once Kendra accused Charlotte of lying about the pregnancy to get me to cancel the trip, Charlotte just cut loose on her. I read the texts, Nina. It was bad."

"And you didn't step in to stop it immediately? You know what, don't answer that. Look, you've got to stop making Kendra feel like she's not a priority. It's unkind, and all the necklaces in the world can't fix that. Yes, I already gave her your birthday present."

"I didn't know. Not until later." He made a grunting noise. "I was trying to make sense of it, and Kendra hadn't responded to me yet. I didn't want to put this on you. I know I've done that a lot over the years, and I'm sorry. I never meant to be that kind of guy. But I want you to know everything so you can take care of our girl."

Nina let out a bitter laugh. "Well, congratulations. Now it's on all of us."

"Nina, listen, I never said those things that Charlotte wrote. I've never even thought those things. Even though our marriage didn't work out, you know I still love Kendra."

It didn't matter. The damage was already done.

Nina looked over at Kendra, still asleep on the couch. The weight of these problems was never meant for a child, but Nina knew all this wasn't just about the divorce—it was a culmination of years of their daughter feeling unseen.

And now? Charlotte had confirmed Kendra's worst fear.

Fisher watched from the doorway, his expression unreadable. But Nina could tell by the way his jaw tightened that he understood what had gone down.

She wrapped up the call and then turned to him. "You heard most of it, I'm sure."

"I did."

Nina clutched the phone so tightly that her fingers ached.

"She thinks I never wanted her at all, Fisher." Tears streamed down her cheeks. "How do I fix a hurt that deep?"

"Nina, guilt is not failure. You are a loving mother, and you do love her, so it'll fall back into place." Fisher spoke calmly, without hesitation. "We don't fix this, Nina. We prove our love consistently by showing up, every day, until she feels it for herself."

Nina drew in a breath, letting his words settle like balm on a fresh wound.

The day stretched long and uneventfully. Kendra moved to her bed, and Rosemary tucked her in as if she'd just come down with the flu, but they all needed rest. The adrenaline crash had left them drained, both physically and emotionally.

Fisher and Tug had lingered for a while, keeping watch from a respectful distance as Nina curled up on the couch, exhaustion winning over the weight of worry. When she drifted off, Fisher felt something shift inside him.

For years, he'd convinced himself he wasn't built for this—for family, for belonging. Maybe the Lord had other plans. But seeing Nina's face now, seeing how much she needed someone steady beside her, he felt that conviction cracking and longed to have a family of his own.

Tug walked over to Rosemary, who sat in her recliner, and kissed her on the cheek. "I love you, sweet girl. Not the day I had in mind for us, but I think our lives just twisted a little tighter together and we're all going to be better for it. I'm going to make some dinner for all of us. I'll be back in a couple of hours."

Rosemary didn't argue. She was probably too tired.

Fisher and Tug walked outside together. They stood in the humid afternoon air, leaning against Fisher's truck and watching the waves slowly roll in. Then, almost at the same time, they both let out a long exhale. The timing made them laugh.

"Dramatic morning," Tug said. "That got my old ticker going. I can skip going to the gym today."

"High intensity, for sure."

Then the front door creaked open, and both were surprised when Kendra stepped outside. Her hands were stuffed deep into her hoodie pocket, and her hair was a little wild from sleep. She shifted from foot to foot, hesitating before saying, "I'm sorry I scared everyone."

Fisher exchanged a glance with Tug.

Tug nodded, folding his arms. "You did."

Kendra walked down the stairs to the driveway. "I didn't know what else to do." She looked up at Fisher. "I know you tried to help me yesterday when I first started texting with my dad's new wife. I'm sorry I didn't confide in you. I just . . ." Her voice wobbled. "I don't know what to believe, you know?"

Her statement was present tense. "I know what it feels like to want someone's attention so bad it hurts," Fisher said. "But you know what I figured out? Sometimes the people who truly see us were right beside us all along."

Kendra sniffled. "But it's not fair. Why am I not enough?"

"Oh, kiddo, you *are* enough. Your dad's choices don't change that. And I know your mom and grandmother would move mountains for you. That's legit." Fisher's heart ached for the day she would be able to say that in the past tense and that it wouldn't be far in her future.

Tug cocked his head. "I don't know what all happened or who said what, but if there's one thing this old man knows, it's that those two redheaded ladies in there . . ." He waved a finger in the air toward the house. "Their hearts beat for you, Kendra." He shot his finger in her direction. "And I pray you'll never scare them like that again."

Her gaze fell to the concrete. "Yes, sir."

Fisher saw her tense her shoulders, like she expected to be lectured again. He wouldn't be the one to do it. Not today.

Tug flipped his keys in his hands. "I'm going to run. I want to fix something for y'all for dinner tonight."

"I'm not going to be hungry," Kendra said. "My stomach's in knots."

Tug's lips twitched. "My cooking has a way of unknotting those twisted guts." He winked. "I'll check on you later, kid. We all love you. All of us. It's real, and you can count on it."

She didn't respond but stood there watching him back out of the driveway.

Fisher waited, studying her, giving her time. Then he said, "*I* ran away once too."

Kendra's posture stiffened, just enough to let him know she was listening.

"I thought love was limited," he continued. "That it ran out, like gas in a tank. That once it was gone, it was gone for good." He released a slow breath, his gaze softening as it met hers. "But

I was wrong. Real love—the kind that matters—doesn't run out. It waits. It forgives. It keeps showing up, even when you don't think you deserve it."

Kendra's chin trembled, her eyes brimming with tears but defiant. "Then why does it hurt so much?"

Fisher's voice stayed low. "Because it matters. And because when you're hurting, it feels like you're all alone. But you're not. Not now. Not ever."

She blinked fast, looking away toward the horizon, but she didn't pull away.

He reached into his pocket, taking out a small rock. It had a faint imperfect heart-shaped pattern etched into it. He set it beside her.

"I found this a long time ago," he said, "when I thought I had nothing left."

Kendra glanced at it, her fingers twitching like she wanted to reach for it but wasn't sure if she should.

Fisher exhaled. "Love isn't finite, kid. You don't run out of it. Your dad loving someone else doesn't mean he loves you any less." His voice was quiet but certain. "And no matter how far you run, whatever you're feeling inside doesn't just disappear. It's still there, waiting."

Kendra let out a shaky breath.

"Face it. But the good news is, you don't have to do it alone." He nudged the rock toward her. "Want to adopt this for a while? It helped me once."

She reached for the rock, turning it over in her palm. Her other hand disappeared into her hoodie pocket. "Thanks, Fisher."

"You get to start with a clean slate whenever you choose. You don't even need permission. Know what your grandmother told me a couple of weeks ago?"

She shrugged.

"It's a simple theory, but it hit home for me. She said we have to leave the past where it happened. We can't live backward. We can only live forward."

"Good, because I never want to relive yesterday."

"I felt the same way when I heard about it, and trust me, I've held on to a lot of yesterday's problems for way too long. No one even knows or cares about the old problems I still worry about." He gave her a minute to let it sink in. "Think tomorrow can be a better day? I do."

"Definitely couldn't be worse." She dipped her head. "I have a lot to make up to Mom."

"No, you don't. You're home. You're safe. You know she loves you. All she needs to know is that you love her too."

"I don't think it's going to be that simple."

"It will, kiddo." Fisher's voice was gentle but firm. "Don't make it any harder than it is."

The front door opened, and Nina rushed down the stairs, her eyes wide. "Is everything okay? Kendra?"

"Yes," Kendra answered. "I just wanted to say something to Tug and Fisher."

"You're not going to—"

"No, ma'am," Kendra interjected. "I'm not going anywhere. I'm right where I'm supposed to be. Safe with you."

Nina clutched her daughter's hand. "It just scared me when I went to check on you and you were gone."

Fisher met Nina's eyes. "We're on the road to recovery, and things are improving. Clean slate. Good decisions. That's our choice every single day."

"We can make that choice," Nina said.

"I want to go to work tomorrow," Kendra said. "Do you think Mr. Paul is going to fire me?"

"I know your job is waiting for you," Fisher replied.

"I'm sorry, Mom." Kendra's voice was small, breaking on the

last word. "I don't know how to fix what's broken inside me, but working with those dogs feels good."

Nina smoothed Kendra's hair back. "You're not broken. You're hurting. But this isn't anything we can't repair. And we'll work through it." She stepped forward, wrapping Kendra in her arms and holding on tight.

Later, after the heaviness of the day had lifted just enough for them to think about food, Tug returned, true to his promise, with a big tray of fried chicken. He had made homemade mashed potatoes, gravy, and coleslaw.

"Dinner's here! Doesn't even matter if you're hungry or not. You can reheat fried chicken or eat it cold for any meal."

"It smells good," Kendra admitted. "You said your cooking would untie the knots in my stomach. You weren't lying."

"Grab whatever you like. We're doing paper plates, so no one has to do dishes. A regular family picnic."

Kendra made her way over, grabbed a drumstick, and took her plate to the table.

Fisher and Nina piled food onto their plates while Tug chatted with Rosemary.

"You are one sweet man, Tug Basnight," Rosemary said. "How did I get so lucky to cross paths with you?"

"Because we were meant to be. All my pleasure," he teased. "You feel like home to me. So, are you going to set a date with me, or are we going to have two houses forever? I miss you every minute I'm away from you."

"Me too." Rosemary's breath hitched. Then she kissed him. "We'll set a date."

He punched a hand into the air, then dipped her and laid a romantic kiss on her.

Kendra gave a loud whistle.

It must be weird to see your grandmother fall in love, but Kendra's reaction tickled Fisher as he watched from across the room. He realized this roomful of people felt like family.

If Tug could find love at his age, maybe there was hope for a guy like *him* too. Maybe, just maybe, his story wasn't finished after all. And maybe Nina was meant to be part of the next chapter.

He studied Nina. She looked tired but was so beautiful inside and out that it made his heart ache to be right where she needed him. Right where he belonged.

Chapter Twenty-Eight

THE NEXT MORNING, NINA TOOK KENDRA TO PAWS TOWN Square. It was a short drive, and Nina couldn't bring herself to let Kendra go alone that morning. Nina was playing it safe, even though Fisher believed that Paul wouldn't fault Kendra for yesterday's events.

The car engine's low rumble hummed in her ears, matching the slow churn of concern weighing on her this morning.

Her mama-bear instincts were still in overdrive, and she knew it. But how was she supposed to relax when her heart had just spent an entire night fearing it might shatter? She needed to come across as relaxed about the situation, though, for Kendra's sake. Or maybe it was more for keeping herself in check. She wished she could make all the worries in her child's heart disappear. If only it were that simple.

Nina turned into the parking lot of Paws. The business was more amazing now that she knew about how Paul had started it. He'd transformed what used to be an abandoned behemoth ghost-box store into something new: a sprawling resort-like facility blending purpose with beauty. The clock tower and open green spaces gave it a timeless feel. It was great to see an abandoned building given new life, built on vision rather than started from scratch.

She cut the engine and turned toward her daughter, offering

a calm smile that she almost believed herself. “Okay, we’re early. You have time to check in with Paul first. Do you want me to go with you?”

Kendra pondered, twisting her fingers, before sighing and shaking her head. “No. I can do it. I’m just feeling overwhelmed.”

“Oh, honey. Being a little overwhelmed is normal. It usually means it’s something that really matters to you. You can do this.”

“Thanks, Mom.” Kendra’s voice shook, but at least they were talking.

Nina felt a quiet sense of victory. Not everything would heal overnight, but this? This was a step. She reached across the console and squeezed Kendra’s hand. “I’m proud of you.”

Days of distance ended as Kendra’s face softened, and Nina saw the familiar spark in her daughter. The girl she’d raised to be brave and strong, even when she felt lost.

“If you need me, I’m a text away.” Nina lifted her phone. “I won’t leave the parking lot until you send me a thumbs-up. Deal?”

Kendra huffed a laugh, rolling her eyes in mock annoyance. “Deal.”

To Nina’s surprise, Kendra leaned over and hugged her. Not a half-hearted hug, but a real one, fierce and warm.

Nina swallowed against the lump in her throat, holding her just a little longer than necessary. She wanted to say so many things. That she loved her more than life itself. That she saw the good in her, even on her worst days. That she’d carry every ounce of Kendra’s hurt if only it meant her daughter wouldn’t have to feel it.

But all that came out was a whispered promise, fierce and sure, as she pressed a kiss to the top of Kendra’s head. “I’m here, Kendra. Always.”

And in that moment, Nina knew there was nothing she wouldn't do to help her find her way back to the light.

When Kendra pulled back, her voice was quieter. "I'm still scared, Mom."

Nina reached up, tucking a loose strand of hair behind her daughter's ear. "That's okay. Fear is just proof that we care about something."

Kendra blinked, her expression thoughtful. "So, how do we know we're doing the right thing?"

Nina's smile softened. "We trust the fear. The right answer isn't always the easy one."

Kendra gave her a look, one eyebrow raised. "That's it?"

Nina chuckled. "Pretty much." But then, turning serious, she placed a hand over Kendra's. "We're going to trust God's timing. We're going to pray every day that we make the right choices, that we uplift each other, and that we talk things through. Because we're a team, honey. And you are never, ever alone in this world. And although we hurt each other, that is only a temporary bruise on our everlasting commitment and love."

Then, to Nina's shock, Kendra nodded. "Can we?"

"Can we what, honey?"

"Pray? Now?"

Nina's breath caught. "Uh, yeah." She hadn't been prepared for that. They weren't one of those pray-out-loud types of families. David had never been a fan of it, and they'd just fallen out of practice after a while.

"I used to love our bedtime prayers," Kendra said.

"Me too. We could do that again."

"That would be nice."

It was a beautiful start to something positive. She reached for her daughter's hands, her voice steady as she willed God to give her the words. With love, she whispered a simple prayer. "Lord, help us find Your peace in all things. Help us trust the plans You've set before us. Even when we're scared. Even when we don't understand. We are leaning into Your plan. Thank You for never leaving us alone. Amen."

Kendra squeezed Nina's fingers tightly, causing Nina's heart to squeeze too. All the nights she'd whispered silent prayers over Kendra's sleeping form, aching for a moment like this, and now, here it was, unexpected and holy.

Kendra exhaled, lifting her chin. "All right. I'm going in."

She opened the car door, but before she got out, Nina caught a flicker of something new in her daughter's eyes. Not defiance for a change but a quiet strength. Determination. And as Kendra walked toward the building, her back a little straighter than before, Nina held on to that hope with everything she had, because this was the first step forward.

I'll be here every step of the way for you, baby girl.

She wasn't sure what the next step for their healing might be, but this morning she knew it was a small step.

It wasn't long before her phone jingled, signaling a message from Kendra. She held her breath as she tapped the screen. Simply two emojis (wasn't that the teenage way?): the thumbs-up and a smiley face.

Sweet relief made Nina hug the phone. Just in case, though, she sat there for a few minutes to be sure.

Kendra was sitting on a bench outside Paws when Nina arrived to pick her up. Nina hoped everything had gone well for her.

Nina rolled down her window to say, "Are you good?" She wished that one day she wouldn't worry at every tiny thing.

"Yeah. Like nothing ever happened. It was a great day."

"Excellent! I was thinking we could walk down to the beach and sit for a bit when we get home. What do you think?"

"Sounds good."

They drove home, and Nina had to bite her lip to keep from asking for details about Kendra's day. Thankfully, it was a short drive. They got out of the car, left their shoes on the porch steps, and headed for the path to the water.

"It's so nice out here," Nina commented. "Why don't I do this every day?"

"We could," Kendra said.

"We should."

They both sat in the sand. Kendra swept her hand, making absent-minded circles and squiggles. The breeze lifted Kendra's hair gently, and for a long moment, they just listened to the waves and the calls of the birds flying above.

Then, after what felt like an eternity, Kendra's voice broke above the sound of nature. "I don't know what's wrong with me, Mom. It's like everything is okay. I was working with the dogs, and I love them, and I think they really love me. They are so happy to see me, and they do everything I tell them."

"That's great. So, what's the problem?"

"I don't know. Sometimes it's like a switch flips." Her hand bunched the fabric of her shirt as she spoke. "I feel like I can't breathe half the time. Like I'm trapped. And I don't even know why I'm so mixed up. It's not being mad or sad. I don't know what it is." Kendra lowered her head.

Nina gave her the moment of quiet reflection, hoping the right words would come. She swallowed the temptation to absorb the emotions. This wasn't about her pain.

She reached for Kendra's hand, expecting resistance, but this time, Kendra let her take it. She wanted Kendra to feel how much that brief touch meant to her. "I think everything is just . . . a lot. What you're feeling could be a panic attack or anxiety. It could just be all the change going on. Being a teenager is tough enough. Then the divorce, losing your grandfather, Mom coming to stay and then moving away. Really, there's a lot happening in our lives."

Kendra nodded.

"If you can't talk to me, I could connect you with Pastor Qualls. Mom loves him, and he seems so approachable. Or I can schedule a doctor's appointment. What do you think might help? I want you to have all the resources you need."

Kendra lifted her chin, trying to control her trembling lips, and held Nina's gaze. "Can we just work through it together for a while?"

"Yes. A little while, though, and we'll do an honest checkpoint, okay?"

"Yes."

"We'll work on keeping our communication open. I don't want you to fall back into that dark place, but I don't think there's anything wrong with you. You're hurt, and those things that Charlotte said . . . honey, anyone would feel the way you're feeling. I love you, and no matter what anyone says, please never doubt it. I'd never do anything that might cause me to lose you."

Kendra squeezed her eyes shut. "I can't trust Dad anymore."

"He's made some bad decisions, but he loves you, even if he has a funny way of showing it. But you don't have to trust him until he earns that back. That's okay." Nina's heart clenched.

"Good."

"Are you ready to see what your grandma is up to?"

"Yeah." Kendra bounced right to her feet and tugged Nina up.

They swept the sand from their clothes and walked up to the house. Nina called out a hello as they walked inside.

"I was wondering what was taking you so long," Rosemary said from the kitchen.

"It smells great in here," Nina said. The aroma of Tug's fried chicken and homemade mashed potatoes filled the room as Rosemary reheated the food from last night. "We walked down to the beach to enjoy nature."

"Isn't it a treasure?" Rosemary gave a sort of shimmy, like a self-hug to bless the beach. "How was your day at work, Kendra?"

"So good, Grandma. You have to come meet the dogs I'm working with. They are so smart. You'll love them. You can walk with us. We just do the regular walking trails. There are other people walking, so it would be okay."

"I'd like that."

A knock at the door interrupted them. "I'll get it," Kendra said.

Nina watched as Kendra opened the door to Tug standing there with The Wife perched on his shoulder and Fisher holding a big brown paper sack.

"Did I miss a party invitation?" Kendra asked, then turned to The Wife and said, "Pretty bird."

Nina stifled a laugh, but it was nice to see Kendra being playful.

The Wife stretched out one wing and pointed her toe. "The Wife is bee-yoooo-tiful," she said, following it up with a wolf whistle and a loud hello.

"She's very humble too," Tug teased as they stepped inside.

Fisher walked in behind Tug and headed straight for the kitchen. "Hey, Nina. I brought something good. You're going to like this." Then he turned back toward Kendra. "And, Kendra, there's going to be a beach-volleyball tournament behind The Tackle Box tomorrow afternoon. You should stop by after work. Free snow cones."

"Maybe I will."

Nina followed him. "What did you bring, Fisher?"

"All the fixings for ice cream sundaes."

"More ice cream? What's the occasion?"

"Happiness," he said with a shrug, but there was more in his eyes, as if giving a quiet promise that he wasn't going anywhere. She hoped she had read that right.

"I like the way you think," she said. She and Fisher stepped away to put the ice cream in the freezer. "I'm not sure ice cream can heal all this. I'm so scared I'll lose her again."

Fisher paused. "It's not the ice cream alone. It's all of us here together. It's love. There's no expiration date on it. Trust her to come back to you, Nina. This is just a little detour. She's a good girl who is having a tough time."

He had a way of making everything feel easier. And his just showing up without her having to drop a hint or ask was something she'd never experienced with other men. *I could get very used to you being around.* "All righty, then. Count me in. Just take the calories out of mine."

"No way. It's the calories that make it tasty. We'll just add a walk on the beach to balance things out."

"You're on."

He bumped her shoulder playfully, and she felt the weight of his presence–solid, grounding.

They rejoined the others.

Rosemary glanced at Tug and then Fisher. "You two are like a traveling surprise party."

Tug leaned closer and kissed her cheek. "Anything to make my girl smile."

The Wife made an abundance of kissing sounds that sent them all into giggles, which only spurred the bird on, ending the kisses with a "K-I-S-S-I-N-G" sing-along.

"Flirt," Rosemary accused Tug. "You and this crazy bird, but that's not a complaint. Never stop."

"Your wish is my command," he said with a wiggle of his

bushy brows. "I can't speak to The Wife's behavior. She's her own bird. A cuckoo bird."

"Cuckoo! Cuckoo! And keep the bluebird in my heart."

"Oh goodness gracious! Make her quiet down, Tug." Rosemary went to a drawer and took out some serving utensils. "I just heated the leftovers. There's plenty. We have to eat dinner before dessert. That's the rule around here. So, let's eat, because a deluxe Supreme Surprise Delight ice cream sundae sounds pretty good to me!"

Nina laughed at Mom's reference. She used to tempt her into good behavior as a kid with a dessert promise all the time. The best ones were always called Supreme Surprise Delights. "That sounds perfect for tonight, Mom."

Everyone gathered around the kitchen island and made a plate, then moved to the dining room table.

Across from Nina, Kendra pushed her mashed potatoes into little swirls, looking more like herself than she had in days.

Tug cleared his throat, lifting his fork with a small smile. "Now, this is what family looks like."

Kendra chuckled. "Is it?"

Tug winked. "It's what *ours* looks like."

Kendra didn't argue. Instead, she broke into a grin.

Rosemary reached for Tug's hand. He squeezed hers, their love quiet, unspoken, but apparent.

Fisher leaned in, whispering to Nina. "That's a good look on them."

Love. Nina glanced at him, warmth blooming in her chest. "It is," she said, looking into his eyes.

He held her gaze. "*We* look pretty good too." He pulled his phone out of his pocket and snapped a selfie. "Look at these two."

She took the phone and laughed at the photo. "It might've been a decent picture if you'd given me half a warning so I could smile." Nina shot him a goofy expression, like the mid-sentence photo he'd captured.

Fisher raised the phone and started counting down. "Fine. Here's your warning. One . . . two . . ."

Before he could finish, Kendra popped up behind them and shouted, "Photobomb!"

Fisher looked at the picture and then showed it to Nina. She stared at the photo, seeing Kendra's grin wide behind them. It was nice that they both wore genuine smiles. This was the snapshot of hope she hadn't dared to dream of just days ago.

Later that night, after Kendra was safe in bed, the storm of worry settled into a heavy quiet. Nina cracked the door open and peeked in to check on Kendra. She stood in the doorway, watching her daughter breathe deeply in sleep. Tomorrow, they'd continue to figure out the next steps. Tonight, they just needed peace.

Chapter Twenty-Nine

FISHER HAD BEEN SWAMPED WITH THE TACKLE BOX'S VOLLEYBALL tournament and refurnishing one of his rental properties, leaving little time for friends. But when Rosemary texted him, inviting him over for a "family night," there was no way he was turning that down.

Rosemary and Tug were a big part of his life already, and now that Kendra and Nina were staying with Rosemary, those visits were the best part of each week. Lately, it was getting harder to imagine a week, much less a lifetime, without someone special in his life. How had he ever convinced himself that he was happy alone?

After they settled around the dinner table, he passed the rolls to the right, then leaned toward Nina. "Seems Kendra is doing much better."

"I think so." Nina watched her daughter talking to Rosemary at the other end of the table. "I feel so much better about everything. We're tackling each day as it comes."

"I was surprised she showed up at the beach-volleyball tournament at The Tackle Box yesterday after work," Fisher said.

Nina's eyebrows lifted. "I hope she'll make some new friends here."

"She will." He chuckled. "She looked like she wanted to play but never joined in."

"She used to love sports. She was on a couple teams, field hockey and softball, before David and I split and our routines got so messy."

"Tell her she's welcome to join one of the volleyball teams. There's an incentive too," Fisher explained. "Local merchants have donated a bunch of prizes. Weekly bracket winners get to pick from T-shirts, beach chairs, gift cards, and all kinds of other stuff."

"That's cool." Nina let out a small hopeful laugh. "Maybe I should get her a volleyball so she can practice. She's got good hand-eye coordination. She'd probably be pretty good."

"I've got extra volleyballs at The Tackle Box. I can lend you one." Then, with a grin, he added, "If you're up for it, we could have a little practice game one day."

Playful curiosity drifted into Nina's expression. "Oh, be careful. I was on the volleyball team in high school, and very good in my prime."

Fisher smirked. "Not worried. Playing on the sand is way harder than playing court volleyball. It's a workout."

"You think I can't do it?" She narrowed her eyes, the challenge unmistakable. "I might surprise you."

Rosemary got up from the table, and Kendra turned her attention to her mom and him.

"Hey, Kendra, your mom just challenged me to a volleyball game. You in? I'll take you both on, two against one. I bet you a pizza I will still win."

Kendra burst into a smile. "Yeah! For sure!"

"Or we can make it a big game. I bet Amanda and Paul will come," Fisher added. "Jesse and Hailey are always up for anything."

"I think we can keep it small for tonight. We'll plan something with Amanda and Paul and the kids next time," said Nina.

Rosemary came back into the room. "I'll keep score and bring the refreshments."

Fisher chuckled. "You're hired!"

Kendra flopped into a chair beside her mother, glancing between her and Rosemary. "Where'd Tug go?"

"He went to get something out of his truck," Rosemary said. "He'll be right back."

"Humph." Kendra hesitated, chewing on the inside of her cheek before saying, "You know, I've noticed Tug has been staying here later and later, Grandma."

Nina's lips twitched, but she stayed quiet, watching the interaction unfold.

"And you've been spending a lot more time over at *his* place too," Kendra added, crossing her arms.

Rosemary shot her a bemused look. "And?"

"Are you two ever going to have a wedding?"

Right on cue, Tug walked into the room, his deep chuckle breaking the quiet. "What's all this now? Are you talking behind my back?"

Kendra didn't back down. "No. I was just asking when you're going to get married." Her voice held a teasing tone, but she looked curious.

Rosemary blushed, a rare sight.

Tug winked at Rosemary, then turned back to Kendra. "Do you think we should get married soon?"

"I do." Kendra gave Tug an approving look. "For an older guy, I think you're pretty cool. Plus, you make Grandma really happy."

Tug glanced over at Rosemary. "Maybe we should ask your grandma what she thinks."

Rosemary beamed, clearly enjoying the moment. "I think he's a keeper."

"Me too," Kendra said. Then her expression turned more serious as she straightened in her seat. "Um, I owe you two an apology," Kendra said, her voice quieter now. "I haven't been fun to be around, and I'm sorry for that."

Rosemary's face softened, and Tug reached over and rested a hand on Kendra's shoulder.

"You've had a lot on your plate, honey," Rosemary said. "We understand."

Kendra didn't respond, but she looked more comfortable having put it out there.

Fisher took it all in, something warm stirring inside him. He hadn't let himself get attached to people in a long time, but these people had somehow settled into his life without him even realizing it. To lighten the mood, he asked, "How about that little volleyball match?"

"On a full stomach?" Kendra twisted with a confused look on her face. "Aren't we supposed to wait forty-five minutes before playing?"

Fisher shrugged. "I think that only pertains to swimming."

"Oh. Well, then you're on," Kendra said. "I've always thought that was a dumb rule anyway. Come on, Mom. Let's show him who's boss."

"Mom, do you and Tug have the rest of this cleanup under control?" Nina asked.

"Sure do. I've got my best helper here." Rosemary stage-whispered to Nina, "I'm referring to The Wife, of course."

"Hey, *I'm* a good helper," Tug teased back.

"Y'all go warm up. Rosemary and I will be out in a minute," Tug said. "I'll referee, and she can keep score."

"I doubt we'll need a referee," Kendra said.

"Um, no offense, but I've seen how competitive your mom is, and I can guarantee you'll need a referee if you are even half the redhead she is!" Tug seemed to enjoy poking fun at her.

They went downstairs. Fisher left for a moment while Kendra and Nina put chairs at the corners to mark a fake volleyball court using the clothesline as the net. Then he came running around the side of the house with a volleyball. "Good thing I had this in the truck. I wouldn't miss this for the world. I love to win."

"Oh, you just wait." Kendra rubbed her hands together. "My mom has a trophy for volleyball from, like, forever ago. She was really good."

"I'm not worried," Fisher said.

"Don't be overconfident. The more you brag, the more that loss is going to sting." Nina shifted her hip with a smirk. "My partner and I are completely in sync these days."

"Better watch out, Fisher!" Kendra was beaming over the banter.

"Is that experience talking?" Fisher's brow rose.

Rosemary waved a napkin in the air as she came down the stairs. "Peace, competitors. No smack-talking." A group groan caused her to pause. "Fine. Bellyache and smack-talk until you're red in the face."

Tug assumed a position on the far side of the makeshift court and pressed his hands to his knees. "Ready? Coin toss for serve."

"Nah. Let the girls serve," Fisher said.

"Oh, no," Nina said. "We're playing fair and square. Then you can't deny we won."

"I don't think you stand a chance."

"It's two against one," she reminded him. "We have some chance even just mathematically!"

Tug flipped the coin, and Fisher won the serve.

"We'll see." Fisher took a step back and sent the volleyball sailing over the net.

Nina set up the ball for Kendra to knock it over, and she did.

Fisher, towering a full foot over Nina and Kendra, eyed the

ball with a mischievous grin, and by the third playful volley, he made his move. "All right, time to end this," he said, winding up for a massive spike.

"Foul!" Nina shouted, both hands in the air in mock protest.

Tug looked confused. "That's *my* job."

Kendra joined in, her hands on her hips. "Yeah, no spiking, Fisher! That's cheating!"

"What? How is that cheating?" He exaggerated a look of innocence.

"It's the nine-inch rule. Everyone knows that, right, Kendra?" Nina flexed her arms, balling her hands into fists, trying to look menacing.

"Yeah, what Mom said."

"There's no such thing," Fisher complained.

"Yeah. Chapter 53, section 12 clearly states that if the other team has a nine-inch or more advantage in height, they cannot spike," Nina said, sounding convincing. "However, the lesser of the two may spike if they can."

"Come on. You're making that up," Fisher said. "I'm just using my natural advantage."

"Natural *giant* advantage," Nina muttered under her breath. "Fisher, that's like playing basketball with the hoop set at six feet. Not fair!"

He chuckled, lowering his hands and conceding with a dramatic bow. "Fine, fine. No spiking. Okay. Let's play your way."

The next few volleys were soft and easy. The girls got their chance to serve, and Kendra's serve surprised them all.

"Where did you learn to serve like that?" Nina asked.

"School, I guess. We played last year. I wasn't good then."

"I'm setting this one up for you. Get him, Kendra." Nina bumped the ball softly straight into the air. Kendra stepped under it and whaled the ball, sending it spinning past Fisher's head like a rocket.

Nina and Kendra looked as shocked as Fisher was. Then they danced around, high-fiving. From that point on, they had him running from left to right, and he wasn't a hundred percent sure that was accidental.

Then, as Nina was about to serve, Kendra pointed and yelled, "Look! Dolphins!"

Fisher whipped around, squinting toward the ocean.

"Gotcha!" Nina shouted, serving the ball to the open spot on his side of the court.

Fisher turned back, watching in slow motion as the ball landed in the sand next to him.

Kendra pretended to straighten her halo. "Oops, my bad. Point for us."

Fisher threw his hands up in mock defeat. "I can't believe I fell for that. All right, I guess it's your point. But I'll get you back!"

Rosemary leaned over the deck railing, grinning. "Nice job, girls. Fisher doesn't know what hit him!"

Fisher grinned back, rolling his eyes. "All right, you two. Game on. But if I win this time, I'm calling the next round no distractions."

Kendra gave a dramatic gasp. "No distractions? That's where all the fun is!"

The game became more friendly, the ball not hitting the ground for almost twenty-four bumps.

Nina threw one of her hands into the air. "I have to give up. Corporate America has sucked the physical abilities out of me. I'm beat!"

"Aw, Mom. We have to get you back into shape."

Nina bent over, trying to catch her breath. "I won't argue with you about that. Wow!"

Fisher tossed the ball into the air and turned to Tug. "Who won?"

Tug whistled. “Rosemary, who won?”

“It must have been a tie,” she said.

“What? Were you keeping score?” Tug asked.

“I guess I forgot.”

At that, they all laughed and then went inside to eat the ice cream sundaes. It had been a good day, start to finish.

When Fisher stood to leave, Nina walked him to the door.

“You know, I don’t think I’ve ever said this to anyone before, but I can’t wait to see you again,” he said, feeling like a twelve-year-old with a crush.

“Really?” She blinked. Then a smile spread across her face, and Fisher sort of melted right there. “I, um, I was going to say something funny, but no . . . I’m going to be honest with you here. I’d really like that.”

A quiet relief washed over him. That was a better response than he could’ve hoped for. He loved the playful jabs, but that sweet answer set his heart on fire. “I’d better go.” He was so tempted to lean in and kiss her, but he knew she wasn’t ready for that yet.

He headed toward his truck, but the moment he slid behind the wheel, one thought lingered. *I should have gone for the kiss.*

He wanted to do something special for Nina. Something that would show her just how much he cared about her and Kendra. But what? As he drove off into the night, his mind began spinning with possibilities.

Chapter Thirty

NINA SAT ON THE DECK WITH HER PHONE PRESSED TO HER ear as she stared out at the ocean. The moonlight shimmered over the water. Any other night, the waves would've been soothing. Instead, being on the phone with the man she'd once promised forever to only made the waves feel menacing.

"I'm sorry neither of us recognized Kendra's pain sooner," she said, her voice soft but steady. She'd practiced how to say it without putting David on the defensive. They both had ownership of this.

There was a long pause on the other end. She could hear him exhale, the weight of her words seeming to settle over him like an anchor.

"Nina, if this is your way of blaming me for her behav—"

"I didn't blame you. We both own the responsibility of being there for her. Co-parenting means making sure she knows she's still our priority no matter how much our lives have changed."

A heavier silence this time. She could picture him with his jaw tight, the way it always was when he felt cornered.

"What is it you want me to do?" he asked, his voice clipped.

Nina sighed, carefully choosing her words. "Don't break your promises to her. I don't know what happened last time, but to Kendra, it felt like you took away the time you'd set aside for her to spend it with your new wife. That felt like a rejection."

"She has a name. Charlotte."

Hearing the name twisted in her gut, remembering the pain the woman had caused her daughter. "Yes, Charlotte. Not the point, though. This is about you. She's your child and you changing the plans feels like rejection to her. You have to keep your promises, David. She's a teenager. These are tough years."

"I keep my promises, Nina. I'll get her for a week this summer. Isn't the time just as important as the when and where?"

"You can't keep dangling things and then switching things up. She needs to be a priority in your life too." She was so frustrated with him. "Fine, David, if you want to be literal. It wasn't a broken promise–it was a change in plans. But whatever we call it, we both need to be careful and consistent with her."

He let out a sharp breath. "I probably could've explained the change in plans better," he acknowledged. "But I guess I felt like I didn't owe her an explanation. We're the parents. We don't have to run our plans by a child for approval. We call the shots."

He frustrated her to no end. "But it doesn't hurt to frame it in a way that she won't take it personally."

"I promised we'd do it another time."

"She's a teenager," Nina reminded him gently. "She's sensitive to all this change, and she admitted to me she's afraid of being forgotten. Of being replaced by Charlotte."

"I guess I played it off," he said. "Maybe even laughed because it sounded so absurd. I might have made the problem worse without meaning to."

Nina's heart clenched. She knew he hadn't meant to hurt Kendra, but the intention didn't erase the pain. "Trust me, it's difficult to figure out."

He sighed. "No, it's not."

A few beats passed before he spoke again, softer this time. "I'll be better about keeping our communication open about

Kendra. But I don't want her to get the wrong idea, or thinking that means we're getting back together."

"I'll make that very clear on my side too."

He hesitated, then said, "My wife . . . Charlotte's a kind and smart woman, Nina. She really is. But she crossed a line with those texts, and I hate that Kendra had to read any of it. I just . . . I still want them to have a chance, you know? I want Kendra to see the good in her, the way I do. I want to be a better father and have family time with her. I want this to work for all of us."

Nina rolled his words over in her mind. Once upon a time, the thought of him loving another woman had felt like a knife to the gut. Now it just felt like part of the story, one she no longer needed to rewrite.

"I believe you, David. I'm sure Charlotte is very nice." She hesitated, then added, "I once thought you were the nicest man I'd ever known."

She didn't say the rest of her thought. That she had still believed that until she met Fisher. Life with David had fizzled with disappointment, and even the good times never held the calm that she felt around Fisher. And Fisher always showed up. He was steady, and he seemed to know when she needed him without even a word from her. It just felt tailor-made for her.

She and David wrapped up the conversation with both of them promising to do better for Kendra. And he promised to at least leave a message on those angsty days when she didn't take his call. To be the bigger person and be a steady positive element in her weeks.

When Nina hung up, she felt lighter, the burden lifted off her shoulders. She'd do her best to keep David in the loop and their interactions positive.

She stepped back into the house, ready to brew a cup of caffeine-free tea, but the scene in the kitchen stopped her in her tracks.

Beneath the soft glow of the range-hood light, Mom and Tug slow danced, their bodies swaying to a scratchy old love song playing on the radio. Tug's hands rested on her mother's waist, and Rosemary's head was nestled against his chest, her eyes closed in contentment. There was no performance, no pretense. Just two people who seemed to know the rhythm of each other's heart.

Nina stood there, overwhelmed by the quiet beauty of it. Her mother wasn't just surviving after Dad, she was *living*. Loving. Choosing joy again.

Maybe for the first time, Nina saw her not as a parent but as a woman still open to love, still worthy of it.

A slow smile rose to her lips as the scent of apple pie filled the kitchen. *They are a good team. And Mom deserves nothing less.*

The world outside felt complicated—divorce, co-parenting, teenage heartbreak—but here, in this quiet little kitchen, love looked simple. It wasn't grand gestures or sweeping declarations; it was showing up, day after day, in small, steady ways. Nina had spent so long thinking love was about fireworks and passion, about proving and chasing and fixing. But this? This was what she'd been missing all along.

Tug caught her eye and grinned, but he didn't stop dancing. Rosemary turned, smiling when she saw Nina.

"I'm sorry. I didn't mean to interrupt." Nina drew a steadying breath.

Rosemary's expression softened with concern. "Are you okay, sweetheart?"

"Yeah," Nina whispered. "I think I am." Her heart tugged, thinking of Kendra in her room, probably asleep, but Nina was no longer searching for peace. It had found her.

"I'm going to go for a walk. You two, don't do anything *I* wouldn't do," she teased with a wink and a wave as she exited.

Nina walked down to the beach. The moon was so bright that she didn't even need to use the flashlight she usually carried after dark. The tide had left behind a new scattering of shells on top of the damp sand, each one glistening. She walked barefoot along the shoreline, the cool water lapping at her toes.

After talking to David, she needed this space around her. She lifted her arms toward the sky. "Why does everything have to be so complicated?" she asked the moon. She whispered a prayer that Kendra could see herself the way Nina saw her: worthy, cherished, unbreakable.

She took a deep breath of the fresh air, hoping she could get her body to relax. To let go a little. Her muscles ached from the tension of dealing with so many emotions over the past few weeks and figuring out how to navigate her feelings about Fisher, a man she wasn't sure she deserved. But standing there, with the endless horizon stretched before her, she realized she liked the way he made her feel.

She started walking and scanned the sand, a habit she'd mastered since coming to Whelk's Island. She picked up a shell. Something about it caused her to close her eyes as she held the shell in her hand, praying for guidance, peace, and confirmation that she should even think about Fisher right now.

A slow breath filled her lungs as she turned the shell over in her hands. A familiar warmth settled in her chest. She thought of when Kendra found that shell with the message. They'd both thought Mom had planted it. She thought of Fisher, of the way he had always been there, even when she wasn't sure how to let him in. She thought of her mother choosing to love again, despite the fear of losing herself.

And then she thought of herself. She was terrified of making the wrong choice. Opening herself up to love again and losing herself wasn't an option. She couldn't get hurt like that again. But maybe love wasn't about losing yourself at all—maybe it was about finding the parts of you that had been waiting to come alive because of someone else.

She curled her fingers around the shell, holding it close as she lifted her gaze. The waves rolled in, steady and unrelenting, a reminder that life would always move forward. And so would she.

It wasn't one of those shells with a message written inside, but she felt the meaning coming through as clearly as if it were. A soft smile touched her lips as she turned back toward the house. She dropped the shell with a silent wish that it might someday land in the hands of someone who needed a special treasure to help gain clarity. Because somewhere in all this, she was now ready.

To heal.

To love.

To give her heart one more chance to find her person. The one who made her truly complete.

Chapter Thirty-One

FISHER WAS LEANING AGAINST HIS TRUCK, WATCHING A seagull ride the breeze in easy loops over the dune, when the familiar sound of Nina's voice brought his attention back to the house.

"Fisher!" She jogged down the wooden steps from Rosemary's deck, barefoot, her hair loose and sun-kissed, her flip-flops dangling from one hand.

"Hey there." He straightened, taking in the sight of her. That easy, natural smile of hers always made something settle in his chest.

Nina swung her arms overhead, stretching. "Thanks for inviting me to breakfast."

"You ready?"

"Sure am. You know, I've been thinking about taking you up on that offer to surf again. It's been a million years, but you said it's like riding a bike and that you have an extra board. Be honest—do you think I'm too old to try?"

Fisher chuckled, shaking his head. "You? Too old? Not a chance. If *I'm* not too old, *you* definitely aren't. Besides, the ocean doesn't care how old we are. It just wants to see if we'll show up."

That earned him a grin. "Good answer."

Kendra came down the steps behind where Nina was standing, curiosity lighting her eyes. "Mom used to be a pretty good surfer, from what Grandma says."

Nina blushed. "I won a couple of trophies when I was a teenager."

Kendra looked at her mom as if seeing her in a new light. Then, her eyes wide with wonder, she glanced out at the waves. "Could *I* try it? I mean, if *you're* going to . . ."

Nina softened. "Yeah, honey. I always loved it at your age. I think you'd enjoy it. Tell you what. Fisher and I will talk about the possibility of lessons for both of us. That way, I don't try to show off and break something."

Kendra crossed her fingers on both hands and then crossed her arms. "Go, then. And hurry back."

Fisher drove them over to a new little crêpe shop that had opened up just for the summer. "Have you been here yet?"

"No, but it's cute," Nina said.

They ordered, and Fisher pressed his forearms to the table as he leaned in. "So, you're ready to surf with me, huh?"

"I believe so," she said. "A little nervous, but yeah, I want to surf with you."

"I like the sound of that." He rubbed his hands together. "I'm game. On one condition."

Nina arched a brow. "Oh? What's that?"

He smirked. "I get to give you your refresher lesson tonight. Just us. Sunset, quiet water . . . a little warm-up before we wrangle your teenager tomorrow."

Nina's cheeks pinked. "Are you getting flirty with me?"

"I sure hope I'm not so out of practice you can't tell." His gaze caught hers, and he thought if it hadn't been for the waitress reaching to set mugs of coffee between them, he might have leaned in and kissed her smiling lips.

"Then you have a deal."

Fisher didn't think he was imagining a wider-than-normal smile and glow on Nina this morning. That made him smile even bigger too.

They ate breakfast, and then he took her back to Rosemary's.

"Until tonight," he said.

"Yes, sir. Want me to meet you down at The Tackle Box?"

"No, I'm going to pick you up and take you to the lesson."

"All righty, then." She slid out of the truck seat and waved as she walked over to the door to her apartment downstairs.

As she disappeared inside, Fisher stayed parked for a beat, staring at the empty passenger seat as though it still held her warmth. He scrubbed a hand over his jaw, grinning like a fool. Tonight couldn't come fast enough. He'd spent a thousand sunsets on a board in the water in his lifetime, but he already knew tonight's would outshine them all.

Just him, Nina, the ocean, and the hope of something new.

The sun dipped low, casting gold and rose over the water as Fisher and Nina walked down to the beach at his favorite spot. She was barefoot, wearing cutoffs and a soft T-shirt knotted at the waist, and carrying a towel and a huge beach bag. She lit up when she saw the two chairs next to a firepit and then shot him a look.

She didn't know there was also a bottle of wine and snacks in a cooler. "Yes, that is for us, after sunset," he explained.

"I like the way you think, Fisher."

He took her beach bag from her and carried it the rest of the way, settling it on a blanket and dropping his T-shirt onto one of the chairs when he turned and noticed her wriggling out of her shorts to reveal her swimsuit. He averted his gaze and carried the two boards down to the water. She raced to catch up as he stuck both boards in the wet sand. Two longboards: the turtle as well as the old pelican board he'd told her about.

"Are you going to let me ride the turtle board or the pelican one?"

"Whichever pleases your heart."

Nina paused, taking a closer look at both boards. "You weren't kidding about the pelican, were you?"

He grinned. "Ugly as sin, but she rides smooth." He nudged it toward her. "I thought you might like to meet her."

She ran a hand along the faded paint. "She's got character."

"She's got soul. Like her rider."

She pressed a finger to her lips. "I think . . . she was meant for me, then." She laughed and the breeze lifted her hair as she waded out with the board next to Fisher.

He crouched and ran through the basics, his voice patient and sure, pointing to the foot placement, the paddle stroke, the balance shifts. "It'll come back to you."

And it did. Before long, Nina was right back in the rhythm—the pull of the water, the dance of balance and breath. Fisher felt a surge of pride as he watched her graceful movements.

"Look at you," he called as they paddled out together. "You didn't forget a thing."

"Liar," she teased.

"I don't know. You're lookin' pretty good. Are you sure we didn't date while I was in Hawaii, lady?"

"I'm pretty sure if that had occurred, I'd have remembered it."

"Yeah, me too. Come on, let's catch these next waves."

When they caught a small rolling wave, they rode it side by

side. Nina laughed, the sound ringing over the surf, and then they paddled out a little farther to wait for the next one.

"I honestly don't think I ever realized the peaceful part of surfing when I was a teen," she said. "This is heaven."

Their boards rocked gently in the quiet water, bumping softly as the waves settled into an easy rhythm. The sun dipped lower, spilling gold across the horizon, and for a moment, it felt like the whole world had slowed to hold its breath.

Fisher reached out, brushing a damp strand of hair from her cheek. His fingers lingered, memorizing the warmth of her skin. "Nina . . ." he said, his voice steady but full of wonder.

She lifted her gaze to his—no fear, no hesitation, just that quiet truth shining between them.

And then he kissed her. Slow, tender. The kind of kiss that didn't rush or demand but instead simply said, *This is real. This is the start of something good.* The ocean cradled them in its soft hush, the heartbeat of the tide the only witness.

When they parted, Nina touched his face, her smile soft, her cheeks pink with warmth. "That was . . . really nice."

"Nice?" Fisher grinned, his forehead resting against hers. "I was aiming for unforgettable."

Her laugh was light, delighted, as she lifted her feet behind her, her toes wiggling in the air. "Look—my toes are curling. That was the best kiss of my life."

He raised a brow. "Now, that sounds like flattery."

"It's not," she said, her voice full of certainty. "It's the truth."

"Only one way to be sure," Fisher murmured. He drew her close again. One hand found her cheek again, and this time his kiss was deeper, slower still. The kind that made the world fall away. A wave could've carried them all the way to shore and he wouldn't have noticed. He was already floating, held aloft by nothing but her and that moment.

Their boards rocked gently as they caught their breath, the

last kiss leaving them both a little giddy, a little breathless. Fisher let his hand glide from her cheek to steady her board.

"Well," he said, his grin easy, "I'd say that refresher lesson went better than I'd hoped."

Nina laughed softly, the sound like music in the salt-tinged air. "Better than *I* hoped. I didn't wipe out once."

"See? You've still got it," he teased. "But I think that's enough warm-up for tonight. Let's head in before the light's gone."

Together, they paddled toward shore, the boards gliding easily over the gentle swells. When they reached the sand, he helped her up, taking her hand as she stepped onto solid ground.

The last sliver of sun melted into the horizon, streaking the sky in pink and lavender. They stood there, barefoot in the cool sand, watching in comfortable silence as the day let go.

Without a word, Fisher walked a few steps ahead and knelt to light the small fire log he'd stashed near the dunes. Soon, a soft flame flickered to life, casting a golden glow around them.

Nina sank onto the sand, pulling her knees close, the warmth of the fire chasing off the evening's chill. Fisher settled beside her, close enough that their shoulders touched, their damp suits slowly drying in the heat.

"This was perfect," she said quietly, watching the flames dance.

Fisher smiled, content. "It was."

They lingered there, letting the night fall fully around them, the ocean's steady song the only sound beyond the crackle of the fire as Fisher opened the wine and they enjoyed the snacks. When the embers burned low, Fisher stood and offered his hand.

"Let's get these boards loaded before I have to carry *you* too," he joked, earning a playful nudge from Nina.

Together, they hauled the boards to the truck, storing them carefully. As they climbed in, the easy quiet between them felt like the start of something they both hoped for but hadn't dared name.

He drove her home and then carried the boards up to Rosemary's, next to Nina's door, safe for tomorrow's lesson.

"Thanks, Fisher," Nina said as they paused by the steps. "For everything tonight. I can't wait to see you tomorrow."

His smile was soft. "Anytime." He leaned and kissed her softly on the cheek.

The next morning on the beach, the wind off the ocean was crisp as Kendra stood beside her mom, eyeing the three surfboards Fisher had brought for them with wide-eyed excitement and a flicker of nerves.

"You sure about this?" Nina asked, ruffling her daughter's hair.

"Yeah. I want to try."

Fisher winked. "You're gonna love it."

They ran through the basics again, this time with Kendra mimicking the moves, giggling when she wobbled, proud when she got it right. The three of them paddled out together, Nina beaming at Kendra's determination.

After they finally came ashore, sandy and tired but grinning, Fisher leaned his board against the dune fence. "How about we make it a group thing tomorrow? I'll see if Amanda and the kids want in."

Kendra brightened. "That'd be awesome, but do we have to do it as early tomorrow?"

"No, I have a couple morning meetings I have to take, but we can make it a late-morning get-together," Nina said. "Does that work for you, Fisher?"

"Thank goodness," Kendra groaned.

Fisher nodded. "Works for me."

The next day, Fisher, Nina, and Kendra were carrying the boards over a dune when Amanda, Hailey, Jesse, and even Paul bounded out of Paul's truck and started dragging surfboards out of the back.

"Wait for us," Hailey called out.

This time, Nina, Amanda, and Paul sat in the sand with coffee, spectating.

The kids were overzealous but doing great. At one point, though, Fisher abandoned the lesson to just push all three of the kids around on the turtle board. Their squeals filled the air, and then they got back to the lesson.

Kendra had just attempted her first solo ride when Tug and Rosemary came down from the house. Tug carried his old surfboard under his arm, and Rosemary carried a lightweight Styrofoam one in bright lime green.

"Oh no," Fisher called. "Tug Basnight, are you crashing my surf lesson?"

"Crashing? I'm enhancing!" Tug boomed, grinning.

Rosemary waved. "I'm just here for moral support. I plan to keep my bum flat on this board the whole time."

But soon, Tug paddled out, caught a small wave with surprising grace, and then paddled over next to Rosemary. She sat on her board, laughing as he clasped her hand, steadying her while she wobbled in place.

Kendra ran up to get a towel. "Look at them, Mom." There was awe in her voice. "They look like otters. You know, how otters hold hands while they sleep so they don't float away from their mate. They mate forever, you know."

"They sure do."

Later, as the boards lay scattered in the sand and everyone stretched out in the sun, Fisher walked over to Tug who was watching the waves come in.

"Tug . . ." he began, unsure how to say it.

"Spit it out, kid." The older man raised a brow. "What's on your mind?"

Fisher hesitated again. "Do you think I am ready for all of this? For Nina. For Kendra. I don't want to let them down."

Tug clapped a hand on his shoulder, firm and reassuring. "Son, sometimes you gotta stop worryin' if you're good enough and just be good."

Fisher allowed the words to sink in, feeling their weight and their truth. The salt air filled his lungs, grounding him. Maybe the simple things were enough.

Soon, they all packed up, excitement on their sunscreen-smeared faces, eager to have another surfing adventure again soon. The kids teased and giggled their way over the dune with their surfboards.

As Fisher carried his boards back up the path, a quiet certainty settled over him that maybe he was right where he was meant to be.

Chapter Thirty-Two

THE DAYS CONTINUED TO PASS IN A WHIRLWIND OF SAWdust, sweat, and fast-growing feelings that Fisher stopped pretending didn't exist. It felt wild and free, like riding a bike with no hands.

But here he was, and he wasn't complaining about it.

He'd spent the evening at The Tackle Box, taking a break from another beach cleanup project he'd spearheaded with the church's summer-camp kids. It had been a solid week of hauling away old debris left from last year's hurricane, smoothing out the dunes, and getting the kids excited about taking care of their island. Giving back had always felt good to Fisher, but this year, it felt different. More personal. Not just a series of serving others but also taking part in and being part of something bigger. And he knew it was because of Nina.

Maybe Whelk's Island is starting to feel like home for her and Kendra too.

While finishing his checklist with the night shift and about to leave The Tackle Box, Fisher was interrupted by Paul, who knocked on the bar as he sidled up. "Hey, man, you free tomorrow?" Paul asked, glancing around at the improvements.

"Can be. What's up?"

Paul looked around. "Been a while since I've been in here. This place looks great."

"Thanks." Fisher looked proud. "Trying to keep my customers happy. That salt air is a bugger on this counter, so I decided to change it out to teak so it would do better in the open-air atmosphere."

"Smart. It works." Paul chuckled. "Well, I need a favor that has nothing to do with customers."

"Sure. What can I do for you?"

"I've got four new military working dogs flying in from overseas. They'll land in Charlotte tomorrow. I'm short a driver who can handle the dogs in case something goes sideways. You've gone with me before, so I hoped you wouldn't mind taking the lead in the second truck."

"Not at all." Fisher didn't even have to think twice. "Count me in."

Paul gave him a knowing look. "You've got a new swagger in your step these days. It's Nina, isn't it? It's written all over your face."

Fisher froze, halfway through wiping down the counter.

"So? What's the deal?" Paul prodded.

Fisher huffed a laugh, shaking his head. "You noticed something there, huh?"

"A blind man could notice it," Paul said with a wry grin.

Fisher exhaled, setting down the rag. "I'm still not quite sure where this could lead, but I do really like spending time with Nina. Kendra too."

Paul grinned. "Love can blindside you like that. Amanda had the same effect on me."

Fisher hesitated, running a hand through his hair. "Do you think they'll stay on Whelk's Island?"

Paul's expression was more serious now. "I don't know. You two haven't talked about it?"

"No. I've been afraid to ask." Fisher swallowed. "Maybe I don't want to know the answer."

"If you're falling in love with her, then you'd better ask, or at least let her know you hope she stays. Marriage is a gift. I didn't know what I was missing until Amanda. I only wish I'd found her sooner. Hey, you don't want to be like Tug and be an old man before you experience real love. I found it. Must be *your* turn now."

"What Tug's got going on with Rosemary is amazing."

Paul gave him a look. "I think the only thing that would make Rosemary happier is to see you in Nina and Kendra's life. I know it can be scary to take on someone else's child, but don't be afraid. Family has a way of being real no matter what the family tree looks like."

"Did you just"—Fisher squinted—"warn me I could lose the best thing I never had?"

"Pretty much. So get honest with her. Pronto, my man." Paul turned to leave. "I'll meet you at Paws at seven-thirty tomorrow morning to get on the road. Does that work for you?"

"Yeah. I'll be there." He watched Paul leave, knowing everything Paul had just said was right: He needed to protect his future with Nina. Because Fisher realized he wasn't afraid of letting someone in—he was more afraid she might walk away.

Fisher and Paul picked up the dogs in Charlotte and brought them to Paws Town Square, where they'd go through a two-week quarantine and a battery of tests to evaluate their condition.

Kendra was there when they arrived.

"Sorry, Kendra. No one gets to work with these guys until the veterinarian checks them out. They've had a long flight and been through some intense times."

"I understand," she said. "Hailey told me you used to work with these kinds of dogs when you were in the Marines."

"I did. These aren't just dogs. They're trained soldiers. An important part of our military, and heroes too."

"Maybe someday I can help train them."

"Maybe," Paul said. "You're doing a great job. I'm glad to have you working here." He glanced at Fisher, then added, "It'll be hard for us if you and your mom decide to go back to Pennsylvania."

"I hadn't thought about that," Kendra said, her mood dipping. "I have to go back there with my dad for a week soon. He's coming to get me for a visit, but then I'll be right back."

"Well, maybe you won't ever leave for good," Fisher added hopefully. "It would be great to have y'all as the newest residents of Whelk's Island."

"Yeah, that would be cool," Kendra said. Then she excused herself to get back to work.

Paul looked at Fisher, quiet until Kendra was out of earshot. "Okay, so you told the kid you want them to stick around. Now tell the woman who really handles the decision."

"Baby steps," Fisher said. "I don't get at least partial credit for baby steps?"

Nina was driving down the beach road when she saw the familiar black SUV in the driveway. David's. Had he really come to pick their daughter up as planned? Early, in fact, which was nice because she was sure Kendra had been watching the clock all day, waiting for him.

Nina's heart clenched when Kendra walked out of the house, gave David her bags, and climbed into the vehicle. There had been so much tension the last time he'd been here.

David shut the hatch on the SUV, then got into the car and eased out of the driveway. Kendra waved frantically from the passenger seat, her face bright with happiness. He caught Nina's gaze and lifted a hand in a small wave before focusing back on the road. She wanted to jump out of her car and give Kendra a hug, but they kept cruising on down the road.

She felt dismissed, and even though Kendra wasn't yet out of the neighborhood, Nina missed her. Nina's working from home and spending all this time with Kendra had really strengthened their relationship. So much so that Nina had already started talking to her manager about working remotely long term.

She parked and pulled her keys from the ignition, barely having time to process her thoughts before a truck rumbled into the driveway behind her.

Fisher.

She turned, her pulse skipping as he stepped out, his usual easygoing smile in place.

"Look at that," he mused, nodding toward the SUV. "She looked happy."

"She did," Nina murmured, still watching the road like she couldn't quite believe it. Then, glancing back at him, she added, "I hope she has fun and they can patch up the divide between them."

Fisher grinned, rocking back on his heels. "And you have a little alone time on your hands. How do you feel about that?"

Something about the way he was looking at her made warmth rise to her cheeks.

He shoved his hands into his pockets. "Well, now that you've got a free evening . . ." His smile turned mischievous. "I hope you don't already have plans."

"Depends," Nina said, crossing her arms. "What did you have in mind?"

His eyes flickered with something playful. "A beach picnic."

She tilted her head. "A picnic? That's your big idea?"

"Oh, ye of little faith," he said with a dramatic sigh. "Trust me, this isn't just any picnic."

"And when is this little shindig going to take place?"

"Let's synchronize our watches," Fisher said.

Nina laughed. "You do know our phones are already synced, right?"

"You're no fun. Fine, I'll pick you up at five."

"I'll be ready."

At exactly 4:55 P.M., Fisher stood at Nina's door, holding a bouquet so large that it nearly hid his grin. The wildflowers were a riot of color, fresh and fragrant, as if he'd tried to bring the whole meadow to her.

Nina's breath caught. "Fisher . . . these are beautiful."

He handed them over, a little sheepish. "Might've gotten carried away."

Rosemary appeared in the doorway, her eyes twinkling with warmth as she took in the scene.

"Well, aren't *you* thoughtful," she said, giving Fisher a knowing nod that somehow made the grand gesture feel exactly right. "Let's get these in water so Nina can enjoy them later."

Nina shot her mother a grateful look, her heart swelling at the quiet way Mom saw the goodness in this man too.

Nina pressed her lips together, hoping they could hold in the laugh. The last thing she wanted to do was hurt his feelings.

"We'll see you later, Mom." Nina and Fisher walked out to his truck and got on the road. "Where are we headed?"

"It's a surprise."

She settled back in her seat. No sense ruining his desire to surprise her.

He pulled into the driveway of a lovely home at the far north end of the beach. The nice end. Farther down than Tug's house, where the more elite residents built their homes.

He came around and opened her door.

"What's this?" she asked as she stepped out.

"One of my favorite places."

"I can see why. It's beautiful. I love that art piece in the front."

He glanced over at the lighthouse made of driftwood. "Me too."

They walked along a private path to the beach lined in luxury vinyl fencing.

"It offers one of the best views around," he said.

They reached the top of the dune, where another driftwood-sculpture piece, of a pelican, was on a post. Next to it, a wind sock fluttered in brilliant shades of blue, the thin material ruffling in the breeze.

Nina spotted the setup of a picnic spread below. A large red beach blanket stretched out over the sand, anchored by a cooler and two sky-blue beach chairs. Along one edge of the blanket, a blow-up inner tube with the center filled with ice had a bottle of wine propped in the middle and a couple of covered trays filling in the rest. Candles flickered inside mason jars, casting a golden glow.

She arched a brow. "Did you plan this all by yourself?"

"Absolutely." Fisher led her to the blanket and offered her a seat before uncorking the bottle of wine. "I even brought chilled glasses that will keep the wine cold."

"Nice touch." She picked up one, turning it in her fingers. "You went all out, huh?"

"Nothing but the best." He poured her a glass. "And before you say anything, yes, I also brought an assortment of gourmet snacks." He lifted the lid off a container, revealing cheeses, crackers, and fresh fruit.

"And yet I saw you eat a gas-station hot dog last week."

He put a hand over his chest. "That was different. That was survival."

"I have never put hot dogs and survival in the same category." She laughed, sipping her wine.

For a while, they ate and talked as the sky melted into deep purples and blues. Nina loved feeling so at ease.

Then Fisher leaned back on his elbows, watching her with an unreadable expression.

"You know," he said, "you are kind of terrible at letting people take care of you."

Nina blinked. "Excuse me?"

He smirked. "You heard me."

She rolled her eyes. "I take care of myself just fine."

"Oh, I know," he said. "But that doesn't mean you have to."

His words settled deep, nudging something inside her. She looked away, watching the waves. "That's a hard thing for me."

"I know," he said. "But I'm patient."

"Oh yeah?"

"Yeah." Fisher leaned in, his voice low. "I'm also persistent."

Nina met his gaze, her heart pounding. The wind tugged at her hair, and Fisher reached out, tucking a loose strand behind her ear.

She felt it then. A shift of clarity had come over her in a wave. *I can't risk losing this man. I've never been this happy.*

"I like you, Nina. A lot. You don't have to respond. I just want you to know without a single doubt where my head is. And my heart." He exhaled slowly.

"I like being here with you," she said, wishing so much they would share another kiss.

"This picnic was sort of impromptu."

"It was. What if I'd been busy? I mean, I am working remotely, you know."

"Then I would've wasted a lot of time on this. I knew it was a risk, but I'm glad that wasn't the case. But it makes me want to ask you on a real proper date. Would you, Nina, go out with me tomorrow night? After work hours?"

"I'd love that."

"Me too." He paused. "I'm working on something."

"Is it for me?"

He grinned. "It is. But you'll have to wait and see."

Chapter Thirty-Three

An actual date. Nina followed Fisher along the narrow trail toward the old lighthouse at the point. Mom had told her about how she and Tug had gone there on one of her famous bucket-list trips. And now Mom and Tug had added an entire list of lighthouses along the East Coast to visit.

Lighthouses had never been on Nina's list of things to see, but she now realized she would go just about anywhere with Fisher.

It was still a while before sunset, but there were already streaks of tangerine and an incredible shade of pink across the sky. Last night's beach picnic had lingered in her mind long after she'd closed her eyes to go to sleep. She'd dreamed about how this evening might go too.

She'd thought that after her nasty divorce from David, she'd be just a solo adventurer for the rest of her life. Tonight she felt like part of a couple, and that made her feel special. The way Fisher had insisted on taking her on a proper date, something for just the two of them, had been a lovely gesture.

Anticipation had driven her thoughts. It had been a hard day to concentrate on work.

The lighthouse stood before them, its towering black-and-white structure weathered by years of watching over this coast.

The black iron railing circled the top, waiting for when the beacon would flicker to life once more.

"Have you ever climbed to the top of a lighthouse?" Fisher asked, tilting his head toward the spiral staircase just inside the entrance.

"Never," Nina said. "I've seen images of this one before. It's taller than it looks in the pictures."

"Well, then," he said, pushing open the heavy wooden door, "tonight's your lucky night. I'm friends with the park ranger who manages this one, and we have permission to go on up even though it's close to closing time."

"Really? You planned this ahead of time?"

"I did."

As they climbed the metal spiral staircase, its clang echoed and the narrow steps made her dizzy. Halfway up, she stumbled, her foot slipping on the uneven tread. Fisher's warm hand closed around hers. The touch steadied her, and she felt the certainty in his moves.

"Whoa, there," he murmured, his thumb brushing over her knuckles before releasing her. The touch was brief, but that fleeting moment caused her heart to tick quicker.

By the time they reached the top and stepped into the open air, she was winded. "I need to get back in shape," she said. "I have to say, I'm surprised Mom and Tug climbed this and plan to visit a bunch of them. This is a hard climb."

"Everything is easier and more fun when you're together and in love."

Nina questioned whether their conversation still centered on Mom and Tug.

At the top, they stood and looked out at the Atlantic Ocean.

"Wow. Do you make this climb often?" she asked, pressing her hands to her hips as she took in the breathtaking view.

"Often enough," Fisher said, watching the waves below.

"Sometimes I like to remind myself what it feels like to stand at the edge of the world."

The sea breeze whipped Nina's hair as she leaned on the railing, her arms spread wide, her laughter carefree. "Like this?" she teased, tilting her head back and shouting into the vastness, "I'm king of the world!"

She looked over to see Fisher watching her with amusement.

"You could be the queen of *my* world," he said without the slightest hint of teasing. "I've admired your resilience and ability to remain composed despite life's recent challenges. But here and now, I'm blown away by your willingness to throw your arms open wide to let me in and share this with you."

She stilled, and her hands lowered as she turned to face him. The weight of what he'd said felt like a welcome hug: unexpected, steady, and impossible to ignore.

A smile played on her lips. "That's a dangerous offer, Fisher."

He held her gaze, a slow grin tugging at the corner of his mouth. "I'm willing to risk it."

Her heart spun as she hoped that what she'd dared to only dream of might come true.

She turned toward the horizon, the vast stretch of ocean churning beneath them. Twilight threatened the sky. The air felt fresh, and she felt almost weightless and so alive with possibilities.

"It's beautiful here," she said.

Fisher leaned against the railing, his gaze soft. "It's got its stories."

"Do tell."

He glanced at her, then back at the ocean. "This lighthouse has been here for over a hundred years. The keeper back then—Samuel Harrison—was said to be one of the last true wickies. His family lived in the cottage below, but one night during a brutal storm, he was the only one left on the island to tend the flame. They say he worked through the night burning every drop of oil he had to keep ships safe."

Nina felt the nip in the air as the sun dropped lower.

"When the storm passed, the sailors made it home. But Samuel?" Fisher's voice lowered. "Some say he never left. That he still keeps watch, sending signs to guide those who feel lost."

Nina arched a brow. "What kind of signs?"

Fisher smiled, slow and sure. "Here on Whelk's Island, folks say if you're meant to find your way, you'll come across a shell with a message inside. Some people think the placement of those shells is actually Samuel's doing—still keeping ships off the rocks, only now it's hearts he watches over too."

Nina's breath caught. "Does everybody who comes to Whelk's Island find a shell? Because Mom found one, and so did Kendra and I."

"No, it's less frequent than one would imagine." His gaze met hers, steady. "But in your case, you, your mom, and Kendra, maybe the whole family, were meant to be here all along."

"Do you believe in that legend? That the shells land in the right people's hands at the right time?" she asked, skepticism lacing her voice.

He shrugged. "I've lived here long enough to know that some things don't need an explanation."

As the first glimmer of light flickered to life in the tower beside them, casting its glow out into the deep blue sea, Nina didn't know about those legends, but she knew this was where she was supposed to be right now.

Maybe it wasn't the lighthouse that guided lost ships home. Maybe it was the simple act of having someone standing in the tower, keeping watch, never giving up hope.

And wasn't that what Fisher had been doing for her? Standing steady. Waiting. Watching over her and Kendra. Never pushing.

Just being there.

"I hope you never let me down," she said. She hadn't meant for the words to surface. Her heart just let the fear roll right off her tongue.

He stepped closer, his eyes as warm as the last light of day. The breeze tugged at his shirt, but he didn't seem to notice. "I won't," he said quietly.

For a moment, they stood together in the hush of the evening, the beacon's glow sweeping across the water like a silent blessing.

Fisher reached for her hand, linking their fingers gently. "Let's stay up here just a little longer," he said quietly, as if speaking too loudly might break the spell.

Nina nodded, her heart steadying in the safety of his closeness. They stood side by side, watching the horizon blur into night, no need for more words.

Chapter Thirty-Four

THE RESTAURANT WAS A SURPRISE. LOCATED IN THE NEXT town over, it was unlike anything Nina had expected. Fisher had kept the destination a secret, saying only, "Trust me," which had made it all the more exciting. No man had ever made the effort to surprise her.

And now, sitting at a table on a wooden deck overlooking the marina—with the aroma of butter, garlic, and fresh seafood filling the air—she had to admit Fisher had outdone himself.

"This is beautiful." Boats bobbed lazily at the dock beneath an inky sky full of stars that didn't even look real.

Fisher reached for his drink. "You sound surprised."

A candle flickered on the table, casting a golden glow between them. "I didn't expect you to be the candlelight-dinner type."

He tilted his head. "You think I only do bonfires and wine?"

"Well, it seems more your speed," she teased.

"I do like bonfires." He cut into his grilled swordfish. "I have many sides, and I can't wait to share them all with you. I'm enjoying learning all the facets of *you* too."

"I guess we bring that out in each other." Nina's insides swirled at the thought. They seemed good together. She took a sip of her iced tea. "So, tell me, Mister-I-am-so-complex-and-have-so-many-sides, what do you dream of?"

Fisher set his fork down, considering the question. "I think I'm living the dream right now."

"This? You don't want more?"

He shook his head, something steady and sure in his eyes. "I used to think all I needed was to keep my head down and do good work. Serve others. Carry on my quiet existence. You've changed all that."

She swallowed, his words settling deep. "How?"

"I can picture more with you. Sunsets, travel, trying new things. Maybe working less and playing more." He twisted his glass. "What about you? What's *your* dream?"

Nina hesitated, feeling exposed. "I don't know," she admitted. "For so long, I thought my dream was to build a strong marriage–something lasting, solid. I wanted a big, successful career, and I got that, but it ended up feeling like just another box to check. And, of course, having Kendra was a real milestone. But when my marriage started to unravel, I realized I wasn't sure what I truly wanted anymore."

Fisher watched her, quiet but engaged. "And now?"

She exhaled, looking out at the water. "Now I think I just want peace. A simpler existence. A life where I'm not constantly off-kilter and failing at something. Or maybe it's not even the fear of failing–it's having to do it all alone."

"You're not failing, Nina." His voice was low, firm. "You're figuring it out."

Her throat tightened. "I feel like I should have already figured it out."

Fisher shook his head. "Who told you life has deadlines?"

"Everything has a deadline. My whole work life is about deadlines." The thought pushed a button that made her feel vulnerable. She dabbed her napkin at the corner of her eye. "I think I've been trying to manage my job and child-rearing the same way."

"Well, I hate to break it to you, but your personal life isn't as predictable as a project." He lifted his glass. "But I know you'll always give everything you do, everything you've got. It's in your DNA. I like that about you. And knowing your mom and daughter—that gives me a pretty good line of sight into how you operate."

"It does. Do you think you can handle three generations of feisty, capable redheaded women?" She grinned, clinking her glass against his.

"It would be my biggest and most satisfying challenge."

They finished dinner, enjoying the view and the fancy treatment of the fine establishment. As they stood to leave, Nina stepped close and Fisher reached out, brushing something from her cheek.

The touch lingered. Nina felt the moment hanging between them, her pulse skipping. She could feel the warmth of his fingers, the gentle calluses on his fingertips.

Then, just as quickly, he pulled away, clearing his throat. "It was an eyelash. Want to make a wish?"

"You bet." She squeezed her eyes tight and wished with every tiny piece of her heart.

As they walked toward his truck, a quiet certainty settled over her. This wasn't just another dinner—this was a turning point. Something real was continuing to unfold between them. Something special she wasn't sure she could stop, even if she wanted to.

At the passenger door, Fisher hesitated, his hand resting on the handle. His eyes met hers in the low light, steady and sure.

"Thank you for tonight," she said softly.

Fisher's slow, easy grin always made her heart flutter. "My pleasure. I meant it, Nina. I can picture us together and a lot more nights like this." He opened the door, but before she could climb in, his hand found hers. Just for a moment. Just enough to let her feel his warmth.

"I'm not going anywhere," he said.

Her chest tightened in the sweetest way. "I'm glad."

And as he helped her into the truck, she knew that whatever came next, she wouldn't be facing it alone.

Chapter Thirty-Five

As Fisher drove down the quiet coastal road back to Whelk's Island with Nina next to him, the reality of the evening he had just spent with her weighed on him.

I'm falling for her. Hard.

He gripped the steering wheel, sneaking a glance at her. She was staring out the window, the ocean stretching out on their right, moonlight glinting off the surface. He wished he knew what she was thinking.

Was she, too, hoping the night wouldn't end? He wanted to keep talking and get to know her more.

Fisher exhaled, adjusting his grip on the wheel. He could feel the tension crackling between them. Not the kind that made you uncomfortable. No, this was the kind that settled deep in your chest, making you ache in the best way.

By the time he pulled into Rosemary's driveway, the air inside the truck was thick and charged. He put the vehicle in park and turned in the seat toward her. She didn't move to get out. Her fingers rested on the door handle, but she didn't open it. Would she just thank him for a nice evening and go inside?

She faced him, her eyes searching his. "Fisher . . ." she whispered.

And that was all it took.

He leaned in, already familiar with the way her breath caught just before their lips met. This wasn't new, but it was still tender territory.

Their kiss was warm and unhurried—less a question this time and more of a promise. Her fingers curled into his shirt, holding on like she didn't want to let go. That was answer enough for Fisher.

He deepened the kiss slightly, letting it linger, one hand at the side of her face, the other resting gently on her leg, anchoring them to this moment. Nina sighed against his mouth, a soft sound that said she wanted this too, whatever this was.

When he finally drew back, he rested his forehead against hers, both of them catching their breath.

"That was . . ." he began, then chuckled low. "Even better than the last time."

Nina brushed her thumb across his collarbone. "It was. I think we're getting the hang of this."

Fisher pulled back just enough to study her face. "We don't have to know what comes next. I just want to be someone who gets to be there, wherever it leads."

She looked at him then—really looked—and nodded. "*I* want that too. I just . . . I don't know what staying looks like. Kendra's still figuring things out. So am I."

"I know," he said quietly. "And I'm not going anywhere. We'll face whatever comes, together."

Her fingers lingered at the edge of his jaw, then dropped to her lap. "Okay," she whispered. "Side by side."

He kissed her again, just once more, sweet and sure.

Her phone rang, the unexpected sound slicing through the moment. She pulled it from her purse, glancing at the screen. "I'm sorry. It's Kendra. I'd better take this."

"Of course." Fisher leaned away, trying to give her some space.

"Hey, sweetheart." Nina tucked her hair behind her ear. "Everything okay?"

"Yeah! I just wanted to say hi. We went to a pizza place, and Dad let me drive in the parking lot after. I didn't hit anything. I was pretty good. Well, sort of."

Nina pressed a grateful hand to her chest. "That's pretty cool. How's it going with Charlotte?" Nina raised her crossed fingers and looked hopefully toward Fisher.

"She apologized." There was a pause, and then Kendra added, "I miss Paws, though. And the island. It's weird, but I kinda can't wait to get back."

Fisher's heart kicked a little at that.

"Oh yeah?" Nina asked casually, but he could hear the same hope stirring in her voice.

"Yeah. I mean, Dad's trying. It's been nice, but it doesn't feel like home, you know?"

Fisher held still, absorbing those words. *Home.* She thought of Whelk's Island as home. That meant something. That meant everything.

"Well, I'll be here waiting when you get back," Nina said.

"Yeah," Kendra said, and then she paused. "Hey, Mom?"

"Yeah?"

Kendra let out a long breath. "Are you happy?"

Fisher's breath caught at Kendra's question. Simple, honest, and somehow it struck deeper than any moment all night. Something flickered across Nina's expression, and he held his breath to see what her answer would be.

She glanced at him, then answered Kendra's question. "I am, sweetheart."

Fisher felt the unexpected tightness in his throat relax.

Kendra made a small noise of approval. "Good. You deserve that."

"Thanks, honey." She hung up, and the significance of the conversation lingered in the air between them.

"She wants to come back," Fisher murmured, more to himself than anything.

"Yes, she does. But I'm glad things are going okay at David's," she said. "She needs that too."

Fisher reached over, brushing a thumb against the back of her hand. "That means there's a chance you could stay on Whelk's Island?"

She hesitated, looking up at him.

"Is it a possibility? Maybe?" he said, hoping to let her know how overjoyed that would make him.

A hesitant "Probably" escaped her lips. Her words were soft, but they were sincere enough to have his pulse riding high like a swell at dawn. "Then I guess that means we need to make some plans."

Nina laughed. "Oh? And what exactly are these big plans?"

He grinned, shifting back into easy conversation. "You'll see. But first, how do you feel about a little festival next week when Kendra gets home?"

Nina tilted her head. "A festival?"

"Outdoor arts-and-crafts festival," Fisher clarified. "Food vendors, live music, overpriced pottery, and some food that isn't considered survival food in your world. You know—the works."

She smiled. "That sounds perfect."

Fisher reached for her hand again, squeezing it once before letting go.

"Great," he said, "because I'd like to take you both. I've been going to it for years, and I'm excited to share it with you."

She gave a little nod, her gaze steady with his. "Then it's a date."

He watched her walk inside, certainty settling deep in his bones. She might not realize it yet, but he was all in. Ready to build their future together one careful step at a time.

Chapter Thirty-Six

THE FESTIVAL WAS ALREADY IN FULL SWING BY THE TIME Fisher pulled up to the entrance, with Nina in the passenger seat and Kendra in the back. She'd been home for just a day, but it was already clear she wasn't the same girl she was when she first arrived on Whelk's Island, burdened so heavily with anger and uncertainty. The time away with her dad had done something—maybe settled some things in her heart.

"I missed this place," she said.

Fisher had been meeting with Paul at Paws when he witnessed the way Kendra seemed to sigh with relief when she walked in for her first shift back, and how she had hugged Rosemary a little longer than usual that night.

She belonged here. And he hoped Nina believed that too.

"Hope you're ready for something special," he said as he climbed out of the truck, then tucked his hands into his pockets.

Nina shot him a teasing look. "You've been hyping this up all morning. I'll be the judge of how special it is."

"Oh, it's good," he promised. "And I've got a surprise for you."

She arched a brow. "You and your surprises."

"Mom used to hate surprises," Kendra said.

Fisher feigned offense. "You could have told me that sooner. What kind of friend are you?"

"A super-duper one," Kendra quipped, earning a chuckle from both of them.

"Yes, you are." He motioned toward the far end of the festival. "Come on, I'll show you."

They weaved through the winding paths of the festival, past booths filled with pottery, paintings, and woven baskets. He took a deep breath, trying to shake the nerves that had crept up on him. He wasn't embarrassed about his interests, but sharing this part of himself felt like a big deal.

As they neared the sculpture exhibit, a voice called out. "Fisher?"

He turned to see a familiar older man wearing an Outer Banks Art Festival staff badge approaching with a wide smile.

"I thought that was you," the man said, clapping him on the shoulder. "Your driftwood sculptures are incredible, as always. That horse of yours? Unbelievable."

Fisher felt his face heat. "Thanks, sir."

Kendra, who had barely been paying attention before, suddenly snapped her gaze toward him. "Wait. *Your* horse? You did those sculptures in that booth?"

Fisher shifted his weight, feeling a little self-conscious. "Yeah. Driftwood's like nature's puzzle. Every piece of wood's been carried by the water, smoothed by sand over time, waiting to fit into the right spot. I just . . . help it find where it belongs."

Nina's eyes gleamed with amusement. "And you weren't going to tell us?"

He glanced down, his voice soft but sure. "That booth, that sign—it's not meant to impress anybody. It's just there because I need the reminder. Keeps me steady. That gratitude's what keeps a man from drifting too far."

For a second, the playful air shifted and Kendra looked at him differently, like she saw more of him than she had before.

The festival staffer chuckled. "Don't let him fool you. He's the highlight every year. Come on, show your friends."

Nina folded her arms, tilting her head at Fisher. "Yes, do show your friends, Fisher."

Fisher's ears pinked. "All right, all right."

They turned the corner into the exhibition space, where the driftwood horse stood at the center, life-size and as if frozen mid-stride. Each piece of sun-bleached wood curved and joined like it had always belonged there: weathered, worn, and woven with the other pieces by unseen hands of tide and wind before Fisher ever touched it. The kind of art that felt grown rather than made.

Kendra stopped short, her mouth falling open. "This is insane. You created this?"

Nina's voice was hushed. "Fisher . . . it's incredible. Like it has its own soul."

He shrugged, shifting his weight. "Told you I was handy."

"This isn't handy. This is art!" Nina corrected, shaking her head. "And this style, it looks incredibly like the sculptures on the property where you took me for that picnic."

"Because they're mine," he admitted. "Those are a little older, but, yeah, the same hands built them."

Kendra turned to him with sudden determination. "Teach me how to do this."

Fisher blinked. "What?"

"This," Kendra said, motioning toward the sculptures. "I want to learn."

He chuckled. "Not so fast, kid. You can't just jump straight into building a life-size horse."

"Why not?"

"Because first," he said, crossing his arms, "you need materials. You can't just go to a store and buy driftwood, not the kind that's good for sculpting. You have to collect it, piece by piece."

Kendra hesitated, then turned to her mom. "Can I?"

"Of course. But if you're going to start a collection, it has to be stacked neatly just outside the gate at Mom's house," Nina said.

Fisher chuckled. "You hear that? No rogue driftwood piles."

Kendra rolled her eyes. "Fine. Neatly stacked. Got it."

"Good, because you're gonna need a lot before we even think about building something," Fisher explained.

Kendra thought for a moment, then smirked. "So . . . if I stack wood outside the gate for a project, does that mean we're staying?"

The question must've caught Nina off guard, because she stilled.

Fisher glanced at her, his heart pounding. This was it. This was the moment when it all fell into place. Kendra wasn't just asking to learn something new—she was asking if Whelk's Island was home. And he knew right then he didn't want only Nina—he wanted *them*.

Nina inhaled, then reached out, brushing a strand of hair from Kendra's face. "I'm still working on it, sweetheart."

Fisher's chest tightened as he wondered what exactly Nina meant by that.

"When do you think you'll know?" Kendra asked.

"I'm not sure, honey. I need some time to think it over. Hey, how about we get some lunch?"

"Okay. I'm kind of starving," Kendra said, and Fisher said he was ready to eat too.

They grabbed lunch from a seafood stall and found a spot in the shade. As they ate, Nina kept sneaking glances at him, curiosity written all over her face.

"So," she said, setting down her drink. "How'd you get into this? Driftwood sculpting isn't a common hobby."

Fisher leaned back, swirling the lemonade in his cup. "Guess you could say I stumbled into it."

She frowned. "Stumbled?"

He took a breath. "The year after my dad died, I wasn't handling it well. Talked very little. Didn't go out much. Was just sort of going through the motions."

Kendra looked down at her plate. "I'm sorry you lost your dad," she said with a tenderness that touched him.

"Thank you, Kendra." He looked at his hands and then gathered his response. "One day, I came across a driftwood sculpture in a magazine. It was of a sailboat. Someone had built it on a beach somewhere. That picture captivated me. I tore it out of the magazine and hung it on my wall."

"Do you still have the picture?" Kendra asked.

"I do. It's framed in one of my rentals." He looked at Nina. "At the driftwood house."

"That one," Nina said, remembering.

"That's cool," Kendra said. "I want to see it."

"I studied the way the wood fit together. No nails. No forcing anything. Just balance, patience, and a lot of time. Driftwood's been on a journey already–rivers, oceans, storms–and somehow it still has more to give. I think that's what hooked me."

Nina's lips parted.

"I know it sounds crazy, but I just felt like I could do it, so I did."

"No, it makes sense," Kendra said.

Nina nodded in agreement.

"Temptation led me to try it," Fisher continued. "It took me three years to finish my first big piece. It wasn't nearly the size of the horse, though."

Kendra pointed at him with her fork. "Three years of anything is a commitment."

"Yeah, well, I almost lost the horse when Hurricane Edwina came knocking. I had to rebuild a good chunk of him."

"But you did," Nina said, watching him closely.

"Yep. And now? You can't even see where I patched him back together," Fisher said. "Given enough time, things find their way back to good as new."

Something flickered in Kendra's expression. "Sometimes better than new, even."

And Fisher knew this wasn't just about the sculpture anymore.

As they lingered over lunch, the warm air thick with the sweet-and-salty smell of kettle corn, Fisher glanced at Nina. She was watching Kendra with the most peaceful look on her face.

He really hoped they were staying on Whelk's Island. It was time for him to stop being careful.

He'd waited for weeks with unwavering resolve, letting things unfold in their own time. But seeing Nina here now—her shoulders looser, her laughter easier—he knew he couldn't risk losing her or this feeling.

A person could shape driftwood into something whole again, piece by piece, tested and worn by the waves but made beautiful by the journey. But love? Now he understood a genuine love was like that, too, and you had to hold on to it before the tide carried it away.

It was time. Time to stop hoping they might have a future and start showing her why she could trust him with hers.

Chapter Thirty-Seven

FISHER WASN'T EXPECTING COMPANY THAT AFTERNOON. He was behind the bar at The Tackle Box, checking the inventory, when he heard someone come in. It was Kendra. The first time Kendra had walked into The Tackle Box alone, she'd been looking for trouble.

She strode toward him, her bike helmet still strapped to her head, her expression serious. "I need your help."

Fisher crossed his arms, feigning suspicion. "Remember that time you came in here and I had to drive you home because your mom was so shaken?"

She rolled her eyes. "That was different. This is important."

He raised a brow. "All right, let's hear it."

She hesitated for half a second, then blurted, "Mom's birthday is coming up. I know something I want to make for her, but I need your help."

He leaned back against the counter. "That so?"

Kendra stuffed her hands into the pockets of her hoodie. "Yeah. I thought maybe you could help me build something real cool."

That was unexpected. "Build what?"

Her answer came without hesitation. "A giant dolphin."

Fisher let out a short laugh. "A giant dolphin?"

She nodded, dead serious.

"Well," he said, rubbing the back of his neck, "I hate to break it to you, kid, but unless your mom's birthday is in about six months, I don't think we've got the time for that. Plus, I'm not sure where she'd put it."

"Yeah." Kendra's face fell slightly, but she nodded, chewing on her lip.

Fisher thought for a moment, then offered, "What about a driftwood bowl? Something pretty she can use to hold the shells she collects. Or for her jewelry."

Her expression brightened. "That's a great idea. It would be perfect for shells. You're so smart."

He smirked. "I have my moments."

She hesitated again, then added, "There's something else."

Fisher waited.

"Will you come to the party?" she asked, shifting her weight from foot to foot. "Grandma's making her favorite cake, and Tug said he knows how to make homemade ice cream. He and Grandma even went to pick peaches for it."

Fisher studied her. "Did you just invite me?"

She hesitated, then looking hopeful, said, "Yeah."

That meant something. "Then I won't miss it."

Kendra grinned. "Thanks!"

He pulled a plastic tote bag from under the counter. "First things first, you need materials. I want you to collect pieces of driftwood about this size." He held his hands about twelve inches apart. "Nothing too big, nothing too small. You're gonna need a good mix of smooth and textured pieces to make it interesting. Fill this up and meet me back here tomorrow."

She took the bag, her excitement barely contained. "I can do that."

"I figured."

And with that, she was off, hopping onto her bike and riding away with purpose.

The next afternoon, while setting up his workspace behind The Tackle Box, Fisher heard Kendra's bike tires making their familiar skidding sound on the oyster-shell sand.

He poked his head out. She dismounted the bike and hurried to him, carrying a huge bag that had been swaying from her handlebars. He realized there were at least two huge pieces of driftwood on the ground behind the bike. It looked like she'd dragged them behind her by tying them with wide red ribbon, probably something she'd found in Rosemary's Christmas boxes. "I got the driftwood!"

She was creative—he had to give her that. "I wouldn't recommend dragging wood behind your bike. That ribbon or whatever it is could get caught in the chain."

"Oh. Yeah." She clenched her teeth. "I didn't think of that."

Fisher took the bag and peeked inside. He pulled out a few pieces of the wood. Some were perfect, some were way too small, and a couple were more like twigs than driftwood.

"Hate to break it to you, kid, but some of these aren't sturdy enough. And those big pieces you've got behind the bike are way too big for this project."

Kendra groaned. "I thought they were cool."

"Oh, they *are* cool. Just not for a bowl. More for, I don't know, building a raft?"

She rolled her eyes. "Fine. I'll get better at picking, but I'm saving them for my gigantic sculpture someday."

"Great. It takes practice." Fisher sorted through the rest of her haul. "All right, these'll work. Let's lay them out and see what we've got."

Settling at the workbench, they arranged the driftwood in a circle. Fisher grabbed a few clamps to hold the base pieces together. "First step, forming the bottom. You want it to be solid so it holds up."

Kendra watched as he showed her how to sand down the rougher edges, making sure the pieces would fit together snugly. "Now we'll start stacking smaller ones on top, weaving them in and out to give it some depth."

Kendra mimicked his movements, picking out different textures and colors. "This is kinda fun," she said.

"Told you."

Once she arranged the pieces, Fisher showed her how to secure them with wood glue and tiny finishing nails. "The goal is to make it seem natural, as if the ocean sculpted it without effort."

Kendra ran a hand over the half-formed bowl. "What can we do to prevent it from scratching the table? Mom freaks out if I even forget to use a coaster."

Fisher grinned. "Smart question." He pulled some soft leather strips from his toolbox. "We'll attach these underneath. They'll give it a nice finish and keep your mom's furniture safe."

Kendra helped him fasten the leather pads. They stepped back to admire their work.

"It's perfect," she whispered.

"One last thing." Fisher handed her a small engraving tool. "You need to sign it. Every artist signs their work."

Kendra hesitated, then etched her initials and the date on the underside of the bowl. She ran her fingers over it, a small smile playing on her lips. "It's my first official piece."

"Won't be your last," Fisher said.

Kendra beamed. "I can't wait to give it to her."

Fisher watched as she packed it up. "She's gonna love it."

With that, Kendra hopped back on her bike, riding off toward home, her excitement palpable.

Fisher leaned against the workbench, watching as Kendra's bike disappeared down the road.

The afternoon sun slanted through the trees, catching on the little scraps of driftwood scattered across the table. He reached for them, moving his fingers without thinking, fitting pieces together the way he always did: trusting his eye, letting the wood tell him what it wanted to be. The workbench creaked against his weight as he clamped two pieces together.

A smooth sun-bleached curve became the top of the heart. A darker salt-worn shard cradled the base. A narrow strip, with its natural swirl, bridged the two sides like it had been made for that spot.

He worked slowly, shaping as he went, letting the textures and lines guide him. The result wasn't fancy, it wasn't polished, but it was real: a small rustic heart that looked like it had grown that way, born of tide and time.

Fisher turned it over in his hands, running his thumb along the edges where the pieces of driftwood met, where nature's story joined with his own.

"Didn't mean to make this," he murmured to no one, his voice low, reverent. "But it sort of made itself, like it was waiting for me to see it."

A slow, satisfied smile spread across his face as he set the piece aside. He was already imagining Nina's face when he gave it to her.

Something so simple, yet it said everything he didn't know how to say out loud.

He thumbed the grain of the wood once more, then wrapped the heart in a scrap of soft cloth and slipped it into his pocket. A quiet promise resting close.

Chapter Thirty-Eight

As Nina approached the front porch, she couldn't help but notice the festive decorations adorning the entrance. Long strands of seashells were interwoven with twinkling fairy lights and a handcrafted sign that read, "Happy Birthday, Nina!" in elegant calligraphy.

Pushing open the door, she was immediately enveloped by the comforting aroma of Mom's macadamia-nut-encrusted pound cake. *My childhood favorite.*

The living room buzzed with laughter and cheerful chatter. Tug, with that charming grin, was setting up a vintage record player in the corner, while Amanda and Paul arranged a colorful assortment of appetizers on the dining table. Fisher supervised Hailey and Jesse as they darted around, their giggles filling the space with youthful energy. He might be the biggest kid of all.

Nina's heart swelled with gratitude. It had been a while since she'd felt so surrounded by love. As she stepped further into the room, Kendra's eyes were sparkling with excitement.

"Mom! You're here!" Kendra rushed over to give her a tight hug. "Happy birthday!"

"Thank you. You completely surprised me," Nina replied, her voice thick with emotion. "This is all so wonderful."

Rosemary wiped her hands on a floral apron and walked over

to hug her. "We wanted to make this day special for you. You being here has been such a gift for me. I couldn't wait to do something for you in return."

Nina glanced around, her eyes landing on a small stack of presents on a side table. "You all have already done so much. You opened your homes to us. Thank you hardly feels enough."

Tug sang badly while putting on a different record. "Just enjoy yourself. That's all the thanks we need."

"Happy birthday, Nina." Fisher pulled her into a side hug. "I hope this will be your happiest year yet."

As the evening progressed, the group gathered around the dining table. It was a delectable spread of homemade dishes. After a hearty meal filled with stories and laughter, it was time for dessert. Rosemary emerged from the kitchen carrying a birthday cake adorned with delicate sugar seashells.

"Make a wish, Mom," Kendra urged as everyone started singing "Happy Birthday."

Nina closed her eyes, the melody of her loved ones' voices washing over her. She didn't need to think hard about her wish. Having Kendra happy and surrounded by such wonderful friends and family was more than she could have ever hoped for, and having Fisher was the icing on the cake. She blew out the candles, opening her eyes to find her mother giving her a knowing nod, as if she could read Nina's thoughts.

"All right, everyone, time for some games!" Amanda announced, clapping her hands.

Paul grinned, producing a deck of cards. "Let's play a round of 'How's Yours?'"

Nina raised an eyebrow. "How do we play that?"

"It's simple," Paul explained. "One person leaves the room, and the rest of us decide on a common characteristic, like 'hair' or 'shoes.' When the person returns, they ask each of us, 'How's yours?' and we respond with a descriptive word. The goal is for them to guess what we're all describing."

Kendra giggled. "I'll go first!"

As Kendra stepped out, the group quickly settled on "socks." When she returned, the room immediately erupted with laughter.

"You first, Tug." Kendra stared at him.

"Damp."

She pointed to her mom.

"Black."

She slumped. "Okay, this won't be easy. Fisher, give me something helpful."

He grinned. "Absent."

"That doesn't even make sense. Black, damp, and absent?"

"My turn." Rosemary raised her hand with excitement.

"Make it good, Grandma."

Rosemary beamed as she said, "Footies."

Kendra thought for a second and then jumped into the air, yelling, "Socks!"

"Mom! That's cheating," Nina said.

"I didn't hear any rules about having to make it impossible to guess," Rosemary replied.

The game continued, and the challenge of conveying the right hint without giving too much away led to uproarious laughter.

After all the games, it was time for presents. Hailey and Jesse bounced on their toes, eager for Nina to open their gift first. She unwrapped a beautifully arranged basket filled with Amanda's homemade aromatic bath salts, gourmet locally made chocolate, and a hand-painted seashell from the kids.

"Thank you so much," Nina said, pulling the children into a hug. "This is lovely."

Amanda looked pleased. “We thought you could use a little pampering.”

Nina’s attention then turned to a large square box wrapped in shiny paper and topped with an oversized bow. She lifted it, noting its surprising weight.

“What could this be?” she mused, glancing at Kendra, who stood nearby, her excitement barely contained.

“Open it and see!” Kendra urged.

As Nina peeled back the wrapping and lifted the lid, her breath caught. Inside was a stunning driftwood bowl, its natural textures and hues artfully arranged.

“Fisher?” Nina asked, looking up in astonishment.

Fisher shook his head, a proud smile on his face. “No, your daughter made that. She collected every piece of driftwood and designed it herself.”

Nina’s eyes filled with tears as she turned to Kendra. “You made this for me?”

Kendra nodded, her own eyes glistening. “Yes, ma’am. I wanted to handcraft something special for you. And it didn’t take me three years like it took someone we know.”

Nina laughed at the inside joke. “My daughter is a prodigy,” she said proudly.

“She learned way faster than I did,” Fisher admitted.

“But really, Mom, I’m sorry I’ve been such a pain. All those terrible things I said. I didn’t mean them. I love you so much.”

“I love you too. Always, all the ways, and forever.” Nina enveloped her daughter in a tight embrace. “Trust me, I gave your grandmother a tough time when I was your age.”

Rosemary chuckled from across the room. “She still does sometimes.”

The room erupted in laughter, easing the emotional intensity of the moment.

“Kendra,” Nina said, pulling back to look into her daughter's eyes, "you just smiling is the biggest gift. But this bowl. It's art. I will treasure it forever."

"Maybe you can put the shells you collect in it," Kendra suggested.

Hailey piped up, "Maeve would've loved a basket like that. Kendra, you're an artist! You should enter the art show next year."

Fisher nodded in agreement. "She's a natural. I couldn't make something that beautiful for years after I got started."

Kendra beamed. "You're a fantastic teacher."

Nina mouthed a heartfelt *Thank you* to Fisher, who responded with a gentle wink.

As the evening continued, Tug and Rosemary exchanged a glance before addressing Nina.

"There's one more gift," Tug began, his eyes twinkling.

Rosemary took Nina's hand. "We'd like you and Kendra to join us on our next bucket-list adventure."

"Really?" Kendra bounced in her seat.

"Yes, it's a dolphin-watching tour and a weekend getaway to Virginia Beach."

Nina's eyes widened in surprise. "That sounds amazing!"

Tug leaned in, his voice full of certainty. "We thought it would be a great way for all of us to spend some quality time together."

After Amanda, Paul, and the kids departed, the house settled into a peaceful calm. Kendra busied herself clearing the dishes while Nina, Fisher, Tug, and Rosemary relaxed on the deck, the sound of the waves providing a soothing backdrop.

"This was a perfect evening," Nina said, and then she sighed with contentment.

Fisher leaned closer, his voice soft. "Would you like to take a walk on the beach?"

Rosemary nudged Nina. "Go on, dear. We'll take care of everything here."

Hand in hand, Nina and Fisher strolled toward the shoreline. As they made their way down the path leading to the beach, the sticky night air wrapped around them like an embrace. The ocean stretched before them, dark and endless, the moon casting a silvery path over the waves. It was the kind of night that made everything feel possible.

Fisher had been quiet for the past few minutes, letting her soak in the moment, and she appreciated that about him. He didn't fill the silence with empty words like so many people did.

She glanced at him, their hands still linked. "Tonight felt like the kind of peace I didn't know I was missing."

"I'm glad."

They reached the damp sand near the water's edge, where the waves rolled in, just barely brushing their toes. He slowed their steps, then stopped altogether.

"I have something for you."

Nina turned to face him, her brow lifting in curiosity. "Fisher, you didn't have to."

He reached into his pocket and pulled out a small box. The way he hesitated before handing it to her sent a soft flutter through her chest.

"I wasn't sure if I should give it to you in front of everyone." He lightly scratched at his jaw.

She took the box from him, tilting her head. "Oh yeah?"

Fisher glanced out at the waves before meeting her eyes again. "Things are going well, and I didn't want to make anything complicated."

Nina's heart skipped. "Complicated?"

He gestured toward the box. "Open it."

She did, carefully peeling back the lid. Nestled inside was a driftwood heart. "I made that from the leftover pieces of Kendra's project. It was nice working with her on your gift. This came from my heart."

Her breath caught. "Fisher . . ."

He took a step closer, his voice steady. "After Kendra finished her bowl, I looked at the leftover scraps and the pieces she didn't need and envisioned putting them together for you. I don't know why, but it felt right. It felt like *us*."

She ran her fingers over the smooth, sanded surface. It was beautiful.

"I care for you, Nina," he said. "Deeply. I made this because after spending all this time with you and Kendra, I've realized something. I like who I am when I'm with you. I don't want this to be something temporary. I want forever. No pressure, but I didn't want to let the moment pass without telling you how I feel."

Nina swallowed hard, the tenderness in his words touching her. This steady, unshakable, and very creative man had found a way to tell her what she had been needing to hear. But there was one thing nagging at her.

"I . . ." She closed the box and held it to her chest. "I need to tell you something, and I don't want it to come out the wrong way."

Fisher's gaze softened. "Go ahead."

She exhaled. "In my marriage, one thing that caused problems was my career. I worked long hours, I was ambitious, and it wasn't something David could handle. He felt overshadowed."

Fisher's lips twitched like he was trying not to laugh.

She frowned. "I'm being serious."

"I know," he said, chuckling. "It's just funny."

Nina scowled. "How is that funny?"

Fisher shook his head, still grinning. "Just that it was even a thing. A marriage is a relationship, and a relationship is a partnership. Every success should be celebrated. I'm sorry you felt you couldn't be your true self."

"You still like to surprise me every day, don't you?" Nina blinked, then let out a self-deprecating laugh. "I just don't want to repeat a mistake. I want us to be a real partnership with us having clear roles and trust in each other."

"Exactly. Equally yoked." His tone shifted back in earnest. "You don't have to worry about me feeling insecure about who you are. I *like* who you are. You could be the CEO of a Fortune 500 company and I'd still be the same guy, fixing up The Tackle Box and making art out of things people throw away."

Her chest tightened at his words. "I don't want to overshadow the love of my life."

"Me being the love of your life will make me shine so bright you'll need sunglasses to get near me. My confidence is fine. No one is ever going to change how comfortable I am in my skin."

She let out a breathy laugh. The sincerity in his voice set her heart on fire for him.

They stood there for a long moment, the waves rolling in and pulling back, the stars blinking above them like tiny sparks of hope.

Nina tilted her head up to him, a slow smile spreading across her lips. "You know, there's only one thing missing from this birthday."

Fisher raised a brow. "Yeah?"

"A birthday kiss under the stars."

His smile deepened. She closed the distance between them, the driftwood heart caught between them as her hands pressed lightly against his chest. His hands settled at her waist as they kissed, softly at first, then deeper, like he had been waiting for this moment just as much as she had.

The night, the ocean, and the laughter from the house in the distance melted away.

When the kiss was complete, Fisher whispered, "Don't forget to make a wish."

Her fingers traced over the heart-shaped driftwood in her hands. Like the wood, she and Fisher had been shaped by time and tide—weathered, yes, but stronger and ready for whatever came next, together. "You've already made it come true."

Chapter Thirty-Nine

NINA AND KENDRA WALKED SIDE BY SIDE ALONG THE WATER's edge, their bare feet sinking into the cool, damp sand. Lately, it seemed like there was always someone with them: Amanda and her kids or Mom or Fisher. As much as she loved the company, it was nice for it to be just the two of them. And this time, Kendra had even left her earbuds behind. That was almost as good as a hug.

"I'm kind of getting used to walking on the beach like this," Kendra said. "The fresh air feels good."

"Well, your old mom here needs the exercise, so thanks for walking with me."

"You sit at that desk a lot, don't you?"

"Yes. At least working from home, I can get up and move around more." Nina had marked out a lunch hour on her schedule and used it to run a quick errand or for things like this, taking a walk on the beach, and it was a pleasant habit to get into. "I'd kind of forgotten how much I used to love being outside."

"Me too. It's a lot prettier here than in our old neighborhood. Plus, there's no chance of seeing dolphins from a sidewalk."

"You can't beat this view," Nina agreed.

"Can I ask you something?" Kendra's voice broke through the quiet, hesitant but sure.

"Of course," Nina said, glancing at her daughter.

Kendra looked down at her feet as they walked. Her fingers traced the edges of her hoodie, the sleeves pulled over her hands. The frumpy zip-up sweatshirt swam over her slender frame, but getting her to shop and dress like a young lady was more than Nina could fight over when they were first heading to Whelk's Island. They had bigger problems then. Thank goodness things seemed to be on the upswing.

"Mom, I was thinking about my last conversation with Dad." Kendra swept her red hair into a messy ponytail, securing it half-heartedly with a plastic claw clip she'd had clipped to her jacket.

Nina swallowed, keeping her expression neutral. "Oh?"

"It wasn't bad or anything. Just different. He was actually listening this time." She paused, kicking her big toe at a small pile of sand. "I told him how I felt, and for once, he didn't brush it off like I was just some dramatic kid. He admitted that he might have handled things wrong."

Nina was quiet for a moment, letting Kendra get her thoughts out. Then she said, "That's huge, honey."

Kendra sighed. "Yeah. I thought it would make me feel better. But it didn't really."

"That's because one conversation can't erase everything that's happened," Nina said softly. "Healing takes time. And trust takes time too. It's a process, not a one-and-done thing."

Kendra's gaze was still distant, like she was processing something bigger. "I think I'm okay with that."

"Is there anything I can do to help you keep moving forward?"

"No." Kendra fell silent for a moment, then glanced up at her mom, a smirk playing on her lips. "You know, I like Fisher."

Nina's heart did a small flip, but she kept her expression calm. "Yeah?"

Kendra's head tilted. "I like the way you act when he's around. You're so relaxed. I've never seen you this way. You were always so stressed out back home."

Nina exhaled, the words settling over her, a revelation she hadn't fully admitted to herself yet. She was different here. Lighter. Happier.

"Maybe I just needed a change," she said, nudging Kendra gently with her elbow.

Kendra gave her a look. "Maybe you just needed Fisher."

Nina laughed. "You sound like your grandmother."

Kendra shrugged. "She's not wrong."

They walked in silence for a while, the ocean stretching actively beside them. Then Kendra stopped.

"Mom?"

"Hmm?"

"Can we make Whelk's Island our forever home for real?"

Nina's steps faltered as she turned to look at her daughter. Kendra's face was expectant.

"We could," Nina said. "You brought it up before, but I wasn't sure if you still felt that way."

"I do," she said with confidence. "Everything feels better here. *I* feel better here."

Nina studied her daughter, noting the relaxation of her shoulders and the absence of doubt and anger in her eyes. "What about school? Are you sure you'd be okay starting over here?"

"Yeah," Kendra said. "I've been thinking about that a lot." She tugged at her ponytail, her eyes focused on the ground.

Nina wanted to urge her to continue but made herself give Kendra time and not push.

"I think . . ." she started, and then she took in a deep breath. "I'd like the chance to start over at a new school. With new friends and maybe be more active in things. Staying here, I could keep working at Paws. Those dogs need me."

You need them too. Nina looked at her daughter. She was no longer her little baby girl. Before long, she'd be driving, but it made Nina's heart ache that Kendra was already having to navigate adult emotions and problems.

"I'm so proud of you, Kendra."

"Thanks, Mom." She swept her foot high in the air, water droplets landing on both of them. "Oops! Sorry. That was an accident."

"Mm-hmm. I hear ya," Nina teased.

"People don't know me here," Kendra said quietly, kicking at the sand again. "So I get to start fresh. Make friends who like me for who I am now, not who they think I'm supposed to be. Maybe find some girls who like the same stuff I do, like art, animals, being outside. Back home, it was harder. It felt like I didn't fit in anymore."

Nina reached for her daughter's hand, giving it a small squeeze. "Staying here would be a new beginning for both of us."

Kendra pumped her fist. "Yes!" She clapped her hands and did a spin. "I was so afraid to ask again."

"Why?"

"Fisher. Moving here. Both are things that aren't my decision to make. I'm just the kid. I didn't want you to be mad."

"I always want to know your opinion. Yes, ultimately, as the parent, it's my decision, but how you feel factors into that."

A few steps later, Kendra stopped and bent to pick up something from the sand. She dusted it off, her fingers brushing over it before holding it up to the sunlight.

"What is it?" Nina asked, stepping closer.

Kendra turned it at an angle, her eyes widening. "Driftwood.

It's kind of a cool piece, the way it looks like it's twisted, isn't it?"

Nina leaned in. "It is."

"I wonder if this could've been part of Tug's Diner."

Nina followed her gaze to the empty lot a ways down the beach. The place where the diner had stood.

"Maybe it was. You know, Tug decided to sell the property after all. It wasn't easy for him, but the developers promised to honor what was there."

"Really?"

"They're planning to put up a permanent marker. I think it'll be a driftwood sign or a bronze plaque or maybe even a mural—something to tell the story of the diner, the surfers, and all the people who found home there," Nina explained. "Tug liked that idea. Said it felt right. Like letting go but not forgetting."

Nina admired Tug's grace in letting go of what he'd built while still ensuring that its story would be remembered. Maybe that was the lesson *she* needed too: that she could honor where she'd been without it holding her back from where she was meant to go.

Kendra smiled, tucking the twisted driftwood into her pocket. "That's pretty cool. It's like part of it will always be here."

Nina tilted her face toward the sky, letting the warmth of the sun kiss her skin. A silent prayer rolled through her, soft and full of gratitude. *Thank You, Lord, for loving us enough to bring us here. Thank You for second chances. Thank You for believing in us even when we didn't believe in ourselves.*

When she lowered her gaze, Kendra was still watching her, a question in her eyes. "What'd you just wish for?" she asked, grinning.

"I didn't make a wish." Her chin lifted. "Just prayed a little thank-you."

Kendra nodded as if she understood.

They turned back toward the house, walking together along the shore, their footprints side by side in the sand. There was a lot to think about: how Mom would react to them wanting to stay in town, where they'd live, renting or selling the house in Pennsylvania, moving everything. Maybe she'd talk to Fisher about it all.

"Would you like me to see if we can visit the school?"

"Yes. Can you?" Kendra looked so excited. "I met a couple of people who go there when I was at Paws. And all the kids my age in Sunday school class go there, so it's not like I wouldn't know anyone."

"I'll call and see when we can visit and check on the transfer process. A change always comes with a lot of moving parts, but at least it's at the beginning of the school year."

Kendra nodded with excitement. "I'm ready."

"Me too. I think this will be a good move for us. I want to start some new habits. Maybe we can help each other find a better balance."

"Yeah, that would be good. Grandma will be so excited that we're gonna stay."

"Let me talk to her first, okay?"

"Yes, ma'am." Kendra pressed her lips together and pretended to insert a key and turn the lock.

Chapter Forty

FRESH OCEAN AIR DRIFTING THROUGH THE OPEN DECK doors slowly brought Nina to life after a night of racing thoughts and intermittent sleep. Her mother moved with ease, deadheading the flowers in the planters with such care, and without a clue of all that had transpired over the past twenty-four hours. Nina took a slow breath, steadying herself as she walked out to join her.

"Good morning, honey," Rosemary said. "You're up early."

"Yeah, it's a beautiful day. Um, Mom, I need to talk to you about something."

Rosemary glanced up, her warm eyes curious. "That sounds serious. Is everything okay?"

"Yes, yes, it is." Nina chose her words carefully. "I had a long talk with Kendra yesterday. She told me she wants to stay on Whelk's Island. For good."

The pruning shears clanked against the chair as Rosemary sat down, her face lighting up. "She does?" She pressed her hand to her heart. "I've been praying about this. I think it's good. You think so, don't you?"

"I do." Nina couldn't help but smile at her mother's instant excitement. "She is optimistic about starting fresh at school here and making new friends. I hope she isn't disappointed."

"Oh, honey, it's wonderful, and she'll be fine. I mean, I

wanted this place to be good for you both. It has changed my life, but I didn't dare hope you would want to stay. Not this soon. It's like a miracle."

Nina let out a small laugh, feeling some of the weight lift off her shoulders. "Kendra is different here. I'm so thankful. I'm different here too. And I love how my relationship with Kendra has renewed."

Rosemary's eyes softened.

"Well, now we just have to figure out the logistics," Nina continued. "Don't worry, we won't be infringing on your hospitality much longer. You've been such a saint to put us up during all this, especially since we'd planned to stay only a few weeks. I have to put my house on the market or maybe rent it out, find a place here, get Kendra enrolled in school . . ." She rubbed a hand over her forehead. "It's a lot, but it feels right."

Rosemary rested her hand on Nina's arm. "Slow down. Make a plan. You probably already started one of those fancy spreadsheets you love so much. We'll hire help to make the move easier. Or maybe . . ." A faint blush touched Rosemary's cheeks, and she cleared her throat. "I've got an idea."

Nina's brows lifted. "What kind of idea?"

"Let me sort it out first. It needs to make sense before I say anything." Rosemary's eyes twinkled. "Just trust me, sweetheart." Then, as if that settled it, she hopped up, almost a little too pleased with herself. "I'm going to get us some coffee and use the fancy creamer to celebrate."

Nina exhaled, knowing better than to push when her mother was being this vague. She'd find out soon enough.

Rosemary stopped at the screen door. "Honey, I'm so glad you're staying. This is the best news I could've gotten."

Nina felt her throat tighten, emotion rising up before she could stop it. "Yeah?"

Rosemary's expression turned serious. "You've spent so much

of your life taking care of everything and everyone. It's about time you let yourself be happy."

The words landed with a surprising weight, because Nina hadn't thought of it that way before. She'd thought about what was best for Kendra, about financial security, about doing the right thing. But happiness? That had never been part of the equation.

Until now.

Rosemary gave her a knowing smile and opened the door. "Speaking of happiness, pay attention to what's blooming between you and Fisher. It seems very special."

Nina blinked. "What are you talking about?"

Rosemary smirked, leaning a little closer. "Oh, sweetheart, I might be old, but I'm not blind. I've seen the way he looks at you."

Heat crept up Nina's neck. "Mom."

"And don't tell me it's nothing. You light up around him." Rosemary tapped a finger on the doorjamb. "That man cares about you, and I think you care about him too. Don't you let him slip away."

Nina fidgeted with the hem of her shirt, stalling. "We're good. We're just taking our time."

"Mm-hmm. Well, my practical daughter, love doesn't have a timeline. People make timelines, but people don't have the answers. Everything is in His time, and I'm not talking Fisher here. All I'm saying is, don't let your head deflect what your heart already knows."

Nina sighed, pressing her fingers to her temples. "I'm not sure I know what I know."

"Then maybe it's time to find out, Nina. Take that man for the test-drive of your life, because I think he deserves a woman as special as you." She flitted inside and left Nina shaking her head, certain her mother hadn't meant that the way it came out. But it was amusing, and it felt pretty good to know Mom was so sure of Fisher, because Nina felt the same way about him.

Rosemary came back out, holding two beautiful coffee mugs with shiny golden handles. One had "I love you" in shiny gold script, and the other said "I love you more."

"Aren't these pretty? Where did you get them?"

"A gift from Tug," she said, her cheeks turning pink as she uttered the words. "I've never felt more loved. Tug, you, and Kendra are here. Life is so good right now."

They tapped their coffee mugs together, and Rosemary said, "To new coastal beginnings and living every day to its full potential."

"I love it!" Nina took a long sip of the creamy coffee. "I'm pretty sure we'd have to walk an extra mile to work this off, but it'll be worth it."

"I know. Such a treat."

Nina's phone rang. "It's Fisher. I'm going to take this in the apartment. Do you mind?"

"Not at all. You go. These flowers are thirsty."

Nina raced inside, excited to talk to him this morning. There was so much to share. "Hey, you."

Fisher's voice was warm. "Hey, yourself. I was just thinking about you."

That made her smile. "Yeah? I might've been thinking about you just the teensiest little bit too. Give me one sec." She took the stairs down and shut the apartment door behind her. "I'm back."

"Yeah, I was waxing my board, and it made me think we should go out surfing again."

She laughed softly. "It's funny you say that. Kendra and I were just talking about that yesterday."

"Oh?" There was a smile in his voice. "Good things, I hope."

"Wonderful things. She told me again that she wants to stay here. For real and for good."

There was a beat of silence, and then, "Really? Do you mean, like, seriously move here to Whelk's Island?"

"Really." Nina felt her own certainty growing the more she said it aloud. "She loves it here, Fisher. And *I* do too. I'll have to sell or at least rent my house to start fresh here. It's a big decision, but—"

"But you have help. *I'll* help." Fisher said quietly. "I didn't want to push, but I've been hoping you would finally see this place as home. You fit here."

"I know." Her heart thumped a little harder. She'd prayed he would think it was good news. "I just told Mom. Then she made me a two-thousand-calorie coffee to celebrate. She's so excited."

"I bet I'm twice as happy as she is. How can I top a two-thousand-calorie coffee to prove it? Let me see . . ."

Nina loved his sense of humor. "Uh-oh. I think I'm worried about what you'll come up with."

"Maybe you should be. But seriously, you know how much I love this town. I'm just thinking how fantastic it is that you feel the same way."

"I do." *And about you.* Nina hesitated. She wanted to say the words, but she held back and the moment passed. Instead, she said, "Even during all the family trouble, I've felt lighter here. Happier. I'm not constantly bracing for the next thing to go wrong."

"That's because you're finally where you're supposed to be." His voice was gentle, like he'd already known this was where she belonged, even before she figured it out for herself.

Nina swallowed past the unexpected tightness in her throat. "You think so?"

"Yes." He paused. "And I think it's brave. You're choosing happiness, choosing what's right for you and Kendra."

She smiled even though he couldn't see it. "You make it sound so simple."

"It is." His voice was steady, sure. "You followed your heart. And if that led you here, I'd say you are brilliant, too, and that Whelk's Island just got a whole lot luckier. No, I take that back. I won't speak for the town. I'll speak for myself. Nina, *I* just got luckier."

Warmth spread throughout her chest. "I was hoping you'd say something like that."

Fisher chuckled. "Well, you called the wrong guy if you were looking for anything less than thrilled. I want you here with me, Nina. I can see our lives together."

"Oh gosh, this is all so crazy and quick, but you are the best part of this decision. It is good for Kendra, but being with you has become really important to me. Actually, this choice is a bit selfish."

"I won't let you ever regret being selfish about this. I promise." A comfortable silence stretched between them before he spoke again. "Wow. So, what's next?"

"Figuring out the details. I'll start looking at houses. Kendra's already excited about school. I guess we just take it one step at a time."

"I can help you with housing and getting moved. I know this place like the back of my hand."

Her heart flipped a little at the offer. "That would be great, Fisher."

"You mean a lot," he said.

The words hit her in a way she wasn't sure she was ready for. It was a little scary and overwhelming, but maybe that was okay. *Didn't I recently tell Kendra that being a little overwhelmed just meant it was something that really mattered? I should take my own advice.*

"Thank you," she said. "I feel the same."

"And, Nina, never hesitate to ask for anything from me." Kindness radiated from his voice.

"I'm not good at it, but I'm going to try really hard to be better about that."

"Meanwhile, we have a surf date to plan."

She grinned. "Kendra would love to go again. I know she had such a great time, and it really helps her. Is that okay?"

"Of course you can bring her!"

"You've won *her* heart too."

"Good. Since our first encounter when you got to town was me ratting her out for trying to buy beer, I guess I should thank my lucky stars she ever wanted to speak to me again. I'm so glad it played out this way instead. So, how about next week?"

"I've got a super-light day next Tuesday, and she has Tuesdays off."

"Perfect. Thanks, Nina. This has turned out to be a special day. I hope you know how much you've already changed my life in this short time. You are everything I needed, and I didn't even know it. I think things are only going to get better."

After she ended the call, she sat cross-legged on her bed, hugging her phone.

This wasn't just a fresh start. It felt like forever—like home. The peaceful kind, where the tide carried those you loved to you and taught you that home is wherever you're together. Home, no matter where.

Chapter Forty-One

NINA SAT AT THE COUNTER AT THE TACKLE BOX, SIPPING on one of Fisher's famous cherry limeades, her phone resting in front of her. Staring past the volleyball nets to the water, she realized she could no longer put off calling David. She didn't want to chance anyone raining on her happiness parade today. She didn't know how he'd react to the news that she and Kendra would be staying on Whelk's Island.

"It's going to be fine." Fisher gave her an encouraging nod. "Call him and get it over with. If he complains about the distance, we can fly her up for visits or meet him halfway. We'll figure out a fair compromise that works for us all."

She exhaled, squared her shoulders, and finally picked up the phone.

David answered on the second ring. "Nina?"

"Hey." It was hard to keep her voice steady. "I figured it was time we talked." She braced herself for the worst.

He paused. No surprise. He'd always hated talks. "Are you going to stay on Whelk's Island?" he asked.

Nina swallowed. "Yeah, we are. Did Kendra call you?"

Another pause, and then he sighed. "No, but I can't say I didn't see this coming."

That threw her off. "Really?"

"I heard it in her voice when we talked last. She sounds happier." He let out a low chuckle. "Which is a miracle, considering where we were at the beginning of the summer. And Nina, you sound happy, and that makes *me* happy too."

"She said her last visit was really good. She felt like you were really listening and including her."

"I'm trying. I'm sorry I hadn't realized how things were slipping away."

Nina softened. "She's not the same kid she was when we left. She's healing. And so am I."

David hesitated. "So, this is it? You're really not coming back?"

"This is it," Nina confirmed, a quiet certainty settling over her. "We're building something here. I know you've had a lot of regrets about how things went down, but I think we both know this is for the best."

A long silence stretched between them. Then, finally, he exhaled. "Yeah, I'm behind it a hundred percent. We'll figure out all the details and visits. No worries. I hope it works out for you, Nina. I really do. I mean, it sounds like this Fisher guy's made a good impression on Kendra too."

She closed her eyes, allowing herself a small smile. She hadn't planned to share any of that with him, but she was glad it was out there. "Thanks, David."

There was nothing left to say. No bitterness. No what-ifs. Just one door closing in the quietest, most peaceful way possible. And that was enough.

She hung up and looked at Fisher, who was standing there with a bar towel over his shoulder. "Well?" he said.

"You were right. Smooth sailing. He said he sort of sensed it coming. He's totally behind it. And, apparently, Kendra talked you up while they were together, because he pretty much gave me his blessing on *you* too."

"Well, there you go. Nothing to worry about. Next time, just take a minute to be thankful and leave the worry on the side of the road. We don't need it."

"You are so good for me."

He leaned across the bar and kissed her. "I love making you smile."

"Not a bad kisser either."

"Need a second chance to rate me?" He kissed her again.

"Well done." She glanced at her phone. "Oh, I missed a text from Mom."

"What's it say?"

"She and Tug want us to bring Kendra to his house tonight for a family meeting and then dinner."

"I'm *family*?" Fisher's chest puffed out. "I like the sound of that."

"Be careful," Nina said. "No telling what kind of drama is cropping up now that warrants a family meeting."

"I'm not scared. I love every ebb and flow we encounter. Bring it on." He caught her hand in his. "Come on, we have time for a walk."

The heat still clung to the air, heavy and thick, even as the sun sagged low behind the dunes. After they took off their shoes, he led her down to the beach, the surf churning so loudly that talking wasn't necessary. Nina kept pace, her toes sinking into the cool sand where the water kept the sun from scorching it.

As the breeze stirred, they headed toward the old pier, still under repair after last year's storm damage, with another rough hurricane season already threatening.

Fisher tipped his chin toward the top of the dune. "Look, they installed the new fence around the marker spot for Tug's Diner."

The fresh fencing framed the new picnic tables, the board storage rack, and the rinse station—simple, sturdy, just the way Tug would want.

His voice was low but full. "It's still so hard for me to walk past here and his diner not be there."

Nina slowed, following his gaze. "It's going to be beautiful. Mom said the Master Gardeners already volunteered to manage the planting as part of their mission. It really is a beautiful tribute."

Fisher's lips curved. "It was so smart of him to think of asking for that. No one expected them to agree. We all thought he was crazy to even waste his time asking, but they didn't blink. Of course, that land is primo. But now the commercial buildout will be a little balanced by something meant for the locals—for us surfers to stash boards, hose off, break for lunch. That's what made the diner home for so many of us. This keeps that spirit going."

Nina looked up at him, touched. "It really does." She reached for his hand, and together they walked on, leaving their footprints in the sand as the long summer light lingered just above the water. The sound of the waves mingled with the promise that some places live on, even when the walls are gone.

Later that evening, Nina, Kendra, and Fisher sat in Tug's living room, their curiosity piqued by the family meeting Rosemary and Tug had called.

Kendra leaned over, whispering to Nina, "What do you think this is about?"

"I have no idea," Nina said, watching the subtle glance Tug and Rosemary exchanged—a warm conspiratorial look that said they were in cahoots on whatever was coming next.

Rosemary cleared her throat, then inhaled and looked at Tug. Her eyes teared up, and Nina's heart lurched.

She glanced over at Fisher, who was already looking at her with wonder.

Mom touched her engagement ring. "Tug makes me so happy. We've been talking today. I accepted this ring in the most breathtaking moment under the aurora borealis. There's never been a question that he's stolen my heart, but I've been so hesitant to make that next step." She paused. "Even though I never thought I'd have this again, I'm here to say I love this man. He loves me, too, and I'm so honored to be engaged to him. I wanted you all to be the first to know we're ready to set a date."

After a beat of silence, Kendra let out a squeal. "So, we're going to have another wedding?"

"Well, just a simple little ceremony, but yes." Rosemary's eyes danced.

Nina clapped a hand to her chest, laughter bubbling out of her. "Mom, that's great!"

Her mother blushed. "I wanted to make sure everything was okay with you and Kendra. And now, after everything we've been through together these past few months, it just makes sense."

Tug grinned. "I knew we'd eventually get here, but it's felt like forever since I gave her that ring."

Kendra bounced on the couch. "Do you have a date in mind?"

"Well," Rosemary said, glancing at Nina, "that actually depends on you two."

Nina's brows lifted. "Us?"

Rosemary took a deep breath, setting her hands on her knees. "I've been thinking about you moving here."

"We will be at the wedding no matter what," Nina said. "Don't you worry about our schedule."

"No, not just that. About my house. About how much you

two love it here. I was wondering if maybe you'd want to take over Palakiko's Retreat."

Nina blinked. "You're serious?"

Tug chuckled. "Dead serious. No wife of mine needs her own house."

"About time, sailor!" The Wife chimed in.

"I couldn't have a bird that only said 'Polly want a cracker.' No." Tug wagged a finger toward The Wife. "You better shape up. I'm going to have a real wife, so what will I call you then? Smarty-pants, maybe."

The Wife squatted, then bounced three times and stretched one leg and wing out. "Pretty bird."

"Pretty bird, it is!" Rosemary laughed. "I'll move in with Tug after the wedding, of course." She patted his leg. "My place is too big for me. You two have already made it a home. I thought instead of putting my house on the market, we'd just sort of move me out and let y'all settle in."

"I've got a whole house full of furniture and a lifetime of belongings here already," Tug explained. "She can just bring her things and a toothbrush and we're all set."

Kendra gasped. "Wait." Her smile was so big that her lips trembled. "You mean we get to live in your house with the elevator, right on the beach?"

"Yes, honey," Rosemary said.

Nina's chest tightened, her emotions crashing over her like a wave. They'd found healing, hope, and a future in that house. She met her mother's gaze. "I'll get an attorney to work up the papers and a fair price."

"We'll have to do the paperwork to transfer the deed, but it's paid for. It was going to be yours eventually, anyway." With a gentle but decisive nod, Rosemary continued, "I'm more sure about this than anything. In fact, it'll be kind of nice to see you enjoying it."

Fisher, who had been silent up until now, let out a low whistle. "Wow. I don't think I've ever witnessed a two-for-one family blessing like this before."

Kendra launched herself at Rosemary, wrapping her in a tight hug. "Best. Grandma. Ever."

Nina swallowed against the lump in her throat. "Mom, I don't even know what to say."

"Say yes and then help me plan the cutest little wedding ever. In fact, just like Paul and Amanda's would suit me just fine."

Nina glanced at Kendra, then at Fisher, and they were both nodding.

"Yes," Nina whispered, and then she laughed, tears blurring her vision. "A million times, yes."

"Wait!" Kendra said with a look of concern. "Will we have to rename the beach house if we move in?" She waited a beat and then added, "Our last name isn't Palakiko, so don't you think the name should be, like, for us?"

Fisher looked as though he agreed.

Nina glanced toward her mom and shrugged. "Well, Palakiko is our family name. I think it sort of still applies."

"Whatever y'all want to do," Rosemary said. "It was the perfect name when y'all came up with it for me. It's only fitting you should rename the beach house for yourselves."

Nina looked in Kendra's direction. "Do you have any ideas?"

Kendra grinned, regaining that spark Nina loved seeing again and again. "Sort of. Since we're moving from inland to the seashore, what about Shore Thing?"

"I think Kendra has a future in marketing and branding," Rosemary said. "I love the play on the word *shore* for *sure.* I get it."

Nina blinked, then laughed. "Shore Thing? Like 'sure thing'? That's perfect."

Kendra's cheeks flushed with pride. "It's like . . . we're sure now. *Sure,* this is where we belong. *Sure,* we've got each other. And it's a pun too."

Nina squeezed her daughter's hand, feeling the weight of all they'd been through lighten in that small, sweet moment. "It's exactly right. Just like us. Not fancy, not perfect, but full of heart."

"And, Fisher, can you maybe help us paint our own driftwood sign for the house?" Kendra asked.

Nina appreciated the kindness her daughter was showing Fisher. He really was such a grounding force for all of them.

Fisher looked surprised, but he didn't hesitate. "Yeah, I'd love to help you make one."

Nina got up and kissed the top of Kendra's head. "This house, this life—we're gonna make it something good, honey. I think Shore Thing is the perfect name for our new home."

"Yay!" Rosemary clapped her hands.

Tug leaped from the chair. "Now that everything is settled, I'm going to grill some shrimp. It won't take long."

After a while, Tug came back with the tray of huge Carolina shrimp with beautiful grill marks across them. "All right, I'm done. Here's a calendar. Pick a date before the shrimp hit the table."

Nina and her mother were caught off guard, but Kendra blurted, "The fifteenth!"

"The fifteenth?" Tug looked pleased. "Well, since this month on the fifteenth is too soon, I'd say September fifteenth is now official."

Kendra skipped around the room.

"September fifteenth it is." Rosemary took the tray of shrimp from Tug and set it on the counter before hugging his neck. "I love you, Tug Basnight."

Later that night, after the celebration settled and Nina, Kendra, and Rosemary had changed into their pajamas at Palakiko's Retreat, Nina snuggled up to her mom on the couch.

"I'm so excited for you, Mom!"

"It's hard to wrap my head around sometimes. It feels too good to be true to have had such grand loves in my life."

"It's true. Tug's great, and I think if Dad had ever met him, they would've been friends."

Rosemary's smile was sweet. "I know. I think that too."

"What are you looking at there?" Nina peered over her arm at her mom's phone.

"Pictures of Paul and Amanda's wedding last year. It was simple but so beautiful. When Tug and I hosted that, I think that's when I realized I was falling in love with him."

"When you know, you know," Nina said.

"Do you think we should have it at Tug's house or here?"

"You mean at *my* new house?" Nina teased. "I think either one works. It would be kind of sweet to have it at Tug's, where you'll be starting your life together."

"I'll ask Pastor Qualls if he'll do the honors. He's always had such a kind, calming way about him, don't you think?" Rosemary's eyes filled with tears as a giggle burst from her. "I'm going to be a bride again."

"A beautiful bride." Nina tried to imagine herself ever making that kind of step. A year ago, it would've been a flat-out no. Now, thanks to Fisher, she'd say yes to that in a hot second.

Family.

And a whole new beginning just waiting to unfold.

Chapter Forty-Two

NINA EXHALED, TAKING IN THE BEAUTY OF THE COASTLINE. Once she left Hawaii, she'd never looked back. She hadn't even missed it all those years she and David lived inland, but being here on the coast had reawakened something deep inside her.

She wiggled her toes into the warm sand, letting the earth hold her steady. The ocean stretched before her, endless and sure, but today she wasn't searching for something just beyond the horizon. She was right where she needed to be.

Kendra, laughing beside her, jumped into the air as a deep wave surprised them by chasing them up the sand. The ocean breeze stirred her daughter's red hair like a lion's mane framing her face. Fisher, his steady presence beside her, was pleasing. The warmth of Fisher's fingers grazing hers as they walked in lockstep as if they'd walked that way for thirty years was just right.

She smiled to herself because the life she had planned had crumbled, and yet somehow a new one she'd never dreamed of had turned out to be the one she needed. She and Fisher watched Tug and Rosemary just ahead, holding hands. Their heads came together as they spoke. The easy way those two fit together was a reminder that love didn't arrive just for people who were looking for it. It happens when it's destined to.

"Look at them," Fisher murmured beside her, nodding toward the couple. "You'd think they've been together forever."

"I was just thinking that." Nina glanced back at her mother, who was smiling at Tug like he'd painted the stars in the sky just for her. A light giggle rose from Nina. "Maybe in their hearts, they have."

Kendra let out a playful groan. "Ugh! They're cute but gross. Old people kissing is weird."

Fisher smirked. "Someday you're going to be an old lady. Your mom kissing someone wouldn't gross you out, would it?"

"I don't know." Kendra shot her mother a mischievous grin. "Well, at least she's younger than Grandma. I might not totally cringe."

Nina rolled her eyes. "Oh, good. I'll cherish that glowing approval."

They walked a little farther, and then Kendra skipped ahead, searching for shells along the shore. Nina slowed her pace, letting her daughter have her moment.

Fisher bumped her shoulder. "You okay?"

She turned to him, her heart full. "Yeah. More than okay."

She had spent so much time waiting for some shift in her life that would make her happy. But life didn't wait—it happened. One wave at a time. And maybe, just maybe, she was finally ready to ride it.

The following week, Fisher and Nina drove up to Pennsylvania to pick up a truckload of her and Kendra's personal things and walk through the house to decide how best to stage it for sale. He'd advised her against managing a rental so far away. He said that if she really wanted rental income, he'd help her find something closer to Whelk's Island.

As they stood in her old kitchen, Nina exhaled.

"It's funny seeing you surrounded by all this stuff," Fisher said. "I've only known you at the beach, and this isn't the style I'd expect. It's stuffier than the Nina I know."

She chuckled. "I *was* stuffier." She pecked him on the lips. "You bring out a playful side of me I forgot all about. It's nice."

He pointed toward the cabinets. "You ready for that next big adventure?"

Nina groaned. "This will be an adventure, for sure." She looked at everything around her. "Why do I have so much stuff? I have every gadget known to humanity."

He poked his head into the pantry overflowing with not just food but also an abundance of pots, pans, and appliances. "Yeah, I've never known someone who had a machine for cutting fancy carrots."

"It's called a spiralizer." The truth was, it had been a wedding gift, and it was still in the box, which was how he'd noticed it on the pantry shelf.

Fisher grinned. "And when's the last time you spiralized anything?"

Nina huffed. "That's not the point."

Fisher just laughed, slipping his arm around her waist. "Well, at least now you don't have to do it alone."

She softened at that, leaning into him just a little. He was right. This time she wasn't handling what came next in her life alone.

After filling a spiral notebook with lists of things to complete, pack, sell, and remember to do when they got back, they made the return trip to Whelk's Island. It had been a long day, but they'd gotten a lot done.

"We're home!" Nina called out as she and Fisher walked into the house.

Rosemary and Kendra came out of the kitchen. "You got back way earlier than we expected," Rosemary said.

"While you were gone, we've been working on something for Grandma and Tug's wedding. It's been a fun day. We barely missed you," said Kendra.

"I missed them a little," Rosemary said. "How did it go?"

Fisher rested his hand on Nina's shoulder. "We made some decisions. Next trip, come with us, Kendra. We're going to bring back everything y'all are keeping. It'll be easier to let a third party set up an estate sale for the rest."

"Works for me," Kendra said.

"It's happening, kiddo. New home. New school. New start that we handle together through both the easy and rough parts."

"I'm not scared anymore, Mom," Kendra said.

Nina turned, studying her daughter's face. The storm in her eyes was gone, replaced with something lighter, something freer. "You mean about starting a new school?"

"About any of it." Kendra grinned. "I know who I am now, and I trust my family."

Nina looked lovingly at her daughter. "Oh, Kendra, I know you're in for a wonderful life. I'm so glad this summer has been kind to you."

Fisher glanced at Nina, then back at Kendra. "And you'll be living so close. I can't complain about that."

Nina laughed. "Oh, so you're relieved I didn't move out of your range?"

Fisher grinned. "Relieved? Yeah. But, Nina . . ." He hesitated for the briefest moment, then took her hand, rubbing his thumb along her palm. "Come here for a second."

She followed him, and Rosemary and Kendra took the hint to go back into the kitchen.

Fisher watched until they cleared the doorway. "Nina, I want more than this someday. I know you've got a lot going on now and we need time to grow this relationship, especially with a child involved, but I want you to know that's where my heart is."

"Thank you, Fisher."

"When we're ready, I want to make this real, like Rosemary and Tug. You and Kendra belong with me."

She stared at him, warmth filling every part of her. "Fisher . . ."

"I've been working on something." He exhaled, a little smile curving his lips. "I've been making updates at the driftwood house. Fixing it up, thinking maybe one day it could be *our* home."

A soft gasp caught her off guard.

"I won't rush things, but I want you to know that I see that future for us. Whenever you're ready, Nina."

Her eyes burned, joy flooding through her. "Fisher, that's exactly what I want."

A muscle jumped in his jaw as he held her gaze, the weight of the moment settling over them both.

"We'll get there," she promised. "But just knowing you've thought about it, that you see us as your future—that means everything."

His lips brushed against hers, slow and full of promise.

Pulling them both back into the moment, Kendra called out, "Didn't y'all get enough alone time on that ride to Pennsylvania?"

"Never enough," Fisher teased.

Nina blushed. "What's up, Kendra?"

"I wanted to show Fisher what I found that day on the beach—the day I asked you if we could move here. Remember?"

"I do." Nina gave Fisher a reassuring nod. "Yeah, come show him."

Kendra opened her palm, revealing the weathered piece of

driftwood. "I found this super-cool hunk of driftwood. I want you to have it."

"Thank you, Kendra." He turned it over in his hand, then held it up, twisting it from one side to the other. "It has a neat shape to it."

"I thought so too. I was hoping that someday we could make something together using this."

"I'm all for that. Yeah, that'll be a great project." Fisher's lips curled into a knowing smile. "I have an idea."

"Awesome," Kendra said. She threw her arms around his neck in a sweet hug. "Thanks, Fisher."

Nina closed her eyes for the briefest of moments. *Thank You. For Whelk's Island. For Fisher. For Kendra finding her way back to a better version of herself. For the peace across every part of my life. For this beautiful second chance.*

Fisher stepped over to join her.

There was love all around them. Every breeze, every wave, every shell, every possibility.

And Nina understood what it meant to have a home no matter where they lived.

Readers Guide

1. The title *Home No Matter Where* invites us to think about what "home" truly means. How did Nina, Kendra, and Rosemary each define it at the start of the story, and how did that change by the end?

2. What themes from this book stuck out to you the most?

3. Fisher is a man who has created a peaceful life for himself, but he's also been holding back from deeper connections. What do you think helped him open his heart?

4. Kendra's rebellion and ultimatum created tension between Nina and Fisher, even if Fisher didn't know the whole story. Why do you think Kendra acted out, and what did she really want deep down?

5. Whelk's Island plays a special role in the characters' healing journeys. How did the setting itself help the family reconnect and find new purpose?

6. The novel explores themes of second chances—not just in romance but in family, parenting, and personal dreams. Which character's second chance touched you the most?

7. The shells with messages show up at just the right time for several characters. How did the messages guide the characters, and what message spoke to you most?

8. Three generations of women share the same roof in this story. How did living together shape the relationships between Nina, Kendra, and Rosemary?

9. How did Nina's relationship with her ex-husband shape the choices she made on Whelk's Island? How did she finally find peace with that part of her past?

10. What does unconditional love look like in this novel? Which moments or gestures best showed it to you?

11. If you found a shell with a message meant just for you, what would you want it to say?

Acknowledgments

Every novel begins as a whisper of an idea, and through the love and encouragement of others, it grows into a story. I couldn't write these books without the friends, colleagues, and family who cheer me on along the way.

First, my heartfelt thanks to my agent, Michelle Grajkowski, whose steady encouragement and smart guidance remind me every day how lucky I am to have her on my side. She's one of those rare women who radiates positivity and wisdom no matter the circumstance, and I'm grateful for her help in finding just the right home for each of my stories.

To my wonderful developmental editor, Jamie Lapeyrolerie, and the entire team at WaterBrook: Thank you for believing in these characters and giving me the space to tell the stories on my heart. Your insight and support help me grow as a writer with every book.

Author friends are such a blessing. I'm grateful for the laughter, brainstorming, and encouragement shared with Lauren Ashwood, Sasha Summers, Karen Schaler, Sheila Roberts, and Jenny Hale. Each of you kept me motivated and inspired as this story came to life.

Thank you to Caitlin Clark, who played Amanda in the Fox Nation movie version of *The Shell Collector*. She has been such a cheerleader and source of strength throughout the writing of this series. Here's hoping all the books become movies!

The Savannah Bound group deserves a special mention. Lisa, thank you for planning that unforgettable writers' getaway. Melissa, Shannon, Vivian, Corneill, Patty—and the joy of spending time with Mary Kay Andrews—what gifts y'all were to this season of writing. The city of Savannah will forever hold a special place in my heart for bringing us together and infusing this book with new energy.

One of the greatest privileges of being an author is the opportunity to give back. I'm grateful for every chance I had to speak to, teach, and encourage other writers during the creation of this novel. Special thanks to Ruby Johnson and Chanda Ricks, whose determination and excitement reminded me of the magic in those early days of dreaming about a book. Watching you set and achieve goals has been an honor, and I'm so glad I get to walk alongside you.

And to the readers of the Shell Collector series—thank you. *The Shell Collector* was the book of my heart, and I never imagined it would become a series. But your love for that story opened the door to the creation of *To Light the Way Forward* and now to this third book, *Home No Matter Where.* Together, we've watched the little town of Whelk's Island grow and, with it, the families and friendships that make these stories shine. Your notes, reviews, and messages remind me daily why I write. You are the reason these books exist, and your enthusiasm made this third novel a true joy to create. Thank you for reading, for sharing, and for being part of this journey with me.

About the Author

USA Today and ECPA bestselling author Nancy Naigle whips up small-town love stories with a whole lot of heart. She began writing while juggling a successful career in finance and life on a seventy-six-acre farm. Now happily retired, this Virginia girl devotes her time to writing, antiquing, enjoying spa days with friends, spending time in the kitchen, and crafting.

Several of Nancy's novels have been adapted for television. You can find the complete list of movies and a free downloadable checklist of all her books in series order on her website, www.nancynaigle.com.

Immerse yourself in the beauty of Whelk's Island.

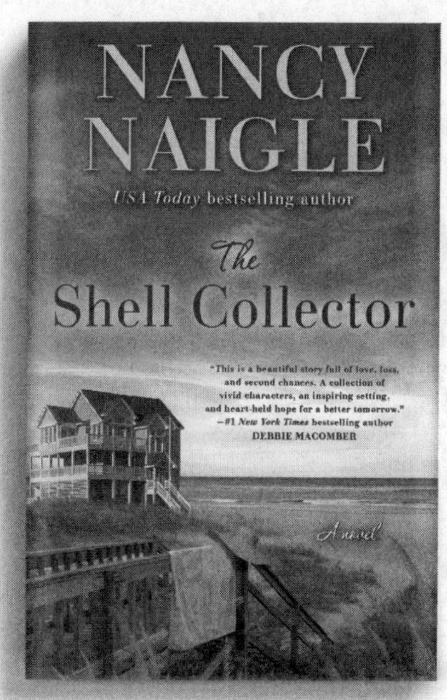

If you were moved by the touching story in *Home No Matter Where,* explore the other captivating novels in the Shell Collector series. *The Shell Collector* and *To Light the Way Forward* are both available now!

Learn more about Nancy Naigle's books at waterbrookmultnomah.com.